"Dance with me," he whispered.

Kennan brought his lips to her ear as he lifted her off the ground and spun in circle after circle. "Ye are the bonniest woman at the gathering, and I cannot bear to watch all the young Highland whelps gawking at you as if you're a prize to be won."

As he twirled, Divana turned to butter in his arms, resting her head against his chest. "I'll dance with ye, Kennan. Ye're my choice always."

He set her down and ran his hands along her arms. She shivered beneath his fingertips. "Are you cold?"

"Nay," she replied.

Looking like a goddess, she tilted her face upward and gazed directly into his eyes. When had she woven her way into his heart? Dipping his chin, he pulled her into his embrace. "Then I aim to kiss you, lass."

PRAISE FOR AMY JARECKI

THE HIGHLAND EARL

"Intense adventure mingles with sensuous love scenes. Fans of romance with strong, socially progressive heroines will thoroughly enjoy this novel."
—Publishers Weekly

"A refreshing take on a historical romance, and Jarecki crafts immersive, sweeping scenes in bustling London and the lowlands of Scotland."
—Shelf Awareness

THE HIGHLAND RENEGADE

"Flirtatious, sensuous romance and adventure fill the pages of this mesmerizing historical, and the undercurrent of Jacobite rebellion raises the tension."
—Publishers Weekly

THE HIGHLAND CHIEFTAIN

A "fast-paced, expertly crafted romance."
—Publishers Weekly

"*The Highland Chieftain* was a smoking romance that was both endearing and sexy!"
—The Genre Minx

THE HIGHLAND GUARDIAN

"Magnetic, sexy romance is at the heart of this novel, made complete with a cast of richly depicted characters, authentic historical detail, and a fast-moving plot."
—Publishers Weekly

"A true gem when it comes to compelling, dynamic characters....With clever, enchanting writing, elements of life-or-death danger and a romance that takes both Reid and Audrey completely by surprise, *The Highland Guardian* is an historical romance so on point it'll leave readers awestruck."
—BookPage

THE HIGHLAND COMMANDER

"Readers craving history entwined with their romance (à la *Outlander*) will find everything they desire in Jarecki's latest. Scottish romance fans rejoice."
—RT Book Reviews

"Sizzles with romance....Jarecki brings the novel to life with vivid historical detail."
—Publishers Weekly

THE HIGHLAND DUKE

"Readers will admire plucky Akira, who, despite her poverty, is fiercely independent and is determined to be no man's mistress. The romance is scintillating and moving, enhanced by fast-paced suspense."
—Publishers Weekly

THE
HIGHLAND
ROGUE

THE HIGHLAND ROGUE

A Lords of the Highlands Novel

AMY JARECKI

FOREVER

New York Boston

Forever
Hachette Book Group
1290 Avenue of the Americas, New York, NY 10104
read-forever.com
twitter.com/readforeverpub

First Edition: March 2020

Forever is an imprint of Grand Central Publishing. The Forever name and logo are trademarks of Hachette Book Group, Inc.

The publisher is not responsible for websites (or their content) that are not owned by the publisher.

The Hachette Speakers Bureau provides a wide range of authors for speaking events. To find out more, go to www.hachettespeakersbureau.com or call (866) 376-6591.

ISBNs: 978-1-5387-5094-0 (mass market), 978-1-5387-5093-3 (ebook)

Printed in the United States of America

OPM

10 9 8 7 6 5 4 3 2 1

To Emily. You are loved.

Acknowledgments

Sincere thanks to all the dedicated people who have helped with this novel. I am truly grateful. My agent, Elaine Spencer, always has my back, as does my publicist, Kim Rozzell. These two women know how to keep me out of trouble. A huge thank-you to my wonderful editor, Leah Hultenschmidt, who is a joy to work with. To the Grand Central Publishing Art Department, especially Craig White and Elizabeth Turner Stokes—the cover of *The Highland Rogue* really pops. The Forever marketing team does a lovely job keeping my books in front of fans, and I am in awe of the social media marketing skills of Estelle Hallick, Jodi Rosoff, and Monisha Lakhotia. Finally, hugs to the copyediting and typesetting department; to Tareth Mitch and Angelina Krahn for her fastidious and diligent copyediting. Bless you all!

THE
HIGHLAND
ROGUE

Chapter One

March 14, 1714
Aboard the Highland Reel
Sailing through the North Channel

A cold sweat seeped through Sir Kennan Cameron's shirt as he shrugged into his leather doublet and pushed out from the captain's cabin of his eighteen-gun ship. His breathing sped, straining against the tightness in his chest. Disbelief consumed his mind.

No. Bloody. Chance.

A tic twitched at the back of his jaw. To mask his alarm, he straightened the tricorne atop his head. They'd been at sea for months. Why now? Why when they were but a day's sailing from his beloved Highlands?

God on the cross, he prayed the report was wrong. "Runner saw Vane's pennant, did you say?"

"Aye." Wheezing, the old quartermaster, Lachie Mor, tried to keep pace, tottering on bowed legs. "'Twas a dread black flag complete with Satan's dancing death."

A dank mist engulfed them as they clambered up the steps to the helm. "How the devil can anyone see a damned thing in this?" Kennan wiped the sleep from his eyes. Accursed pirates. It was typical of a varlet like Jackson Vane to mount a dawn attack; navigating in this soup was impossible for the best of sailors.

The boatswain, Mr. MacNeil, met them at the ship's wheel. "The lad spent the entire night in the crow's nest. Said he saw the flag above the fog as it rolled in just afore sunrise."

By the eerie haze in the east, the sun was making a paltry attempt of showing itself. "Where is the cabin boy now?"

"Here, sir." Runner's voice came from across the deck, though the outline of his form was barely discernable.

Kennan beckoned the lad forward as lightning flashed, followed by a thunderous clap. And with it a downpour released its fury. "Are you certain it was Vane's flag?" he asked, ignoring the rain. "Did you have a clear view, or were you waking from a wee nap?"

The lad stood square and looked him in the eye. "I was fully awake. I ken what I saw."

"How far out?" asked Lachie Mor.

"Hard to say. The Jolly Roger was like a phantom waving above the mist without a ship." At the age of sixteen, Runner had proven himself an able seaman and wasn't one to tell tall tales.

Kennan turned to MacNeil. "Man the cannons at once."

"I've already given the order, sir."

"Damn them to Hades," growled Lachie Mor. "Vane

has a gargantuan pair of cods if he aims to attack this close to Britain."

Mr. MacNeil gripped the wheel, his knife-scarred face white as bed linens. "Mayhap, but if he does, the queen's navy will not be alerted until our bones are at the bottom of the sea."

"Wheesht. You're talking as if we're already doomed." As the words slipped through Kennan's lips, the hairs on his nape pricked. And when he peered ahead, the tendrils of breath billowing from his nose turned to ice along with the air in his lungs. With the rain, the fog had lifted a bit, and he almost wished it hadn't. Dead ahead, not one but three schooners raced toward them at full tilt—each one flying a black flag with skull and bones.

"Tack hard to port!" Kennan bellowed, opening his spyglass. He twisted the copper casing to sharpen the image, but the mist and rain were still too thick to discern much detail. Hell, he needed nothing more— by the speed and bent of the approaching armada, Vane intended to attack. Damnation! How could he know what lay beneath the false bottom of the hold? And why the devil did Vane wait if he intended to plunder? Why now when the *Highland Reel* was but a day's sailing from home?

"Outrun them?" Mor asked over the screeching of the booms of all three masts while they swung across the deck.

"Or what?" Kennan slammed his spyglass shut, his gaze scanning the faces of his crew for any sign of a traitor. "If we stand and fight, we're dead men."

"But there's nay time!" MacNeil shouted, his arms shaking as he fought the resistance of the wheel.

Ahead the enemy ships divided, one sailing broadside

to port, the other to starboard, and the third making a sharp turn, cutting across the *Highland Reel*'s bow.

"Lord save us," grumbled Lachie Mor.

"We're nearly home, damn it all. By God's grace I'll be sitting by my father's hearth this eve! Fire a cannon from each side and let them know we'll not surrender without a fight." Kennan grabbed Runner by the arm and headed aft at a run. "Come with me."

"Aye, sir." With a spark in his eyes, the lad grinned as if heading to a gathering filled with bonny lassies rather than sailing straight for certain death. "Are we going to send them to hell, sir?"

"You'd best believe it." Kennan ushered Runner to one of the skiffs they used to ferry sailors to the shore. "Climb in."

The boy's smile dropped like a lead weight. "Beg your pardon?"

"You heard me."

"Och, what about the battle?"

Kennan patted the side of the boat, a steely edge to his jaw. "Aye, there's going to be one hell of a fight, but you'll not be wielding your sword this day."

"But I'm nearly as big as a man." Runner—Baltazar his Christian name—tipped up his rain-soaked chin and squared his shoulders while two consecutive cannon blasts from the gun deck shook the timbers. "I'd be milk-livered if I didn't stand with the others."

When lightning burst and thunder brayed, Kennan stepped nearer the boy. "Nay, lad. You'll be alive."

Before the young whelp said another word, Kennan hoisted the cabin boy into the skiff and swung out the wench. "Row northwest and you'll hit land. Take a transport to Achnacarry and ask for an audience with Lochiel.

Tell him of our adventures. Our fortune. Tell him we nearly made it."

"All isn't lost." Runner's voice shot up while he gripped the side of the boat. The skiff teetered in midair, dangling over the side of the ship. "We've a ferocious crew, sir. We'll fight them!"

"Aye, we will." With a swing of his sword, Kennan cut the restraining rope and sent the skiff plummeting to the sea to the tune of Runner's adolescent shrieks. Nay, it wasn't pretty, but as captain of the *Highland Reel*, he wasn't about to let the boy face certain doom. If they didn't come out of this alive, at least someone would take word to Lochiel, the great chieftain of Clan Cameron, Kennan's da.

"Remember!" He cupped his hands around his mouth and shouted to the boy, praying he'd be heard above the mounting blasts from enemy cannons.

Curses to Hades. One more bloody day and they would have sailed into Loch Eil, each sailor wealthier than he'd ever dreamed. A shiver snaked up Kennan's spine. Had one of his crew deceived him? Or was something even more sinister afoot?

When he turned, the schooners had formed their trap. Three to one. He'd never admit it to a soul, but the odds of surviving this day were nil. "Fire at will!" he roared. Thrusting his sword above his head, he ran back to the helm, his pistols and dirk straining on his belt. He sheathed the sword and grabbed his musket from Lachie Mor's hands. "To arms!"

The entire ship shuddered as the cannons below decks let lose their arsenal. The pirate ships fired shots across bow and stern, but not a missile hit the *Highland Reel*. And Kennan knew why. The treasure aboard

was enough to tempt any pirate on the high seas. They
hadn't dallied when they left Nassau, but someone
had beat his ship to British waters—someone fast and
shrewd enough to ruin him. Unless that someone had
sailed ahead?

Who?

Mistress Evans?

Unlikely.

Not only had the woman supplied his ship, the widow
had been more than accommodating in Nassau—very
accommodating indeed.

*I pledge my oath, if I survive this day, only God will be
able to save the Judas who betrayed me.*

As Kennan charged his weapon, crewmen with their
muskets kneeled behind the hull. He hardly noticed the
rain drenching his clothes as he took aim, glad the mist
no longer impeded his view. At broadside, the enemy
ships heaved to. And Lord save the poor bastard looking
straight at his sights.

"Muskets, fire!" His finger closed around the trigger,
making the gun explode with a deafening blast. The
stench of sulfur burned his nostrils as smoke billowed
from the barrel, but not before the pirate catapulted backward with the impact of the lead ball hitting him square
between the eyes.

Pandemonium reigned with volleys of musket and
cannon fire. One of the schooners listed in the water from
a hit to her hull, but the battle had only begun.

With a roar, the brigands on two sides levered planks
into place. Kennan drew his flintlock pistol and fired, hitting his mark. Meanwhile, his men shoved the boards to
the water, only as soon as one crashed to the sea, another
followed.

He glanced at the quartermaster. "Are you ready for the fight of your life?"

"Ready to send them to the icy depths, sir." As Lachie Mor spoke, pirates swung onto the ship from the rigging above while others leaped from the blasted planks. The first to cross were welcomed with shots of lead to their bellies, but within two blinks of an eye, the top deck of Kennan's beloved barque swarmed with fighting men. The clashing of swords replaced the boom of gunfire, but the screams of the fallen carried above it all.

Kennan and his most trusted man, Lachie Mor, stood side by side, protecting the helm. Each pirate who dared to ascend the stairs met with a thrust of a Highland great sword.

"Watch your two o'clock!" bellowed Lachie Mor.

A brigand swung in from the rigging, and Kennan spun just in time to deflect the cutlass aimed at his neck. Rain stung his eyes. No time to stop, he thrust with his dirk, deflecting deathly jabs with his sword.

Vane's pirates kept coming, leaping over the rail and swinging from ropes, dropping onto the deck, cutting men down with ruthless terror—as if Vane and his devils had descended from the black clouds overhead.

Kennan gripped his dirk tight in his fist while his sword hissed and struck their cutlasses—fighting four at once, then eight. Mor crashed backward through the rail, leaving Kennan to fend off the onslaught on his own. The iron taste of blood filled his mouth.

His blood or another's?

It mattered not. Nor were the rigors of his daily training of any consequence, not while fighting for his very breath. His arms burned and strained with the weight of the sword in his hand.

Backed against the bulkhead, Kennan fought like a madman—a stab to the left, a thrust with his dirk. He hopped to the side, blocking an attack aimed at his heart. On and on he continued, ignoring the searing burn as his muscles screamed for respite.

"Arrgh!" he cried, a cutlass slicing across his midriff. As hot blood oozed into the waistband of his kilt, he fought harder, honing his senses, deflecting every strike as it hurled toward him. He slashed his dirk across an attacker's throat while skewering another on his blade. Kicking, he shoved the pirate away and drew back his sword. With the next clanging clash of iron, his weapon flew from his fist and clattered to the deck.

God on the cross, a behemoth of a man bore down upon him—two missing teeth and ugly as sin. Pressing his back against the timbers, Kennan sliced his dirk through the air. "Stay back, ye bloody Goliath!"

Six blades leveled at Kennan's neck while his pulse beat a fierce rhythm at the base of his throat. Gasping for breath, he looked beyond the enemy as the giant stripped the dirk from his fingers. Not one of his crewmen still standing wielded a weapon. In less than an hour the fortune he'd fought so hard to win was forfeit to the vilest British pirate who sailed the seas.

"Your ship is lost, Cameron, and so is your precious cargo."

Kennan had met Jackson Vane only once in his life, but there was no mistaking the sound of the man's grating voice. He wore a black neckcloth, which some claimed hid a scar so deep that it had changed his voice forever.

Coming into view, the bastard tugged at the cloth now. His scowl was as grisly as his black-whiskered face. "Bind his wrists."

There was no use struggling. Not with so many blades

ready to cut Kennan to the quick. But as the hemp rope wrapped around and slashed into his wrists, he scanned the deck for survivors. The pirates had already gathered the stragglers. Neither Lachie Mor nor Mr. MacNeil were among them.

A weight the size of an anchor swelled in his gut. He should have prevented this—should have been more vigilant. Damnation, he'd been asleep in his cabin while the bastard lay in wait. He should have sailed a different route—gone up the eastern shore of Scotland and down through the western isles. Doing so would have added a sennight or more to the voyage, but that would have been little price to pay.

If only he had the choice now.

"Bring this heap of worthless rot under way, men!" shouted Vane. "Set a course for hell, where no Jack Tar will find us."

A pirate struck Kennan in the back with the butt of his musket. "Move your arse."

The *sgian dubh* and pouch of coins Kennan always wore strapped to the inside of his thigh rubbed as he stumbled forward, straight into the face of Satan. "You've taken my ship, now 'tis your duty to send off the survivors in a skiff," he spat at Vane, ice in his voice.

A twisted sneer split the pirate's black whiskers. "Aye, we'll be casting them off. But they'll need to be strong swimmers. Drag them to the plank!"

The behemoth approached with a noose. Kennan elbowed the man on his right and lurched forward, striking Goliath's chest with his forehead. But his efforts proved futile as two brigands restrained his arms while the big man slipped the rope over Kennan's head. "I'll enjoy watching ye swing."

"Move your arse," growled a vile cur, clubbing Kennan in the back with the hilt of his cutlass.

As the brigand dragged him toward midship, Kennan wrapped his fingers around the noose and tugged it away from his windpipe. Everything hurt. The cut across his stomach stung and throbbed. His muscles burned, and all for naught. He'd lost his bloody ship. Worse—his men either were dead or would soon be swimming for their lives in the icy sea.

The pirates drew out their murderous crime, humiliating every prisoner with taunts, pilfering jewelry, clan pins, and any clothing worth a farthing from their bodies. Some men were completely nude as the pirates forced them onto the plank by point of bayonet. The most heartrending part? Every condemned soul looked Kennan in the eye with haunting stares of disbelief, silently pleading for help.

Cuthbert, the loyal first mate, was the last of the crew from the *Highland Reel* to suffer humiliation. Bless him, he didn't tarry and allow the bastards to plunder his effects. He took a running leap over the side to the roars of the crowd. "I'll meet the lot of ye in hellllll!"

After the dunking splash came from Cuthbert's body hitting the surf, Jackson Vane cracked a switch against his palm, his grin growing more menacing as he sauntered toward Kennan. "Now 'tis your turn, O captain of the briny deep."

"You're a vile excuse for a man," Kennan seethed, baring his teeth. "There is no reason you could not have spared them—sent them off in a damned skiff for God's sake."

"Is that so?" Vane glared with eyes as black and glassy as obsidian. "By your reputation I would have thought you more callous."

His *reputation*? Kennan had done a bit of pirating, but nothing to compare with Vane. "I have no idea to what you are referring."

"You stole into Versailles and plundered a man's gold—quite daring of you. But I admire a chap with courage, albeit foolhardy. Tell me, why did you leave him alive?"

The anchor in Kennan's gut sank to his toes. Dear God, he should have ended the scoundrel's life in France. Claude Dubois was a traitor and a snake. The man had tricked them all into believing he supported the Jacobite cause. Moreover, the bastard had lied his way into Kennan's trust and stolen gold intended to support James Stuart's succession to the throne of Britain. Kennan had merely taken back that which rightfully belonged to the prince.

"Dubois is my Judas? Where is the thief?"

"Waiting to watch you hang." Dubois stepped out from the crowd, grinning wide as if he were proud of the missing front tooth—the gap left after Kennan had removed the upper central with a pair of tongs. "I've been waiting too long to claim my due."

The French cutthroat had deceived everyone. A spy for King Louis, Dubois had wormed his way into Queen Anne's court with intent to stage a coup. Had he been successful, all of Britain would currently be a province of France.

"Nothing was your due." Kennan clenched his fists and took a swing even though the cur was beyond his reach. His effort earned him a yank from the noose. Coughing, he stretched his neck. "You stole the gold not only from me, but from Prince James."

"You were always inordinately gullible, Cameron." Dubois threw his head back with a grating laugh. "I had you eating from my hand."

"And now you're eating from mine." Vane gave Dubois a smirk before he thrust up his hands and strutted in a circle. "What say you, men? Hang the Cameron bastard or feed him to the sharks?"

In a heartbeat, the blood thrumming through Kennan's veins turned as thick as mud. He'd most likely die if he walked the plank, but he'd never survive if he let these bastards string him from the mast. He glanced across the sea. A speck of land darkened the horizon. Was it too far?

"Hang him!" came repeated shouts while Goliath flung the rope over the main boom.

As the accursed beast reached for the rope's end, Kennan dove for the dagger sheathed at the bastard's waist, and slashed it across the pirate's throat. In the time it took to blink, he raced for the plank, loosening the noose and casting it over his head. A musket cracked behind him just as he leaped. The shot seared the outside of his shoulder, tearing through his doublet and shirt, cleaving his flesh.

"Aaaaaaaaaaah!" he hollered, his legs still running as the sea approached.

In the nick of time he pulled his feet together and pointed his toes. He crashed into waves as though he'd slammed into a stone wall at full tilt. Icy salt water engulfed him, attacking with the sting of a thousand wasps made even more excruciating by the freezing snow of Ben Nevis in winter. His breath rushed from his lungs as he fought for the surface, keeping the dagger tight in his fist. As his head popped through the water, musket balls pierced the waves around him with sharp slaps, far sharper than the pattering raindrops on his face.

Taking in a deep breath, Kennan dived under, using

every bit of remaining strength to swim away from his beloved *Highland Reel*. When he next surfaced, the ship had sailed too far for the sights of a musket. Waves crashed over his head while he treaded water, searching for survivors. And, as his teeth chattered, he spotted not a soul. Damn. Any men still alive would have started swimming two or three leagues back. And it didn't take a seer to know when a man found himself overboard in waters this cold, he'd be lucky to survive for an hour.

If there are any survivors.

His stomach roiled, though all trepidation vanished at the sight of a dark gray dorsal fin fast approaching from the north. Then another. And another.

Still clenching the dagger in his fist, he faced the sharks head-on.

Chapter Two

*D*ivana tossed a clam into her basket, then took a moment of respite, leaning on her shovel and brushing the tendrils of hair away from her face. The sea was rough after the storm, and the wind still blew a gale. Though on Hyskeir, the wind never stopped. At best it was breezy, and oft blowing so hard that she had to lean forward and fight to walk a straight line. She ought to be accustomed to it by now.

But she wasn't.

Mayhap one day I'll be rescued from this isle and travel to a place where 'tis warm and sunny.

Of course on the Hebridean isle, the only warmth and sun she ever experienced was the odd summer's day, but it never lasted more than a fleeting moment.

As she returned to her work, a sudden bout of gooseflesh rose upon her skin, and an odd sensation prickled her neck, as if caressed by the breath of a ghost.

Inhaling sharply, she gazed out over the dark and menacing swells of the sea. Something glimmered on the water—something with eyes. Her heart stuttered as she stepped forward for a better glimpse, but as the waves crested and fell, the sea creature vanished.

"Mischievous selkie," she mumbled, pushing her shovel into the sand. No, Divana didn't really believe in mystical creatures. If they did exist, she doubted she'd have been stranded on Hyskeir for so long without earning a wee bit of kindness. The fairy folk surely ought to see good in her heart by now. Oh, to imagine if they took her away on a fantastical adventure. Perhaps, if they were real, she would have been taken to the fairy kingdom to marry a handsome prince.

But no. There she stood, hunting for clams. Alone.

As the water filled her hole, it bubbled. At the sign of an escaping clam, she shoveled faster. "Where'd ye go, ye wee beastie?" With a few more scoops, she spotted the clam, dropped to her knees, and wrapped her fingers around the shell right before the slippery mollusk dug deeper. "Ye're nay spiriting away this day, not from me, ye sprite!"

With a chuckle, she tossed her prize into the basket.

As she straightened, the ghostly sensation she'd felt on her neck returned full force. Gasping, she froze, her knees sinking into the sand.

A man crouched at the edge of the surf, his hands on his thighs, a dagger in one fist. Stark, bloodshot eyes stared at her while he panted through blue lips. Water dripped from his hair and clothing. Blood seeped across his stomach, spreading through the fibers of his shirt.

Clutching her shovel across her body, Divana sprang to her feet and skittered away. "Stay back!"

The man's eyes widened, though he made not a move. "Fire," he said, his blue lips quivering.

She glanced back to the bothy, smoke curling above it from the small blaze inside.

"Blanket," he said, his voice forceful and strained as he staggered closer.

"But—"

"Please," he bit out sharply, crossing his arms and shivering like seagrass bent sideways by the wind. "I-I'll nay harm you."

Divana gaped. She hadn't spoken to another soul in two years, and now a large, half-drowned, bleeding man appeared from the sea without a boat. But before she thought of something to say, the Highlander set off, weaving and stumbling toward the bothy, his back hunched, water bubbling from his woolen hose.

Gripping her shovel, she followed. Saint Columba, what ought she do? The wee shelter was her only refuge. "Stop! You mustn't go in there."

Completely ignoring her, the ragged man continued toward her home, walking like a drunkard.

Aye, it was the only place on Hyskeir one could escape the weather, though the thatch leaked and the wind whistled through the rushes—and on the coldest of winter's days, the fire did nothing to warm the tiny hovel.

She surged after him, ready to give him a good wallop. "That is me home. Mine, I say!"

The fiend didn't respond, just pushed inside through the worn sealskin shroud.

Divana stopped and stared. Good heavens, what

was she to do now? Where had this barbarian come from? Why was he bleeding? Was he a pirate? By the look of him, he was half crazed. Worse, he'd barged into her home uninvited as if he owned the entire isle.

Regardless of what he'd said, what might he do to her? And why, after two years, couldn't someone arrive with a blasted boat?

She paced outside the doorway, clutching her beloved shovel.

Should I smack him atop the head? What if I hurt him? What if I killed him?

What if he is a good sort? And how will I ken?

She shuddered, scarcely able to breathe. How could she hurt a man, even if he did barge into her home? She ought to at least try to ask some questions first. After all, the fellow had been wounded...but how had he sustained his injuries? What happened? Why?

What if she went inside and he tried to ravish her?

Divana's stomach turned over as she ran her fingers across her mouth.

That is me home he marched into like an overbearing brute. I ought not allow it. She pounded her shovel on the ground. *I shan't be cast from me own hearth!*

Divana inhaled deeply, summoned her courage, and marched through the doorway.

"Saint Columba's bones!"

The scoundrel had removed his doublet and shirt and crouched over the peat fire with his hands extended. His bare back was riddled with white scars, and a vicious wound on his shoulder bled. When he turned, it wasn't the mat of blond curls on his chest that drew her eye first. The man's well-muscled stomach had been sliced open from flank to flank. Och, he'd been through the wars for certain.

Divana clenched her shovel tightly. "Do not come near me."

His complexion green, he rubbed his trembling hands. "I need a blanket."

"Ah…" What should she do? Help him? Blast it, of course she should. Never in her life ought she turn her back on a soul in need. Not like her kin had done to her. Divana's gaze shot to her pallet and the only blanket that wasn't threadbare. "Very well, but ye cannot stay. This is me home."

Saying nothing, he swayed and dropped to his haunches. *Is he sick with the fever?*

"Did ye not hear me?" she asked, her fingers twisting over the worn wooden shaft.

"I'll pay…," he mumbled, his head lolling.

A man of means? Not that money would be of any use here. She tilted her chin upward and narrowed her eyes. "If ye have coin, then why have ye washed up on the beach like a lump of driftwood?"

"Pirates attacked…" A lock of his tangled hair fell over an eye. "Please. The blanket."

"Pirates?" That single word made a shiver course across her skin. Divana had heard tell about pirates pillaging and plundering the high seas. They were ruthless and savage. They were murderers.

'Tis a wonder he's alive.

Without a moment's hesitation, Divana took the coveted plaid from her pallet and held it out. "Use this, but as soon as ye've dried, ye must leave me be—"

As she handed him the blanket, he slumped to the dirt floor, his eyes closed. Worse, she spotted yet another wound—big, ugly, and bloody, looking as if a sea monster had tried to take a bite out of his thigh.

Puckered skin in the shape of an arc riddled his flesh like minced meat. Something shiny and white gleamed from one of the fissures. Leaning, Divana looked closer, then plucked away a tooth and held it up. Good Lord, this man hadn't just been set upon by pirates, he'd suffered a shark attack.

"Are ye awake?" she whispered.

When he didn't budge, she draped the blanket over him. Who was this soul? From whence had he come? Had he a good heart or bad? What horrors had he seen that had brought him to this remote isle? And now that he was there, what should she do with him?

What if he died?

Dear Holy Father, please. Not another!

* * *

Divana stirred the pot of kelp and water. Warm steam moistened her face as she leaned over and checked to see if it had begun boiling. There weren't many herbs on Hyskeir, but her mother had oft used a seaweed poultice on cuts and burns. The only problem was she couldn't recall if Ma had added anything but water to the mixture. Though even if she had, it most likely wasn't available.

"How are ye feeling?" she asked the man, but he gave no reply. The dank air in the bothy carried a new scent. His scent. A mixture of sea salt and musk. It was heady yet alluring in an odd way.

After she let the mixture boil for a few moments longer, she ladled some of the thick, sticky muck into a bowl-size clamshell and set it aside to cool. "I've a poultice for your wounds, sir. Me ma always said seaweed staves off corruption, and I would not want your injuries to grow putrid."

The man lay still, stretched out on the dirt floor. His hair was nearly dry—a light brown color with wheaten wisps framing his face. In repose his was a braw face. Expressive brows arched above his closed eyes—dark eyelashes forming crescents on his cheeks. He seemed rather young, though deep lines etched the corners of his eyes and mouth as if he spent a great deal of time squinting in the sun.

Divana moistened a bit of cloth and cleaned her hands with the lye soap she'd made last year. Then she kneeled beside the Highlander and drew the cloth across his brow and cleansed his face with gentle brushes.

The Highlander's nose suited his face—masculine, sturdy, rectangular. He drew in a breath through slightly pursed lips that were chapped so much, blood-encrusted scabs filled the cracks. Divana scooped a bit of duck fat onto her finger and ran it over his lips, surprised to find them full and pillowy soft beneath the abrasions.

Though the stubble peppering his face had made him look dangerous at first, in slumber he appeared rather harmless. She folded the blanket down to his hips. The red and green plaid he wore was still damp, and he shivered, gooseflesh rising over his fair skin—far fairer than his tanned face and hands. The muscles across his belly were taut like bands of iron. Even his chest, rising and falling with each slow breath, was powerful yet riddled with puckered scars. He'd been savagely sliced across his belly. Divana peered closer. The wound hadn't exposed his insides, thank heavens. She took his thick leather doublet and held it toward the light. It had been slashed right open.

"I reckon this coat saved ye."

There was a jagged cut directly across his shoulder, but the flesh looked like minced meat.

She retrieved the clamshell and blew on the poultice. "I do not reckon this'll hurt." Scraping her teeth over her bottom lip, she shifted her gaze to his eyes. "But we'll soon ken if it does, will we not?"

The big Highlander didn't move as she used her fingers to work the seaweed concoction into the wound on his stomach, being sure to glob it on thick. The mixture didn't adhere as well to his shoulder and slid to the ground. Divana scooped a handful and held it against his arm for a time, then shifted her gaze to the blanket, beneath which the shark bites needed tending as well.

She felt herself blush as she bared the man's thigh. Soft brown curls covered his leg from the ankle up his shin and then under his kilt. Though her blood stirred with curiosity, Divana didn't dare push the wool higher. Heavens, he even had hair on the tops of his toes.

"But that's nay why I've exposed your leg, is it?" she said softly. To stave off her loneliness, she oft hummed a tune, and she did so now—more to slow the questions racing through her mind. *Who are you? Where did you come from? What happened to the pirates? And how did you escape the sharks?*

All these questions plagued her, but she'd never uncover the answers if her poultice didn't work. He might grow fevered, and such a thing must not happen. Fevered people died, and Divana knew more about death than most anyone.

She stopped singing and looked at the man's face. "Ye cannot die. Please..." She set down the clamshell and leaned over his bonny face.

"Live," she whispered while a haunting chill spread over her skin.

Chapter Three

*E*verything throbbed. The worst of his misery? The relentless pressure in Kennan's head, but at least the damned shivers had stopped. He lay on hard ground, a shoulder blade grinding into stone, the smell of earth strong in his nostrils.

Where am I?

He hissed as clashing swords and booming cannons rang in his ears. Grunting, he ground his molars, reliving the fight, yet aware he was no longer aboard the *Highland Reel.*

God blind me. How many of his men had perished?

I should have been more vigilant. I should have sacrificed myself and my cargo before the battle began.

Damn it all to hell, I should have drowned with the lot of them.

What he wouldn't give to bring his crewmen back. Every last one. Their lives were worth more than the treasure in the hull. More than his worthless life, for certain. The slice across his midriff burned as he relived the hell, tortured by the terrors from a mere hour of violent battle early that fateful morn. One moment he'd been fighting beside Lachie Mor, and the next, the old sailor had vanished—plummeted to the sea.

Had he swum to safety? Or had he met his end?

Damn Jackson Vane to hell!

Kennan thrashed until his head hit a stone, bringing consciousness nearer.

Where am I?

He opened his eyes, barely managing to squint. The bloody rock beneath his head ground into his temple. Not but an arm's reach was a firepit. Smoke hung in the air above like the breath of a dragon ready to send him to Hades.

Rolling to his back, he stretched his leg and winced. "Ugh." One of the sharks had tried to eat him alive—right before Kennan had thrust the dagger into the beast's eye. Only then a miracle had happened. As the shark's blood turned the water red, the rest of the mongrels swam away nearly faster than they'd attacked.

Rustling came from nearby. "Are ye awake?" asked a woman, her voice soft. Soothing.

He ran his tongue over parched lips while thirst suddenly consumed him. "Aye."

Above, his doublet, shirt, and woolen hose came into view, hanging from the only crossbeam. And beside him rested his gold brooch with the Cameron crest. Och, he remembered now. The redheaded lass had been alone on the beach digging for clams, her feet bare. She had cowered when she saw him. Hell, he most likely posed a gruesome sight—bloodied and exhausted from his fight both in and out of the water. Kennan moved his fingers to his shoulder and hissed. Pulling his hand away, he examined something green and slimy.

He raised his head. "What's this?"

The woman leaned over him, looking sleepy eyed and holding a clamshell with the green muck. "I made a seaweed poultice for your wounds."

Seaweed and salt. Damnation, it stung. "It stinks. Hurts as well."

"Leave it be. 'Twill keep the pus at bay."

"You a healer?"

"Not by half." She shifted her eyes aside. "'Tis a relief to see ye're awake."

The bothy hadn't a single window, and no light shone around the fur covering the doorway. "How long have I been here?"

"Hours. 'Tis almost morn."

He dropped back and draped his arm over his forehead. "I feel weaker than a bairn."

"Perhaps ye need a meal," she said, fetching a pot— her feet still bare. "I've boiled some clams. Are ye hungry?"

Kennan wasn't until she mentioned it, but suddenly he was ravenous. "Aye. Thirsty as well." He sat up too fast and his head swam while the blanket fell to his waist. The lass had caked the wound across his gut with her wicked remedy, too.

The woman's inordinately long tresses swept forward as she levered a cast-iron pot to the ground in front of him and sat opposite. He gave the vessel a cursory glance, then peered around the bothy. It might be better than a tent, but the shelter was crude for certain. "Do you live here?"

"Mm-hmm." She placed a chipped wooden cup in

front of him—one that looked like it might be better off tossed in the middens.

"Anyone else?"

She looked up, her eyes intense and blue as sky. Her fiery red hair was mussed, still needing a good brushing, same as it had on the shore. Her skin appeared windblown with rosy cheeks. Pockmarks riddled the right side of her chin. But the fear in her shocking blue eyes made his breath stop.

He took a long drink of water, then cleared his throat. "Forgive me. My name is Kennan...Sir Kennan Cameron."

"Saint Columba's bones." Her gaze grew more intense with her unseemly oath. "Ye're a knight?"

"I am, though my rank did nothing to prevent me from being in this predicament at the moment." He took another drink of water, letting the sweetness flow over his tongue. "And you? What is your name?"

"Divana...Campbell."

That figured. Not only had he washed ashore onto some godforsaken island, he'd happened upon a bloody Campbell. "What is this place?"

"Hyskeir."

He closed his eyes and pictured his map of western Scotland. "A speck...west of Rùm?"

"Aye."

"I thought this place was too barren to support humanity."

"It is."

"But you're here."

"Only me."

"How the blazes did you end up all the way out on a wee Hebridean isle alone?"

"'Tis a long story. One I care not to relay." Divana pushed the pot toward him. "Now eat afore the clams turn cold."

Kennan took an opened shell and tore off the meat with his teeth. The single bite increased his hunger and he devoured five more.

The lass stared as if she'd never seen a man before. Or a barbarian. He didn't need a mirror to know he posed a grisly sight.

Wiping the juice dribbling down his chin with the back of his hand, he examined her as well. The light from a tallow candle in a seashell flickered across her face. Even her unkempt hair looked like polished copper. The lass had a spark in her eyes—the look of a fighter. If she had been surviving alone on a wee isle, he didn't doubt her spirit.

"You wouldn't have a flagon of whisky sitting about?" he asked.

She snorted, loudly. "Whisky? Are ye daft?"

"Mayhap I am." Taking another clam, he again glanced about the crude shelter. Made of stone, it was cave-like with a thatched roof, the crossbeam so low, he'd needed to stoop when he stepped inside. Along the far wall was a pallet with eider duck feathers strewn everywhere.

Nothing about this woman or her circumstances made sense. "Do you have a boat?"

She reached for a clam and pointed it from wall to wall. "If I did, I would not be living here, now would I?"

"Nay?" Kennan licked his lips. "Then why are you?"

She scraped off the meat, licked her lips, and rocked back, her face taking on a shadow that spoke of fear, horror, and something else.

Sadness.

Aye, that was it. This woman carried a heavy burden. "Ye ask too many questions."

"That's what a person does when he wants to come to know someone better." Kennan tugged his shirt down from the beam above. Finding it dry, he pulled it over his head, making the wound across his belly sear and the ache in his shoulder practically blind him. Trying not to show any sign of discomfort, he ran his hands through his salt-encrusted hair. Dear God, he must look a fright. Perhaps if he made an attempt to appear more presentable, the lass might be willing to explain what the devil had happened to her. He tied the shirt's laces, though his neckcloth had fallen off sometime between the battle on the ship and the fight with the sharks.

"Forgive me. I was thoughtless to address you without a shirt." He ought to have put on his doublet as well, but the thought of shrugging into damp leather made him hesitate. The shirt had been bloody painful enough.

Divana drew a hand to her chest and smiled—a quite lovely smile, as if she was truly taken aback by his attempt at thoughtfulness. Most women Kennan knew would have already given him a good chiding about his lack of manners, especially his sister.

Kennan cleared his throat. "Now tell me, where do you hail from, lass?"

"Connel."

Campbell lands—that made sense. "And where's your kin?"

"Gone."

"Still in Connel?"

"Nay. They're in heaven."

"All of them?"

"Aye. Ma, Da, me wee brother, Eann."

He eyed her as he ate another clam. "What happened?"

Wiping her hand across her nose, she looked to the ground. "Th- they sent us here to die."

Kennan gaped at her while a sickly lump dropped to his stomach. What? He shoved away the wooden cup. He'd heard tell of clans sending away their kin to protect the others. "Smallpox?" he whispered, scarcely able to utter the word. Where had he bloody landed?

She didn't look up, shame written across her face. "Two years past."

"God on the cross!" He pushed to his feet, hitting his head on the damned beam. Stars darted through his vision while he tried to shake off his dizziness. "You brought me into a den of death?"

Divana stood as well. A good two heads shorter, the lass thrust her fists on to her hips. "Ye marched in here afore ye were invited—I told ye not to go inside, but ye wouldn't listen to the likes of me, now would ye?"

Kennan tried to focus on her face, but the damned blow to his head rendered him as dizzy as a mad ewe. How much blood had he lost? He reached for the beam but missed, managing to stumble toward the lass with his hands outstretched. "Why in Hades did you not stop me?" he asked, his voice cracking as he staggered to keep himself from falling on his face.

The wench skittered away, grabbing her blasted shovel. "I kent ye were a scoundrel! Stay back or I'll thwack ye."

He almost laughed. He would have if his knees weren't about to buckle, or worse, he wasn't about to contract smallpox and die. But no self-respecting Highlander would let a slip of a lass threaten him with a shovel. "You ken I'd seize that damned spade from your fingertips if you gave it a swing."

She took another step away, putting her back against the wall. "Ye would never!"

"You think not?" Even riddled with wounds, his knees wobbling and weak, a wee lass wouldn't pose a challenge.

"But ye said ye're a knight. That means ye live by a code of chivalry—ye're a queen's man."

Indeed, Kennan lived by a code of chivalry, but he'd never call himself a queen's man. He took a step toward the doorway, but his head swam so much, he was forced to brace himself on the wall. God save him, he was in no shape to go anywhere. "How long ago did your kin pass?"

"I told ye two years. It has been ages."

Had enough time lapsed to clear the sickness from the isle? If it hadn't, he was already as good as dead. Weaving like a drunkard, he bent toward her and examined the scars on her chin. "You were inflicted, were you not?"

"Aye, but it didn't kill me."

"And now? Are you well?"

"The rash and fever has nay returned."

It hadn't returned? She'd survived.

What were his chances? After he'd watched his men die, he deserved to fall ill and succumb to smallpox on this godforsaken isle.

His head spun faster as Kennan tried to think.

He was weak—too weak to attempt to swim to Rùm. Worse, the cold would kill any man before he made it halfway. Without a boat, a treacherous swim was his only option. He looked the ginger-haired lass over from head to toe. If the dread speckled monster still lingered in this place, his chances were grim. Blood streamed from the cut on his abdomen and pooled on his shirt again—blood mixed with Divana's deep green poultice. What an untenable state of affairs. If small-pox didn't slay him, his festering wounds most likely would do the job.

Chapter Four

Snowflakes splattered Divana's face when she popped her head out the sealskin doorway. Ugh. Another blustery March morn had arrived. At least the snow rarely amounted to much on the isle, though the chill made things miserable. Ducking back inside, she clutched her moth-eaten arisaid about her shoulders. The Highlander still slumbered, covered by her best blanket. The other two were threadbare, but better than nothing.

After she wrapped one over her head and shoulders, she moved to Sir Kennan's pallet and tapped his foot. 'Twas a shame his shoes didn't make it during his swim, else she might have borrowed them to allay the cold, even if his feet were much larger.

"Are ye awake?" she asked softly. He'd slept two full days, this being the third. He ought to have had enough sleep by now, and the longer he slept the more worried she grew.

When he didn't stir, she stooped and felt his forehead.

Thank heavens he wasn't running a fever, though he had a bit of a knot where he'd smacked his head on the crossbeam. Better yet, there were no signs of red spots, either.

Perhaps the threat of infection was gone. That would make sense. If this man didn't contract smallpox in this very place where Ma, Da, and her wee brother had suffered and died, then Divana could be certain the dread sickness was gone for good.

But why hadn't Sir Kennan stirred? Her gaze shifted to his abdomen. The bleeding had stopped, but she'd best make another poultice for his wounds.

She smoothed her fingers over the stubble on his jaw and chin. It was blond, not red like her father's had been. The light color of his beard contrasted with his hair. With one finger, she drew a line across his mustache. The beard softened the angles of his face, but Divana wavered as to whether it made him look friendlier or more menacing. He needed to open his eyes. Then she'd know.

"Please wake. I'm ever so worried about ye, and I've nay the skills to set ye to rights." She hadn't been able to save her kin—and it frightened her to her toes to think Sir Kennan mightn't survive as well. And because she was all but useless as a healer.

If only they weren't stranded on this godforsaken isle, she might actually be of some help to the poor man. All she managed was to dribble water into his mouth and apply seaweed poultices. She closed her eyes and clasped her hands. "Dear Jesus, if ye have not forgotten me, please, please, please save Sir Kennan. I cannot survive another death. I haven't been acquainted with him but for a short time, but in me heart I ken he's a good man—and he said he wouldn't harm me. And I believe him. I do. Please...do not let him die."

She opened her eyes, a wee bit blurry with tears. Blinking them away, she smoothed the back of her hand over his forehead just like her ma had done to her when she'd first taken ill. Through her worry, she managed a sad smile. "Can ye believe it? There's a real live knight in me bothy—a Cameron, no less."

Aye, in the Highlands, the name Cameron was nearly as feared as Campbell. Though even Divana knew their clans had always feuded through the ages. Presently, Campbells sided with the crown, and Camerons were suspected of being staunch Jacobites. Though Divana cared not for any it. Whoever sat on the throne in London had never affected her one way or the other. Who gave a fig about clan feuds and forays now? Truth be told, now that she was no longer afraid of Sir Kennan, it was nice to have someone here—someone to care for.

Sighing, she pulled the blanket up to his chin and looked toward the doorway. One thing about living on a barren skerry like Hyskeir, simply finding enough food to stay alive was a daily chore. During the past two autumns, Divana had harvested salt from the rocks and dried enough eider duck meat to see her through the winter, but her stores were gone now. So were the ducks until a few days past. She'd spied a flock dallying about, and soon half the shore would be overrun by them...and there would be eggs as well.

Clutching her blanket taut beneath her chin, she collected her slingshot and headed out into the blustery cold. Her feet—wide, calloused, and unseemly—always bore the brunt of the cold. But she'd never owned a pair of shoes. Aye, she'd seen Sir Kennan look at them, and had turned her toes inward while her cheeks had burned something awful. What a fright she must pose to a man like Cameron. Her dress was torn at the elbows and stained, though she did wash it whenever it was warm enough to do so. She owned one petticoat, and that was in tatters. Thank heavens it was hidden beneath her skirt.

The island was so small, it took little time to walk to the end and back. On the east side were craggy rocks that were difficult to traverse, and on the west was a beach where the eider ducks nested. Seals as well. Some wayward traveler must have killed a seal and stayed in the bothy before she'd arrived, because sealskin covered the doorway—very warm sealskin. If only she had a musket or a bow and arrow, she might try for a seal. Then she'd have a warm fur to wrap around her shoulders in winter— lots of meat and fat to put up as well.

But Divana shuddered at the thought of killing a seal. How could she do it? Or even think of such a thing? She didn't much like killing ducks, either. And she wouldn't if she had any other choice.

At the south of the island was a small cove, but Sir Kennan had come ashore in the north—right near the bothy—one of the best spots for hunting clams when the tide was low.

She stopped atop the lea of seagrass and searched the western shore. Ah, yes, more ducks had arrived and, by the squawking overhead, more were soon to be nesting. She crept very slowly until she reached an enormous rock she used as a duck blind. Plucking a fist-size stone from the ground, she loaded her slingshot. Then she moved at a snail's pace to peer around the rock.

Not but twenty paces down the incline, a female sat alone.

"Lord, bless the wee creature," Divana whispered under her breath. With a flick of her wrist, she wound up her slingshot. One circle, two, three!

* * *

Kennan opened his eyes after the lass left the bothy. He'd stirred when she brushed her fingers over his beard. And though he'd heard her whispered prayers, his mind hadn't let him come fully awake—not until she was gone.

His mouth parched and his entire body feeling as if it weighed fifty stone, he willed himself to sit upright. The movement restarted the pounding in his skull, and he pressed the heels of his hands to his temples to quash it. When he stretched, the wound across his belly burned. Aye, the shoulder and leg stung as well, but he'd been asleep too long—abed too long.

At his side, Divana had left the chipped cup filled with water. He picked it up and drank. The water tasted better than he'd had in a long time—as if from a Highland spring. He used the last of it to splash his face, then ran his fingers through his hair. This time, he was mindful of the crossbeam when he stood.

His doublet was dry, though the leather stiff. When he shrugged into it, his shoulder burned like he'd been sliced open with a dull blade. He leaned against the wall to steady his breath and will away the pain.

I'm growing bloody soft.

This was no time to lie low and lick his wounds. He owed it to his men to make Jackson Vane pay for every lost member of the *Highland Reel*'s crew— Vane *and* miserable Dubois. *I should have run my dirk across that Frenchman's throat when I had the chance in Versailles.*

Kennan fully intended to reclaim his silver as well. With a plan forming in his mind, one day he'd face the pirate and take back his due.

But first Kennan needed to find a way off the island and head for his family lands in Achnacarry. There he'd stand before his father and damn the consequences.

As he stepped outside, the brisk wind served to provide the wakeup he needed. Turning, he caught the flutter of Divana's skirts before she disappeared over the crag. He'd sailed past this wee isle several times before, but he'd never given it much thought aside from allowing for a wide berth. Many a ship had fallen victim to low-set skerry isles like Hyskeir—in rough seas they were difficult to see. The odds for rescue were slim since Divana had admitted being alone for two years. Any sailor worth his salt wouldn't give this isle a cursory glance—Kennan hadn't.

He hissed as sharp rocks prodded the soles of his feet. He'd had to kick off his shoes when he fought the sharks and swam for his life, but he missed his brogues now. Aye, he was soft all right. That slip of a woman had crossed over the stones as if she'd been barefoot all her life. Perhaps she had.

He stopped when he crested the hillock. Divana crouched behind a boulder, swinging a slingshot toward a flock of eider ducks.

Och, so the wee lassie eats more than clams. No wonder her pallet had been peppered with feathers. Doubtless, it looked a fair bit more comfortable than the dirt floor.

With her release, the hiss of her rock cut through the wind as it hurtled toward the duck. Kennan moved closer while he watched the unsuspecting eider collapse. "I'm duly impressed. I do not think I have a man in my crew able to do any better."

She whipped around, her expression startled, but as soon as she saw him, her lips eased into a lovely smile. "Ye're awake."

He liked her smile. It was warm and friendly, and made him grin back. "Aye, though my head feels as though it is filled with wool."

"I'm nay surprised, ye've been asleep for two days."

Good God, had it been that long? "Then it is past time for me to be on the mend."

Her brow furrowed. "Do ye mean that?"

"Bloody oath, I do." He winked, remembering the worry in her voice when she'd prayed over him. "I'm no milk-livered varlet set to spend the rest of my days moaning on a pallet."

Sighing, Divana drew her hands over her heart. "I'm so happy to see ye aren't planning to die."

"Me?" He started toward the flock. "Never—well, not yet anyway."

She followed. "I'm glad to hear it."

He picked up the fallen duck and held it aloft while the wool in his head seemed to swell. God's blood, he hated weakness—especially in himself. "What do you aim to do with this beauty? Soup or roast it over the fire?"

"Can ye fashion a spit?"

"Is there any wood about?"

"Bits of driftwood along the shore." She took the duck by the legs and gave it a once-over. "Are ye feeling well enough to be up and about?"

"Yes on both counts." He tried not to sway where he stood, but he did, nonetheless. "The sooner I rebuild my strength, the sooner I can leave this island."

"Oh?" Another shadow of sadness darkened her crystal-blue eyes. "And how do ye intend to go? Swim?"

Kennan stumbled as he began to follow her back to the bothy. "The thought has crossed my mind."

"I cannot."

"Can't swim?" He almost offered to teach her before he caught himself. Once he left this little rock, he'd most likely never see the lass again. And he most certainly didn't plan to be here more than a few days. "Tell me, on a clear day, can you see the isle of Rùm?"

"I think so." She pointed—in the right direction. "I can see a slip of land over there."

"Good, then we can signal them with a fire."

She stared out across the rough seas, scraping her teeth over her bottom lip. "I doubt they will come."

"Because of the smallpox?"

Fear filled her eyes as she nodded, telling of the horrors the poor lass had endured. "They abandoned me," she whispered.

"But that was quite some time ago. Perhaps they'll be curious if they see a fire," he said, trying to sound encouraging.

By the shake of her head, she wasn't convinced. "What will ye burn? The peat won't last if we build a bonfire. I've been careful to ration it."

"But there's driftwood, you say?"

"Aye, though 'tis of no use for a fire—'tis too smoky."

"Smoke might draw more attention." Kennan offered a reassuring smile. "That's what we'll do, collect a pile of driftwood and dry it in the bothy."

Divana stopped outside the doorway and snatched the eider from his grasp. "Och, ye've only just arrived. Can ye not leave matters be?"

He scrubbed his face with his knuckles. Why was she acting so testily? What else was she afraid of? "I haven't grown ill."

"Nay, ye have not, have ye?" she said, pushing through the sealskin shroud.

Kennan followed. "Do you not want to leave this isle?"

"I'd like nothing more," she sniped as if growing angrier by the moment.

"Then we shall build a beacon and burn it as brightly as we can."

"We?" She set the duck on a rock near the firepit and straightened, brushing her hands down her shabby dress. "Do ye mean to say ye'll take me with ye?"

"Och, lass. I'd nay leave a soul, man or woman, stranded on a barren isle."

Chapter Five

*I*t didn't take long for Divana to grow accustomed to having a guest. She'd been ever so lonely, engaging in conversation with someone other than herself raised her spirits higher than they'd been in over two years. As the days passed, Sir Kennan grew stronger and his beard fuller. Though he had a dagger, it wasn't sharp enough to shave. But Divana didn't mind.

This evening, she sat weaving a basket from reeds she'd been soaking when he came inside, his arms laden with driftwood. How he managed to carry such a heavy load with wounds still healing amazed her. He complained not once, though at night his grunts and moans disclosed the pain he must be feeling.

He shook a bit, flinging droplets of water. "'Tis raining."

She pointed her reed upward at the leaking roof that had started dripping in the corner. "I ken."

"Och, I'd best see to repairing that on the morrow."

He turned in a circle, then set to stacking the pieces atop a pile already half-dry.

"I do not ken where ye'll put any more. The bothy is already so full, there's hardly room for us to sit."

He grinned over his shoulder. Goodness, with the beard and a lock of hair dangling over his eye, he looked wild and dangerous. Yet Divana's stomach fluttered all the same. Her silly stomach had been doing a great deal of fluttering of late, and it had nothing to do with hunger.

"They'll nay come if we do not make a fire large enough to broadcast our presence," he said, carefully placing the last stick on top of the heap, then held his palms out while he backed away. Thank heavens the stack held.

"Surely the folk on Rùm have seen the blaze these past three nights. And last eve was so clear—mayhap the clearest night in months."

He brushed off his hands, wincing as he sat on his pallet—aye, he was still in pain for certain. "No one's paid us a visit, have they? We must keep the flame lit until someone grows so curious, they cannot help but sail across the channel and investigate." He winced again. "It could take months."

Divana wove her reed through the basket's spokes. "Aye, they'll arrive with muskets at the ready, knowing how fate enjoys torturing me." She had been afraid when Kennan first built the signal fire. Aye, she'd dreamed about being rescued. But now that there was a chance of it, she feared they'd come and taunt her—mayhap even try to kill her.

"They may have muskets, but I'll talk them out of firing."

Under, over, under, over, she worked the next reed.

"Aren't ye the confident one?" She puzzled, though. Hadn't he been overrun by pirates? What kind of talking had he done then?

"I have to be." He picked up a piece of driftwood he'd been whittling and examined it. "The captain of a ship must maintain order—and with that comes knowing what to say and when to say it."

Divana's hands stilled. "*Captain*, did ye say?" He hadn't spoken much about his past or what had happened— wounds and all. And after listening to his tormented moans in the night, she hadn't pressed him.

Sir Kennan's grin was replaced by a shadowy grimace—one that spoke of the horrors he must have faced. But Divana was no stranger to horrors. She'd lived with the memory of the ravages of smallpox for the past two years.

"Aye," he replied, setting to work by the light of a tallow candle as if he'd said everything there was on the topic.

But Divana needed to learn more. "What happened?"

He pursed his lips and inclined the dagger as if he were carving something very intricate. "You do not want to hear it."

Another reason she hadn't asked about his past was because his conversation was empty and haunted, just like this one. He didn't want to talk about the ordeal. She wove the reeds for a time, chewing the inside of her cheek before she regarded him across the fire. "If someone comes and takes us off this isle, where will ye go?"

"Home to begin with."

"What's it like?"

The grin returned as he held out the figurine—taking shape and looking like a person. "Achnacarry is a village and a fortress, built by my ancestors to protect and defend Clan Cameron."

"Are ye related to the clan chief?"

"He's my da."

The basket slipped in her fingertips. She'd been taking care of the son of a chieftain? And there she sat in tatters. What must he think of her? "Good heavens. A knight and the son of a chieftain?" she said, unable to hide the wonder in her voice. "Do ye have many brothers and sisters?"

"Two younger brothers who are in St Andrews at university, a sister who married the laird of Clan Grant, and a wee half brother who's only two."

Divana grasped another reed and wove it through the tines even faster. "Then ye're the heir?" she whispered.

He scraped his knife, a roll of driftwood curling from the blade. "Last I checked, though the Great Lochiel may reconsider when he discovers I've not only lost my ship and my crew, I've lost most of my bloody fortune."

"Oh, dear."

He tossed the figurine toward the firepit, but it bounced on a rock and landed at Divana's feet. She picked it up and held it to the light. He'd been carving a woman with long skirts and hair. "This is good."

Saying nothing, he stabbed the knife into a driftwood log.

Bless it, no matter where Divana tried to steer the conversation, it seemed to make him more distant. She set the figurine beside her. "At least ye have kin to return to."

A grimace crossed his face as if her words had delivered a slap. "Forgive me. The ordeal that landed you on this isle must have been harrowing, indeed."

She hated to think on it. Perhaps that's why she'd

let Sir Kennan be and hadn't pestered him. Still, the sickly churning of her insides brought by his words made prickly heat spread down her arms. "Aye," she whispered. It seemed it was her turn to grow quiet.

"Death is never pretty."

The threat of tears burned the backs of her eyes. "Watching your kin die rips your heart out and throws it to the sea forever."

He was quiet for a time, then took a deep breath. "Pray tell, what is your age?"

Divana wasn't certain. Poor folk in the Highlands never paid much mind to birthdays—though she'd heard tell of expensive gifts given by the wealthy—by people the likes of Kennan's kin. "I reckon I'm nineteen, near enough."

"You do not know?"

"Why?" She reached for another reed. "'Tis easy to lose count."

"How old were you when you came to the isle?"

"Seventeen, near enough." Why didn't he let it rest? Divana busied herself weaving the reeds. Why should he care about her age? She was fully grown and marriageable—not that she ever dared to dream she'd find a husband. "What is your age, sir? Ye may be a captain, but ye do not appear to be much older than I."

"Oh, how wrong you are, lass. I'm eight and twenty. Nearly a decade your senior." He stretched out his legs and crossed his ankles. "What about your clan? Campbell is a powerful name in the Highlands. Do you have an auntie or an uncle who will take you in?"

She never wanted to see another hateful soul from Connel again. Her hands stilled as she remembered the day, fevered and so ill she couldn't sit up, yet they'd heartlessly poked and prodded and forced Divana and her family out into the cold air and onto a galley. "No one who would want me."

"What did you do afore you came to Hyskeir?"

"We had a wee croft that took most of our time. 'Twas me uncle who insisted they take us away—sent us to die with naught but the clothes on our backs, he did." She stared at her hands, her face growing hot. But every day since the fever cleared, Divana had yearned to leave the isle—of finding a caring family to take her in, mayhap employ her as a servant. She scraped her teeth over her bottom lip. Kennan spoke well of his family, and his da was the chieftain of Clan Cameron. Dare she ask? Taking a deep breath, she let out with it. "If we are rescued, will ye let me follow ye to your lands?" Every muscle in her body tensed as she waited for his reply.

He frowned, stroking his fingers down his beard as if he hadn't thought of what might happen to her once they reached the mainland. "My life is complicated..."

Her heart raced. Once they left the isle, she would need to earn coin. "I-I'd be no trouble. I can cook and clean and mend and tend sheep."

Chuckling, he tossed a square of peat on the fire. "Not to mention dig clams and kill eider ducks with a slingshot from twenty paces."

Divana sat taller. "See? I ought to be of use to ye...or...or someone."

"Hmm." He looked aside, frowning again. "Mayhap you'd make a fine scullery maid at Achnacarry."

"Truly?" She clasped her hands beneath her chin. "Do ye think I could be a servant in a grand castle?"

"I cannot see why you wouldn't do well. After all, you've just given me a summary of your virtues. I'm certain my stepmother would find a position for you..." He turned the bird over the fire, his makeshift spit managing to hold steady without dropping their dinner into the flames like it did the first time they tried to roast a duck. "At Achnacarry you'd have a fine bed, clothes, and you'd never want for another meal."

Honestly? He'd do that for her? She could stay with the family and earn her own coin? "What about shoes?"

"All our servants wear shoes."

Heat rose to her cheeks and she covered them with cool fingers, hoping he wouldn't notice if she was blushing. "I've never owned a pair."

"No shoes?" he asked as if being barefoot were a sin, though few of the crofter's children in Connel were able to afford them. "Well then, I reckon you'll be happier at Achnacarry than anywhere you've lived in all your days."

Divana held up her basket and pretended to examine it, though she was hiding her smile. If Sir Kennan's bonfire did indeed bring a ship, she'd no longer be alone. She'd live and work in a castle. At Achnacarry, mayhap she'd even chance to see Sir Kennan from time to time... at least when he wasn't away being a sea captain.

* * *

One side of the bothy was hewn from the steep wall of the bluff, while the other three consisted of stones bonded together with crumbling mortar. In truth, if Divana stayed on Hyskeir another year, the walls would likely fall to pieces around her. The roof had all but blown away, and Kennan lay on his aching belly, pushing twisted clumps of thatch into any crevice that looked as if it might spring a leak. But with every shove, the existing thatch crumbled a bit more.

I should have left the bloody roof alone.

There was nothing on the isle to use for proper repairs. The fact that Divana had survived alone this long was a miracle, if not a testament to her resourcefulness. He pushed in another clump of twisted thatch, and a gust of wind caught the miserable thing and blew it to the ground.

"Fie!"

There had to be something on this godforsaken isle he could use to tie the thatch down. Aye, he might braid the seagrass into a rope, but they'd most likely see a boat from Rùm before the plant dried and was ready to use. While scavenging for driftwood, he'd spotted bits of rubbish washed up on the shore. Perhaps if he scouted about, he might find some wire or a length of rope that wasn't so eaten away by salt water it was useless.

He'd collected the driftwood on the northern tip, but on the south shore, there was a wee cove where bits and pieces of castoffs from ships were more likely to gather. Unfortunately, his feet didn't seem to be growing any tougher. So, as he'd done since the surf spat him out on this blessed isle, Kennan treaded lightly over the jagged stones. Yesterday he'd walked the circumference of the isle, a trek that took about an hour. He'd spotted the cove but hadn't ventured down to the water because the rocks were jagged and filled with nesting ducks.

Divana said the eiders all arrived within a few days. Good timing, he reckoned, because it took an awful lot of clams to sate a man's hunger. Not to mention the poor lass looked as if she needed a month of feasting to add some meat to her slender bones.

Once he arrived at the precipice, the climb down sharp rocks brought a few more cuts to his feet and hands, and a good scrape to a knee. But the trip wasn't entirely in vain.

The tide was on its way out and, after using a stick of driftwood to dig about the rocks, Kennan found a rusted length of chain and a glass fishing float attached to some netting that hadn't yet rotted.

The tangled mesh was just a bit of scrap, but Kennan held up the blue glass orb and laughed as if he'd found a treasure. Who would have thought a snarled mop of fishing net would raise his spirits? For the love of God, he'd just lost a king's ransom in treasure, and now he was thrilled to be able to fix the leaks on the roof of a decrepit bothy on a remote Hebridean isle.

He'd go back, secure the thatch, and then pile the driftwood and pray the rain would stay at bay for the night. Bless it, he needed to find a way home. Kennan chastised himself for allowing himself a moment of good humor. Time was wasting while Jackson Vane and the wretched Claude Dubois enjoyed the spoils of the pirate's thievery.

Damn them to hell.

After he climbed back up the crag with the wire and netting, a splash of water and a high-pitched squawk rose over the roar of the surf.

Oddly, the noise sounded nearby, but Kennan saw not a thing. Could it have been a duck? A tern, perhaps? Most likely, but Kennan never ignored a twist in his gut, and on an isle this size, it wouldn't take but a moment to inspect. With luck, someone had seen his beacon and come ashore.

He hastened toward the noise only to stop dead in his tracks. Aye, now he remembered the pool. He'd seen it before. It was supplied with fresh spring water, and a burn from its outlet led to the sea. But when Kennan had ventured past yesterday, there wasn't a naked woman standing knee deep, bathing.

Gulping, Kennan blinked, his heart stuttering and completely knocked from its rhythm. Like a daft Highlander, he stared, gasped, and damned near drooled. He should have shifted his gaze away and gone about the business of repairing the roof, but how was a man to avert his eyes from a glimpse of perfection? Divana's long, red tresses contrasted with the smoothest, creamiest skin he'd ever seen. Oblivious to his presence, she scooped water with her hands, then swirled lye soap up slender thighs. Her movement was graceful and feminine, like a swan preening on a glassy pool.

He crouched low behind the seagrass, trying to convince himself to turn away. His heart hammered a wicked rhythm, and something stirred he should definitely be ignoring. How long had it been since he'd enjoyed the company of a woman?

But this was not a woman he ought to begin to consider bedding. To take advantage of her trust would be nothing shy of unconscionable.

Kennan's thoughts muddled and blurred when Divana collected her locks at her nape and tied them in a knot. Wearing rags that barely covered her bones, she'd looked like an urchin—albeit a bonny one. How could he have guessed what loveliness lay beneath?

Kennan stretched his fingers, longing to cup those exquisite breasts and kiss them, worship them, caress them. Succulent pink buds stood proud, made rosier by the cold water. Kennan's gaze trailed to her waist—it was smaller than he'd imagined—and the flare of her hips so very tempting.

When a flock of eider ducks squawked overhead, her gaze darted upward. Before he was seen, Kennan crouched and backed away. The lass must never know that he'd been watching. Never know how much she'd stirred his blood.

He mustn't forget the woman had welcomed him into her tiny home and cared for him at his weakest hour. Only an unprincipled rogue would take advantage and force himself upon such an angel. Divana was kind and generous and deserved far better than a privateer who'd lost his fortune—a man who'd sworn an oath of revenge against the vilest pirate on the high seas. Hell, once Kennan left this isle and saw her safely settled, he'd sail away. The voyage might well last for years. He hadn't yet taken a wife because he still had an adventurer's spirit. There was no use starting something with Divana he'd never be able to finish.

Chapter Six

April 14th, 1714
One month since the Highland Reel *fell victim to*
Jackson Vane's pirates

 T his shovel is nearly rusted clean through," Kennan said while he tossed a clam into the basket. By the way he moved, he looked as if he'd never been injured.

Divana chewed her bottom lip, gazing longingly at the rusty blade. She hated for things to wear out, because once they were gone, there was no replacing them. "Well, do not break it. 'Tis the only one I have."

He stretched his back, then crossed his ankles and stood akimbo, leaning on the shaft. "Did you bring it from Connel?"

"Nay." She walked in a circle while searching the sand for air pockets. She'd spent every night for the past month with this man, she may as well tell him the lot of it. "Men with kerchiefs tied over their faces burst into our cottage at night, forced us out of bed with the points of their bayonets—me uncle in the lead, mind ye, as if he thought we would not recognize me da's brother with his face covered." She clenched her fists and let out an angered grunt. "We were lucky to leave with blankets wrapped about our shoulders."

"Only blankets—no valise, no food?"

"We were at death's door—scarcely able to hold our heads up, let alone think to ask. None of them reckoned we would live out the week."

"So, everything here was already in the bothy?"

"Aye."

"Do you ken who left it?"

"No idea. But I reckon by the long, narrow shape of the shovel, someone most likely came to stay during the summer to collect peat."

Sir Kennan shoved the blade into the sand and scooped out an enormous hole, one that would have taken Divana three digs to make. "I'll wager your guess is close to the mark."

It bubbled straightaway and she pointed. "Haste, he's escaping."

The big Highlander dug deeper. "Och, you're a hard taskmaster."

She threw her head back to laugh but instead a gasp caught in her throat. "Sir Kennan! Look!"

Clam forgotten, he followed her gaze. "I'll be damned."

Divana hadn't allowed herself to hope his bonfire would do its job, but clear as he was digging clams beside her, a single-masted galley approached from the east, its sail billowing with wind.

"I cannot believe it."

Kennan raised his hand to shade his eyes. A tic twitched in his jaw as he pulled Divana behind him. "Redcoats."

The protective gesture made her tingle for a moment, but not for long—not with soldiers drawing near. Unable to help herself, she leaned far enough aside to see them. "Ye mean they've sent dragoons to fetch us?"

"They're not a crew of fishermen, for certain," he said over his shoulder. "I'll do the talking. There's only one thing that matters and it is escaping this isle. I'll sell my bloody soul if I must."

She gulped, staring at the approaching boat. "Do ye think they'll harm us?"

"Not if we don't provoke them. I've just..." The tic twitched again.

"What?"

"I had an altercation with the queen's dragoons last year in Dundee when a customs officer miscalculated the duties on my shipment."

"An altercation? Was anyone injured?"

"Unfortunately, an all-out brawl burst forth on the pier. We were lucky to escape with our lives."

"Good heavens. Why did ye not tell me about this sooner?"

He gave her a look as if to say there were thousands of secrets he still harbored. "It never came up in conversation."

If Sir Kennan was avoiding dragoons, why was he returning to the Highlands? "But were ye not sailing home when ye were set upon by the pirates?"

"Aye—though I was heading for Achnacarry, where I'd have the protection of clan and kin."

"Saint Columba, are we in peril?"

"I think not. Besides, Dundee is in the Lowlands, clear on the other side of Scotland. And neither me nor my crew started the fighting."

This changed things a great deal. She wrung her hands, a stone sinking in her stomach as she watched the galley approach. "Who did?"

"The first shot was fired from the pier."

"'Tis an abomination. Government troops were shooting at a knight of the...of the..." She gave him a nudge. "What were ye knighted for?"

"To begin with, my da's a knight. I was admitted to his order—the Order of the Thistle—for services to the queen in the War of the Spanish Succession."

"Well, that ought to count for something."

"Except I'd wager Queen Anne has no idea I exist. She's not overly enamored with Scotland—or her subjects up here." Sir Kennan sliced his hand through the air. "Enough talk. That galley will soon run aground on the shore, and the closer she comes, the more likely they'll hear anything we say. Just remember, I am innocent in all that has transpired."

"All?"

"Shhhh." He waved his hands above his head. "Hail, ye mates!"

"Move away from the shore," bellowed a stocky man wearing a red coat and a tricorne with a white plume.

Kennan grasped Divana's hand and urged her back, though he kept his face toward the boat. His hand was warm and filled her with confidence even though the men on the approaching ship were scowling something fierce—one was even aiming his musket at them just as she'd predicted.

"Those dragoons look none too friendly," she whispered.

They furled the sail while oarsmen took their places and rowed the boat onto the beach.

"Drop anchor," bellowed the man with the tricorne, standing at the stern. As the crew went about securing the galley, he looked at Sir Kennan yet made no attempt to disembark. "I am Sergeant Corbyn with the queen's dragoons." He had a square, clean-shaven face, and strands of brown hair blew into his squinting eyes.

"Sir Kennan Cameron, and Miss Divana Campbell, at your service." Kennan started forward, but the man held up his palm, making him stop.

Bowing, the decorated knight spread his palms to his sides. "We are...shipwrecked."

The sergeant put his boot on a bench and rested his elbow on his knee. "MacLeod of Rùm reported your beacon—said this isle was infected."

"Nay!" Divana hollered, but Kennan silenced her with a slice of his hand.

"I've been here a month. I'm the one who lit the fires at night and I've suffered no ailment—and as a knight of the Order of the Thistle, you have my word there is no sickness here."

"Cameron did you say?" Sergeant Corbyn spoke with an English accent. He stroked his chin and glanced away. "Hmm."

"My father is Sir Ewen Cameron, clan chief, called the Great Lochiel. I served Queen Anne in the War of the Spanish Succession, and one month past, my ship was set upon by Jackson Vane in these very waters."

The sergeant straightened and threw out his hands. "Vane? Why, he's a queen's privateer."

The man beside her grew so rigid, Divana felt the heat of ire radiating off him. "He's a scoundrel and a pirate,"

Kennan seethed. "He killed my crew and took my ship as well as my coin and cargo."

"Is that so?"

"Aye, I give you my oath."

"What is the name of this vessel?"

"The *Highland*...ah...*Lass*. Aye, the *Highland Lass* it is."

Divana gaped, but she said not a word. If what Kennan had told her was true, he might bargain for trouble by telling them the real name of his ship.

He took another step toward the galley. "As you can see, the pair of us are as healthy as newborn lambs. Please, can you take us as far as Fort William?"

She puzzled all the more. Fort William was but a day's ride from Connel. Did he change his mind and intend to leave her with her heartless kin?

Sergeant Corbyn gave a nod to one of his men. "You'll climb into the bow and stay there. But we're not sailing all the way through the Sound of Mull and up Loch Linnhe for a castaway, no matter who you say you are. I don't give a rat's arse if you're a bloody duke, you'll undergo quarantine in Mallaig."

"Quarantine?" Sir Kennan snorted as he threw out his hands. "But there's no need, I—"

"Do you want off this isle or nay?"

After a moment's hesitation, Kennan glanced from the boat to Divana, his lips forming a white line. "Aye, we'll go with you."

"Men, affix your kerchiefs over your noses and mouths and give the passengers a wide berth."

"May I have a moment to collect my belongings?" Divana asked, her legs suddenly weak. Things were happening far too quickly. Yes, Kennan had promised her a position at his family's keep—she'd have protection there as well. But the last time she was among society, her own kin had abandoned her.

She gripped her tattered skirts. She hadn't a single nice garment to wear, nothing suitable for meeting anyone, let alone a chieftain. What if the Camerons rejected her?

Giving a wink, Kennan grasped her elbow. "I'd best help the lass and hurry her along."

She faced him and licked her lips. Within a month she'd come to trust this man. Why did she fear now? They'd just discussed her spade being almost rusted through. She'd die if she stayed behind.

"Haste ye," said the sergeant. "We want to make good use of this day's fine weather."

* * *

On the sea galley, a dragoon used an oar to give Kennan and Divana kerchiefs to tie over their noses and mouths. Kennan snatched his with a scowl. "We're nay bloody ailing, you maggots. If we were afflicted, Miss Campbell would have perished two years past, and I would be at death's door."

"Shut it," growled one of the soldiers.

Kennan shot the man a leer as he tied the damned kerchief in place. Had there been any other option, he never would have set foot in this boat.

"What do ye reckon they'll do with us?" Divana whispered after the galley got under way.

"Lord kens, the bloody back-stabbers. If only we'd been rescued by a fisherman, not a sergeant with a dim-witted crew. Blast my miserable luck of late."

"Do ye think he kens about..." She inclined her head over her shoulder. "What ye told me?"

Kennan rubbed his hand on his thigh, the thumb brushing the hilt of the *sgian dubh* he'd lashed in place when they'd gone back to the bothy to collect their effects. "I think not. But one thing being a ship's captain has taught me is never leave anything to chance. And never to forget I have friends in high places. Sailing away from that very incident I mentioned earlier, I helped the Earl of Mar clear his name and return to his post on Queen Anne's cabinet."

The lass's round eyes sparkled with her amazement. "Ye're acquainted with an earl?"

He winked—even in the face of adversity, his chest swelled like a king's. "I have friends as well as enemies everywhere."

"I hope more friends. A person can do without adversaries."

"Och, I wish it were so." Ever since he leapt from his own ship's plank, Kennan had been plotting his revenge. And Jackson Vane had become the second greatest adversary in his life. Aye, Vane would pay, but the man Kennan truly wanted to ruin was Claude Dubois. During the negotiations for peace between France and Britain, Dubois had weaseled his way into the queen's court, claiming to be an emissary from King Louis. He also tried to rally the Jacobite leaders against the queen, though in truth he was in London sending information to the French king, who was plotting an invasion of Britain.

Right now, however, revenge had naught but take a rear seat to the problem at hand. There was no time to waste being detained in quarantine by a sergeant hell-bent on proving himself.

With a strong westerly wind, the sailing didn't take more than an hour. Kennan and Divana were forced to disembark at the points of bayonets while the townsfolk looked on as if the castaways were common thieves. Mallaig was no more than a small fishing village, dotted with cottages and one sizable warehouse hewn of stone, used for smoking and salting fish. And it came as no surprise to Kennan when the bastards led them there.

A narrow, muddied road came from the west into town, following the shoreline. He knew it well enough—had ridden to Mallaig once with his da when he was a lad, but he'd sailed past the sleepy village more times than he could count.

Once inside the warehouse, he blinked rapidly to adjust his vision to the dim light. It smelled of pungent fish with a more pleasant overtone of hickory smoke. Divana coughed, waving her hand in front of her face. They walked past a row of women salting fish. Above, two men worked in the tower where the haddock were drying, suspended from wooden poles. Thus far, there were no other redcoats in sight.

"Turn right," Sergeant Corbyn barked. "Then up the steps."

The spiral stairs were narrow, and Kennan crouched to avoid hitting his head. They emptied onto a landing open to the tower on one side with naught but a rail to prevent someone from falling.

Divana stepped beside Kennan, her fingers lightly brushing the back of his arm. "This place smells awful," she whispered.

"You'll be retained in here," said Corbyn, opening the door to an empty room that looked like it might have once been used for storage.

Kennan didn't budge. "How long do you intend to hold us?"

"It will be a fortnight before the physician is back in these parts."

Divana clutched Kennan's arm. "Two weeks? Are ye not taking things a bit far? We're nay criminals."

"She's right," he said. "How many times must I say, if we were afflicted with the dread sickness, we'd already be dead."

Corbyn rested his hand on the hilt of his sword. "Orders from my lieutenant are not negotiable, and you'll stay here until you've been cleared by a proper physician."

Kennan's mind raced. He didn't have time to rot in a smelly warehouse while Jackson Vane sailed farther from Scotland. Damn, he was so close to home he could taste it. "I'd like to send word to my father, Lochiel. Let him know I'm still breathing."

A dragoon shoved him toward the minuscule chamber. "You're full of requests, are you not?"

"Thinks he's Lochiel himself," griped another.

Divana tightened her grip on Kennan's arm. "He's the heir, and ye're treating him like a petty thief."

The sailor smirked, tapping her with the flat edge of his bayonet. "You'd best watch yourself, wench."

Using the palm of his hand, Kennan pushed the gun's muzzle aside. "Leave her be."

The man thrust his weapon in Kennan's face. "Tupping her, are ye?"

As Kennan gripped the barrel, it took but a flick of his wrist for him to wrest the damned musket from the bastard's hands. He whipped the weapon around, moving the butt against his shoulder, only to face four enemy barrels pointed at his eyeballs. It seemed he'd been faced with a similar situation only one month prior.

Corbyn drew his flintlock and aimed it at Divana's

head, the snake. "Return the musket to the sentinel, or I'll shoot her dead."

Kennan bared his teeth, shifting the firearm toward the sergeant. He nearly squeezed the trigger. Nearly. But on top of everything else, he didn't need the redcoats chasing him for murder. "Certainly. If you agree to bring a quill, parchment, and a pot of ink."

"Word will be sent to your father. Now return the musket before my finger decides to twitch."

Chapter Seven

*C*lutching her basket to her chest, Divana stood against the stone wall of the small chamber. It smelled of fish and salt and was as cold as the bothy. Things hadn't changed on the mainland—the soldiers treated them like vermin. At least on the isle, she'd been safe. "We never should have left Hyskeir."

Kennan shook the latch. When his efforts proved fruitless, he marched to the window. "We'll not be here long."

Divana set her basket on the floor and joined him. "Nay? The sergeant said it would be at least a fortnight afore the doctor comes."

"Wheesht." Kennan held up his palm, then pointed down below where Sergeant Corbyn and the dragoons were exiting the mill. Divana clapped a hand over her mouth to silence her gasp.

"Are you truly going to send word to Lochiel?"

asked one of the soldiers, his voice muffled through the glass pane.

Corbyn stopped and looked up toward the window— both Kennan and Divana stepped aside. "No bloody chance. If Lochiel discovers we're holding his son, he'll have half the fighting men within fifty miles beating down the door."

"But why are you holding them?" asked the surly sentry who'd provoked him with his bayonet. "Clearly, neither one is ill."

"Perhaps not, but Kennan Cameron is no saint. Mark me, he's a Jacobite and so is his backbiting father. Dispatch a retinue to Fort William. I want to know more about our captive before we entertain his release."

"And the girl?"

"She's a vagrant—a clear victim of smallpox. I don't give a rat's arse what happens to her."

Ready to scream, Divana drew her fists over her lips as she glanced to Kennan. "I—"

He held up a finger, silencing her.

"Nothing a bath and a decent dress wouldn't fix," one of the men below continued. "She's bonny."

"Forget the dress." They all laughed. "A lass like that ought to be naked and across my bed."

Shaking her head, Divana covered her ears and backed away from the window. "They're vile," she whispered while the horrors of being taken captive and dumped on Hyskeir tormented her mind.

"Och, lassie," Kennan growled under his breath. In two strides, he wrapped her in his arms. "Do not listen to those flea-bitten maggots. They have no idea what they're on about."

Scarcely able to breathe, she grasped his waist and

clung as if her next breath depended on his protection. It had been too long since another person had touched her with care, had talked to her, had been a friend to her, and now there was a very real threat of losing him. "But they want to arrest ye and—and then those animals will come after me."

He pressed his lips to her forehead. His mouth was warm and soft and ever so comforting. "Nay, nay," he cooed. "I'll never allow it."

"What if they take ye away?" She buried her face in his chest, wishing his powerful arms would surround her for the rest of her days. How could she ever trust anyone but Kennan? "I-I'm so frightened."

"Don't be. I'll not allow anything to happen to you."

He smoothed a big, solid hand down her hair. Had he any idea of the comfort he imparted with his touch? Divana clung to him tighter. "How do ye ken?"

Drawing a hand to her cheek, his gentle fingers soothed her as he coaxed her to raise her chin and look at his face. As he focused on only her, his green eyes filled with compassion while the corners of his mouth turned up. "Ye ken you're not helpless, lass."

Trying not to cry, she drew in a stuttered breath. "Against dragoons?"

"Aye." He blessed her with a confident grin. "Did you put your slingshot in your basket?"

"I did. A stone as well."

"Then you're not helpless. You've seen what a wee rock does to a duck?"

She nodded, the sound of his voice giving her strength.

"Imagine what it would do to a man's head."

She remembered back to her childhood—a Sunday sermon at the old kirk. "Like David and Goliath?"

"Now you're thinking." He brushed her cheek with his finger. "Never forget you have a skill few men can match."

When footsteps sounded on the stairs, Kennan lowered his hands and turned his ear toward the door. Divana glanced from wall to wall. Their chamber was empty aside from the straw strewn across the floor and a bucket in the corner. She shuddered to think what it was used for.

Kennan rattled the latch, giving it a good jerk.

"Leave the door alone, you swine," bellowed a guard from beyond.

"We're hungry. Haven't eaten since breakfast."

"You'll be fed after the rest of us." The man chuckled. "If there's anything left."

Backing up, Kennan cupped a hand to the side of his mouth and whispered, "We'll need to be careful what we say." Then he returned to the window and placed both his palms on the pane. It creaked a bit.

Divana slipped beside him. "What are ye doing?"

"'Tis loose," he whispered.

She glanced down to the cobblestones. "Jump all that way?" she asked, so quietly, she barely heard herself.

Kennan pointed up to the exposed beams. "They'll help us."

"How?"

"Go to the door and listen. If the guard makes a sound, whistle."

"I can't whistle."

"Then clear your throat."

Divana did as she was told until Kennan took the blanket from her basket. She dashed across the floor and grasped one end. "Ye cannot use that!"

"Keep your voice down," he whispered, pulling the

sgian dubh from beneath his kilt. "Do you want to remain here at the mercy of Sergeant Corbyn for the next fortnight?"

Biting her lip, she stared forlornly at her blanket. "Nay."

"Then trust me."

It wasn't easy, but she returned to the door and listened while Kennan cut her best blanket—the only blanket she'd brought, the only one she liked—into four lengthwise strips. What was he planning, and how would they stay warm at night? Before she asked, a door down below slammed and another set of footsteps started up the stairs.

"Ahem," she said, clearing her throat and flicking her hand at the Highlander.

Kennan swiftly slid his knife up his sleeve and crammed the blanket pieces into the basket.

"What have you there?" asked the guard beyond the door.

"Bread and water for the prisoners," said an unfamiliar voice.

"Is that so?" A key scraped the lock. "If it were me, I'd let them starve."

* * *

Even Kennan felt the cold as he rubbed Divana's arm. With her head nestled against his chest, she'd drifted off to sleep an hour or so past. Moonbeams shone in through the window, illuminating her face. She was so young yet had endured too much suffering. And through it all, she was cheerful, friendly, and as lovely as an angel. In a world filled with scoundrels, she shone as bright and pure as a primrose blooming in the midst of a mire.

He brushed the hair away from her forehead and kissed her temple. "I vow to guard you with my life," he whispered into her coppery tresses. Her fresh scent reminded him of a newborn lamb and, as Kennan closed his eyes, the need to protect her swelled through him.

But he knew a lass like Divana could never be more to him than a passing fancy. And the woman in his arms was too precious for anyone to love and cast aside. Kennan was the heir to one of the most powerful chieftainships in the Highlands. Men like him married for lands and titles—to strengthen the bonds between clans.

Hell, his sister Janet had married into the feuding Clan Grant, and with that single act, she'd put an end to centuries of unrest and boundary battles. Though, in truth, Janet had married for love, and the Grant laird had ultimately saved his life.

A man can find allies in the strangest places.

Besides, Kennan couldn't think of marriage to anyone at the moment. It would be unfair to wed a woman and then take to the high seas for years.

He smiled at Divana while she slept. Had they met under different circumstances, he never would have come to know her—her strength, her kindness, and her fears. What lass wouldn't be afraid to face the harsh world after being left to die on a godforsaken island by her own damned clan?

A light snore came from the other side of the door, at long last. Kennan let Divana sleep for a time while the guard's snores grew louder. Only then did he squeeze her shoulder. "'Tis time to wake."

Moaning, she sat upright and stretched. "Is it morn already?"

"Nay. Fetch your basket." He gripped his *sgian dubh*

and ran it around the window's frame. Placing his palms on the pane, he pressed with alternating force, trying to carefully dislodge it from the sill without sending the glass crashing to the ground below. The blasted thing gave a fraction but was too deep in the grooves to come out.

"What's the matter?" Divana asked, looking over his shoulder.

"She's stuck."

"Do not break it."

Kennan clenched his teeth. The window gave more up and down than it did from side to side. "I'm trying my damnedest." He grasped the lass by the shoulder and urged her to shift to the place where he'd been standing. "I need your help. Put your palms on the pane, push it upward, and hold it there. I'll see if I can lever it out with my *sgian dubh*."

"What if it breaks?" she asked, moving her hands into place.

"Then we'll make a racket loud enough to wake the dead."

"Och, that's reassuring."

She raised the glass while Kennan slipped his knife under and drew out, but the blasted glass stuck on the right. "Is it centered?"

"Pardon?"

"Move it a hair to the left."

As she shifted, he clenched his teeth, drawing the hilt toward his body. Finally, the glass gave way, but before Divana released her hands, the pane plummeted out the window.

"No!" Kennan shouted in a whisper as he lurched out the hole with his upper body. His heart stuck in his throat as he caught the glass with the tips of his fingers while his *sgian dubh* clanked on the cobblestones below.

"Good glory," Divana exclaimed, her voice hushed but very high in pitch.

"You can say that again." Kennan didn't even breathe as he slowly drew the glass into the chamber and set it on the floor. Staring at each other, they stood motionless, listening until the guard's snores pealed through the timbers. "Hand me the blanket."

After they'd eaten their meager meal of bread and water, he had tied the four strips together, creating a makeshift rope. He swung one end over a rafter beam and tied it firm, then tossed the length out the window. "You go first. It doesn't reach all the way, but the drop won't be far once you've reached the end."

"Are ye certain it will hold?"

He tested it himself. "If it can hold me, it'll hold you for certain. Now haste afore someone comes along."

"All right then." She squared her shoulders, clapped her hands to his cheeks, and gave him a kiss on the lips. "For luck."

Kennan's heart decided to leap in fifty different directions as the corner of his mouth ticked up. He cleared his throat and painted on a serious expression. Good God, he mustn't let on how much her kindly gesture affected him. "You'll be fine and I'll be right behind."

After she made it safely to the footpath, it took but a moment for Kennan to join her. He retrieved his knife and grasped Divana's hand. "This way."

Together they hastened to the stable of an old crofter—a man he and his father had visited when Kennan was a lad—a man who ought to be trustworthy.

"I think we should keep going," Divana said.

"We need a horse first."

"Ye aim to steal a horse?" She yanked her hand away

from his. "Nay! If we're caught, they'll send us to the gallows for certain."

"Not if I pay for the beast." Walking through the dark aisle, he popped his head into three stalls until he found an old garron pony standing in the shadows. "This fellow will do."

Fortunately, the pony's bridle was hanging on a nail beside the stall. Kennan untied his pouch from around his upper thigh. Once he'd taken to the sea, he'd started the habit of keeping the pouch and *sgian dubh* lashed to his thigh, certain not only the knife but also the coin would be of use one day.

Divana's feet crunched over the hay as she stepped beside him. "They didn't search ye there, did they?"

"Nay—'tis why I carry a blade and coin near my loins. A man never kens when his life will hang on a precipice, and with these, I am never penniless or unarmed." As he shook five coins into his palm, the gold glimmered with the fleeting rays of moonlight. "These ought to satisfy the old crofter."

"Saint Columba! Are those sovereigns?" she asked, tracing a finger over a coin. "I've never seen one afore."

"Aye." Kennan closed his fist around them, then let them fall into the horse's grain bucket. For good measure, he removed his clan badge from his shoulder and dropped it in as well. "Five of those beauties will more than pay for this old nag and 'twill keep my da's friend from hastening to the soldiers."

After he bridled the pony, it took nearly no strength to set Divana across his withers.

"How long will it take us to reach Achnacarry?" she asked as he climbed up behind her.

He reached around the lass and took up the reins, the

familiar stirring coming to life again. He liked having her there where he could protect her from brigands like Corbyn. Where he could hold her close to his body. Breathe in her scent. Feel the shift of her hip against his.

Kennan shook his head, sat taller, and tapped his heels. "'Tis a good day's journey, but we'll be following the glens. The route is more direct, but far less traveled."

"Is it faster?"

"That depends on the weather." He tapped the reins and headed inland and south, setting a path for Loch Morar, where they'd find no roads and, God willing, no soldiers.

Chapter Eight

*S*waying with the motion of the horse, Divana curled into Kennan's warmth. Though it was windy and cold, there was nowhere in all of Christendom she'd rather be. Surrounded by his arms made all the fear of being captured melt away. As Divana rested against his powerful chest, watching the midnight-blue silhouettes of the Highlands slowly pass by, she realized that, together, they could overcome anything.

Kennan walked the horse along the south shore of Loch Morar while the moonlight glistened off the rippling waves. "You ought to close your eyes, lass."

She looked up and met his gaze. Even in the dark his eyes sparkled with kindness. "It wouldn't be fair of me to sleep."

"We still have a long journey ahead."

"How far do ye reckon?"

He inclined his head, his silky beard brushing her

forehead. "Just yonder is the inlet—from there we follow the glen until we reach Loch Arkaig—Cameron lands."

"Then we're nearly there?"

"Och, my kin's lands are vast. Achnacarry sits beyond on the River Arkaig. We'll not arrive afore midmorning for certain."

"I don't mind." She shifted her seat a bit, nestling between Kennan's powerful thighs. A contented sigh slipped through her lips. "Ye're warm enough to be a brazier."

"I'm happy to hear your ladyship approves."

"Ladyship?"

"I'm teasing."

"Your mother is a lady, is she not?"

"She was. My stepmother is Lady Lochiel now."

Divana pursed her lips, feeling like a heel. "Sorry."

She fidgeted with the horse's mane while an unpleasant pause swelled through the air. There was one she'd yearned to discuss for sennights. Her mouth grew dry as she ran her trembling fingers through the horse's mane.

I need to stop fidgeting and just have out with it.

"And when ye wed, your wife will be a lady as well?" There. She'd said what needed to be said. But why did she want to leap off the pony and run to the hills?

"If I ever marry, she will be," the man said matter-of-factly, as if they weren't talking about the most important decision of his life.

She flipped the mane hairs to and fro. "Do ye want to marry?"

"I haven't given it much thought, aside from the fact I'm expected to choose a bride one day to carry on with the Cameron line."

Divana licked her lips and dared to look at his mouth.

Aye, before they mounted the horse, she'd risked all by kissing him. And though she'd said it was for luck, there was no mistaking the charged energy between them. If only he'd see fit to kiss her—really kiss her on the mouth without an excuse. "But ye do not want to?"

"Grave matters have taken precedence at the moment. A wife brings a great deal of responsibility. Something which I am not at liberty to give."

"I wouldn't reckon she'd be much trouble at all. I think a wife ought to be a help to her husband, nay hinder him." Smiling, Divana closed her eyes and pictured herself in a garden of roses. *Lady Divana.* Then she jolted and sat straight.

"What is it?"

She rapidly shook her head. "Nothing."

Kennan's arms tightened around her. "Did you see something?"

"Nay, I just had a bad thought is all." It was a glorious, wonderful thought and one she should never again entertain. But still, now that she'd spent so much time with Sir Kennan, it was hard to imagine not being with him for the rest of her days.

I'd best think of something else to talk about afore I go off and kiss him again.

"Tell me more about Achnacarry."

"In the first place, you'll be safe there."

"Even if Sergeant Corbyn comes after us?"

"He might try, but we are not ailing, and no matter what he said about the lieutenant's orders, he cannot hold us without grounds. I highly suspect the only orders Corbyn was acting on were his own."

"Even though ye had the mishap on the pier in Dundee?"

"Even then. And if that matter should ever return to

haunt me, I'm certain the Earl of Mar will petition the queen for a pardon."

Divana shifted to ease the pain in her backside from riding for so long. "It must be nice to have such lofty acquaintances."

"It is," Kennan said, his voice straining. He must be a wee bit saddle sore as well.

"Do ye think the folk in Achnacarry will like me?"

"You?" He chuckled. "Och, you're the most likeable lass I've ever met. My kin will adore you. Besides, 'tis like an enormous family. Da has hundreds of servants."

"Are they all kin?"

"They're all loyal to Clan Cameron. My father can raise an army of a thousand men with a snap of his fingers."

"He must be a powerful laird."

"He is—old and wise as well. Some say he'll never die, the Great Lochiel they call him." The rushing of a river filled the air. "This is where the footing can be a bit dicey. 'Tis a blessing we have a clear night and a bright moon to travel by."

"It is a blessing. If only we had a blanket, we'd both be toasty warm." She bit her lip. The blanket had been used for their escape. She shouldn't have mentioned it.

"Are you cold, lass?"

"A little, though it would be far worse without your arms around me." She glanced up to his face. The whites of his eyes looked brighter and the green almost black.

"When we arrive I'll see to it you have new clothes, a cloak, and all the blankets you want."

"Ye would do that for me?"

"You took me in when I was half-drowned, did you not?"

"Aye." She brushed a finger over his beard, the hair soft and curly. "Will I oft see ye there?"

"Truth be told, I'm not oft home and I—" He pursed his lips.

"You what?"

"I've a score to settle with Jackson Vane."

"But he's far away. Do ye nay need a new ship?"

His expression grew distant with his curt nod. "A ship and a crew."

"I don't suppose your da has a spare sea galley he can lend ye."

"Do not sound so certain. My da is as shrewd as he is wise."

"Nay unlike his son I reckon."

"Nay, I'm half the man my father is. Besides, it will take a bigger ship than a sea galley to find that bastard," Kennan said with a low growl followed by an uncomfortable silence.

Divana closed her eyes for a time. She preferred not to talk about seeking revenge on Vane or anything to do with Kennan sailing away. He didn't know that she'd been awake when he pressed his lips to her forehead and vowed to guard her with his life. Did that mean forever or just until they reached Cameron lands?

She yawned. "Do ye think Sergeant Corbyn kens we've escaped by now?"

"I'm hoping they don't realize we're missing until morning."

* * *

"There she is!" Kennan shouted, resisting the urge to demand a canter from the weary garron pony.

Divana sat taller, the curves of her bottom rocking between his thighs as they'd done so many times throughout the journey. He was exhausted and sore, and yet, his mind had run the gamut of all the positions in which he'd enjoy seeing the lass's hind end, and none of them had anything to do with riding a horse and everything to do with her riding him. Preferably in a bed—but that didn't even matter now.

He'd spent too much time with this woman in his arms. It was enough to torture any man who'd abstained from the sport of the bedchamber for as long as Kennan had done.

To erase his errant thoughts, he drew in a deep breath of crisp Highland air.

"Saint Columba," Divana exclaimed, not masking the awe in her voice. "'Tis magnificent."

Kennan never tired of the sight of home. Achnacarry had been the clan seat for generations. The keep in the center of the fortress had been built by the fourth clan chief and nearly every one of his ancestors had added something since—the curtain walls, the east and west wings, the vast stables, the immaculate gardens. Though he knew one day he'd be laird, he had never been eager to assume the title from his da. By the stars, his father might very well outlive him, especially now that Kennan had vowed to go after the most heinous pirate on the high seas.

Shouts came from the top of the guardhouse, followed by a cacophony of barking deerhounds. Before they reached the gates, the enormous portcullis raised and out ran a pair of dogs, followed by—

Kennan nearly fell off his horse. "I'll be damned."

"What is it?" Divana asked.

"A face from the dead."

"Huh?"

Runner charged toward them and grasped the pony's bridle. "God on the cross, you're alive!"

"That fiendish pirate cannot get the better of me." Kennan pointed ahead, while Runner stood gape mouthed, staring at Divana. "Good Lord, do you see that? Lachie Mor and Mr. MacNeil cheated death as well."

"Aye, and nearly half the crew." The lad gave the lass a grin, then grabbed the pony's bridle and pulled the poor animal forward until Kennan stopped him under the archway.

Mobbed by clan and kin, he hopped down and then helped Divana to her feet.

Lachie gripped his palm in a powerful handshake. "I kent that bastard didn't send you to hell."

"Never!" Kennan craned his neck, looking toward the keep. "Where's Lochiel?"

"I'm coming, bless it!" Da marched from the keep with Kennan's stepmother following closely behind.

Hastening forward, Kennan shook his father's hand. "By God, 'tis good to be home."

"You cannot ken what a relief it is to see your face, son. The lot of us feared the worst."

"But I never gave up hope," said Lady Lochiel, giving Kennan a kiss on the cheek. She shifted her gaze to Divana. "Who is this?"

The poor lass clutched her hands over her heart, staring at the ground, her face apple red.

"Do not be shy." Kennan stepped back and took her elbow. "This is Divana. If it weren't for this wee lassie, I would have frozen my bones on Hyskeir."

"Hyskeir?" asked Lachie Mor, sounding alarmed—he must have known about the smallpox.

"I was there a month." Kennan swirled a calming hand

around Divana's shoulder. "We were rescued more or less by a sergeant who's a bit too big for his breeches—locked us in the mill at Mallaig. But I wasn't about to sit on my backside and wait until they decided to release us."

"Then are we to expect a visit from the queen's dragoons?" Da asked.

Kennan gave a single nod. "I'd reckon so."

"'Tis not the first time, the brigands." Da thrust his thumb toward the keep. "Go have a wash and find some shoes. Then I'll meet you in the library."

Kennan glanced at his shabby attire, but his clothes were nowhere near as badly worn as Divana's tattered dress. "Lady Lochiel, I've promised this lassie she'll be given a good home with clothes, shoes, a bed, and all the blankets she desires. Do you reckon you can find a position for her at Achnacarry?"

"Hmm." Lady Lochiel frowned, giving the lass an exaggerated once-over. "Very well, if anyone can set the gel to rights, 'tis Mistress Barton. And she can always use another set of hands. Come with me, lass."

Divana gave Kennan's hand a squeeze, her blue eyes filled with trepidation. "Will I see ye later?"

"Aye. I'll find you. Now go with my stepmother. Mistress Barton is the housekeeper and there's none better."

The lass gave a nod, but she looked anything other than convinced. And Kennan had deliberately withheld her surname. They'd learn she was a Campbell soon enough, and it was best to have his kin discover what a treasure she was before they started jumping to conclusions.

Once she'd started away, he grasped Lachie Mor's shoulder. "How many men survived?"

"Sixteen, counting you, sir."

"Damn." He'd lost fifteen because of that bloody pirate. The treasure could be replaced, but those men's lives were gone forever. A fist-size lump stretched in his throat. "It is all my fault."

"God, no, sir. You fought with the strength of ten men. Had it not been for you every last one of us would have been cut to the quick."

Kennan couldn't take credit—not when there were so many dead. "Praise the saints you and the survivors are strong swimmers."

Lachie slapped the cabin boy on the back. "Perhaps, though the losses would be far worse if Runner hadn't been there with the skiff. We'd have all met our end if not for him."

"The lad said you sent him down afore Vane attacked," said Da, rocking back on his heels. "Wise of you."

Kennan let out a long breath he hadn't realized he was holding. "Thank God I did."

Chapter Nine

Divana had never been inside a grand manse, let alone a castle. When she stepped across the threshold, she was immediately transfixed. The entry alone was enormous. Dark paneling stretched to the ceiling, adorned with portrait after portrait of Kennan's ancestors. The black-and-white-checked marble floor was immaculate and warm to her toes—mayhap because of the enormous logs burning in the hearth, three of which must have measured at least five feet long apiece.

"There you are, Mistress Barton," said Her Ladyship, moving toward a woman dressed in black, wearing a white apron and coif. "This is Divana...from Hyskeir. Evidently she's been *tending* Sir Kennan whilst he's been shipwrecked..."

Divana didn't hear the rest, for directly in front of her was a life-size portrait of Sir Kennan himself—except he didn't look like the man she'd come to know. He was dressed in full Highland regalia with a sword at his hip, a dirk sheathed to the right of his sporran, and a musket in his hand. His bonnet was adorned with a plume of grouse feathers. The glint in his eye was fierce as he stared into the distance with a hard set to his jaw.

"Miss?"

Divana startled when Mistress Barton touched her elbow.

"You must have had a terrible ordeal." The housekeeper's careworn face expressed concern. "Come along, and you can tell me all about it while we set you to rights."

Divana glanced over her shoulder. Lady Lochiel was gone. The men's voices resounded from beyond the door, yet nothing seemed real. "'Tis as if I've stepped into a fairy story."

"Aye, there's something magical about Achnacarry." Mistress Barton led her through a small doorway and into a narrow corridor painted white. It was stark and nothing like the opulence of the entry. "And once a person enters into service here, they never want to leave."

"Sir Kennan said I'd make a good maid."

"Have you any experience?"

"Experience?"

"Folding linens, making beds, dusting, washing, preparing the table, setting fires."

"Yes, ma'am, I've done all that—have done since I was a wee lass."

"Wonderful, then I can confidently say that there will be plenty for you to do."

Without a word of hello, they walked straight through an enormous kitchen where people worked, chopping and washing and turning a spit in a fireplace large enough to stand in. Herbs hug from hooks on the ceiling, and raw chickens lined a table. A rather plump woman holding a cleaver looked up. "Och, what are ye on about now, Mistress Barton, bringing vagrants through my kitchens?"

"This is Divana. She's been shipwrecked with Sir Kennan," the housekeeper said over her shoulder, then beckoned with her hand. "Do not fall behind, dear. We're just passing through."

They exited the rear door. Outside, the woman strode directly to a stone building with smoke billowing from its chimney. "This is the servants' bathhouse. Ladies are allowed to bathe before midday, and the lads are allowed in anytime after. I suggest taking your bath first thing when you rise. Besides, it will most likely be your duty to see the water's changed every morn."

"Does Sir Kennan take his bath out here?"

"Of course not. All members of the family bathe in their chambers."

Inside, warm steam enveloped her. Kettles hung suspended from blackened iron hooks over another enormous fire. The Camerons certainly must be wealthy to be able to keep so many fires burning all at once.

Mistress Barton took a cloth from the shelf and used it to remove one of the kettles. She poured it into the bath, then repeated with a second. "There's soap on the tray, and drying cloths on the table. Remove your clothes and climb in whilst I'll find you something suitable to wear."

"Thank you."

"And do ensure you wash your hair, dear. It looks as if it hasn't been brushed in months."

"I didn't have a brush on Hyskeir—I used me fingers."

"Well, that explains it." The woman placed the empty kettle beside others near the door, then spoke over her shoulder. "Were you alone on the isle before Sir Kennan arrived?"

"Aye."

"Why?"

Divana chewed her lip. With her next words, she might end up thrown out while the housekeeper barred the gates. But they'd find out soon enough. *May as well have out with it now.* "Two years past, me uncle took me and me kin there to die. But I didn't. I was the only one who beat the sickness. Had to bury the others."

"Good Lord, you poor child," said the housekeeper before she stepped out the door.

Divana stared after her. No yelling? No fear? No being forced up the tower by the point of a bayonet and locked there for ages?

Mayhap Achnacarry was as nice as Kennan described. And the bathwater looked too tempting to ignore. Divana removed her clothes, carefully folded them, and set them on the chair. As she stepped into the warm water, she sighed audibly. It had been too long since she had enjoyed a tub of warm water. She drew the cake of soap to her nose and inhaled. The scent of roses brought another sigh.

Och aye, this is heaven.

Sliding down, she immersed her body and savored the bliss, closing her eyes and stirring the water with her fingers. Fancy that. She could bathe there every morning if she pleased.

The warmth felt so heavenly, she reclined and let the water ease way the stiffness from sitting a horse for hour upon hour. Goodness she was bone weary. So much so, she wouldn't complain if they showed her to the barn, gave her a pallet, and told her to sleep until the morrow.

But Mistress Barton had said she'd return, and Divana

didn't want to appear a laggard—especially not to the woman who oversaw the female servants. She lathered her hair until it was slippery with soap and washed from head to toe, paying special attention to the encrusted dirt on her feet and hands.

When the water grew cool, she stood. Good heavens, the bath had turned murky brown.

Grabbing a cloth, she dashed to the hearth and made quick work of rubbing herself dry and wringing out her hair.

As the door opened, a whoosh of cold air swept inside. "Here we are," said Mistress Barton, sounding official and marching to the chair. "A shift, stays, a kirtle, an apron, stockings, garters, and I hope these slippers fit."

Divana stared, gripping the drying cloth in front of her naked body. Stays? She'd never worn them. And the slippers were leather with red ribbons. "I hope I haven't taken someone's things."

"They belong to Fiona—you'll be sleeping in a box bed with her. She's about your size, and I've ordered new clothes for the both of you. The mistress doesn't care to see anyone in her employ dressed in rags." Mistress Barton gathered Divana's clothing. "And these are suited for nothing but the fire."

"Nay! Those are the only clothes I own—Sir Kennan tore my blanket to escape from the mill, and I've naught in my basket but a rock, a slingshot, and a bit of driftwood whittled by..." She didn't finish. What might the house-keeper think if she knew how much time Divana and Kennan had spent together? They'd slept in a one-room bothy, for heaven's sake. Even a poor lass like her knew such a thing wasn't done—at least not among society when there were other places to sleep.

"Well, then you'll fare far better here." The matron offered a warm smile right before she threw the clothing onto the flames. "Come now, pull the shift over your head and I'll help you with the stays."

Divana complied, not certain about anything. Now that she was a servant, would she ever see Kennan? Where was he? Would he set sail soon and forget she'd ever existed?

The linen shift was soft against her skin without a single hole—and the woolen kirtle was finely woven and warmer than anything she'd ever worn. Real woolen stockings and garters, too. But even with all the niceties, a thickness constricted Divana's throat. The shoes pinched a bit, though she kept mum and didn't complain.

She'd come to Achnacarry because there she'd still be a part of Kennan's world. But after her bath, she suddenly felt as alone as she'd been on Hyskeir.

Heavenly Father, please do not let him forget me.

* * *

Fiona was a healthy-looking lass with brown hair and rosy cheeks. Thank goodness she was a bit bigger around than Divana, because wearing her stays already made it difficult to breathe.

Divana stood in front of a mirror while Fiona worked a comb through Divana's hair. "I do not believe I've ever seen so many knots."

"Mayhap we should cut it."

Fiona gaped. "Cut this bonny mane of red? 'Twould be a sacrilege."

"I'm sorry ye've been tasked with combing it."

"Nonsense. Mistress Barton excused me from replenishing the water in the bathhouse. For that, I'd comb ten heads of knotted hair."

Divana couldn't help but chuckle. Replenishing the water in the bathhouse seemed easy compared to daily survival on Hyskeir. "How long have ye been at Achnacarry?"

"All of my life. My father is the stable master, and Ma is a lady's maid." Fiona worked through a clump and started at the ends of another. "I'm hoping to be a lady's maid one day."

"For Her Ladyship?"

"Aye, if Ma retires, or for Sir Kennan's wife—or one of the other sons' wives. If they would ever grow serious and wed. Since Miss Janet married Laird Grant, there hasn't been a need for a second lady's maid."

Though Divana had spoken to Kennan about his eventual marriage, having someone mention his nuptials as if they were written on the stars and about to happen on the morrow made her hackles rise. She took in a breath and let it out slowly.

Sir Kennan is not for me. How many times must I remind meself of that fact?

Regardless of their differences in station, he'd come to mean so much to her in such a short time. And now that they had been rescued, things would change entirely. He wouldn't be whittling driftwood across the bothy, his green eyes shifting her way now and again. He wouldn't be helping her dig for clams or fixing the thatch on the roof. He was the son of a great laird, a sea captain. And by the size of Achnacarry, he was likely one of the most sought after bachelors in the Highlands.

How will I endure it?

She regarded her reflection and turned her chin, running her fingers along the pocked scars. Divana had known they were there, but it had been difficult to picture them. Before she'd been stricken with smallpox, there wasn't a blemish on her face aside from a splay of freckles across her nose. Kennan would most likely want a wife with creamy smooth skin without a single spot.

Fiona tugged the comb so hard, if felt as if Divana's hair would come out at the roots. "You'll be working alongside me to begin with."

Gulping, Divana tried to smile, though her heart was twisting in a hundred knots. "I should like that." Hopefully, she sounded sincere. In truth she just wanted to crumple to the floor and weep. So much had happened since they'd left Hyskeir. It was difficult enough not to have Kennan nearby to answer questions or to protect her with his brawny arms. Yes, she wanted to enter into service and make her own coin. She desperately wanted to find a place to call home. But things had changed so fast, it overwhelmed her.

"Tell me, what is your age?" asked Fiona.

Blinking back the sting of tears, Divana cleared her throat. "I reckon I'm nineteen, or near enough. Ye?"

"Nineteen as well."

"We're the same age?" Divana's spirits dove a bit further. "Here ye are in training to be a lady's maid and I've never had a position in a castle afore."

"You'll be fine. Besides, you'll have me to show you what to do." Fiona tugged Divana's tresses around to the back and set to braiding. "Now tell me, how long were you marooned with Sir Kennan?"

Divana didn't miss the mischief in Fiona's eyes. Though she craved friendship, it was best to keep her feelings under wraps. "I suppose it caused quite a stir when we rode through the gates together looking like a pair of ragamuffins, did it not?"

"Aye, the entire castle is buzzing with gossip."

"I do not think 'tis nice to gossip."

"Are you jesting?" Fiona's comb paused while she laughed aloud. "At Achnacarry life would be ever so dull without it. They're saying you suffered a dread illness."

"I did, but I'm well now."

"So, what happened between you and the Cameron heir?"

"I suppose Ken—er—*Sir* Kennan is sharing the story with his da as we speak." Divana took in a deep breath, trying to stretch her annoying stays. "All I ken is he washed ashore after the *Highland Reel* was lost. Have you not heard the tale from Lachie Mor?"

Chapter Ten

Shaven and dressed in a decent suit of clothes, yet exhausted clear to his bones, Kennan cast a forlorn glance to his four-poster bed before he left his chamber and headed for the library. He'd rehearsed the explanation of the battle in his head a hundred times, but nonetheless, facing his father wouldn't be easy. What son who'd lost his ship, half his crew, and a fortune could stand in front of the Great Lochiel and hold his head high?

I cannot.

But Kennan must own up to and look his demons in the eye. Only then would he be free to seek the reckoning he craved clear to his very bones. Arriving at the library far faster than he'd intended, he stood for a moment and rubbed his weary eyes.

May as well have it done with.

He opened the door and popped his head inside. "Are you ready to receive me, sir?"

Lochiel put down his correspondence and motioned for Kennan to take a seat across the table. "For a moment I thought you might have fallen victim to your pillow."

"Nay, though I'd be lying if I didn't admit it beckoned." Kennan sat on the edge of the chair, his back erect. "I suppose 'tis best to start at the beginning—confess my sins, so to speak."

"We're all sinners, lad." Da slowly turned the globe and tapped a spot that Kennan was unable to see. "Lachie Mor filled me in on most of it. Vane attacked with three schooners. No captain in all of Christendom would have been able to fend off an attack of that magnitude with one wee ship. You fought until the end—five at once, I'm told."

Kennan nodded while his father took a breath.

"Vane made you watch your men walk the plank. Runner managed to save many. But they lost you. Afore you met your supposed demise, a mighty gale blew through the channel, the *Reel* sailed off too fast for the lads to keep her in their sights. Nary a man thought my son had met his end, but they all vowed you were lost at sea." Da reached for a flagon of whisky and two goblets. "Does that about sum it up?"

"Aye—I couldn't have abbreviated any better."

"And the rest of it?" Pulling the stopper, Da sniffed it. "You washed ashore on Hyskeir. What about the lass? Why have you brought her here?"

"Divana fed me. Took me in when I was at death's door. During the fighting, I sustained a near-mortal cut across my stomach. Once they caught me, a Goliath of a brute put a noose around my neck. Thank God the bastards decided to toy about afore they strung me up from the

Reel's mast. As I made my escape and leapt overboard, I was shot in the arm, then had a nice disagreement with a mob of sharks. I was half-dead when I crawled onto the shore." Kennan's scars throbbed as if he'd suffered his injuries only a day prior. "Divana was living in a decrepit bothy on the isle. I mightn't have made it back alive if it weren't for her kindness."

"Then she's welcome here."

"Thank you. She's had a rough time of it. The bloody Campbells dumped the lass and her kin on the isle to die." Kennan pursed his lips. The word *smallpox* had a way of striking fear in the hearts of the toughest of men. Hell, even he had shrunk from the woman when he first discovered the reason for her exile.

"By the marks on her face, I can imagine." Da poured the whisky, then pushed a goblet to Kennan. "She's completely healed?" Of course, he knew. He was bloody Lochiel.

He raised the drink to his lips. "I wouldn't have brought her here if she weren't."

"I thought no less." Glancing aside, Lochiel frowned. "She's a Campbell, you say?"

"Was," Kennan clarified, "She cares never to set eyes on her kin again."

"Good." The old man sat back and savored a swallow of fine Highland spirit. Kennan, too. "So now you're home, what do you aim to do?"

"I'd be lying if I told you I hadn't spent every waking hour plotting revenge."

Da held his cup aloft. "Hear, hear. Word is Vane is skulking somewhere in the Caribbean."

"I don't doubt it. He's most likely whoring and spending my coin. Dammit, Da, I recovered a king's ransom in silver, not to mention vast quantities of rum and silks."

"Then you must go after it."

"I'd like nothing more, but I need a ship—one with big bloody guns and a crew thrice the size of the last."

"I've thought the same as well."

Kennan pushed his goblet away. One sip of whisky and his fatigue returned with full force. "Aye, but none of our galleys are large enough for a sea voyage deep into the Atlantic."

"I'll write to the Baronet of Sleat. He's a shrewd businessman. With your proven captainship and the promise of a piece of the spoils, I'd wager he might sell us one of his fleet to further our cause."

"Sleat, aye?" It had been years since Kennan captained the old brig for the baronet, sailing packing salt up and down the British seaboard and over to the Continent. Hell, he'd even sailed her to Spain. "'Tis worth inquiring, I'll say."

Da reached for a slip of parchment. "I'll write him straightaway."

Before his father picked up his quill, Kennan placed his hand atop the parchment. "I'm a grown man. The letter ought to come from me."

Da frowned, but then slid the paper across the table. "Very well. Then I'll contact your uncle in Glasgow. If Sleat doesn't bite, Sir Broden may have some ideas as well. After all, 'tis your gold we'll be spending."

It was. Prince James had generously paid Kennan for his efforts in taking back a fortune in gold from Claude Dubois at Versailles with the help of the Earl and Countess of Mar. Some of his share he'd spent to purchase the cargo he'd lost on the *Highland Reel*. The remainder was in a strongbox hidden behind a false wall in his chamber—possibly enough to purchase an old ship from an ally.

"Good thinking."

"I'm certain it comes as no shock when I say this state of affairs makes me ill." Da poured himself another dram. "I'll tell ye true, son, if it didn't take two years to commission a ship, I'd order one built this very day. No man attacks my kin without paying in blood."

* * *

Kennan had planned to find Divana after his meeting with his father, but it wasn't to be. He'd also wanted to meet with Lachie Mor and Mr. MacNeil, but Da had detained him, talking more about Vane and matters at home. Over the course of several hours, they'd managed to consume the entire flagon of whisky, after which Kennan had barely made it back to his bed before the exhaustion of riding all night overcame him.

But first thing the next morn, he woke early and, after visiting the kitchens, found the lass working in the dining hall with Fiona. And it didn't surprise him to see Divana on her knees shoveling ash from the hearth while Fiona flitted about with a duster.

"There you are," Kennan said, walking straight toward the Campbell lass.

Fiona gasped, dipping into a ridiculously low curtsy. "Sir! My, you're up early."

Looking back at the maid, Divana cringed while she pushed to her feet and attempted a curtsy while brushing the ash from her apron. "Good morn, sir."

"Ah..." Scratching his freshly shaven chin, Kennan

looked between the two. Suddenly everything had changed. He was the master and Divana the servant. Somehow he hadn't anticipated an instant change in their friendship. But then, why wouldn't there be? 'Twas the way of things...and he cared for it not one bit.

As she straightened, he leaned in and looked her over from head to toe. Though dressed simply, she looked as radiant as a queen. He'd never seen her hair brushed and flowing about her shoulders like copper silk. Was it the ray of light shining in from the window that made her eyes sparkle, her face glow, her unsure smile absolutely captivating?

"Is something amiss, sir?" asked Fiona.

"N-no." Still staring at Divana, he wiped a hand across his mouth. "I...ah...wanted to ensure Divana was...uh. Are you well, lass?"

She turned a brilliant shade of scarlet, making her all the more alluring. "Quite well, thank ye. Fiona has been very helpful."

Kennan's gaze slipped to the other maid, but not for long. "And you slept soundly?"

"Och, I've never been so comfortable."

"And my mother is taking good care of you?"

Divana folded her hands, appearing more uncomfortable than he'd ever seen her. "I've not seen Her Ladyship since she introduced me to Mistress Barton, but ye were right, there's plenty to eat, and there's heaps of blankets on our bed—"

"Our bed?" he asked, ready to strangle the fiend.

"She's sharing with me, of course," said Fiona.

"Right." Kennan rubbed the back of his neck. He'd rather thought Divana would have a bed all to herself, but what did he know about the maids' quarters? "Well, then, is there anything you need?"

Divana chewed her bottom lip as she cast her gaze downward. "'Tis most likely not proper of me to say—'cause I was told not to speak to any of his lairdship's kin—"

"Unless spoken to," Fiona added.

"Aye...if ye must ken, these shoes pinch my feet something awful." A black slipper slid out from beneath her hem.

"Divana!" Fiona chided.

Kennan moved closer for a better look at the offending shoe. "No bother. I asked." Indeed, Divana's foot looked a bit cramped—most likely because she'd gone without shoes her whole life. "I will ensure the cobbler fashions a pair that fits."

Fiona flourished her duster. "Och, that is ever so gracious of you, sir."

He looked to the maid and she arched her brows, giving a nervous smile. "Would you mind leaving us for a moment?"

"You and Divana?"

"Aye, if you would, please."

Fiona curtsied. "Very well, sir." She glanced between them, blinking as if she didn't know what to make of the situation or if she ought to leave them alone. "I-I'll just take my duster to the entry if you should need me."

Divana brushed a bit of soot from her apron. "I'll be along after I've swept the ash from the hearth."

Once Fiona slipped out the door, Divana threw out her hands. "I am sorry if I was impertinent. But ye asked and I'm just not accustomed to wearing shoes."

"I thought not, but the cobbler can make you a pair with a wee bit wider fit that shouldn't pinch so."

She crossed her arms and paced. "Ye must think me a shrew with such big feet."

"They're not nearly as large as mine."

"That's because you're a man."

"Yes." And he was ever so aware of it at the moment.

She whipped around and faced him, her eyes ablaze with dozens of emotions—anger, hurt, confusion, and fear. "Things feel different between us now."

He almost asked, "How so?" But since yesterday morning, things had suddenly grown quite awkward. "Och, there's no need for you to be formal in my presence. That's why I sent Fiona away."

"She has been kind to me." Divana turned in a circle, making her skirts billow. "She braided my hair yesterday, and this morn when she brushed it, she said it was too bonny to tie back again." She drew her tresses through her hand. "I hope Mistress Barton doesn't reprimand me."

Kennan couldn't help but capture a lock and twirl the silken strand around his finger. He'd missed her company last night as he lay in his bed, alone in a chamber five times the size of the bothy. The lass was funny and, no matter the hardship she faced, she was always smiling and cheerful. "If she does, I ought to reprimand her back." He drew the hair to his nose and inhaled. Good God, she smelled like woman and roses. Before his knees grew weak, he released the curl. "Your hair should always be thus unbound."

Divana chuckled and reached toward his freshly shaven chin but drew her hand away before she touched him. "Ye look so different."

"So do you."

"Well, I ought to, I suppose. I had the most wonderful bath in all me days. Though I ken not what I'll do if Fiona wants her shift and kirtle back because Mistress Barton burned me clothes." Divana smoothed her hands down her rib cage. "I reckon I wouldn't mind if she took these stays back, though. They're miserably uncomfortable. I would have said that first if we were alone."

He grinned, loving her candidness. Why weren't more women so blatantly honest about such things? "I've oft wondered how women put up with those constricting contrivances."

"Well, if I must wear them to be able to stay on at Achnacarry, I'll do it."

"I'm glad you're happy here."

"It is better than Hyskeir." She blushed and looked to the floor. "Far better."

"Agreed."

"But what about Sergeant Corbyn and the dragoons? Are we safe?"

"If you ask me, there's no safer fortress in all of Scotland than Achnacarry. And as I said before, they had no grounds on which to hold us."

"Aside from the incident in Dundee."

"Aye, well, there's that." He almost grasped her hand but stopped himself. "But I've strong allies. And my father is sending a missive to the colonel at Fort William for good measure."

"Your da is close with the colonel?"

"They're on amicable terms."

"So no one will come and haul us to the pillory?"

"I hope not." His fingers itched to touch her—to pull the woman into his arms and make promises he couldn't keep. "Da says this is your clan now."

"I like that." With her hands behind her back she swayed, looking coy and ever so kissable. "Yesterday your men seemed overjoyed to see ye."

"Och aye, and more were spared than I'd dared to dream."

"Everyone is saying ye'll go after Vane straightaway."

Kennan nodded, a lump forming in his throat. But he'd told her he was a man of the sea—often gone. He mustn't allow his feelings for her to overpower his resolve—not when there was so much at stake.

"So, when are ye leaving?"

"Dunno. I need to commandeer a ship first."

"I wouldn't think that would be easy to do."

"Nay, but it helps to have—"

"Strong allies?"

"Aye."

Her bottom lip pouted ever so slightly. "I do not want ye to go."

"Not to worry, lass. These things take time, and once my crew and I are ready to set sail, you will have endeared yourself to all who walk these halls."

"Mayhap." She gestured toward the hearth, the spark in her eyes shaded by the dim light. "Well, there's work to be done and I mustn't dally about."

"Right." Kennan gripped one of the dining chairs. It didn't seem right for her to be cleaning soot from the fireplace and setting fires. She ought to be a lady's maid or a head housekeeper—or attain some lofty position.

He ground his molars.

The lass must start somewhere, mustn't she? He couldn't just march up to his stepmother and insist that she create a position for a lass who had never served on a big estate before.

Divana had said herself, she'd never been so comfortable. She had a warm bed, food, clothes, and meaningful work. But somehow, that didn't seem enough.

He released his iron grip and bowed. "Then I'll bid you good day."

Chapter Eleven

Two weeks later

*A*t the side of the keep, Divana cranked the handle above the well until the bucket appeared. After filling two pails, she started toward the kitchen, just as a dozen dragoons rode through the gates. At the sight of the redcoats, prickles fired across her skin. But when she recognized Sergeant Corbyn trotting at the head of the retinue, one pail dropped from her fingertips and washed over the cobblestones.

Divana's heart nearly hammered out of her chest. Before she was spotted, she quickly turned away. She could scarcely breathe as she darted around the far side of the well and crouched behind it, daring to peek at Corbyn. He sat his horse as if he carried a proclamation from the queen herself.

When the redcoats stopped, silence filled the courtyard.

Armed Cameron guardsmen looked on from the curtain walls while an important-looking man strode from the guardhouse and addressed the soldiers. "I'm Lochiel's man-at-arms. State your business."

Corbyn glared down his nose at the man. "Kennan Cameron escaped from our quarantine. The man is suspected of contracting an infectious disease. Same with the wench with whom he was traveling. They must be quarantined at once."

Divana's fingernails bit into her palms. She'd been quarantined for two miserable years, was that not enough? Besides, two weeks had already passed since they left Hyskeir, and nary a soul had contracted smallpox.

"Why the devil are the queen's dragoons in my courtyard, led by the navy of all things?" demanded Sir Ewen, hastening down the steps of the keep.

The sergeant shifted his attention to the laird, though he still wore an air of arrogance. "Sir, I demand you turn over your pirate son immediately."

At the sound of *pirate*, Sir Ewen stroked the palm of his hand along the hilt of his dirk. "I have four sons, none of whom are pirates."

"You know to whom I am referring."

"Do I?" Ewen sauntered up to Corbyn and grasped the horse's bridle. "Unfortunately, the only son in residence has not yet reached his second birthday."

"Then I demand you tell me where he is."

"I beg your pardon, Sergeant, but you are speaking in riddles."

"Kennan Cameron," Corbyn bit out. "Where is he?"

The Great Lochiel's expression turned dark. "I do not care for your tone. And it would be *Sir* Kennan to the likes of you."

Corbyn cast his beady-eyed gaze up to the keep. "If he's here, he's putting the rest of you at risk." He eyed the men on the curtain wall, then raised his voice. "Risk of contracting the dread smallpox."

"Then I applaud my son for staying away," said Lochiel. "What with a bairn above stairs, it would be unthinkable for any of my kin to deliberately bring sickness into this house."

"Has he sent word of his whereabouts?"

"He has not."

"Unfortunate, because there's also the matter of inciting a riot in Dundee, which *Sir* Kennan must answer for."

Divana clapped a hand over her mouth. *Och nay!*

Lochiel scowled. "So this is your reason for your less than amicable visit. Sources tell me the whole debacle was started on the pier—by government troops no less."

"What sources?" demanded the sergeant in a very disrespectful tone.

"You're stepping on thin ice. I suggest you take your retinue and return from whence you came."

"Cameron may not have come cowering to his clan as of yet, but he will and we'll be watching until he does."

"And then what, arrest him for his good health?"

"And rioting, piracy, and anything else I can uncover about his lawlessness."

"You're grievously misled on every count." Sir Ewen thrust up his hands, gesturing to the men watching from the surrounding wall above. "I'd have a word with the Earl of Mar afore you go off incriminating my son for defending his ship, his crew, and his cargo from assault by a disgruntled customs officer intent on padding his pockets by charging duties twice that imposed by the crown!"

The sergeant squared his shoulders. "So say you."

It seemed as if Sir Ewen had simply put his hand on Corbyn's wrist, but by the way the dragoon cringed, twisting toward the older man with his face turning red, it wasn't a friendly gesture in the slightest. "Do not attempt to travel down this road, Mr. Corbyn," seethed Lochiel. "I can see to it you are demoted to a post cleaning the bilges on Her Majesty's most worm-infested ship."

"You are trying to coerce me and put me off the scent, but I'll not be dissuaded." As Lochiel stepped away, the sergeant picked up his reins. "We will meet again."

"I truly hope not. I'll be having words with the colonel at Fort William anon, mark me."

Divana ducked behind the well, clutching her chest. Where was Kennan? Had he been listening? As the soldiers rode off, she picked up the full bucket and skirted toward the house. Standing in the kitchen's doorway, Kennan held up his palm, his face tense.

She thrust her finger over her shoulder, pointing in the direction of Corbyn and his mob of dragoons. "They're after you," she whispered, exaggerating the words with her lips.

His second palm joined his first, urging her to stay put. "Wait," he mouthed in reply.

Once the sound of shod horses faded, he hastened toward her. "Why the devil were you out here?"

It wasn't exactly the greeting she'd hoped to receive. She'd scarcely seen the man in the last fortnight. Straightening, she raised the bucket. "I was drawing water for Cook."

"Well, you shouldn't have been out in the open." He took the pail and placed a hand on the small of her back, leading her inside.

Cook greeted them with her fists on her hips. "At last, I thought you'd gone all the way to the river to fetch my water."

Kennan set the bucket on the table. "Henceforth, Divana will not be fetching water."

"I beg your pardon?" Divana nearly tripped as he took ahold of her hand and pulled her into the servants' dining hall. Thank heavens it was empty, or else he'd have caused a spectacle. "Did ye hear Mr. Corbyn? He wants to arrest ye—and me as well."

"He'll have no luck at Achnacarry. I kent he was fishing when he held us."

"And now he kens about Dundee."

His feet planted wide, Kennan pounded a fist onto the table. "Dundee was not of my doing."

"Aye, but he could make things very unpleasant for you until the matter is settled." Divana paced, her mind racing—Saint Columba, Corbyn even wanted to arrest her. "'Tis dangerous for us to dally here."

"Nay, it is the safest place we can be at the moment."

She gripped the back of a chair, about to crack it over his head. "I wish we had never left Hyskeir." There they had been equals. There they were free to speak and laugh and tell stories about their lives.

Kennan's stance immediately softened as he stepped toward her. "Are my kin being unkind?"

She clutched her fingers tightly around the bent wood. How could she tell him of the agonizing love in her heart? "Nay."

"Are you in want of something?" He stroked a hand down his chin as his gaze roved from her head to her hem. "Och, your shoes. How daft you must think me. Come, we'll visit the cobbler anon."

He took her hand and pulled her back outside, of all places. He was too strong for her not to follow, but she made a good show of tugging against him, not quite trying to wrench away. "I thought I wasn't supposed to be seen out of doors."

"You must be careful. And no dawdling in the courtyard."

"What about ye? The soldiers were here naught but five minutes ago, and here we are taking a wee stroll."

"Wheesht. I can take care of myself."

"Ye make no sense at all."

He gave her a sidewise grin. Why did he have to go off and do that? And how did he always manage to turn her heart into a puddle with a glance? He looked like a devil, and a pirate, and too tempting not to embrace. Instead she gripped his hand tighter. "Ye oughtn't look at me like that."

"Like what?"

It took all the fortitude in her being to ease her hand away from his. "Ye ken."

The ringing of the smithy shop neared as Kennan headed out the postern gate. Clansmen and women lived in the cottages beyond the castle. The tiny village boasted a smithy, a cobbler, a tailor, and a family that sold herbs— at least according to Fiona.

"I want you to be happy here."

"Who said I wasn't happy?"

"But you just told me you wished we'd never left Hyskeir."

Divana stopped. "That's because—" She looked to the skies with a tsk of her tongue. Why must he make everything so difficult?

"Because?" he persisted.

"Because when we were alone on the isle I could talk to ye any time I wanted—without causing a stir, without it being *improper*." She threw her arms out in an arc. "Here I'm merely a lowly scullery maid, not fit to tie your brogues."

"Hogwash. You are speaking to me now." His gaze shifted left and then right. "I do not see a guard hastening toward us with intent to throw you in the tower's goal."

"'Tis not what I meant, and ye ken it." She shoved him in the shoulder for good measure. "Do ye not?"

He frowned, a long breath hissing through his lips. "I'll speak to my mother about promoting you to house-maid."

"Och aye, that would endear all the servants to me all the more, especially Fiona, who's worked for your kin all her life."

His mouth twisted as he took a step back. "Well then, what is it you want?"

"If 'tis not clear, then I'm nay about to tell ye." Divana pulled on the latch and stepped into the shop—of course Kennan followed. And thank heavens he did. She had no idea what to say to a cobbler, nor could she afford to pay for shoes—not even with the wages she'd received just yesterday.

The shop smelled of leather, salt, and tallow while a man wearing spectacles looked up from a table, hammer in hand. "Sir Kennan, 'tis always a pleasure to see you."

Kennan made the introductions, and Divana was instructed to sit in a chair while the cobbler traced around her foot.

Oh, how her insides were twisted in knots. She didn't mind her work at Achnacarry, and all that came with it—most of what came with it. But more than anything she hated the vast divide that had instantaneously separated her from Kennan Cameron.

As the cobbler measured her foot, her hand slipped to her apron's pocket and smoothed over the figurine he'd whittled in the driftwood. How she longed to watch him across the fire with no one else about. How she longed to hear his stories of sailing the seas. If only she'd realized how precious those days were, she never would have boarded Sergeant Corbyn's galley.

"Are you looking forward to the Beltane festivities on the morrow?" asked the cobbler.

"I—" Divana bit her lip and glanced at Kennan.

"Of course she is." Kennan grinned again—that same look as before, except this time he winked as well. Blast it, she liked his attention and didn't like it all at once. It made her too nervous, too vulnerable, and far too blissful. *Curse him!* "And I'll be the first to ask her to dance."

* * *

Tankard of ale in hand, Kennan stood beside his father, watching the children laugh and dance around the may-pole, weaving their colorful ribbons.

"A missive just arrived from Sleat," Kennan said behind his ale.

Da nearly spilled froth down the front of his doublet. "Why did you not fetch me sooner?"

"I kent you were here—besides, the messenger delivered the note no more than a quarter hour ago."

"Do not keep me in suspense. What news from the baronet?"

"My old brig, the *Lady Heather*, is in dry dock in Port Glasgow."

"Bloody hell. Does he not have another ship?"

"He thought I ought to oversee her repairs—as I've done in the past. Said he'd sell her to me with a share of the spoils as we discussed."

"Are ye certain? Och, I do not recommend traveling to Port Glasgow with that bloodhound sergeant sniffing about."

"I ken that ship nearly better than the *Reel*—and Sleat is offering her at a price we'd not see anywhere else. But only I can ensure everything is outfitted to my satisfaction. Besides, I need more men."

"I don't like it."

"And I'm nay about to sail into the choppy Atlantic with a ship that's not seaworthy."

Da took a long drink from his ale, his expression grim. "Do not worry. We'll ride at night. Sail a Cameron galley from Loch Eil."

"How many men do you plan to take to Port Glasgow?"

"Lachie Mor, Mr. MacNeil, and a handful of others."

"You ought to take the Cameron army," Da said, clapping his hand against his tankard as the maypole dancers took their bows.

"Aye? And that wouldn't draw attention?" Kennan spied Divana on Fiona's arm. Holy Moses, she wore a blue gown with a scooped neckline that revealed two lovely, unforgettable breasts. "Nay," he croaked. "'Tis best to draw as little attention as possible until we've had word from Mar."

"The earl ought to request a pardon from the queen," Da continued. "After all, she might have lost her throne if it weren't for the pair of you thwarting King Louis's attempt to invade."

Kennan was hardly listening. For the love of God, how

did the wee urchin grow more radiant by the day? She wore her hair down, flowing like red silk, and her smile was nearly as bright as the Beltane bonfire itself. "I'm certain 'tis only a matter of time," he managed to say. "Word is Anne is quite ill."

"Aye, and all the more reason for Mar to act quickly."

Kennan sipped thoughtfully, forcing his gaze away from Divana. "Sergeant Corbyn is the least of my worries."

"Agreed." Da gave his tankard to a passing footman and exchanged it for another. "Though I'd like to show the festering pustule his place."

"Perhaps we'll have the chance afore all this is done." Kennan finished his drink. "But 'tis Beltane and I intend to enjoy it."

"Good on you, lad. But do not bugger one of my serving wenches or there'll be hell to pay."

"Never."

Kennan strolled around the gathering until he stopped directly behind Divana. In truth, he'd prefer to swing an ax and chop wood for an entire day rather than dance, but he'd made the lass a promise, and he always made good on his word.

Except before he tapped her shoulder, Runner skipped up with his bonnet in hand. "Will ye dance the reel with me?"

Divana turned enough for Kennan to see her face, and she looked terrified. "Och, I'm nay much good at dancing."

Runner grabbed for her hands and tugged. "Not to worry, I'll help ye. Besides, ye look too bonny to be standing on the fringes."

Kennan clenched his fists as he watched the lad drag Divana to the patch of grass they used for dancing. How dare the adolescent slaver all over the woman, telling her she looked bonny? And now she was out there standing in the women's row, the eye of every male Cameron focused on her wholesome beauty. Damnation, she outshone every woman present.

"Is all well, sir?" asked Lachie Mor, stepping beside him with a tankard of ale in hand.

"Aye, it will be when we set out for Glasgow."

"Agreed. I think the missus is growing tired of having me home."

"Tell her to enjoy your company whilst she can. I reckon you'll be gone for a fair stretch soon."

When Divana turned the wrong way and stumbled into the lass beside her, Kennan couldn't help his grin. The poor gel apologized and grew more flustered until Runner locked her elbow with his and rowdily spun her in a circle.

"Smiling at the Campbell lass, are you?" asked Mor.

"She's not much of a dancer."

"Nor are you." The quartermaster laughed. "She's fetching, I'll say."

"Why the blazes is everyone talking about how bonny Divana looks? Good Lord, everyone's openly gawking as if they've never seen a woman before."

"You like her do you?"

"What has that got to do with anything?"

The damned gap-toothed wastrel shrugged as he started off, wobbling on his bowlegs. "I thought as much."

Kennan grumbled under his breath. Everyone wanted to be a smart-arse. Of course. It was Beltane. By the end of the evening the pairing would start—lassie's choice. His gut clenched. He wasn't about to let some randy Highlander haul Divana off into the brush and have his way. And Kennan knew it could happen. The ale flowed freely, the weather was fine for once, and the promise of spring was on the air. Hell, it was a recipe for disaster.

As the reel ended, he marched straight up to Divana. If nothing else, it was his duty to protect her, especially tonight. She smiled at him, her face flushed. "Sir Kennan. I'm afraid I'm nay as graceful as the others."

Wiping a hand across his eyes, he offered his elbow. "Would you care to take a wee stroll with me?"

She placed her fingers in the crook of his arm. They were far more delicate than he'd remembered, making his skin tingle beneath. "Ye do not want to dance?"

"I'm nay much of a dancer. I prefer a more intimate crowd."

"For dancing? That makes it difficult when there's a gathering of so many people."

"I mostly watch the others kick up their heels."

"That can be fun, too."

"Did you have dancing lessons as a lass?"

"Nay. We danced, though. Whenever there was a gathering—I guess I do not remember the steps all that well."

Kennan stopped and faced her. Though they were in the shadows beyond the light of the fire, the music still swirled around them. "We could dance here where no one will see us."

"Here? With ye?"

"Aye." He brushed a wisp of hair away from her face. "Though 'tis Beltane, lass. That means you choose to dance with whomever you please."

She grinned, her white teeth gleaming blue in the moonlight. "My choice?"

He stepped nearer and was blessed with the fragrance

of rose and the unmistakable scent of Divana. "Yes," he whispered.

Drawing a sharp breath, she tilted her chin up, her gaze locking with his.

Damn it all, his body shouldn't be responding like a stag, but his mind refused to take charge. Holding both her hands, he started in a slow circle. "Dancing like this is more diverting."

Luminescent blue eyes filled with trust gazed up at him. "It is intoxicating."

He pulled her nearer. "So you agree?"

Together they stepped out. "To what?"

"Dance with me," he whispered, bringing his lips to her ear as he lifted her off the ground and spun in circle after circle. "You are the bonniest woman at the gathering, and I cannot bear to watch all the young Highland whelps gawking at you as if you're a prize to be won."

As he twirled, she turned to butter in his arms, resting her head against his chest. "I'll dance with ye, Kennan. Ye're my choice always."

He set her down and ran his hands along her arms. She shivered beneath his fingertips. "Are you cold?"

"Nay," she replied, her breasts heaving—begging to be caressed, kissed, fondled, adored. Looking like a goddess, she tilted her face upward and gazed directly into his eyes.

When had she woven her way into his heart? Dipping his chin, he pulled her into his embrace. "Then I aim to kiss you, lass."

Chapter Twelve

*H*eaven. Floating in Kennan's arms must be exactly what it was like to be floating on a heavenly cloud. As soon as his lips touched hers, Divana turned to liquid honey in his arms, sighing against his mouth, praying his kiss would never end.

And it didn't.

He brushed the parting of her mouth with a warm tongue, as if asking permission to taste her. Holding on for dear life, wanting to please him with every fiber of her body, Divana timidly opened her lips, wishing, craving, needing to prove worthy of his affection. As she let him in, his tongue swept inside her mouth, making her body gush with want. Making something coil deep inside, as though she'd die if he dared pull away.

Her thirst for him turned unquenchable when he drew her flush against him, the friction from the contact of their bodies sending a wave of desire swirling in her breasts. Every inch of her flesh inflamed while his hands slid down and gripped her buttocks, drawing her hips even nearer.

Something hard came between them, causing a deep ache between her legs. Divana's head swam with the power of the emotions pulsing through her blood—feelings she barely comprehended.

She gasped at his lips skimming her neck. "What's happening to me?"

"'Tis the magic of Beltane," he growled, his warm tongue caressing the tops of her breasts.

Gripping his arms, Divana forced her eyes open. Beltane? It was a pagan holiday. Suddenly chilled, disappointment gripped her. She knew enough about the holiday to realize Kennan's affection could not possibly be real. He'd been addled by the ale or the thrum of the music or the charge of excitement in the air. Tomorrow she would wake a scullery maid, and the man with his warm, sensuous lips kissing her breasts would still be the heir to the Cameron chieftainship—a knight of such a lofty rank, a lass like Divana had no hope of winning his love. And no matter how utterly marvelous it felt to be in his arms, remaining there was wrong.

"Nay," she clipped, pushing him away. "I am no harlot!"

A crease formed between Kennan's brows as his eyes filled with bewilderment. "N-n-no, you're not."

"Then why did ye do...do...do *that*!"

"Kiss you?"

"Aye."

"Every man at the gathering has a mind to do the same."

She rubbed her fingers across her lips, trying to erase the tingling. "But I thought it was *my* choice!"

"It is." He spread his big palms to his sides, a deeper

crease furrowing his forehead. "Forgive me. Did you not want me to kiss you?"

She clutched her fists under her chin. "It is not the wanting of your affection that scares me."

He inched forward, one eye squinting as if he didn't quite understand. "Nay?"

"'Tis just that kissing ye is too…too *wonderful!*"

"But…I…um…" He ran his fingers over the golden clan brooch at his shoulder—yet another sign of his high-born station. "I beg your pardon?"

She huffed out a sigh. "A-a-and awful!"

Unable to remain there a moment longer, Divana dashed for the servants' entrance. How was she to explain her feelings to him—the heir to the Cameron dynasty? Kissing Sir Kennan Cameron filled her with more desire than she'd ever experienced in her life. How could it not be sinful to feel so inexplicably fantastic? Worse, since she'd been at Achnacarry, every time she set eyes on the Highlander made her desire him all the more.

He can never be mine! Dashing up the steps, tears stung her eyes. *I must never dance with him again.*

With an enormous sob, she almost burst through the door of the small chamber she shared with Fiona—except it was already ajar.

A flash of movement made Divana stop as if she'd slammed into a wall. A sigh came from within.

Making not a sound, she peered through the opening. The sight made her gasp and blink rapidly, trying to make sense of the shocking figures entwined within. She ought to run, but her limbs had frozen stiff. Saint Columba, 'twas the most outlandish sight she'd ever seen. Had she plunged into a ritual of pagan Beltane sin?

Garry, a stable hand, wore only a shirt, his kilt around his ankles, his hairy arse completely bare. Another sigh filled the chamber. He stood behind Fiona, her skirts pulled nearly over her head, while he plunged himself in and out of her from behind.

Divana clenched her fists, ready to barrel in and give Garry a good kick in his naked backside, but from the sweet sounds of pleasure coming from Fiona, she liked it—liked what he was doing to her a great deal.

Taking a step back, Divana wanted to hide her eyes, yet her fists remained stiff at her sides. As Fiona's moans grew, Garry moved faster and faster, throwing his head back with his panting breath.

"Oh, oh, oh, now!" the lass cried.

A deep bellow erupted from the stable hand's throat as he withdrew, spurting like a stallion and collapsing over the lass, gasping as if he'd run for miles.

In a blink, Divana reclaimed her wits and stepped aside, shoving her back against the wall. She buried her face in her hands. What horrors had she just witnessed?

Good glory, when she'd kissed Kennan, the hardness between them was his manhood. Did he desire her in that…that…that completely unusual way?

Divana trembled, surprised not to be completely disgusted by the thought of doing…that…with Kennan.

"We'd best hurry," said Fiona from inside the chamber. "Ma will be searching for me."

"We ought to tell her, ye ken."

"Never. She'd take the switch to me."

He'd best offer to marry her, the lout!

Not wanting to be caught, Divana tiptoed down a flight of steps and waited on the landing until she heard footsteps and giggles approaching. Pursing her lips, she did her best to look taken aback. "Fiona, no lads are allowed in the women's quarters."

"Shhh." The lass dashed toward her and grasped her hands. "Ye must promise not to tell. Pleeease. It would mean my position if you did."

Divana squeezed her fingers and gave a nod. "Och, after all ye've done for me, I'd never speak out against ye." Then she shifted her gaze to Garry. "But I'll have your promise that ye'll respect this young maid always."

"Ah…" He shot a dubious glance to Fiona, who winked. "I-I…uh…always. Of course."

"Very well then. Good evening," Divana said, praying she hadn't turned as red as a scarlet rose. She gripped her trembling hands against her midriff, unable to race up the stairs fast enough. Beltane certainly was as wild as everyone claimed. And it made her all too self-aware. Too many emotions pulsed through her. She needed to crawl under the bedclothes and think.

Survival might be easier at Achnacarry, but living under Lochiel's roof was far more complicated.

* * *

The sun dipped low in the western sky as Kennan tightened the girth of his horse's saddle. It would take about two hours to ride to Corpach on Loch Eil, where Clan Cameron moored their galleys. From the loch, given good winds, they could expect a half day's sailing to Port Glasgow.

"There you are, lad," said Da, hastening into the stables and waving a letter. "A missive just arrived from Mar."

Kennan gave his horse's shoulder a pat and met his father halfway down the aisle. "I hope it is good news."

Da shoved the parchment into his hand. "Do not tarry, open the blasted thing."

Kennan examined the seal, then ran his thumb beneath the wax and shook the letter open.

"Come, lad. What does it say?"

He gave his father a look before he tilted the missive toward the light and read.

"Well?" Da persisted.

"He opens with a bit of jesting at first...says he's surprised I'm not in the Americas making a name for myself."

"What about the bloody incident in Dundee?"

Kennan read on. "Och, here it is. The queen issued a pardon for the debacle over six months past...he's not surprised that Fort William's information is dated...aaaand he also dispatched a missive to the colonel to ensure their records were set to rights."

"And under no circumstances are any pernicious sergeants to badger you further?" Da asked.

"Aye, that about sums it up." Kennan folded the letter and stuffed it into his doublet. "Well, that's one thorn in my side easily removed."

"Thank God."

"Agreed." Kennan strolled back to his horse. "With this I'll be free to spend a bit more time in port, recruiting the hands I need for the journey. I'll purchase supplies as well."

"You're still planning to return home, are you not? Spend a few more days with your old man?"

Kennan gave his father a firm pat on the shoulder.

"There's no chance I'll sail without my core crew."
Mounting, he took up the reins. "I hope to return in a
month...and whilst I'm away, would you please watch
over Divana?"

"The wee Campbell lass?"

"Aye. She has no family here. 'Twould be nice to see
Lady Lochiel take the maid under her wing—entrust her
with more responsibilities. After all, if it weren't for her,
I mightn't have made it home."

"Very well, I'll have a word with Jean."

"My thanks." Kennan saluted his father, then rode his
horse out to the courtyard where Lachie Mor and three of
his best men were waiting. "Are you ready to ride?"

The old quartermaster grinned, the gap between his
front his teeth made darker by twilight. "Bloody oath,
I've been ready for ages."

As they headed through the postern gate, a high-pitched
voice rang out, echoing between the curtain walls. "Sir
Kennan, wait!"

Reining his horse to a stop, he glanced back. Divana
ran toward him with a basket in hand. His heart twisted.
Seeing the dregs of sunlight flicker through her coppery
hair as she sprinted across the cobbles was too reminiscent of a simpler time. She was right to have stopped him
at Beltane. He'd lost his mind when he kissed her. And
blast it all, he must never hurt the lass.

If only he'd been born a crofter, he might have
proposed. That's what she deserved.

Breathing heavily, she stopped beside him, her cheeks
rosy, her smile a tad unsure. "I packed some food for
ye and the men—things ye mightn't have thought to
bring."

The delicious aroma of freshly baked shortbread wafted

from beneath the cloth covering the basket's contents. Though it wasn't easy to fasten a basket to his saddle. "That's very thoughtful of you. Would you mind wrapping the victuals in the cloth and placing them into my saddlebags?"

She glanced behind him as she bit her lip. "Oh. Of course."

He leaned down and lowered his voice. "But those biscuits smell too good to ignore. May I have one for the road?"

"Aye." Her expression brightened as she gave him a warm triangle of shortbread. "And ye'll be returning soon, will ye not?"

"As soon as I can, and whilst I'm gone, my father will ensure you are cared for."

She unfastened the buckles on his leather bag and pushed in the parcel. "Your da?" she asked, wincing.

"Does my news make you unhappy?"

"He's a wee bit frightening," she whispered.

Kennan knew very well how menacing Lochiel appeared. He scowled and strolled about the halls of Achnacarry like an ogre at times. In fact, as a lad, Kennan had been terrified of his father, but the great chieftain was kindhearted toward his allies—though naught could be said for his enemies. "Perhaps, but he's a good man."

"I wish you weren't leaving."

God, how her words cut him to the quick. If circumstances were different, he'd be able to stay. But Kennan would be a coward if he didn't face Vane. He'd never be able to live with himself.

"I'm a sea captain, remember? 'Tis what I do." He kissed his fingers, then raised his shortbread in thanks. "I'll see you soon, lassie."

What was it about the redheaded woman? As her vivid blue eyes met his gaze, his heart twisted. It seemed the damned organ was doing too much twisting of late. Again Kennan regretted his actions at Beltane. Why had he grown so jealous when Runner told her she looked bonny? Or when he noticed every man at the gathering was watching her dance? He should have been relieved to see her garner so such attention.

Bless it, Divana would make a fine Highland wife. She was loving and selfless and bonny on top of it all. With luck, by the time he returned, she'd be courting a strapping young man from Clan Cameron.

Kennan gripped his reins tighter, demanding a fast trot from his horse. If some young whelp did so much as steal a kiss, he'd challenge the rake to a duel.

"Ye seem a wee bit agitated, sir," said Lachie Mor, riding beside him. "I would have thought after the news from Mar you'd be racing for Loch Eil with your hair afire."

"I'm anxious to sail to Glasgow is all."

"You're twisted in knots over what to do with the lass."

"Hold your tongue."

The old quartermaster chuckled but kept his opinions at bay. Aye, Kennan cared what happened to Divana, but that's where it had to end. The sooner she found another, the better. Why, she wouldn't be simply courting, she'd most likely find her spouse while Kennan was off chasing Vane—and God only knew how long he'd be away.

The last of the light faded and the men rode quietly, keeping an eye out for soldiers and highwaymen. A weight lifted from his shoulders when the waters of Loch Eil sparkled in the moonlight...right before he saw the glimmer of a musket barrel swing his way.

"Ambu—!" The word hadn't completely left his lips as the gun flashed. Before the deafening blast touched his ears, the world turned white around him as the musket ball hit and hurled him backward to the ground.

The last thing Kennan heard was Lachie Mor shout, "Ye bloody murdering bastard. He's carrying a pardon from the queen!"

Chapter Thirteen

*U*nable to sleep, Divana wrapped a plaid around her shoulders and climbed the stairs to the curtain walls. Atop the ramparts, she could see for miles. Mountains surrounded the castle, and the village of Achnacarry down below was even smaller than Connel. To the north, the River Arkaig rolled toward the loch with a calming and steady hum. When they escaped from the mill at Mallaig, Kennan had taken her along the narrow loch and they'd seen not a soul, as if they were the only two people in all the world.

Divana chuckled to herself. The most exhilarating time of her life had been escaping with Kennan—especially sharing a pony with the brawny knight. She'd never forget how the heat from his body soothed her, protected her, made her feel as if someone in her life actually cared.

But this night she felt neither loved nor cared for. Kennan was off to Glasgow to see about his ship. True, he might come home for a sennight or two, but then he'd be away again, navigating seas unknown in his hunt for Jackson Vane, undertaking a dangerous pursuit of one of the most feared pirates in all of Christendom.

As she sighed, a tendril of breath coiled on the air. There she stood on the wall-walk of a grand castle. Fate had brought her here. And being a scullery maid afforded her far more comforts than she'd enjoyed living with her family in a two-room cottage with its dirt floor. And she wasn't completely unhappy. Goodness, Divana ought to be content to live and work among Clan Cameron for the rest of her days. Perhaps she would be...if Kennan weren't so very important to the clan. But one day he would be laird of the castle. One day he would have a wife and family.

A tear slipped down her cheek as she tried to see beyond the dark outlines of mountains. If she left this place, where would she go? What would she do? How would she live? On Hyskeir finding food was a daily chore. It was painfully lonely and ever so cold. Did she truly want to return to such a life?

I'm being a daft curmudgeon. I've naught but to accept my lot and thank the stars Clan Cameron has opened their arms and their doors to me.

On her third trip around the wall-walk, the cadence of horses approaching the postern gate resounded from the south. Clutching her blanket tightly about her shoulders, Divana leaned out a crenel and strained to see.

"Two horses approach!" shouted a guard from the tower.

Though it oughtn't be anyone in Kennan's retinue, Divana jumped as high as possible, craning her neck for a better look. There! As the dark figures neared, she saw only the silhouette of one rider—and something bulky bouncing on the second horse.

"Open the gate!" cried the rider in an adolescent tone, one that sounded a great deal like Baltazar's—Runner, they called him.

Divana clutched her fists over her heart as the gates screeched open. But she broke into a run as soon as she realized a man's body was draped over the back of the second horse. In a heartbeat her blood turned to ice, her breath caught in her throat. No one needed to tell her who it was.

Dear God, he cannot be dead!

Her feet barely touched the stone steps as she raced down the endless spiral stairwell. When she dashed out into the south courtyard, Runner had dismounted while three guardsmen raced toward him. "'Tis Sir Kennan—he's been shot in the shoulder and thrown from his horse. Quickly! Fetch his da!"

All three men headed for the keep while the big Highlander's back heaved, hanging upside down over the back of a horse, the animal snorting from exertion.

"Wait!" Divana shouted, relieved to see him breathing. "One of ye alert His Lairdship. The other two, help Sir Kennan to his chamber."

They gaped at her for a moment.

"Now, please! Make haste."

While the two returned, she raced to Kennan's side and placed her hand against his forehead. "Who did this?"

Runner untied the ropes that had kept Kennan's body in place. "'Twas that scoundrel sergeant—he and his dragoons were lying in wait at Loch Eil—and after the captain received a pardon from the queen herself."

"This is unbelievable." Divana's voice trembled as she

wiped streams of blood from Kennan's beautiful face, willing him to open his eyes. "Do ye ken how to find the healer?"

Throwing his thumb over his shoulder, Runner gave a nod. "Aye, Mistress Ava lives just yonder."

"Fetch her at once." Divana secured the horse's lead line while the two guards stepped near. "Have a care moving him. Can ye see which shoulder is injured?"

"'Tis his left."

Her stomach twisted. "Saint Columba's bones."

Kennan grunted as they slid him from the horse. Though the sound was pained, it filled her with reassurance.

"I'll carry him above stairs," said the largest, hoisting the injured heir over his shoulder. "'Tis the only way to ensure we do not jostle his arm."

"Thank ye." Divana followed. "Ye're home, Sir Kennan, and we'll set ye to rights." What else could she say? "Please don't die"? "I cannot survive without you"? "I love you more than the air I breathe"?

The poor Highlander moaned and grunted as the burly man trudged through the servants' entrance and up the narrow rear stairs. Divana took a moment to stop in the kitchen to grab a pail of water and some clean cloths, then quickly took two steps at a time until she found the guard heading down the third-floor passageway.

"I'll open the door," she said as the water sloshed over the rim of the pail.

"Divana," Kennan mumbled, his eyes still closed. "I kent you'd be here."

"Of course," she said, casting a bashful glance at the guards as she ushered them into the chamber. The passageway sconce reflected a stream of sweat on the heir's brow. "Put him on the bed straightaway, thank ye." She rushed forward, set the pail on the floor and put the rags on the bedside table, then pulled down the bedclothes. "Your strength is impressive. Sir Kennan is so large, I do not ken of any other men who would have been able to haul him up three flights of stairs."

"Comes from carting hay on me back and swinging an ax, I reckon," said the largest while they carefully laid Kennan on his back.

The shorter one then stepped away and brushed his hands. "Is there anything else you'll be needing, miss?"

"I'm not certain," she said, tucking the bedclothes in. "I hope the healer will arrive shortly. Sir Kennan will most likely need some willow bark tea... I've brought water and rags."

"What about hot water?"

Divana set to lighting the candles. "Aye... and anything you reckon Mistress Ava will need."

"I'll fetch it," said the shorter man.

Kennan moaned, his eyes closed. But he still wore his leather doublet and shirt.

Divana rushed to his side, bent over him, and examined his shoulder—at least what she could see. He was in dire straits with blood pooled thickly on his clothes. "We'll need to remove these garments."

The big guard cringed. "With a musket ball in his shoulder?"

"Cut them off," said a matronly woman from the doorway with Sir Ewen and Lady Jean standing behind her.

"Straightaway, Mistress Ava," said the guard, drawing his dirk.

Ever so relieved to see the healer, Divana backed away from the bed while the grim-faced lord and lady of the castle neared. "What can I do to help?" she asked.

The matron pointed. "Gather those rags and stand at the foot of the bed. Be ready to sop up blood if need be."

After cutting away Kennan's shirt and doublet, the guard sidled toward the door. "I'll go help Randy with the hot water."

"What happened?" Sir Ewen demanded in a booming voice as he moved to the far side of the bed.

Lady Lochiel followed, her face drawn and tired. "The poor lad."

Divana twisted the cloth in her hands. "Baltazar said Sergeant Corbyn and his dragoons ambushed them at Loch Eil."

The chieftain's face blazed with anger. "Bloody hell, I'll see to it that demon of a dragoon is dragged before a court martial and hanged for this."

Divana pursed her lips to stop herself from expressing her opinion. If it were up to her, she'd ensure the sergeant received a good-size rock in the side of the head and forget the court-martial.

Kennan appeared to be sleeping soundly while Mistress Ava stooped over him, running a moistened rag around an angry and puckered wound. "I don't think the ball went in very far." She glanced back at Divana. "Have a look at his doublet. It may have saved his shoulder."

Retrieving the jacket from the floor, she held it up. "'Tis made of thick leather." She poked her finger through the musket ball hole. "But it went clean through."

"I always say a heavy leather doublet is as good as armor," Sir Ewen said.

"More importantly, can you dig the ball out?" asked Lady Lochiel.

"Aye." Mistress Ava looked across the bed. "But I reckon you ought to wait in your chamber, m'lady. This procedure is not meant to be seen by a gentlewoman such as yourself."

Her Ladyship turned a tad green. "Of course."

The healer shifted her attention to the laird. "Would you mind holding your son's ankles?"

Lochiel moved to the end of the bed while his wife took her leave. "Very well."

Mistress Ava beckoned Divana. "Stand beside me. Are you ready with the cloths?"

"Aye, ma'am."

The matron removed a bottle from her basket and unstoppered it. "I'll first pour a tincture of Saint-John's-wort over the wound to help stave off infection."

"He will nay die will he?" Divana asked, gripping the cloths in clenched fists. Kennan had not survived pirates and a shark attack only to succumb to an injury on his own lands.

"Make no bones about it, a musket shot of any sort can turn putrid, but our Kennan is a strong lad." Mistress Ava's lips formed a thin line as she returned the bottle to her basket and pulled out a small knife. "Now brace yourself."

Divana's stomach squelched, but she swallowed the bile and leaned in with her cloth at the ready, watching the woman's dagger angle toward Kennan's mottled flesh. Had Sergeant Corbyn shot him knowing about the missive from Mar and the queen's pardon?

Kennan had been in such a hurry to charge off to Glasgow. If only he had waited a sennight, this mightn't have happened. But now, staring at him bleeding on the bed, Divana would give an entire year's pay to be in his place, to suffer his pain.

She cringed as the knife pierced the skin. Kennan's

eyes flashed open. Bucking like a calf in a castrating pen, he bellowed.

"Easy, son," growled Lochiel, struggling to restrain the kicking legs.

Mistress Ava's hand remained steady while she twisted the knife, baring her teeth. "I nearly have it."

Dear God, please, please make his suffering be over.

And if as an answer to a prayer, the ball popped out, straight into the healer's fingers, and with it came a gush of red blood. Divana surged forward with a cloth.

"Press as hard as you can," commanded Mistress Ava, holding up the musket ball. "I'll wager he'll want this for a keepsake."

At the foot of the bed, Sir Ewen released his son's ankles. "I'll wager he'll be shoving that wee bit o' lead down Corbyn's throat."

Divana stretched for another cloth. "At this rate, Sir Kennan is making enemies faster than he's making allies."

"Och, I'll see to the sergeant myself. Once the lad is back on his feet, he'll be itching to chase after Vane—'tis where his priorities lie, mark me."

Her arms burned from applying constant pressure, but she wasn't about to stop. Every time she changed cloths, the blood ran like a mountain burn.

"Would you like me to give you a spell, lass?" asked Lochiel. Holy Moses, the chieftain of Clan Cameron was offering to take a turn?

"No, m'laird, I think the flow is slowing."

Mistress Ava set a pot on the bedside table. "This is a salve to help heal the wound."

"Are you not going to stitch it?" asked Divana.

"I'll bring some leeches in the morning. 'Tis best if

we leave it to air." The healer looked to Lochiel. "Ye ken these wounds. Someone must sit with Sir Kennan to ensure he doesn't grow fevered."

"I'm not leaving his side." Divana threw back her shoulders as she grabbed another cloth and firmly held it in place. She did not make poultices and hold vigil over him on Hyskeir only to lose him now. "Not until this very man wakes and tells me to go."

Emboldened, she eyed Lochiel, the leader of one of the most powerful clans in the Highlands. Though in truth, she cared less if he was a king. She wasn't leaving. "And though ye're his da, and a grand chieftain, and I respect ye for it, not even the likes of ye can tell me to go."

"Are you certain, lass?" His gray eyes filled with concern rather than contempt. "You need your sleep just like everyone else. I could send in a night guardsman."

"I'll have no other tend him." She pulled away the cloth and checked the wound. Praise be, the bleeding had ebbed some. "Thank ye for your thoughtfulness, sir."

Lochiel gave a nod. "I should be thanking you, lass. 'Tis understandable why my son thinks highly of you."

With those words, tingles spread across her skin. Kennan thought highly of her? Now, why hadn't he bothered to say so himself? She bowed her head to hide her smile. "Good night to ye, m'laird."

* * *

After the bleeding stopped, Divana leaned on the post of Kennan's bed for a time. Since the healer had left, Kennan seemed so peaceful in slumber, his deep breathing the only sound. A sense of calm fell over her as it had when no pecking order existed and they'd been but two people working to survive on a lone isle. Yet their time on Hyskeir seemed like another world away. And though tending him emboldened her, she never would have hoped for a tragedy to befall the man to bring them together again.

"Ye should have let your men go without ye..." She sighed, running her fingers down the post. "But I suppose it doesn't matter now."

He tossed his head, his brows pinching as if he were in pain.

"Let me fluff your pillows. That'll make ye more comfortable." Divana ran her fingertips over the heavy damask coverlet as she walked to the head of the bed. "Look at ye, living in luxury with a chamber four times the size of the bothy and a stately bed large enough for an entire family. Why, ye have enough feather pillows to make a pallet for a king."

Reaching behind him, she punched the cushions inward, trying not to jostle him overmuch.

Again, Kennan moaned and knit his brows.

"Is your shoulder ailing ye?" she asked, glancing downward and gasping. "Oh, dear."

Runner had mentioned the captain had been thrown from his horse, but everyone was so fraught with the musket ball in his shoulder no one noticed the bruise spreading down the back of his neck. Honestly, if Divana hadn't been leaning over him, she wouldn't have seen it.

Ever so lightly, she rubbed her fingers toward the back of his neck. When everything felt normal, she continued upward and found a knot the size of her elbow.

Kennan grunted and winced.

"Saint Columba, ye've struck your head something terrible for certain."

Wringing her hands, she turned toward the door. Should she have someone fetch the healer? But what more would Mistress Ava do? It wasn't as if she could stitch a lump. She'd left the salve, and a guard had brought up a tincture of willow bark tea for the pain. The knot on his head clearly must hurt something awful.

Divana spooned a bit of tea between his slightly parted lips and watched his Adam's apple move as he swallowed. After half the cup was gone, she rolled him to his uninjured side.

"That ought to make ye more comfortable."

At the washstand, she poured water from the ewer and doused a cloth, then cooled Kennan's head with it. "Ye're going to grow well. I refuse to think otherwise." She leaned over and kissed his cheek, breathing in the masculine scent of him—of the man she'd come to know in the bothy. "Now rest and let your body heal itself. Have not a care. I'll be here until you wake, *mo cridhe*."

Aye, he had become her heart, her courage. And she vowed to be his strength in his hour of need.

God willing, she would move heaven and hell to see her Highlander smile once again.

Chapter Fourteen

*S*omewhere in the recesses of his mind, Kennan knew he was home. He'd suffered a severe blow to the head once before when he'd fought a band of dragoons while fleeing the Samhain gathering at Inverlochy with his sister. The red-coated bastards had bludgeoned him half to death, and he remembered very little of the incident.

Now, as he drifted in and out of consciousness, he again found his memory lacking. If only he were able to wake and to ask what had happened, but there was a terrible pounding at the back of his head and, every time he tried to move, searing pain shot through his shoulder as if someone had prodded him with a red-hot fire poker.

During fleeting moments of consciousness, he sensed Divana's presence. Cool cloths were replaced on his forehead time and again. Sometimes Da's voice would resonate through the chamber. But mostly the dear lassie's soothing voice gave him ease.

When she sang a ditty, he'd wanted to open his eyes and smile. "*A lusty young smith at his vise stood a-filing...*" In Kennan's mind's eye, he saw her swaying with the tune on the beach at Hyskeir, her mien carefree and dreamy, her hair billowing in the wind. Perhaps he managed a smile when she held forth about a "buxom young damsel." He wanted to open his eyes so badly but must have drifted off before the song ended.

When next his consciousness returned, her voice cooed to him again.

"I never thought I'd work in a fine house like Achnacarry," she said softly as if speaking to herself. "I always thought I'd end up a crofter's wife like my ma. Wives must know so very many things—making candles and soap, cooking, cleaning, stitching clothes, knitting and darning. I even learned to weave a bit. I think I rather like weaving."

"I reckon you'd make a fine weaver—you'd be good at anything you set your mind to." Kennan's throat sounded dry and hoarse as his eyes opened.

A sharp gasp came from the bedside. "Ye're awake!"

His tongue ran over chapped lips. There he lay, once again being tended by his redheaded spitfire. How did this state of affairs come to pass? "Water."

"At once." She took a cup from the table and gently slid a hand behind his head. "Can ye sit up a wee bit, else I can spoon it into your mouth as I've been doing."

He felt as weak as a bairn, but he managed to clench his muscles, lift his head, and drink. Groaning, he dropped back to the pillow. "How long have I been abed?"

"Three days."

"Damn." He closed his eyes and pressed the heel of his hand against his forehead. His thoughts were a complete jumble. Hadn't he been traveling somewhere? "How the bloody hell did I end up at home?"

"Do ye not remember being shot?" Divana set the cup on the table. "Ye were thrown from your horse as well—sustained quite a nasty bump to the back of your head."

"Och, that explains the endless throbbing."

It took a great deal of strength to pull himself up against the headboard, but he bore down and tried not to grunt. "I remember now. The men and I were headed to Glasgow." He scrubbed his hands over his face. "But everything after that is mired in blackness. Tell me, where's the *Lady Heather*?"

"Why, Lachie Mor and the men went on to Glasgow to oversee her refitting, just as ye'd planned."

"No, no, no. There is too much to be done. I must be there as well." Kennan pushed away the bedclothes and moved his feet over the side of the bed.

The lass jammed her fists into her hips. "Ye've been on the brink of death for three days and ye'll set foot out of that bed over me dead body."

"I'll not allow a woman to tell me—" His bloody knees buckled as he took his weight onto his feet.

"Nay!" Divana caught him under the arms—uncannily strong for a wee lass. "How dare ye give me such a scare when I've had naught but a wink of sleep in three long days, worrying about whether ye'll live or die." With a gentle push she coaxed him to the mattress. "Back in bed with ye afore me heart fails."

"But you don't understand," he said, his voice cracking with the dryness.

"I understand everything quite well. Now if ye'll lie back, I'll tell ye why."

Kennan eyed her. "Good God, I must regain my strength at once."

"Agreed, but ye'll accomplish nothing by falling on your bonny face." She shoved a lump of cheese into his hand. "Eat this, ye surlyheaded boar."

He took the food and clipped a bite, reaching for the water on his own. "I'm listening."

She told him about being ambushed by Sergeant Corbyn at the bend in the road before they arrived at Loch Eil. "The next day your father rode to Fort William and insisted the colonel put the varlet behind bars."

"And did he?"

"Aye, he's faced a court-martial as well. He's headed for the gallows, where he belongs."

Kennan scowled. "Unfortunate. I'd like to challenge the fiend to a duel of swords."

"I think with your feud with Jackson Vane, ye've enough enemies ye're hankering to fight." She gave him a bannock, and Kennan craned his neck to see what else she might be hoarding on the table. "A missive arrived just this morn, and Lachie Mor reported he has things in hand in Glasgow."

"A missive? I want to see it straightaway." Damnation, why must his head pound so?

"I'll fetch it for ye, but your da has read the contents and said Lachie estimates the repairs will take a month. He's already working to recruit seasoned sailors to fill out the crew."

"A month, aye?"

"Aye. That means ye'll at least have a bit o' time to rebuild your strength. Ye need to be able to use your arm if ye're planning to confront a rascal like Vane and his mob of pirates."

Kennan gulped down a bite of bannock, though he had no appetite. "I can heal along the voyage."

"Och, I wouldn't be putting the cart afore the horse about now. Ye cannot fool me. Ye nearly fell on your face when ye tried to stand." She shook her finger under his nose, looking as if she wanted to thrash him. "I'll tell ye true, ye ungrateful mollusk, I'll thwack ye with the fire poker if ye do anything to hurt yourself again. After all the time I spent tending your bedside, the least ye can do is have a care for your *damned* self!"

Kennan winced at her curse. She'd never before uttered a foul word. She was madder than a mother badger protecting her young—or him to be honest. And why shouldn't she be? She'd been tending him without sleep for three days. That would make anyone irritable.

He patted the bed beside him, the fog in his mind clearing a bit. "Did my father mention if Lachie Mor is satisfied with the refitting progress?"

She sat. "Aye, he said they're ahead of schedule."

"And he's already interviewing the men we need?"

"See, ye've nothing to worry about with Lachie and Mr. MacNeil taking up the reins—naught but healing."

He hoped the quartermaster wasn't keeping the purse strings too tight. He'd best be hiring able sailors and enough of them to fight an army.

Kennan fingered a wisp of her hair as he'd oft done. It was silky and feminine and felt like peace—smelled of serenity as well. Of course serenity wasn't a fragrance, but her flowery scent was more than fragrant. It calmed the beast in his soul.

"Thank you for tending me." He brushed a finger over her cheek and along the scarred flesh on her jaw. "The few times I woke, you were always here, were you not?"

She nodded, a tear slipping from her eye. "I would never leave your side and let ye die."

"You're an angel. Far too good a woman for the likes of me." He grinned, making his lips crack. As he wiped away her tear, he ground his molars. "I'm too cantankerous to die—especially now. There's far too much life remaining that must be lived."

Her teeth flashed white with a smile as she wiped her eyes. "Now that is what I wanted to hear ye say." She stood. "If ye promise to stay abed, I'll fetch your missive from the table."

Before Kennan answered, the door swung open. "Praise God and all the saints!" boomed Da as he strode inside. "I was afraid you'd never wake."

"Ye ken no one can keep me abed for long."

"Never could."

Divana gave Kennan the letter—addressed to him but already opened.

Da leaned over the bed. "I hope you don't mind I took the liberty of reading Lachie Mor's note."

Kennan unfolded the parchment. "There are no secrets between us."

Da patted Divana on the shoulder. "This lass hasn't left your side. I reckon she ought to head for her chamber for a good night's sleep."

Kennan looked to the window and then to the mantel. Eight o'clock. Divana should go no matter how much he wished for her to stay.

"If ye wouldn't mind, I'd like to make up a pallet in here," she said. "Sir Kennan has only just opened his eyes, m'laird. I reckon 'tis still too soon to leave him alone."

* * *

At the sound of creaking floorboards, Divana roused from a deep sleep and sprang from her pallet. "Ye should have awakened me!"

Wearing only a plaid tied around his hips, Kennan gave her a sidewise glance from the washstand. "Why? You were sleeping peacefully."

"But ye might have fallen."

"'Tisn't my legs that are sore, lass." He winced when he tried to pick up the ewer with his left hand, then switched to his right. "I've been downtrodden enough times to ken the only way for a man to regain his strength is if he pushes himself."

She supposed he was right. After all, he'd pushed himself a great deal on Hyskeir. Most likely, she'd do the same. "What can I do to help?"

"I'm starved."

"Good."

"Hmm?" he asked, splashing his face with water.

"Last eve I ordered—"

"Good morn." Fiona stood in the doorway holding an enormous breakfast tray, but she took one look at Kennan and gasped. "Are you not ready to break your fast, sir?"

"I'm past ready." He splashed under his arms. "Put the tray on the table in front of the hearth."

"You'll not be taking your meal in bed?" asked Divana.

"No, I absolutely will not."

Fiona did as told, then looked at Divana as if she were shocked—she, the lass who'd been above stairs with Garry on Beltane, the wee harlot.

"Would ye be needing anything else?" Fiona asked.

The two women looked expectantly at Kennan, who, bare chested, faced them with a hand planted on his hip. "It smells delicious."

"Divana ordered the tray. Since ye were injured, she's become quite good at ordering everyone about."

"Fiona!" Divana scolded.

"Perhaps that's why I'm standing here on my own two feet at this very moment." Kennan smirked and flicked his hand. "That will be all, thank you."

Divana headed straight for the table and held the chair. "I haven't been ordering people about."

He took the back of the chair and wrested it from her grasp. "Nay? Then I must ask you not to order me about, either."

"I beg your pardon? I've done no such thing."

He didn't argue. After all, he must forgive her for her wee tirade yesterday. She'd been exhausted. "I'll seat myself from here on out."

"Very well."

He gestured across the table to the opposite chair. "Join me. There's enough food here to feed a crew of ornery sailors."

"One ornery captain is enough," she whispered under her breath.

"What was that?"

Divana drew in a breath before she sat. "I kent ye'd be hungry, so I asked Cook to send up porridge, eggs, sausages, haggis, and toast."

He speared a sausage with his fork. "No ale?"

She picked up the teapot and poured. "According to Mistress Ava, tea is better for your constitution."

He ate the sausage, reached for a piece of toast, and dipped it in the egg yolk. "I generally prefer a pint of ale with my breakfast."

"I'm only trying to help."

He didn't respond as his mouth appeared to be too full.

"Are ye sore?" she asked.

He swallowed. "Been sorer."

"Good." Divana wrapped a sausage in her toast. She supposed that was Kennan's way of saying he was sore but he'd endure. She examined him while she chewed. "'Cause if ye're feeling as well as ye say, then 'tis nigh time to step outside for some fresh air."

He saluted with his cup. "Now that's something I can agree to. This chamber has grown awfully stuffy."

She used the wee spoon from the salt cellar to sprinkle her egg. Truly, she hadn't expected Kennan to agree so readily. After all, he must not only walk down three flights of stairs, but also climb them on the way back. And there was no chance he'd allow one of the men to help him unless he was out senseless.

What might they do that wouldn't be too taxing? Of course, if she asked him, he'd insist on some activity requiring such an outlay of exertion, he'd collapse...However, if that happened, the guards would be able to carry him above stairs. She took a bite of egg. "The lilacs in the garden are in bloom."

"Ah yes. They were planted by my mother, God rest her soul."

"Then I'm certain it would please her to have ye enjoy them."

"You're right."

Divana nearly dropped her fork. He'd agreed without so much as a single objection. Perhaps the knock on the head had done him some good. "I'm glad of it." She sat a bit taller. "I think I like ye better when ye agree with me."

His tongue slipped to the corner of his mouth, licking a morsel there. "Is that so?"

Her gaze slipped from his eyes to the tawny curls on

his chest. Heavens, the man clearly had lost little strength in the past three days. How did he manage it? Always to look so braw no matter his state?

"There's a clean shirt, hose, and kilt on the trunk. I'll visit the privy whilst ye dress." Lochiel had brought in a new doublet for Kennan as well, but she wasn't going to suggest he try to put it on. Not when his shoulder looked like a gnarled patch of angry and swollen flesh. Goodness, he still had red marks where Mistress Ava had applied the leeches.

Divana made quick work of tending to her needs and, when she returned to Kennan's bedchamber, he was dressed and seated at his writing table. His quill fluttered through the air with strokes of his pen.

"What are ye writing?"

"I need to dispatch a letter to Lachie Mor. Let him know I'm healing well and thank him for stepping up his effort—ensure he has enlisted all the men we need— skilled men of fine character."

"I'm certain he'll appreciate hearing from ye."

"He's a good hand."

Divana looked longingly over his shoulder, wishing she'd learned to read. "Ye should be proud to have Lachie Mor do your bidding."

"I am." He rested the quill in the holder and sanded the parchment. "I'll just seal this and then we can pay a visit to the garden."

She didn't know whether it was the food or the fact that she'd agreed with him, but choosing to let him set the pace for his recovery seemed like the right thing to do. Though once they'd started down the spiral stairs, she wondered if her judgment had been sound. Kennan's face grew drawn and pained as he cradled his left arm.

Divana stopped at the first-floor landing. "Let me go fashion a sling."

He scowled. "I do not need a bloody sling."

"Very well then." She gave him a squint. "Ye might try stepping up your pace. Ye're lagging."

"Bloody miserable taskmaster," he mumbled from behind as she started off.

Grinning, she purposely pattered down the steps at a quick tack, then feigned amusement as he lumbered after her. But he didn't complain, just gestured forward. "Lead on."

"Aye, master."

He grumbled again, but this time she didn't catch what he'd said. It didn't matter. He was hurting yet determined to keep going. No matter how much she cringed on the inside, she wouldn't let him see anything but a bright and cheery face.

"Here we are," she said, sliding onto a bench amid a sea of lilac. She didn't pat it. She didn't suggest he sit beside her. She merely smiled and took of deep breath of the heady fragrance on the air.

Kennan more or less collapsed beside her, his chest heaving. "Damnation." Several minutes passed before he spoke again. "Forgive me for being a cantankerous grumbler. I shouldn't have barked at you this morn."

"Apology accepted. I imagine I'd be doing a fair bit of grousing if someone shot me in the shoulder."

"It is not you with whom I am angry."

"I ken."

He lumbered to his feet, cupped a clump of lilacs, and inhaled. "Ma loved to sit here on fine days and read."

"I'll wager she was an extraordinary woman."

"None better."

"Do you miss her?"

He plucked the bunch he'd been admiring. "Every day."

"I miss me kin as well, especially me ma."

Turning, he sat again, but this time he presented her with the lilacs. "For you. These blooms are as bonny as your smile."

Her heart swelled as if dozens of butterflies set to flight, levitating her chest and limbs. As she breathed in the scent, Divana knew without a single doubt there was nothing she wouldn't do for this man.

Chapter Fifteen

*Y*ou've managed to live nineteen years without riding a horse?" Kennan asked as he and Divana walked into the stables. Three days had passed since he'd barely made it to the garden before collapsing on the bench, doing his best to act as if he hadn't needed to catch his breath. Nonetheless, his strength was returning, albeit far too slowly for the likes of a sea captain. He pushed himself every day, refusing to give in to the pain. Thank God the throbbing in his head had finally eased, and his shoulder was mending, or so Kennan ventured to believe.

"I've been on the back of a horse afore—like when we rode from Mallaig, but me da couldn't afford a mule let alone a pony—very few crofters in Connel have the coin to buy horses."

"Then 'tis about time you learned."

Garry met them with a pitchfork in hand. "'Tis a fine day for riding."

"Indeed," said Kennan. After they'd agreed to a wee

riding lesson, the lass had packed a satchel with bread and cheese, and Kennan had added a bottle of wine and two wooden cups that wouldn't break—they weren't even chipped. "Please saddle your most even-tempered gelding for Miss Divana and put a halter and lead line on him."

"Straightaway." Garry gave Divana a once-over—taking a bit too long for Kennan's taste. "Sidesaddle?"

Unsure, she shifted her gaze to Kennan. "Ah—aye?"

"Aye," he clipped, stepping between the lass and the stable hand. Good Lord, her skirts would hike up to her knees or further if she sat astride. It was already difficult enough to keep his emotions in check, but if she trotted around the round pen bare legged, she'd have every young buck in Achnacarry hankering to bed her—especially Garry it appeared.

"Shall I saddle yours, sir?"

"Yes, but I'll not ride until Miss Divana has been comfortable in the round pen."

As Garry set to task, Kennan stroked the nose of a horse watching them with his head poked over the door to his stall. "All horses have different temperaments, but I've found they're likely to be less ornery if you use a light touch."

She patted the sorrel's neck. "Ye mean pet them?"

"Petting never hurts. But when riding sidesaddle, you kick with your heel and tap with your crop—start lightly. Only use as much pressure as you need to move the beast along."

"Truly? What about spurs and all that?"

"You'll not need spurs today. In fact, when I see how they can be misused, I wish they'd never been invented."

"Here we are," said Garry, leading an old gelding up to the mounting block. "This fella is as gentle as a lamb."

Kennan offered his hand and helped Divana step up, relishing the feel of her cool fingers tickling his palm.

But the lass wasn't looking at him. She eyed the stable hand rather intently. "Have ye convinced Fiona to marry ye yet?"

Garry blanched. "Er...ah...nay."

"I wouldn't dawdle about. She's a good lass and deserves better I reckon."

Kennan gave the lad a pointed frown. "Do we need to have a conversation?"

"No, sir."

"Then I suggest you take Miss Divana to heart, if I understand the undercurrent of her meaning." He stepped near the stable hand and lowered his lips to the man's ear. "And if I hear word of foul play, you'll be heading to the altar at the point of my dirk, ye ken?"

Passing the riding crop to Divana, Garry did not meet Kennan's gaze. "Aye, sir."

He straightened and gave the lad a wink. "Well then, I'm glad we've had this wee chat."

Divana waved the small whip. "I'm supposed to tap me pony with this?"

"Wait until we're outside." Kennan slipped a spare bridle onto his arm and grasped the gelding's lead line. "Is your knee secured over the upper pommel?"

"The what?"

As Garry strode away, Kennan stepped around to the "on side" of the horse and patted the pommel. "You hook your right knee here—it will give you balance." He then slid the iron stirrup over her left foot. "And your toes go in the stirrup like so."

"Ah—that feels more secure."

He led her out to the round pen and gave her a few pointers before he started the horse walking. "You're looking fine, but if you relax your seat in harmony with the horse's motion, both of you will be a mite more comfortable."

After a few turns around the ring, Divana's rigid posture eased a bit too much.

"Keep your head up as if you're balancing a book atop."

She immediately stiffened, making the horse sidestep. "How am I supposed to relax my seat and keep my head fixed at the same time?"

"Picture it this way—if you're nervous and tense, the horse will be nervous and tense. If you relax, then your horse relaxes, but you don't want to relax so much you lose control of your mount."

She snarled, her eyes fierce—good God, he enjoyed her spirit. "Och, 'tis easy for ye to say."

"All right then, what was that ditty you were singing about the young smith? Didn't it have a chorus?"

"Ye heard that?"

"I did."

She adjusted herself in her seat, tapping her crop while the horse snorted and bobbed his head. "*Rum, rum, rum. In and out, fiddly dum.*"

"Good, now sing that over and over as the horse moves."

Once Divana's mind was taken off riding and she shifted to enjoying herself, her posture adjusted itself like magic. "That's better."

Smiling, she wriggled her shoulders. "He seems to like the song."

"Aye, and he likes that you're not tense." Kennan let out a bit of rope. "Are you ready to try a trot?"

"Whilst I sing?"

"Why not?"

A great many clansmen stopped and watched with amusement on their faces. Divana didn't seem to notice, her unbound hair flapping from beneath her bonnet as she naturally posted with the rhythm of the horse.

After Kennan buckled the bridle in place and spent the greater part of an hour teaching her how to control the reins, her heel, and the riding crop, all to the tune of "The Lusty Young Smith," he gritted his teeth against the tearing pain in his shoulder as he hoisted himself astride his horse.

"Ye should have used a mounting block," said Divana, pointing to the bloodstain spreading at his shoulder.

"Not on your life."

Together they rode across the lea and along the River Arkaig trail. He liked Divana's company—she calmed him like no other. Though the lass was open with her opinions, she didn't nag. He liked her smile, the healthy glow of her skin, the way she looked at him and listened as if everything he said was remarkable and important.

"Where are we going?" she asked.

"I thought we'd take our nooning up yonder in a clearing where my brothers and I used to cast stones and see who could throw the farthest."

"Aside from their portraits, I haven't seen your brothers. Will they come home from university soon?"

"Mayhap in the summer."

"Och, university," she said dreamily. "What I wouldn't give to learn to read and write."

Kennan nearly offered to teach her, but he wouldn't be there much longer. He'd only begin lessons and he'd be off—and she'd forget everything while he was away.

"Perhaps I can find a book of letters for you. The alphabet is the best place to start."

"Oh, would ye? I'd be ever so grateful." She batted a tree limb with her riding crop. "Did ye attend university as well?"

"I did—the University of Glasgow. Studied a course on maritime and seafaring. That was where I fell into good standing with the Baronet of Sleat."

"And you captained ships for him?"

"Aye, the very *Lady Heather* in refitting at the moment."

Divana's expression grew distant at the mention of his ship. She lightly tapped her crop, making the horse trot for a few steps. "Did ye like university?"

"I'll say the years were invaluable. I made many allies and met friends who have become great men, but I prefer the sea."

"Why? Ye almost lost your life afore ye washed ashore on Hyskeir."

"There are a great many risks with sailing, but the rewards are boundless."

"Like plundering silver?"

He chuckled. "A man can earn his fortune if all the stars align. But there's nothing like a spray of salt water in your face whilst you're battling a wicked tempest, fighting to keep your ship afloat and your crew alive."

"Goodness, that sounds frightening." She shivered a bit. "Mayhap exciting as well."

"It certainly isn't boring. There's always something to do aboard a ship, even when there's no wind."

As they reached the clearing, Kennan reined his horse to a halt. "Here we are."

Divana stopped beside him, smiling as if she hadn't a care, her gaze shifting to take in the beauty of the green canopy of weeping willows and the carpet of bluebells. "I already love it here. 'Tis peaceful."

He hopped down from his mount, then held up his right hand. "Allow me to help you alight."

"But ye're still injured."

"Only one shoulder is sore." He beckoned with his fingers. "Now come, lass, we haven't all day."

As she placed a hand on his right shoulder, he clutched her waist and slowly let her slide down his body. The curve of Divana's hip molded to him as though she was meant to be there. The wind picked up her hair, whipping silken tresses around his neck and across his nose, the feminine fragrance enough to tame a wild beast. But what melted his heart was the way she smiled at him—as if he were the only man in the world. He adored her smile, especially when the sun sparkled in her lovely blue eyes.

"The color of a shallow sea," he whispered while he lowered her to the ground ever so slowly.

Her tiny gasp brought with it an internal storm of lust he intensely craved to act upon. Her lids lowered as she shifted her gaze to his lips, and a pink tongue slipped out, tempting him. "I do not suppose me riding lesson will end up like Beltane?"

"Beltane?"

She swiped her fingers across her mouth. "Ye ken. Do not make me say it."

The kiss. His muscles tensed. She'd been the one to back away. But why? "Of course not."

As Kennan released her waist, a flash of disappointment crossed her face. She skittered back and brushed out her skirts. "I'll fetch the satchel."

Confounded, Kennan untied the plaid from the back of

his saddle. Did she want to kiss him or not? According to his father, the woman had spent the three days he was unconscious standing over him like a mother hen. What was it between them?

Obviously they both knew they had no future. She was of marriageable age, more beautiful than any lass he'd seen in the Highlands. And he'd be sailing off to sea for an indeterminate amount of time. Pledging his love and showering her with kisses would be a rakish thing to do—even though he'd acted the rake in the past, he absolutely must not act upon his lust with Divana.

They had developed some inexplicable bond, something entwined their souls. He would give his life for her, and he highly suspected she might do the same for him.

Though it couldn't be.

He absolutely must not—*would* not—make promises to the lass. Doing so would only cut her to the quick when he ended up breaking those promises.

Perhaps he shouldn't encourage her. But then teaching her to ride had been his idea. How the bloody hell was he to stop encouraging himself? Naught but a moment ago she had raised her chin and puckered her lips. He would have kissed her, and out there in the clearing of the river with no one else about, he might have gone further—much further.

* * *

Over and over Divana told herself she was not in love with Sir Kennan and there was no chance in Hades he was in love with her. And that meant no kissing. No gazing into each other's eyes. No moving too close on the blanket they were sharing at the river's edge.

Why was it she and this Highlander could be having a wonderful time, and all of a sudden it would grow serious, she'd go as mushy as porridge inside and say something daft, and then they'd end up at odds?

For the love of Saint Columba, she didn't want to make him angry. They had but a few sennights together and then he'd be gone—off on a sea voyage to chase after Britain's most vile pirate. Worse, he might never return. He'd nearly been killed the last time he had an altercation with the brigand. Moreover, it didn't take a scholar to know how dangerous it was to sail the high seas, what with sea monsters and reefs that tore gargantuan holes through ships' hulls. She'd heard the tales.

Divana choked on a bit of cheese. Clutching her throat, her face grew warm as she coughed.

Kennan immediately reached for the cup of wine and held it to her. "Are you unwell?"

Divana patted her chest, her eyes watering. She took the cup and drank greedily, swallowing down the cheese. "Thank you," she managed in a strained voice. "I'm fine."

He gave her a look while he tore off a bit of bread with his teeth. "You've grown quiet all of a sudden."

Above, a flock of swallows had taken to flight. If only she had wings, she'd fly away with them—find her prince in a warm country on the Continent. "Och, I reckon my coughing was enough to scare away all the birds within fifty paces."

"Nay." He took the cup from her fingers and drank even though he had a cup of his own. "Before then you seemed withdrawn."

Who wouldn't grow silent when faced with a man she desperately wanted and could never have? A man who intended to leave her without a backward glance. Withdrawn? She ought to push him away and tell him not to come near.

The drastic thought made her pick up the bottle and pour more wine. She'd been elated when Kennan suggested riding. Of course, she'd suggested bringing the food, but the outing had been his idea. If she'd said no, perhaps he might have found another lass to ride with, and that simply wouldn't do. Bless it, if all she had was a handful of days to enjoy his company, then she'd spend every moment with him—even if he was shredding her heart to bits.

"Take me with ye," she blurted before she thought the better of it.

He gestured toward the river with a sweep of his hand. "I *have* brought you with me."

"Ye ken that's not what I mean. Take me on your voyage."

He rocked back and tossed the wine bottle's cork, easily catching it. "Och, ye ken I cannot."

"Why? Once ye're away, there'll be naught for me here."

"There's plenty for you. Mistress Barton tells me you're a hard laborer—that you accomplish far more in a day than Fiona."

"Too right, I work hard and I'd work even harder on your ship. I can clean and cook. I even learned some of the healing arts from Mistress Ava." Divana clasped her hands. Aye, she'd plead if she must. "Please. I'll earn me keep, I will."

He brushed a knuckle across her cheek. "I ken you'd work your fingers to the bone, but a ship is no place for a woman."

"So ye aim to leave me here with nothing but a mob of Camerons."

He threw the cork into the grass. "Wait a moment, those are my kin you're grumbling about."

"Aye, but they're not *me* kin."

"Are you saying you want to go back to Connel?"

She stared, her mouth agape. How could she make him understand? "Nay. Me place is wherever ye are. If I do not go with ye, I cannot tend ye when ye're hurt or sick. Why can ye not see how I feel?"

"Och, lass." He looked out toward the river. "You must realize I've been sailing for eight years and I haven't needed a woman to tend me in all that time."

"Obviously not." Divana stood and began shoving the remains of their meal into the satchel. "Ye nay need anyone, do ye?"

"What have I said to make you so upset?"

She threw the blasted bag at him. "If ye do not ken, then ye are as daft as a cock with his head cut off!"

She marched to her horse and untied the reins from the tree.

"Wait." Kennan wadded up the blanket. "I'll help you mount."

No! The last thing she wanted was for him to come near—to put his hands on her once again. Divana led the pony to a fallen tree and climbed up. Slipping her foot in the stirrup, she hoisted herself into the saddle and slipped her knee over the upper pommel.

"Ye see? I can do it meself."

Chapter Sixteen

*A*s time passed, Kennan's unrest grew. Though, with every new day, he gained mobility in his left arm. He spent most of his time working to regain his strength, stretching and running. He chopped wood with the lads and spent afternoons in the smithy shack swinging a heavy hammer, molding red-hot iron into hooks and stirrups and horseshoes.

Today he carried his sword out to the practice field, which also was used for clan gatherings. He headed for a sparring post, but movement at the far end by the shooting targets caught his eye.

Divana.

After their riding lesson, she'd returned to her duties of the household and steered clear of him. And Mistress Barton had promoted her to Cook's assistant, which Kennan had nothing to do with. Indeed, the lass earned the promotion on her own. Of course, he missed their daily interactions, though he'd done nothing to seek her out. He was a damned heel in so many ways.

She was right to push him away. The lass could never be serious about traveling with him. The ship of a privateer was no place for a lady, even a woman as independent and robust as Divana. Though, in truth, she might be heartier than a few sailors he knew. Still, a woman aboard was never advisable among a crew of randy men, especially when at sea for months at a time. No matter how much he'd enjoy her company, he could not allow it.

He watched as she loaded her slingshot and whipped it above her head three times. Lunging forward with a graceful release, she held her pose while the rock smashed into the bull's-eye of the straw target.

Kennan chuckled to himself. He probably didn't know one other person in all of Scotland able to wield a slingshot as accurately as Divana Campbell.

Bloody oath, I envy the man who wins that woman's heart.

The thought brought a scowl to his lips.

He removed his shirt and slung it over the fence. Then, drawing his sword, he addressed an oak sparring post with both hands on the hilt. The movement burned a bit, but the work he'd done chopping wood had helped loosen up the sinews some.

He eyed his target and took three breaths through his teeth, willing his inner strength to surface. Bellowing his Gaelic war cry, "*Aonaibh Ri Chéile!*" Kennan attacked, his blade hissing through the air as he spun in place and struck the solid wood, demanding every thread of power, bone, and sinew he could muster. With the impact, searing pain shot from his hands, up his arms, across his shoulders and neck, reverberating in his head until his skull rattled.

"Ugh!" Kennan grunted as if he'd been punched in the gut.

He glanced over his shoulder at Divana. She released another rock, hitting her target as if her arm were a cannon. Thank God she hadn't stopped to watch him. The damned oak post was two hands thick and solid as petrified wood. He knew better than to unleash all his strength on a sparring pole hewn of oak. But just thinking about Divana with any other man made him want to unleash his ire on someone or something.

Leveling his blade, he addressed the post again. "I'm a patient man."

Lunging right, he struck with a side slice, then spun to the left, his sword singing as he cut into the oak—his target a man's flank. Over his head, he attacked with a death strike to the head. A jab to the gut, driving his blade upward to slice through vitals that would end a man's life before he hit the deck.

On and on, Kennan fought his demons—his mind racing back to the battle aboard the *Highland Reel*. No doubt he'd face the same pirates again, and this time he'd fight them to the end. As soon as his crew set sail, they'd practice for hours, honing their strength and their endurance. No army would match them, and no ambush would send him into the sea, fighting bloodthirsty sharks.

"Ye've healed a great deal, have ye not?"

Kennan's gut clenched as he heard Divana's voice come from behind. He spun and faced her, his weapon high in on guard, out of habit. She took a step away, her hands entwined with the leather slingshot. "Ye look as if ye are about to attack me with your mammoth sword."

He immediately lowered the weapon. "Forgive me. 'Tis the training. When faced with the need to turn, the swordsman raises his blade—both for safety and to ready himself for an attack."

"I see." Her gaze meandered down to his chest, then to the waistband of his kilt, then up to the angry scar on his shoulder. "Is it hurting?"

"Less every day."

"I'm glad." Sidestepping, she picked up a wooden sword—one the men usually used for sparring. She brandished it with a flick of her wrist, making it whirl in a circle as an experienced swordsman might do. "I've always wanted to learn to wield one of these."

"Have you ever done so?"

"Nay—only watched me da swing an old rusty blade that had been handed down from his father."

"By the way you're holding that waster, I might have guessed you'd had a lesson or two."

She made a cross slice, showing a natural ability. "Never."

Kennan sheathed his sword and picked up a wooden waster identical to the one in her hands. "A sword is too heavy for a woman."

She sliced the practice weapon back and forth. "This isn't heavy in the slightest."

Without unsheathing it, he removed his sword belt and handed her his Scottish great sword. "There's a fair bit of difference between the waster and the actual blade."

She weighed it in her hands. "I see—this might be difficult to wield in a long battle, but not too heavy at first."

"Many a man has lost his life on account of being ill prepared for a long fight." He took the sword and leaned it against the fence. "I'd hate to see any woman embroiled in strife, but you are so skilled with a rock and a wee strip of leather, I'd advise you to keep your distance and take out your enemies one by one."

"So, ye're saying ye think I might be useful in battle?"

He eyed her. What was she driving toward? He opted for a neutral reply. "I reckon if you were a man, you'd be invaluable."

She drew a deep inhale through her nose, leveling her gaze with unquestioned fury. Again she brandished the waster. "Will ye show me how to use this?"

"One doesn't learn to wield a sword in one session."

"One can begin to learn."

"But a little knowledge can be fatal."

"So can nay knowledge at all."

"Very well." He addressed the post, holding the weapon in both hands. "There are eight basic positions and from each you can either defend a strike or attack. If your opponent is advancing, you defend until you see an opening."

"Ye mean a mistake?"

"Of sorts. Say I aim for a killing strike to your neck." He demonstrated, carefully placing the waster against the pulse throbbing at the base of her slender neck. "Bob beneath my blade."

She ducked under and wove to her left as if he'd told her to do so. "Like this?"

"Aye. And since my strike missed, I'm carried to my left with more force than I'd intended." He followed through and pointed to his side. "Now my flank is open to you."

Divana lunged with her weapon. "So I go in for the kill?"

Kennan dropped and rolled away from her pointy tip. "You can try, lassie."

"All right." She moved back to a ready stance—the

lass mightn't know it, but she'd learned well from her da. "Shall we start at the beginning?"

"'Tis always smart."

He moved through a form of the positions. "On guard, head, left shoulder, left gut, left leg, right shoulder, right gut, right leg."

Her feet stumbled as she raised the weapon to her side. "On guard?"

"Close—you did it just a moment ago without knowing." He moved in behind her and grasped her wrists. "When you are on guard you hold the hilt up and out, whilst eyeing your opponent, ready for his attack."

"Or her attack."

Kennan cleared his throat. "Hmm." The scent of roses distracted him as he moved her hands up. "This is a very important position. Here you block deathly strikes to your head and neck."

"Very well." Divana's voice grew breathless, her shoulders relaxing against his chest.

From behind, he craned his neck and observed her face as he took her through the motions. "If you want to become an accomplished swordswoman, you must first master these eight defenses."

"I can do that."

"You'll practice every day?"

She turned enough to look him in the eye. "I can when I'm not needed in the kitchens."

His breath caught in his chest. It felt so inexplicably good to keep her so close, to hold his arms around her. "I...ah..." He licked his lips, trying to convince himself he mustn't kiss the soft, irresistible woman—but she was so tempting, her bow-shaped lips so utterly inviting. "Mayhap we should go through it once more?"

"I'd like that."

Kennan's knees turned to boneless mollusks as he dipped his chin and studied the curve of her neck. "On guard," he purred at the side of her ear. Having been taught swordsmanship since the age of seven, going through the basic motions was like breathing. But his student excelled admirably. Divana's arms were like clay in his hands as she intently studied each exact placement.

"Right leg." He whispered the final position as his lips caressed her creamy flesh.

She drew in a gasp but didn't push him away. "Ye will be my undoing, Sir Kennan Cameron." The words came out low and sultry, as if she were fighting the same inner demons tormenting him.

Unable to help himself, he applied a gentle kiss at the base of her throat—right atop the pulse quivering in a steady rhythm.

Her inhale came in a stuttered gasp, her lithe body shifting against him.

Though it nearly tore him to bits, he forced himself to lower his arms to his sides. "Forgive me. I did not intend to take liberties."

A lovely blush spread up her neck, the wee pulse thrumming faster. "We are so similar ye and I, yet separated by an uncrossable divide."

Chapter Seventeen

*D*ivana stared at nothing while she worked the butter churn—an unending rhythm of up and down. With her mind stuck in a muddled mire, at least the monotony of churning didn't require her to be terribly attentive. She'd done everything she could think of to convince Kennan to take her to sea, and yet her efforts resulted in failure.

Worse, Lachie Mor had arrived at Achnacarry two nights ago, and since, the castle was in upheaval. Of course the men weren't allowed inside the castle—they camped in the stables or beyond the wall. But working in the kitchens was like being in the midst of the wars. Cook madly prepared food while stores arrived by the wagonload.

When the crewmen weren't on the practice field with their captain, they were preparing for the voyage. Every time Divana stepped outside, Kennan was in conversation with his da or Lachie Mor or Mr. MacNeil or even Cook.

He was so wrapped up in his affairs, he paid no mind whatsoever to her aside from a smile here, a hello there. And though the great Cameron captain had relegated Divana to the depths of uselessness, Runner, at the age of sixteen, had been promoted to ship's mate.

"Baltazar," she said as the boy strode into the kitchens and retrieved a large basket from the table.

"Aye?"

Her hand stilled on the churn. "Do ye ken if Sir Kennan has named a replacement for cabin boy?"

Snorting, Runner looked at her as though she'd grown two heads. "Nay. Not all ships have cabin boys."

"What about cabin lassies?" she mumbled under her breath while she resumed her rocking, her arm numb from the repetitive movement.

"How is that butter coming?" asked Cook, wiping her hands on her apron while the lad slipped away without answering her question. "Sir Kennan needs it afore they set out to board the *Lady Heather*."

Divana's spine snapped straight. "When are they leaving?"

"Och, have ye not heard the commotion? They're hitching the wagons now."

Her gaze shot to the window. "Now? Ye must be jesting!"

"Nay. They'll be off just as soon as I parcel up the last of the stores. Good heavens, by the list I received from Sir Kennan, he'll be at sea for months afore he replenishes."

Divana gripped her stomach. *Months* before he replenished? How long would he be away? And why hadn't he mentioned a single word about his departure date to her?

Cook opened the lid and peered inside the churn. "Och, this is fine butter. You've an arm like an iron crank."

Divana swirled the handle around as she pushed to her feet. "Comes from years of practice with the slingshot."

"I beg your pardon?"

"Never mind me." She backed toward the door. "Would ye permit me to step out for a time? After all that churning, I reckon I need a wee bit of air."

Cook hefted up the churn and cradled it in her sturdy arms. "Och, you've been working since daylight, lass. Take a slice of shortbread and go give your legs a good stretch."

If there was one thing Divana couldn't resist, it was Cook's shortbread. She took a wedge and clipped off a bite with her teeth. Her eyes rolled back when the sweet, buttery pastry melted on her tongue. But as soon as she stepped outside and looked toward the stables, the pleasure vanished.

Gripping the biscuit in her fist, she stood in the shadows of the bathhouse and watched the hub of activity beyond. The men were busy loading barrels, carpenter's supplies, baskets, and Lord knew what else onto wagons. They rolled up enormous pieces of canvas and coiled rope while oxen stood harnessed, stamping their feet as if itching to go.

"Finished with your churning?" Runner asked, approaching with an enormous grin. He was one of the few allowed in the inner courtyard. "There's always excitement on the air when a ship's about to set sail."

She wanted to bat the feathered bonnet off his head. "Och, such a thing is easy for ye to say."

"Whyever do ye sound so woeful?" The boy drew a dirk form his belt and stabbed it through the air, his eyes filled with excitement. "We're heading on a grand adventure, and now I'm a full-blown mate, the captain will let me fight pirates for certain."

"A laddie of sixteen?" she spat out.

"Nearly seventeen, mind ye."

"Aye, that makes all the difference." Divana didn't hide the sarcasm in her voice. It burned her to the core to look at the proud young man, going to sea with Sir Kennan because he happened to have the right sex between his legs while she was forced to remain behind.

She eyed the lad. "Baltazar," she said, using his Christian name, which always commanded his attention whenever she spoke it. "If ye had to make a guess, how long would ye say ye'll be away?"

"Forever, if my opinion mattered." The lad grinned as if he were embarking on the adventure of a lifetime. "But I reckon it'll take a good six months to a year to find the *Reel*. And then the captain will have to figure a plan to steal her back. I'm thinking that will take ages, knowing the likes of Jackson Vane. Once we've taken the ship, we'll most likely need to call into port for repairs— which may take a few months, depending on damages and supplies." He scratched the fuzzy hairs on his chin. "Och, repairs might take an entire year. And 'tis up to God and the wind on how long sailing home will be." He gave her an assured nod. "Mayhap two years."

Divana drew a hand over her sinking heart. "Two years?" She'd be an old spinster by then. And what was there for her at Achnacarry? Garry had finally proposed to Fiona, and once they were wed, they planned to move into a cottage in the village. Without Fiona, work would be tedious to say the least.

"Runner, stop your dawdling and help load these

planks," Lachie Mor shouted as he slapped a cat-o'-nine-tails in his leathery palm.

Alone again, Divana wandered through the bustle with hardly a soul glancing her way. Even Kennan stood at the far end of the outer courtyard surrounded by men as he pointed this way and that. True, by the bustle, he had a great deal of responsibility, though she still tried to will him to look her way.

When finally he did, his features grew dark. He uttered something to one of the crewmen and headed her way. "There you are."

Her stupid heart fluttered. "I thought ye were about to set off without saying good-bye."

"Never." He ran a hand across his mouth, shifting his eyes. "The last of the stores came in yesterday afternoon. 'Twas late when we made the decision to load the wagons."

Her heart sank to her toes. "So then ye'll be gone for two years or more?"

"Most likely."

"Ah…" What could she say? He'd made his decision. "Think of me when ye spread butter on your ship's biscuits. I churned it meself."

"I will."

Did he not know she was falling apart on the inside?

"Sir Kennan!" Lachie Mor hollered.

The sea captain looked toward the quartermaster, then back at her. "I haven't much time."

"Nay," she snapped. "I'm certain his question is more important."

Kennan's expression grew darker. "It might be more urgent, but not more important."

"Whatever ye say."

He brushed his knuckle over her cheek. "I shall miss you, please know that. However..." His jaw twitched.

Did she dare hope? "Aye?"

"I do not want you to worry about me. You're a beautiful young woman, free to make your own choices, and it is time for you to move on with your life."

"Sir Kennan!" Lachie Mor shouted.

Wiping her eyes, Divana refused to cry in front of him. She was free to make her own decisions? What if what she wanted was not possible? The only man she had ever loved, the man who had protected her and freed her from her island prison, was leaving. Worse, he was telling her to move on with her life.

"Go. Ye are needed," she said, turning and fleeing.

"Divana!" Kennan called after her.

"Bless it," Lachie boomed. "How many sheep are we to take aboard?"

Clapping her hands over her ears, Divana didn't want to hear it. She wanted to run away and forget she'd ever met Kennan Cameron even though the Highlander was burned onto her memory forever—his kindness, his friendly banter, the caring way he'd taught her to wield a sword.

By the time she stopped, her slice of shortbread had disappeared and she was well away from the bustle, standing among dozens of barrels. Most were already sealed, but the one beside her was completely empty. Her stomach squeezed as she checked over each shoulder. Many of the men had shifted their attention to loading the livestock onto a wagon—and it appeared the sheep weren't about to go without a fight. On the way up the ramp, a lamb jumped through a gap in a makeshift fence. With frantic bleating, the lamb's mother knocked the barrier down as she leapt from the ramp, leading the way for the rest of the flock while sailors scattered to round them up.

Within the blink of an eye, Divana raced into the keep and ran up the winding stairs until she reached her chamber. She spread a thick plaid on the bed and tossed the few items she'd collected since arriving at Achnacarry—a comb, flint, a candle, a spare shift, a brush for her teeth, a drying cloth, slingshot, and the most precious item of all, the carving Kennan had whittled on Hyskeir. Swiftly she folded in the sides and made a roll.

After tiptoeing to the kitchen larder, she took an old grain sack and swiped a loaf of bread, a handful of dried meat, some bannocks, and two bottles of watered wine. Tucking everything under her arm, she stood at the corner of the doorway and waited until the corridor was clear. Only then did she rush out to the bathhouse, where she propped her back against the wall and stood, pretending she wasn't catching her breath, trying to appear as if it were an ordinary spring day. Thank heavens the men were still rounding up the mob of sheep.

Divana looked toward the barrels—they hadn't yet been touched—and nary a soul was near them.

After a sailor brushed past not even giving her a second glance, she strolled at a normal pace until she reached the barrel, turned full circle, and dropped her things inside. She chanced another scan of the courtyard and set the lid on a neighboring barrel. Planting both hands on the rim, she hefted herself up, straightening her arms. The barrel teetered as she raised her knee. Encumbered by her skirts, she couldn't swing her miserable leg high enough.

Curses!

The men had all but three of the sheep loaded on the wagon.

Divana's gaze darted to a quarter barrel. If she didn't hide now, she'd be caught for certain. Quickly, she shoved the smaller cask beside her empty barrel. Using the wee cask as a step she climbed atop, grabbed her skirts, and leaped inside, landing on the watered wine and twisting her ankle.

"Ow!" she hissed, rubbing away the pain. Holding her breath, she dared to peek over the rim. Thank goodness Lachie Mor wasn't marching over, swinging his cat-o'-nine-tails in a rage. In fact, no one had seemed to notice. She snatched the cover and pulled it over her head.

Sitting for a moment, she blinked while her eyes adjusted to the dim light. A sliver of daylight shone through the cork hole and her knees were a bit cramped, but there was no chance in Hades she'd entertain a change of heart now.

Divana's heartbeat thundered in her ears as heavy footsteps neared. Would she be caught?

"Why haven't these barrels been loaded?" bellowed the quartermaster, thumping the side of Divana's cask, nearly making her squeal. Her erratic pulse hammered. And if she'd jolted any higher, she would hit her head on the lid and give her hiding place away. Trying to calm her racing heart, she clapped her hands over her mouth and held her breath, ready for the humiliation to come.

A myriad of footsteps crunched about her barrel.

Did the quartermaster know she was within? Had anyone seen her?

Her question was answered when someone laid her barrel on its side and rolled it! Divana clutched her possessions tightly to her breast as she squeezed her eyes shut and tried to swallow back the bile and shortbread being sloshed in her stomach.

If I can survive on Hyskeir—I can survive this!

* * *

But Divana was wrong.

She'd never sailed beyond the Inner Hebrides or on a voyage lasting more than an hour or two. At first, aside from Divana's not being able to see, everything seemed to be fine. Once they'd carted her aboard, she chewed on a bit of dried meat and drank some watered wine. But a few hours later, the hull began to groan like a retching dragon. Worse, Divana's stomach followed suit, and she spent the next day curled up at the bottom of the barrel praying for either relief or death—whichever came first. Several times she had surged upward, retching over the side of the barrel, positive her insides had emptied and she was about to die.

By the time the seasickness had run its course, she had no idea how much time had passed. The hold was dark and already stank of excrement from the animals they'd taken aboard, though a crew of men came down daily to siphon out the water. Nonetheless, inches of tainted sludge sloshed outside her barrel.

During daylight hours, a faint ray of light shone through the lattice portal in the deck above. A bit more light came through when men removed the cover to clean the bilges. But they never saw her—she made certain of it. The rats stayed hidden as well. Those hideous varlets pattered about only when it was dark. And for some reason they weren't afraid of her. Divana had to pull the cover over her head when she slept and ate to keep them from crawling into the cask with her. Of course she'd learned her lesson the hard way when she awakened to a rat in her lap with his head in her sack, finishing off the last of her bread.

And now she'd gone a whole day without eating a morsel. Her stomach growled and clawed at her insides like the early days on Hyskeir—before she'd perfected throwing the slingshot—before she knew all the tricks about clamming.

The problem was now that she'd stowed away, she had no idea how to feed herself. What if she was discovered and Kennan decided to return to Scotland? Or abandon her on an isle like Hyskeir for the rest of her days just as her own kin—people she'd loved—had done?

And what if a roguish sailor found her? Some of the shipmates had come from Glasgow, and from the little she'd seen of them on their visits to the hold, they weren't as friendly as the folks at Achnacarry had been. Kennan had warned her about wily crewmen. She needed to steer clear of them.

If only she could find Runner, he'd help her for certain.

Lachie Mor would most likely throw her overboard. And the boatswain, Mr. MacNeil, had a knife scar that ran from his forehead to his chin. A lass only needed to look at that man to know he was surly. Who knew what he was capable of? If only Kennan would visit the hold, she'd be brave enough to show herself then. After all, he was the reason she was in this predicament. As the captain of the ship, he had to make an inspection sooner or later. Right?

Long after the light faded, Divana removed her slippers and used her toes to feel her way, carefully walking across the tops of the barrels, crouching and bending her knees in tandem with the rocking of the ship. Halfway, she stopped and glanced back into the darkness while her stomach growled and clawed with hunger. No, she mustn't go back now, lest she have no strength whatsoever come morn. She counted twenty barrels to where the ladder ought to be, but as she reached forward her hands felt nothing.

It has to be here.

Dropping to her hands and knees, she stretched as far as she could until her fingers brushed a wooden post.

Praise be!

She climbed upward toward the faint light until she reached the lattice, then pushed it aft as the men had done. When it wouldn't budge, she pushed harder.

Still nothing.

A creaking sound came from above. Divana crouched, her gaze snapping toward the direction of the noise. An unlit lantern swung from a beam, and behind it a sconce glowed with a yellow light. The ship's sounds were different up there, and she held very still, clinging to the rung while she listened. Snores came from the distance, the slap of waves against the hull. The creak of timbers, even the flap of canvas sails, cut through the chilly night air.

Once certain she was alone, she tried moving the lattice again. This time it budged about a half inch before jamming, but not before Divana caught sight of a wooden dowel.

Curses!

She braced her feet on one rung and held on to the top with her right, stretching out with her left. Her hand barely fit through the gap. Clenching her teeth, Divana stretched, trying to close the gap. Her fingers brushed the dowel, but it was too far to gain a hold. Her neck cramped as she strained to see her target. Inching up on her toes and extending her grasp on the rung, she stretched farther until her fingers wrapped around the pin. Her entire body wobbled as she dangled with one toe on the ladder and two fingers gripping the rung.

Just a wee bit more.

With a grunt she used all her strength to lever up the peg from its hold. As it released, her body swung down and around, crashing into the ladder. Up top, the dowel hit the deck with a hollow clank as loud as a smithy's hammer.

Divana wrapped her arms around the ladder and hung on for dear life while she imagined the entire crew waking with a start and charging into the mid-deck with weapons drawn. Though it was chilly, a bead of sweat streamed down the side of her face.

As her breathing calmed, she heard not a single footfall approach. She glanced into the blackness of the hold. The pattering of scampering rats sounded below.

Should I go back?

To the tune of her growling stomach, she strengthened her resolve. Divana hadn't stowed away to cower and die in a barrel—a fate far worse than living alone and abandoned on a deserted isle.

It didn't take long to shift the trapdoor enough to slip out. On the mid-deck the air was fresher, and the wafting aroma from a pottage led her forward to the galley while her mouth watered. And she was right. A large pot secured to an old brick hob simmered with brine and salt pork. Overcome with hunger, she grabbed a wooden spoon and ladled a few bites into her mouth, burning her tongue. Round ship's biscuits caught her eye next. She chewed as fast as she could, devouring the food like a starved dog.

But the dry biscuit stuck in her mouth, her saliva like glue. In the corner was a tapped beer cask and beside it a basket full of wooden cups. She filled one and greedily drank while ale streamed from the corner of her mouth.

But it wasn't enough and the longer she stayed, the greater the chances of being caught. She filled her cup once again, then set to spreading a cloth and filling the center with biscuits. She tied the ends and cradled it in her arms, then picked up her cup and headed off.

Except Lachie Mor blocked her escape. His blue eyes blazed, his mouth hidden by a face full of grizzled whiskers.

"Saint Columba," she uttered, freezing where she stood, the food in her belly turning to lead.

"What the bloody blazes are you doing here?"

Divana glanced beyond his shoulder while clutching the food in her arms. If a lass could wilt and die, this would be the moment. Visions of being whipped and humiliated in front of the crew danced through her mind. Should she run? But to where? "I . . . ah . . . stowed away."

"Aye. That part is obvious, but why?" Rather than take her by the scuff of the neck, the man leaned against the galley's jamb. "The captain never allows women aboard."

Her tongue slipped to something caught between her molars and probed. "Whyever not?"

"On account of they cause trouble."

"I'm no trouble. I swear it."

"I beg to differ. You've just caused me a great deal of consternation."

"But I can help. I-I'll do anything. I can—"

"Och, there are some things you'll not do, mark me." He poked his head out of the galley and looked to and fro. "Who kens you're here?"

"No one."

"Are you certain?"

"I've been hiding in a barrel in the hold since we sailed."

"For four bloody days?"

"Has it been that long?" This conversation was going nowhere. She clutched the sea biscuits tighter. Bless it, she wasn't about to starve—not when there was an abundance of food. "What do ye aim to do with me?"

He scowled. "I ought to bend you over my knee and give you a good hiding."

She took a step back. "Ye wouldn't do that."

"I would if it were up to me. But seeing the captain has a soft spot for you, I've no choice but to hand you over to him and hope he sees fit to do the honors."

A soft spot? Perhaps public humiliation might be worth the pain, especially if it was issued by the captain. Would Kennan take a switch to her backside?

"Now, I need you to step lightly, lass. I'll take you to his cabin, but we must ensure no one sees."

"Why?"

"'Cause if the men ken there's a woman on board, there'll be anarchy."

"But there are women ashore," she whispered.

"That's different."

"I fail to see why."

"Wheesht. Keep your head down and follow me."

Chapter Eighteen

*K*ennan's eyes flashed open with the rap on his cabin door.

"Captain?" Lachie Mor's voice rumbled through the timbers. Hearing the quartermaster's voice at this hour meant nothing good.

As he jolted up, the bedclothes slid to Kennan's waist. "Come."

Footsteps shuffled while Lachie led with his lamp, making it impossible to see a thing. "We've a stowaway."

Kennan stood, dragging the plaid around his hips and knotting it. "A stowaway? Why the devil did you bring him up here?" It wasn't like Lachie to awaken him in the middle of the night on account of a useless varlet.

The quartermaster stretched to hang his lamp on a ceiling hook. Only then did Kennan get a good look at the prisoner. He shook his head and blinked.

Then he swiped a hand across his eyes, just to ensure they hadn't deceived him.

Nay. It was Divana Campbell, just as plain as ink on parchment.

And she stood with shoulders back and chin high like Zenobia facing the Romans.

He ought to be spitting with ire. He ought to give her a good chiding for disobeying him. Yet, if he weren't in the middle of the Atlantic, he'd be ever so happy to see her. He sauntered forward, rubbing his fingertips. If only the quartermaster weren't standing like a slavering bulldog, Kennan might pull the woman into his arms and forget her defiance. But right now he had to be a captain to his men first. "What the blazes are you doing aboard my ship, lassie?" he demanded.

Divana glanced at Lachie, who gave her elbow a shove. "Go on. May as well have out with it."

Before she spoke, her gaze slipped to Kennan's chest. Her teeth grazed her bottom lip while her eyes dipped lower before meandering back up to his face. She'd seen him without a shirt before, but if he knew anything about women, she'd just undressed him without uttering a word. He gulped as she stared into his eyes without so much as a flinch.

And she looked so damned self-righteous. Did she not know he'd be within his rights to hang her for stowing away? Cleary not by the purse of her lips, the arch of a single, saucy eyebrow.

"Who in all of Scotland do ye think ye are forcing me to bide me time at Achnacarry whilst you sail away on the high seas for Lord kens how long?" She jammed her fists into her hips. God, she was bonny when angry. "And after I sat by your sickbed without a lick of sleep night after night. Twice, mind ye!"

Hadn't he explained it clearly enough? Females didn't

go to sea with a ship full of randy sailors. "Women do not sail on merchant ships—not unless they're—" *Paying passengers.*

"Why not?"

Lachie Mor smirked. "On account the lads will start behaving like stags during the rut."

Slicing his hand through the air to demand silence, Kennan shifted his attention to the quartermaster. "Who else kens she's aboard?"

"Only me." When the old man thwacked Divana's shoulder, Kennan's blood boiled. "Aye, lass?"

Then Lachie swallowed his grin when she elbowed him back, the spitfire. "Aye."

"Leave us," Kennan said.

As the quartermaster closed the door behind him, Kennan pulled out a chair from his walnut dining table and gestured for Divana to sit. God's bones, she smelled like the bilges.

"I'm nay going back to Scotland."

He'd already considered calling into port at Bermuda and paying for a transport to take her home. In fact, he still might. "At Achnacarry you have plenty to eat, you have shelter and the protection of Clan Cameron. I kent you'd be well cared for there."

"What is all that without ye?"

"Good Lord, Divana. Many women—no, *all* women bide their time at home whilst their men are a-sea."

"Well, I'm not '*all* women,' mind ye. If ye've forgotten, I can take care of meself quite nicely."

"Except when you're living in a castle with my father and my kin, it seems."

"I was working as a servant in your castle. And I'm nay here on account of being unable to manage."

"Were you forced to remain there? Was anyone unkind? I've asked you before and you've always denied mistreatment."

"Why must ye make me say it?" She pushed to her feet with such vehemence, the chair teetered. "I cannot abide being without ye. I ken ye do not love me. I ken ye look upon me as wretched and undeserving—but whether ye like it or nay, I am bound to ye, Kennan Cameron. If it weren't for ye, I would still be alone on Hyskeir digging for clams and hunting eiders. But ye rescued me, and now I'm lost, I say, lost and just as alone as I was on that wee isle."

"You are neither wretched nor undeserving. You are resolute and capable, and I have severely misjudged your tenacity." Kennan turned away and strolled to the windows looking out over the stern, the foaming wake calming compared to the tempest in his cabin. This woman had done so much to help him. Moreover, he liked her. Not only that, she had been the object of his dreams since sailing from Scotland. She was funny and thoughtful and, bless it, she was as bonny as a rose. He glanced at her over his shoulder. What the hell was he supposed to do with her now? Marry the lass?

That might keep her safe from the crew, but it sure would send Lochiel into a rage. Kennan was duty-bound to marry an heiress. Da surely alluded to it often enough. *Clan and kin are your first priority*, Da had said more times than Kennan could remember.

"Ye need a cabin boy, do ye not?" she asked, her voice cutting through his thoughts.

Kennan faced her, looking at the lass from head to toe. She was shorter than Runner by a hand and slim enough that it wouldn't be difficult to hide her breasts. "You'll have to cut your hair," he said, wishing he hadn't. God, he loved her mane of coppery locks.

She pulled her tresses into a tail over her shoulder. "If it means ye'll allow me to stay, then aye."

"There's no other way," he insisted.

"It will grow back in time."

"You'll have to sleep on a pallet in here. I'll not take a chance on anyone discovering your sex."

"Och, Kennan!" She dashed across the floor and wrapped her arms around him, showering his cheeks with kisses. "Thank ye, thank ye, thank ye!"

He closed his eyes, trying to fight his reaction, but how was a man supposed to resist a bonny lass kissing him? Especially when she felt so good in his arms? Before he pushed her away, he brushed his lips over her forehead, the mere effort making his heart twist. Bless it, the depth of his affection hadn't waned in the slightest. Nonetheless, he stiffened and affected a gruff voice. "If you're planning to impersonate a lad, there'll be no hugging and kissing, ye ken?"

She dropped her hands to her sides and stood at attention. "Aye, sir."

"And you'll climb to the crow's nest and man your watch." *Only when the weather is fine, bless it.*

That lovely, defiant chin ticked up. "I'm nay afraid."

"And you'll do my bidding."

"Haven't I always done that?"

"You have—barring your presence in my cabin." His mind riffled through all the reasons this was a bad idea while he pulled the wooden tub out from under his four-poster bed. "Who on the crew might recognize you—that is after we've fashioned a disguise?"

"Runner for certain. Lachie Mor, of course. Mayhap

Mr. MacNeil—but most everyone else was away in Glasgow. And they were at Achnacarry only a few days. I reckon ye had them all too busy to pay a mind to me— besides, I'll look far different once I don a disguise."

"Very well." Those three he trusted to keep mum— as long as he spoke with them come dawn. He poured the contents of his ewer into the tub, the water barely covering the bottom. "Ye'll have to wash in seawater. 'Tis what the rest of us use."

Her entire face blushed. "Wash?"

He sniffed and made a sour face. "I take it you've been stowing away near the bilges?"

She nodded, toying with the lace on her kirtle. "Ye'll promise to turn your back?"

"Promise." Kennan fetched two of the seawater pails stationed for dousing fires. She still had no idea he'd already seen her bathe—an image that plagued him most nights. Not plagued, exactly, perhaps tortured, befuddled. Nay, Kennan was *never* befuddled.

"And ye'll don a shirt this instant," she demanded— the cheek of her.

"Beg your pardon?" he asked, pouring the water.

"How is a lass supposed to remain thick-skinned when the captain is tending her bath wearing nothing save a plaid tucked about his hips?"

His damned loins stirred. Fie, they more than stirred. There was a bloody tent growing at the front of the wool. Quickly, he pulled a shirt over his head, thankful it was long enough to cover his hips. "You've seen my chest before."

"Aye." She twirled a lock of hair around her finger. The sooner he chopped off those distracting tresses, the less alluring she'd be.

And he'd just agreed to turn her into a cabin boy and pretend she was a lad? For how long?

Lord save me.

* * *

If Divana had known being caught in the galley would result in earning her a pallet in the captain's cabin, she might have actually tried to be caught by the quartermaster a few days earlier. Though, if she were caught too soon, Kennan would have taken her home for certain.

She swirled the bar of pine-scented soap on a wet cloth while she looked over her shoulder. The braw captain sat at his writing table with his back to her, his quill making loops and flickering like a warbler's tail. The light from the lamp danced, making him appear larger and his hair more golden, more surreal. Yet he was asleep when Lachie Mor had knocked.

"I apologize for waking ye. I'll wager ye're awfully tired."

"Not to worry," he said, slightly raising his head. "I'm awakened often when at sea. A captain's work is never done."

She scrubbed her face and hair—it seemed so short now that he'd cut it to her shoulders. Every time she ran her fingers through it, her tresses dropped while her hand kept going. 'Twas as if she'd lost a limb. "I'll be finished directly."

His quill stilled for a moment. "Take your time."

"What are ye writing?"

"I'm recording the day's events in the ship's journal."

"Do ye not do that afore ye retire?"

"I do, but since rousing I've recalled another entry which needed to be made."

Was he writing about her? If only Divana could read, she'd know. "I wish I kent my letters."

This time his chin turned in line with his shoulder—not quite looking, curse it all. "Would you like to learn?"

"Och, I'd give all me pay from Achnacarry to be able to read and write."

"Very well. I'll teach you."

As soon as her fingers touched the bar, the slippery soap shot beneath her knees. "Ye will? Truly?"

"We'll be on this ship a long time. I'd guess you'll be able to read anything of your choosing by the time we return."

"And ye're nay too busy for the likes of me?" she asked, finally gripping the soap.

"Do not misunderstand, daily routines aboard ship are taxing. However, I'd think a lesson before you turn in each night will suffice—neither of us will be too occupied for that. Most days, anyway."

Could things grow better? Not only would she be alone with Kennan every night, he'd be teaching her letters! Divana stretched out a leg and pushed bubbles between her toes.

Kennan rose and stretched, keeping his back turned. Clearly, he was bent on keeping his promise. "I'll set to making up a pallet."

She rinsed her feet. "I can do that."

"Nay, you'd best finish your bath and don the clothes I set out."

"I'm done." After checking to ensure his back was still turned, she stood and reached for the drying cloth. Curses, why had she told him not to look? He hadn't stolen a wee peek the entire time she was in the tub. And why not? She knew he liked her—mayhap he didn't want to marry her, but he'd kissed her before and rather passionately.

Perhaps he was angry. After all, she'd disobeyed him. And now he was stuck having her in his chamber for the duration of the journey.

But Divana had time to win his affections—two whole years if she was lucky. Now that they were together, she was bound to find some way to make him fall in love with her. Then perhaps he mightn't want to marry a high-born gentlewoman. If he truly loved her, he would never abandon her even if he was away captaining a ship now and again.

Right?

She held up the square linen garment Kennan had set out beside the breeches. A tie was sewn at each of four corners. "What am I supposed to do with this square thing?"

"They're drawers."

"Drawers? I haven't seen ye wear these afore."

"They're worn with breeches—cover a man's private parts."

"Over the top or beneath?"

"Are you covered?"

She pulled the drying cloth up high enough to conceal most everything. "Aye."

"Allow me to demonstrate." He took the drawers and tied the two corners around his waist from front to back, then he pulled the length through his legs and tied the other two from back to front. "See? Easy."

"Who wears such things?"

"Any number of men—including myself when I'm

wearing breeches." He held the trousers up. "The falls are buttoned in the front."

"I ken that."

He handed her the drawers and turned his back. "Carry on, then."

With all the ties, Divana managed to keep the breeches on without having them drop to her knees. But then she held up the enormous bandage he intended for her to use to bind her breasts. "How am I supposed to wind this around me?"

Spreading a plaid on his hands and knees, his body grew still. "Do you need help?"

"I suppose I could stretch it out across the floor and roll it up."

"May I turn?"

She didn't dare breathe as she clutched the cloth in front of her, knowing she was barely covered. "Aye."

Kennan's eyes grew dark as they shifted from her face and meandered downward. The muscles in his jaw flexed as he stood and moved toward her. "You'll need to figure out how to do this yourself." His voice had grown gruffer than usual. But he made quick work of wrapping the cloth around her torso four times before he tucked in the edge.

He stood back and gave her a once-over. "God's bloody stones," he growled.

She glanced downward. "What is it?"

He tossed her the shirt. "Put this on."

She did as told while he stood back and crossed his arms, a disapproving slant to his brows. "You still look too bloody female."

She flicked her damp tresses. "With my hair shorn?"

"Your hair has nothing to do with it." He brushed his

hand over the floorboards, then smeared her face. "A bit of dirt will help."

"Och, I just bathed, ye ken."

"Aye, and you smell a great deal better." He opened his trunk and retrieved a man's feathered bonnet. "Wear this low over your brow and try to scowl as much as possible."

She put it on. "What about shoes?"

His gaze dropped to her toes while his tongue tapped his upper lip. "Are you still more comfortable in bare feet?"

She turned one foot inward. "I reckon so."

"Mine are far too large and you cannot skip across the main deck wearing a pair of women's slippers. You'll have to go without until we call into port." He took a step nearer and pinched the front of her shirt. "I'll buy you a pair of square-toes."

A sharp gasp slipped through her lips as he tugged her closer—so close his breath warmed her forehead. Divana dared to look into his eyes. He stood very still, the reflection in those mysterious pools of green ravenous.

"A-are ye hungry?" she whispered.

His lips parted slightly while his gaze fell to her mouth. "Starved."

Aye, she knew exactly what he meant. The hardest part of being so near him was no touching and no kissing. As she rose onto her toes, her body couldn't manage to remember the rules. *Just one wee kiss.* She studied the fullness of his masculine lips while a torrent of energy swirled throughout her body.

Time slowed as his chin dipped. And with her next blink, he swept her into his arms and covered her mouth.

Riding a wave of unbridled longing, Divana grasped

his cheeks as she closed the distance. The day's growth on his face felt like sandpaper beneath her fingers, the masculinity of it serving to heighten her need. His tongue swept into her mouth with bold strokes, every bit as raw and unapologetic as it was seductive.

Her toes curled as she matched his fervor swirl for swirl. Why had she pushed him away at Beltane? Why, when she'd wanted him so desperately?

Divana threw her head back as he trailed tiny kisses along her neck, making her body tingle in places she must never mention. She grew numb as he lifted her into his arms and carried her across the floor and set her on the bed.

As he gazed upon her with glistening eyes, she reached up for another kiss. Grinning, he avoided her mouth and pressed his lips to her forehead. "Sleep well, my angel."

Then with a deep sigh he backed to the pallet and lay down.

"What are ye doing?" She sat up. "That is me bed ye're on. Ye are the captain. Ye're supposed to sleep here."

He pulled a plaid over his shoulders. "There's no chance in hell I'll let a woman sleep on the floor whist I languish on a feather mattress."

"But—"

"Och, lass. You promised to follow orders. Now close your eyes and go to sleep."

Divana saluted the bed-curtains. "Aye, captain!"

"And one more thing," he said, stretching up to his table and turning down the lantern.

"Hmm?"

"Remember you're a lad—and lads do not tempt their captains with wee kisses. Not ever again."

Divana rolled to her side. His form was dark and

shadowy through the blue moonlight shining in from the windows. "What about the other way around?"

"Wheesht!"

Smiling, she dropped to her back and pulled the bed-clothes right under her chin. After nights of sleeping in a cramped barrel with rats scurrying about, curling into the downy comfort of Kennan's mattress was near enough to heavenly. There she was, Divana Campbell, a lass cast out and condemned by her clan, sailing the high seas with Kennan Cameron—the only man she had ever loved.

Now all she had to do was figure out how to convince him to kiss her again...and again...and again.

Chapter Nineteen

A southwester filled the sails with chilly air while Kennan stood on the quarterdeck, gazing down at the rugged faces of his crew. They hailed from all walks of life, some from Cameron crofts—those men he'd trust with his life. Though roughly half the rest was composed of the gruff and bedraggled newcomers from Glasgow.

They stood at attention, their beards full, the craggy squints to their eyes fixed in place by years of sun, sailing, and whisky. Only the passage of time would ferret out the trustworthy on this voyage—though Kennan doubted he'd ever allow the man on the end too near. They called him Ethan. He was shorter than most, thin, and ornery, though during the trials at Achnacarry, he'd proved skilled with a dirk and sword. Perhaps he'd passed Lachie Mor's jaundiced eye with his fighting prowess. Nonetheless, Ethan was one to watch.

On the other end, Divana stood beside Runner, who'd

been assigned to show her the ropes. The lad had been given instructions not to allow "Davy" out of his sight—though Runner, Lachie Mor, and Mr. MacNeil were privy to Divana's true identity and sworn to secrecy. The problem? As far as Kennan was concerned, Davy still looked like the redheaded lass who, on the isle of Hyskeir, had twisted his heart around her little finger. No set of breeches or a feathered cap could hide the lassie's feminine allure.

Damn it all.

If anything happened to her, Kennan would never forgive himself.

And, though this voyage was about revenge and reclaiming that which was rightfully his, he'd do his damnedest to keep her safe—starting with his present address to the crew. "I'm certain many of you have heard we've found a stowaway."

Dissent rumbled from the ranks, whistled back to attention by the boatswain, Mr. MacNeil. On the deck, the quartermaster gave Divana a shove in the shoulder—blast Lachie's manhandling. Kennan noted he'd need to have a word with the man posthaste.

"Though he spirited aboard in a barrel, I ken this lad," Kennan continued. "His name is Davy Campbell, the youngest son of Laird Alexander Campbell of Ardslignish—"

"A bloody Campbell?" griped Ethan, elbowing the sailor beside him.

Kennan gave the man a dead-eyed stare—an expression so fierce, few ever deigned to challenge him. "It is my duty to see to his protection until I'm able to return the lad to his kin. He will fulfill the role of cabin boy and will be taking direction from Runner. But hear me now, and hear me clear, I'll tolerate no mistreatment. The lad may be a stowaway, but he's as close as kin to me. If any man aboard has a grievance with him, you'll bring it to me or your quartermaster first."

"Aye, aye!" boomed Lachie Mor.

"Aye, aye, Captain!" the men shouted in unison.

"Very well." Kennan pulled his spyglass from his belt and slapped it against his palm. "We've made good headway thus far and I commend you all. Keep your minds and hands on task, and we'll anchor off Nassau within the month, God and wind willing. Dismissed!"

Divana flashed a bonny smile and gave him a wave. God's stones, he'd need to school her on masculine behavior. She ought to be adjusting her crotch and scowling at him. But Lachie Mor thumped the top of her cap and ordered Runner to set her to swabbing the decks.

After the two moved on, Kennan motioned for the quartermaster to join him on the upper deck.

"I reckon your chat went well, Captain," said Lachie, his gap-toothed grin disappearing beneath his dappled gray whiskers.

"Mayhap. However, I do not care for your rough treatment of our new cabin boy."

"I beg your pardon?" Lachie checked over his shoulder and moved to the rail. "I ought to be kicking her—er—him up the backside. 'Tis what I'd do with any other young whelp stowaway."

"Aye, but he's nay just anyone. He's the son of a clan chief. I've given you reason enough for leniency."

"Bloody hell, did your time on Hyskeir turn ye soft?"

Kennan leaned in and leveled his gaze with the quartermaster. "I'll bid you remember your place, sir. Mind you, after I plunged into the sea, I fought off a mob of basking sharks with nothing but my hands and a bloody English pirate's dull-bladed dagger. Got a nice ring of teeth branded on my thigh to serve as a constant memory. And the woman on Hyskeir? If it weren't for her, there'd be seagrass sprouting from my corpse about now. So, aye, give the lass—er—lad his due."

Lachie Mor scratched his beard. "Bloody women. They're why I prefer to be a-sea. Wenches are always causing trouble. Especially that one—and I'm not bloody blind. She has eyes for ye, no question in me mind."

"Och aye? The woman's a bloody saint."

"And I'd venture to guess you've a greater soft spot for her than you're letting on. Ye'd best watch yourself, Captain."

Kennan gave the quartermaster a playful jab with his elbow. "Mind your own affairs, ye onion-eyed varlet."

"'Tis exactly what I intend to do—and my affairs concern the orderly running of this ship."

"I'm glad ye ken your priorities." Kennan opened his spyglass and raised it to his eye. "Just have a care. We do not need a weeping cabin boy on our hands."

"God forbid." The old man tottered back down the steps, grumbling under his breath. "I'll burn in hell afore we have a ship full of weepy-eyed, lad-impersonating women."

* * *

"Go on, just a bit higher," said Runner as if they weren't about to fall to their deaths.

Divana clung to the rigging and glanced downward. Mistake. Her stomach squeezed and turned over—more aptly, it did a flying leap. "But 'tis so far to the deck," she squeaked, all attempts at sounding like a lad vanishing. "What if a big wave comes and flings us into the sea?"

"Och, I've been keeping watch in the crow's nest for years and I've never been flung. Asides, there's a rope up there to hold ye in."

Cringing, she slowly shifted her gaze to the offending nest. A barrel sawed in half, it reminded her of a gigantic slingshot—one made for people, especially her. "Are ye certain 'tis necessary to have a lookout up there at all times?"

"Not to worry, Davy," Runner said with a hint of laughter in his voice. "The captain advised you're only allowed up the rigging during calm seas."

What appeared to be miles away, Kennan stood on the quarterdeck, his posture as rigid as a statue, staring at them—at her. *Blast him for watching.* Did he not think her capable of climbing up to the crow's nest? And how was it not preferential treatment to tell Runner not to let her go up there except in calm seas? She steeled her nerves and pulled herself upward.

"Baltazar," she said, trying to make her voice deeper and more confident. "What is it you like about keeping watch up here?"

"You'd best not keep calling me by my Christian name, else someone will guess you're not a lad."

"Well, we cannot abide that." She cleared her throat, trying for an even deeper tone. "Runner, tell me what you like about the blessed crow's nest." There—she practically sounded like a gruff old tar.

He continued his assent. "No one bothers me when I'm keeping watch."

That wasn't exactly the answer she was expecting. "Do the men heckle you?"

"Aye, on account of being the youngest." He hopped over the side of the barrel and offered his hand. "'Tis why they call me Runner. 'Hey, lad, fetch me a scrap of bread...clean the bilges...empty the pails of p—.' Ye ken, they saved all the foul jobs for me whilst the crew laughed."

After a backward glance to the captain, Divana ignored the offered hand and pulled herself into the nest, queasy stomach and all. "That doesn't sound fair."

"Life aboard ship isn't always fair."

As she looked out, the wits she'd used to pull herself up collapsed into a heap. Saint Columba, she was higher up than she'd ever been in her life—mayhap the wall-walk at Achnacarry was higher, but it wasn't swaying. She grasped the dangling rope and stared at the round wooden floor beneath her toes. It didn't seem sturdy in the slightest.

"W-why did you put up with it?" she managed to croak, trying to continue the conversation.

"There wasn't much I could do—the lowest ranked man is given the most unsavory tasks." He thumped his chest. "But I aim to fix that."

Aside from quavering and jolting with every gust of wind, the space was cramped with two people in the nest, not allowing much room for limbs. Divana wrapped her arms around her knees, letting her shoulder press into the lad. "On account of being promoted?"

"That, and the captain rewards his men for service. If we recapture our fortune, every man will receive his share."

"Coin, aye?"

"Enough to purchase a parcel of land—mayhap a pony or two and a suit of clothes."

"'Tis generous of Sir Kennan."

"Och, he's the *captain* when aboard, ye ken."

She dared to peek over the rim. The aforementioned captain was engaged in conversation with Mr. MacNeil, who was pointing to the sails billowing aft.

"Do you ken the names of all these sails?"

"I do."

For the first time since she climbed up the rigging, Divana dared to look beyond the decks. "Oh my, the sea is so vast—and I cannot see another vessel anywhere."

"Once we enter the trade routes, you see them often enough." Runner stood, grabbed a rope, and leaned so far out the nest, if it snapped, he'd fall to his death.

"Careful!"

"I can swing down to the decks from here if I want." Laughing, he hoisted himself out of the nest and swung around the mast. "All ye need to ken when you're working as a spotter is when ye see a ship, there are three very important things to look for—the type and size of the vessel—so we can gauge how many guns she's carrying. How low she is in the water—so we ken if her hull's laden with cargo. And what sort of flag she's flying. Black flags are the worst, especially if they have a skull and bones."

She shuddered. "Pirates."

"Aye."

She checked the pennant flapping at the top of the center mast. "Kennan flies the Saint Andrew's cross."

"He does."

"Och, I kent it. The captain would never fly a black flag."

"Not in these waters."

"What do you mean?"

"The black skull and bones is meant to strike fear in the hearts of sailors when ye aim to take their ship."

"But Kennan would never take anyone's ship..."

"*Captain*, mind you. And not unless they're his enemy."

"Like Jackson Vane?"

"You'd best believe it—*Davy*." Runner winked. "Are ye accustomed to your new name as of yet?"

She shrugged. "I suppose 'tis not too unlike Divana."

"Just repeat it over and over 'cause I reckon it'll be a year or two afore anyone uses your real name again—unless..."

"Unless."

He twisted his mouth and looked toward the quarterdeck. "Unless someone discovers you're really a lass."

Chapter Twenty

*K*ennan leaned back in his velvet-upholstered dining chair while Divana sat at the table practicing her letters.

It had been a fortnight since she'd first been brought to his cabin, a fortnight of torture. Torture because at night when they were locked in his cabin, he'd lean over her to teach her something new or to listen to her beguiling voice as she sounded out a word. Every time he was within arm's reach, she captivated him.

Nights were the worst, having a woman's scent fill the cabin, calling to him. Yet he'd vowed to protect the lass, not ravish her.

Days weren't much better. Every time she climbed to the crow's nest, his miserable heart stuck in his throat. And it put him on edge while she was up there—he groused at anyone who stood in his way. Damn, he kept one eye on the lass at all times. She wasn't as sure with the rigging as Runner—one slip and she'd be injured, mayhap killed. And when she was working on deck, it was an utter distraction with the way her breeches hugged her hips. Worse, Kennan was ready to lash out with the cat-o'-nine-tails whenever anyone gave her lip—though she could give it right back, bless her.

He watched Divana's quill move as she bit the corner of her mouth, trying to make every stroke perfect—perfect like the crescent of her petite nose, the splay of red eyelashes half-cast as she studied, the slender arc of her waist.

He rubbed the ache in his damned loins. Was he to be hard throughout the entire voyage?

Divana glanced up and smiled, turning the parchment his way. "What do ye think?"

She should have been a scholar. Her handwriting was artful with hardly any blotches—which wasn't easy on a sailing ship. He gave a nod of approval. "I'll give you top levels for this."

She retrieved the paper, a bit of color springing to her cheeks. "Ye're nay just saying that to make me feel better?"

"'Tisn't in my nature to give credit when it isn't due—especially top levels."

Her blush grew redder as she gazed at him out of the corner of her eye. He'd received such a look before, and not only from her. It was a feminine shift of the eye, informing him of the desire lurking deep within—whether she knew it or not. "Does that mean I've earned a favor?"

Kennan adjusted his seat, trying to push away his errant thoughts—like pulling off her shirt and slowly unwinding the bindings covering her breasts. Like unbuttoning her falls and ripping her breeches from those sumptuous hips.

"Ah...perhaps," he mumbled. "What sort of favor?"

She pushed back her chair, her gaze focused on him. And when she sauntered near, her hips swayed with every lingering step.

Kennan's breath caught as she placed her hand on his shoulder.

"Ye ken Fiona and Garry are engaged to be wed?" she whispered in his ear, her voice as sultry as the air of the southern sea.

"I'd heard."

"I saw them."

When Kennan tried to swallow, his Adam's apple stuck in his throat, swelling to the size of a shinty ball. The tingling beneath her fingertips, her warm breath on his neck, meant one thing, and he didn't know if he could resist. His gaze met hers, and those vibrant blues confirmed it. Passion thrummed through her blood, driving her mad just as it did to him.

Divana's gaze slid to his lap. "They were rutting."

The corner of his mouth ticked up, along with another part of his body—the place where she was staring. "Rutting?"

A pink tongue slipped over her lip as she nodded, placing her hands on the table. "Fiona's skirts were hiked up all the way to her..."

"Hips?"

Divana arched her back and spread her legs. "And Garry was behind."

Good God, the lout had taken his intended like a dog?

"Would you?" Her gaze slipped to the bulge beneath his kilt. "Want to?"

If Kennan thought he was hard, he'd been fooling himself. His cock lengthened to the point of excruciating pain. God's stones, he'd win a battle fighting with his rod as stiff as iron. "Do you ken what you're saying, lass?" he asked, his voice low and strained.

She blushed, her eyes so filled with want, they were practically black. "I ken I haven't been able to think of much else but rutting with ye."

He gulped, blinking to clear the stars in his vision, hoping to bring some bloody sense to his addled mind. "To begin with, 'tisn't rutting—at least not with me it won't be. And secondly, you're supposed to be saving yourself for your husband. You're a-a *nice* lass." He'd nearly said *well-bred*, but she'd argue such a claim in a heartbeat.

"Fiona is a nice lass."

"But she's engaged to be married."

"She wasn't when I saw them." Divana straightened, fingering the buttons on her falls and staring at the floor. "Do you not want me?"

Kennan dug in his heels and shoved his chair back, tugging her between his legs. "'Tis not a question of want, 'tis a question of honor."

"And if I ru—ah—do *that* with ye, I will lose me honor?"

"Nay, I will lose mine. I promised to watch out for you, not ravish you."

"I'm tired of saving meself for another when all I want is ye."

Her shoulders fell along with her frown. Hell, even a tear spilled from her eye.

Unable to help himself, he wrapped her in his arms and tilted that lovely face to his. "God, I want you, Divana."

Their lips fused as her sigh vibrated through him— all the way down to his cock. He was powerless to push her away, not when she felt so good in his arms. Not when she wanted him as much as he craved her. Kennan plunged his tongue into her mouth and took his plunder. He'd kissed her before, but never had he tasted her wildness, experienced her urgency and unbridled passion.

Discarding all the barriers and reasons he'd constructed to prevent himself from taking her, he collected the woman in his embrace and took her to the bed. Within a few ticks of the wall clock he'd removed her garments, unwrapped her bindings, and had her bare, staring at the creamiest skin he'd ever seen.

Fully clothed, he kneeled between her legs and smoothed his hands from her shoulders to her breasts, swirling his thumbs around her hardened nipples. Downward he went, drinking her in. "You are so bloody beautiful."

"Ye reckon so?" she asked, panting erotically.

"You have no idea how alluring you are. How long has it been since we met? That's how long I've resisted you."

"Near three months," she said, reaching for his hands. "But I've longed for you more, I ken it."

"Hush."

"I want to see ye bare as well."

He rocked back on his haunches and chuckled, whipping the shirt over his head. "It takes but a few flicks of the fingers to disrobe a Highlander," he said, unfastening his belt and letting his plaid fall around his knees.

"Saint Columba," she said as if his member astounded her.

And her reaction made him harder.

She rolled over and pushed up to her hands and knees. "Is this right?"

Och aye, what a glorious bottom presented to him—legs wide—the slick wetness of her core open to him. All he needed to do was slip inside, grab those shapely hips, and thrust. God, how he wanted to tup her now. "Nay," he managed in a strangled whisper, coaxing her hips back to the mattress. "I'd never ask you to lower yourself that way."

She turned, crossing her arms over her breasts, concern and, perhaps, shame reflected in her eyes. "But how?"

Careful not to crush her, he stretched over her and nuzzled into her neck. "I'll show you, lass, if it is truly what you want." He had to ask once more before he completely lost control.

"Aye. 'Tis all I want. I stowed away because I want to be with ye."

"Do ye ken a child can be conceived?"

She nodded. "Even if you spill outside? That's what Garry did."

Good Lord, she'd seen it all. "Withdrawing helps, but there are no sure remedies. I want you to ken this afore we..."

"I still want ye to..."

"And the first time there's pain."

"I am not afraid."

"After watching you climb the rigging I didn't think you would be," he growled against her ear. "Now let me take you to heaven."

He trailed kisses from her throat down to her breast and fondled her nipple with his tongue. Though small, her breasts fit perfectly in the cups of his palms. And he plied them as she writhed beneath him.

"I cannot explain the need coiling tighter and tighter inside me. I feel as though I want to merge my body with yours and feel all of you. Especially. Ah!" she gasped as he moved his hand down to her nest of red curls and slid his finger into her parting.

"Spread your knees for me, lass."

Sighing, Divana closed her eyes and opened like an orchid displaying her sacred beauty. He worked slick moisture around her tiny button, watching her face transform from tense to enchanted bliss. Only when she was breathless and rocking her hips did he slip his finger inside.

She opened her eyes and pushed up. "Kennan!"

"Lie back and close your eyes and dream of me entering you."

"A-are ye certain I'll not explode like a cannon?"

"Nay—but I promise the explosion will be worth it."

He stretched her with two fingers, then three. And finally he thrust with his fingers while lapping the swollen pebble that would send her over the edge.

Divana shook her head from side to side, her hips churning with the rhythm of his fingers until all at once a gasp caught in her throat and she shattered, into dozens of tiny pulses.

* * *

If Kennan told Divana she had died and gone to heaven, she would have believed him. She ought to be embarrassed to her core, lying atop the bed without a stitch covering her. But nay. She felt like a queen, prostrate to her king and ready to give him anything he asked.

As he drew back, his member tapped his belly.

She might not know much about rutting, but he'd left

something very important unfinished. "What about your pleasure?"

He ran his fingers up her thighs. "Och, we're nay finished. Not by half."

She started to turn and present her buttocks to him. "Of course."

"Stay."

"On me back?"

"Aye, 'tis where I want you."

"But—"

"You're not swivving with Garry, you're making...ah...*love* to me."

"Making love?"

His Adam's apple bobbed as he glanced aside. "Aye, that's what they call it when two people like each other."

"I see."

He shifted to her side and kissed her as his fingers began a magical dance, swirling around her breasts. "And afore we go any further, I aim to make you writhe with rapture."

"Again?"

"Sh."

But this time as his hands explored her, Divana did some exploring of her own. She delighted in the sleek softness of his skin contrasting with the curls on his chest, and when he took her breast in his mouth, she teased his teat with thumb and forefinger. By his rumbling moan, he liked it.

"Squeeze," he said before his tongue swirled around her tender flesh.

Divana reveled in the delight of his moan as she teased him. Next she trailed her fingers down his body and smoothed them over his triangle of tawny hair, just as he was doing to her. Oh, goodness, he was right. It was so much more invigorating to feel him—to watch the pleasure on his face. When he slid his finger lower—to the place where she didn't even dare to touch—she bit her lip and stared at his member while her breath grew ragged.

"Go on," he said, his voice deep and raspy.

With one finger she touched him, then gasped. "'Tis rock hard, but soft as velvet."

He took her hand and wrapped her fingers around his shaft. "Grip it firm but do not squeeze, then slide up and down from root to tip."

"'Tis moist at the top."

He nuzzled her neck and slipped a finger inside her. "Because I want to be here."

Twice she'd tried to present her bum to him, and twice he'd indicated it was an indelicate position. What did he want? "Show me."

Chuckling, he moved between her thighs. "I thought you'd never ask."

Hadn't she been asking all along?

"The question is," he continued, rubbing his member along her slick channel, "how much do you want this?"

She dug her fingers into his buttocks, arching up to him, needing more friction. "Ye ken how much I want ye...inside me." Had those naughty words actually escaped her lips? Yes, she wanted him with every fiber of her body. She wanted him more than she'd ever wanted anything in her life, and by the way he was rubbing up and down, he'd soon be sending her over the edge just as he'd done with his tongue. "Please."

Suddenly, he entered her—but it wasn't like his fingers. He more than filled her as she stretched to receive him. "See?" She panted. "'Tisn't all that bad."

"But there's a lot more to go."

"More?" she squeaked.

"Are you ready?"

She gripped him, arching her back. "I am."

And then he broke through. Hot pain seared inside her as she hissed and clenched her teeth.

He held very still, his features stretched. "Does it hurt overmuch?"

She moved her hips. "'Tis a good kind of pain."

"I'll try to go slow."

He did at first, but even though there was pain, the need pulsing through her blood demanded a faster tempo. She writhed beneath him, gasping as she clung to his backside. His breathing sped with the cadence of his thrusts.

"Come for me, Divana!"

As she clung to him, the glorious wave of passion took her to the stars for the second time that night. And with it came Kennan's bellow. He withdrew and spilled onto her belly. Perspiration peppered his brow while he continued to pant, hovering above her.

She gazed into those delicious green eyes. "That was astonishing."

"You are astonishing." He nuzzled into her neck. "I've known it all along. I just have been afraid of hurting you."

"Because ye must..."

He tapped her lips with his finger. "We are bonded now, you and I. Nothing else matters."

Oh, how his words warmed her.

"How are you feeling? Are you sore?"

"A little. 'Tis nay bad, though."

"I'm glad of it." Grinning, he rolled to his side and cleaned her stomach with his shirt. "You must remember, lass. When the cabin door is unlocked, you are still Davy and I'm the captain. Nothing has changed as far as the crew is concerned. Ye ken?"

Rather than respond, she kissed him. A great deal had changed. But Divana understood what he meant.

Chapter Twenty-One

*D*ivana stood in front of the mirror bolted to the wall above Kennan's ornately carved trunk and tied her hair back with a leather thong, then donned her feathered cap. "Are ye looking forward to our arrival in Nassau?" By their heading, they were expected to reach the Bahamian island today if not on the morrow.

"Indeed. I've waited a long time for this."

He moved behind her and trailed feathery kisses along her neck. Would the floating ever cease? She hoped not.

"Do ye reckon Captain Vane will be there?"

Kennan opened the trunk and retrieved his weapons. "'Tis a possibility."

"What if he's not?"

"Then we'll resupply and move on." He shoved his dirk into his belt. "Come, 'tis time for my morning inspection."

"And I'll be in the crow's nest today."

"Would you like me to assign someone else? This close to Nassau, there's a chance we'll meet with trouble."

"Would that not be preferential treatment?"

Kennan's gaze meandered down her body. "Are you growing accustomed to the height?"

"I've learned how to tie meself in. Me arms are stronger as well."

"I could assign you to the galley."

She shifted her fists to her hips and gave a saucy snort. "Why didn't ye do that in the first place?"

"Galley work is usually reserved for the older sailors, or those with injuries who cannot stand up to the rigors of manning the decks."

"So galley work is preferential treatment as well?"

"If I give the order, no one will balk."

"At least not when ye're nearby." She twirled to the door. "No sense changing things now. Besides, with Nassau so near, I might actually see something interesting when I'm on watch."

On the way out, Kennan patted her backside. "You're too bonny to impersonate a lad."

Divana giggled, then clapped a hand over her mouth, praying no one heard. "Sto-op."

As they stepped onto the deck, Ethan glared over from his post, manning the crank to the bilge pump. "Mornin', Captain," he said, though he was scowling at Divana like he always did.

Kennan looked to the cloudless skies as he assumed his role, gripping the lapels of his doublet, not giving Divana a second glance. He started up the steps to the quarterdeck. "'Tis a fine morning, indeed."

"Davy," barked Lachie Mor. "Coil these ropes afore you climb the rigging."

Divana snapped to attention. "Aye, aye, sir."

She always tried to ignore Kennan while she worked, but after last night, she felt as if someone had released a vat of bubbles inside her. She'd slept the entire night in the Highlander's arms. If only she could dance across the deck and sing! Shout to the skies that she was utterly, inexplicably in love.

Stealing a wee peek, she found the braw captain had moved to the helm. He was watching her, too, and gave her a nod. Was he thinking about her as well? Thinking about...Saint Columba's bones, how was she to endure the entire day until they were alone again?

"Ye are awful friendly with the captain," said a reedy voice from behind, making prickles nettle Divana's back.

She didn't need to turn to know it was Ethan. If anyone had something awful to say, it always seemed to be him. She gave a sharp nod. "He has been kind, taking me under his wing."

"Och, lassie, ye're no' fooling me."

Her hands froze on the rope as heat flushed through her blood. *Lassie?* "What are ye on about now?" she barked in her deepest voice. "Have ye gone daft?"

"I ken who ye are. Figured it out when ye were making eyes at the captain." He leaned down, the stench of sour breath wafting into her face. "Do no' deny it, else I'll make a ruckus, but I remember, I do. Ye're the kitchen maid from Achnacarry."

She wound the rope with vigor. "Ye're mad."

Ethan gripped her shoulder like a vise. "I saw ye churnin' butter when I went to fetch stores—and ye were talkin' to Runner."

Divana's mind raced. Pursing her lips, she pushed the varlet aside. "Leave me be."

"Tell ye what." Ethan waggled his brows, shifting his gaze to her breasts. "You give me what I need and I'll keep your secret."

She set to coiling as fast as possible, refusing to respond. This was exactly why Kennan wanted her to impersonate a lad. Disgusting brigands like Ethan were whoremongers of the worst sort.

He licked his lips. "Worry not, lass. Though I'd be the first in line to sample your wares, I'd be the last to invite the captain's ire. All I want is your share of the spoils."

"What makes you think there will be any plunder?" Runner had mentioned there might be, but there were no assurances, were there?

"Och, now I ken you're a bloody female. Ye may have your sights on Lochiel's son, but the rest of us are here for just rewards."

"Even though there may be none?"

"If the captain doesn't want a mutiny, there will be."

She moved slower, pretending to ensure the rope was tidy. "Are ye saying the men are planning to turn against Sir Kennan?"

"I'm bloody saying they will if they think he's lied to them about the likes of ye. If they catch wind of his deceit, they'll reckon he's lied about other things as well." He grabbed her by the wrist and twisted. "And I'll stir up the crew something fierce if ye spout a word of this to a goddamned soul. Moreover, I'll make your life so miserable ye'll wish ye had never been born."

"Remove your hand from Davy's wrist," growled Lachie Mor, moving to the rail with a dirk in his fist. "Now, I say."

Immediately snapping to attention, Ethan released his grip. "Just having a wee chat, sir."

"You can talk all you want when you're not on bloody duty. Now off with you."

Before he sauntered away, Ethan gave her a pointed look. "I'm watching."

After he'd gone, Divana secured the end of the rope into the coil and hefted it over a belaying pin. "Thank ye, sir."

The quartermaster frowned, his bushy eyebrows drawing together. "You never should have stowed away. The sea is no place for a woman."

She paced in a circle while she watched Lachie Mor head aft. Blast it all, if it was payment the varlet wanted, then so be it. Divana didn't give a fig about riches. She'd been poor all her life. She'd scraped and clawed for her daily food. The dearest thing to her heart? The wee carving Kennan had made on Hyskeir. She didn't need a purse of silver, and a cask of rum would do her no good whatsoever.

Runner signaled to her from the crow's nest and, for the first time since she began this voyage, she was overjoyed to climb the rigging. The pox to Ethan and his threats. She might let him steal from her, but she'd *never* allow him to cross Kennan!

"What took ye so long?" asked Runner, giving her a hand to scramble over the side of the nest.

"I had to coil the ropes first." She brushed herself off. "May I ask ye a question?"

"Make it fast 'cause I have something to show ye."

"Are the men content?"

The lad gave a lopsided grin. "They'll be a whole lot more bloody content after a few nights ashore."

Feigning an affronted gasp, she shoved him in the shoulder. "'Twas not what I meant—are they receiving a fair wage?"

"Aye. Anyone aboard who might be unhappy is addled

in the mind." Runner grasped her arm and pointed. "Now look yonder. I waited until ye climbed up so ye'd be the one to holler down to the quarterdeck."

Divana shaded her eyes, squinting until she saw the faintest outline of something dark on the horizon. "Saint Columba! Is that what I think it is?"

"'Tis land, or my name isn't Baltazar MacGee." Runner slung an arm around her shoulders. "Ye'd best alert them now, Davy."

If she weren't so high off the deck, she might take his hand and dance a jig. Instead, she cupped her hands over her mouth, careful to keep her voice deep. "Land ho!"

* * *

Lachie Mor stepped into Kennan's cabin. "The skiff is ready, Captain."

The ship was always peaceful when at anchor, and more so today, protected in the harbor between Nassau and Hog Island. Seated at his writing desk, Kennan replaced the quill in its holder and wiped the sweat from his brow. "My thanks. I'll be there directly."

At the table, Divana closed the book detailing the types of sailing ships. She'd already learned her letters and taken to reading like a fish to water. Her smile was fresh as spring, and it appeared the sweltering air affected her little. She hopped to her feet. "I'm ready as well."

"I think 'tis best if you remained aboard ship."

"Stay here? Whilst ye walk on dry land? But I'm not on watch. I-I've been looking forward to going ashore ever so much." She clasped her hands over her heart. "Please, ye cannot expect me to remain behind. I've never been anywhere away from the Highlands."

Kennan put his tricorne on his head. He hadn't mentioned his misgivings to the lass because she'd be disappointed. "I'm sorry but—"

"Ye cannot make me miss Nassau. Not when Runner has told me so many stories about the place."

Kennan imagined the tall tales the lad had spun. "The isle is not but a den of thieves since the governor's office was sacked ten years past." Groaning, he looked to the lantern, gently swaying from its hook in the ceiling. What if she were hurt? He'd never forgive himself. "Besides, I'm nay stepping ashore for pleasure. I'll not be stopping at the markets or bartering for cloth. I'm seeking information and that is all."

She stepped in front of the bloody door and spread her arms as if she could stop him from leaving. "Very well, but I see no reason why I cannot tag along. I promise ye'll hardly ken I'm about. Besides, ye might need an errand boy."

"Not on Nassau. There's no chance I'll let you out of my sight amongst those slippery snakes—I wouldn't trust a one of them."

"Did ye say out of your sight?" She beamed—a glorious smile that made the freckles across her nose stretch and her eyes sparkle like a shallow sea. "So ye'll let me go with ye?"

Kennan eyed her, a low growl rumbling in his throat. How was a man to resist such a face, especially when those eyes continually bewitched him?

"Have I ever given ye cause to doubt my loyalty?"

"Nay." He tugged down the sleeves of his coat, kicking himself for being so bloody soft. "Come along, then, we haven't much time."

It wasn't long before his men pulled the skiff onto the

beach and Kennan hopped out with Divana and Lachie Mor. It nearly killed him not to carry her through the ankle-deep water, but bare feet and all she leaped over the side of the boat and waded to the shore with the others. Clearly, she'd taken Runner's lessons to heart. In truth, having the cabin boy with him might make people less suspicious.

"I'll head for the taverns," said Lachie Mor. "See what I can uncover there."

Kennan straightened his sword belt. "And I'll hunt down an honest merchant in this den of thieves."

The quartermaster snorted. "I wouldn't count on it."

"Perhaps, but I ken someone who isn't overly fond of Jackson Vane."

"I wish ye luck, then," said Lachie Mor as he headed for the din of the town.

Kennan placed his hand on Divana's shoulder and tilted his lips toward her ear. "Stay near."

"Who are we going to see?"

"There's a woman I can trust."

"A woman?" Not one for hiding her emotions, Divana crossed her arms and scrunched her nose. "I thought ye said not to trust anyone here."

He headed up the beach toward the market. To be honest, Kennan had his reservations about visiting Helen Evans for a host of reasons. "Let's just say she hates Jackson Vane as much as I."

As they strode along the main street, he saw the place hadn't changed much since he was last there. Ramshackle wooden shops stood side by side, with the odd two-story brothel, whores adorning their balconies. Sweaty, tanned men strutted in groups—uniformed in black leather vests, and knee breeches of all sorts. They scowled, the skin around their eyes etched from years of squinting in the blistering sun. Every varlet walked with his shoulders back, resting his hand on the hilt of a cutlass or the handle of a flintlock pistol.

A woman held up a coconut as they passed her stall. "God's nectar, this is. Only cost ye two pennies."

Kennan ignored her while Divana tapped his elbow. "What are those?"

"Coconuts."

"Have ye tried them?"

"Aye."

"I sure am thirsty."

He shot her a look. "Wheesht. Remember what I said."

As they passed stalls with silks, sizzling sticks of pork, and necklaces made from shells, the lass whimpered. But she didn't speak until a whore called down from a second-story window. "Two shags for the price of one, gov'ner."

"What's this? Fresh meat?" said another with a howling laugh.

"Are those jezebels?" Divana asked.

"Pay them no mind," he grumbled under his breath, wagering every last one of them carried the pox.

"Saint Columba," she whispered, hastening her step. "We're certainly nay in Scotland anymore, are we?"

"Are you sorry you came?"

"Och, nay—'tis fascinating."

After they'd passed through the market, the houses became a tad more respectable looking. But most showed signs of disrepair, even after the year or so since he'd last walked these dirt roads, made white by the sand. He spotted Helen Evans's house up the hill, not far from the governor's mansion at the top, which stood in ruins with black soot around its hollow windows.

Kennan's gut turned over. He didn't relish a meeting with Helen. They hadn't parted on good terms after their affair had gone on for too long. He never should have bedded the woman. He'd been heading for Scotland a wealthy man—and she didn't care to have him leave—or for the fact that he'd earned his fortune. She'd wanted him to join her fleet—become another notch in her bedpost. Fifteen years his senior, the woman preferred men who needed her money, and she expected her lovers to make their home ports in Nassau. Over time Kennan had discovered her affinity for well-bred younger men—and they were in short supply on this godforsaken island.

As Kennan and Divana ascended the wooden steps to the portico, the door opened and they were met with an enormous grin from Helen's butler. "Hi-hi, boss." He wore a red coat with gold trim, topped by a crisp linen neckcloth.

"Msizi!" Kennan shook the old African warrior's weathered hand. "I ought to have known you'd still be here."

"No'tin' would take me away from missus."

"Good man." He gestured to Divana. "This is my cabin boy, Davy."

Msizi's reddened eyes shifted to the lass. "A lad ye say?" He chuckled. "Anyone who look like dat aren't no lad."

Leave it to Msizi to take one look and uncover the truth. The man was the only real seer Kennan had ever known. Changing the subject, he patted the butler's shoulder and gestured inside. "Is Mistress Evans in?"

"Ya, ya. I reckon she'll be keen to hear the sip sip from England."

"But I'm Scottish."

"Ya, ya, boss." He gestured to a settee in the modest entrance hall. Helen ran her trading company from her parlor, and trade partners never saw more of the house than that.

Kennan followed Divana to the seat. "I want you to wait here whilst I have a word with Mistress Evans."

"She's married?"

"Widowed."

Divana crossed her arms and her legs, her bare foot swinging to an unheard tempo of a snare. "Are ye certain ye will not need to keep a watchful eye on me whilst ye're chatting with the widow?"

"You'll be safe here, but if you venture outside, I'll have Lachie Mor take the cat-o'-nine-tails to your backside."

She gaped, her lips forming a lovely O. "Ye wouldn't."

"Don't tempt me."

"The missus will see ye now," said Msizi as he stepped into the entry.

Kennan arched his eyebrow at Divana before he stood.

"Do not ye worry, Captain," she said, her voice deep enough for an adolescent lad, while somewhere at the rear of the house a door closed. "I'll be waiting right here."

He gave a curt bow of his head. "I'll see you anon."

In the parlor, Helen sat in her wing-backed chair and raised her hand as Kennan entered. "Will wonders never cease? I thought I'd see snow in Nassau before you set foot in my house again."

He grasped her fingers and applied a well-practiced kiss to the back of her hand, her skin chilly. Not a stunning beauty, the woman regarded him with icy blue eyes—a gaze holding a world of secrets—wicked things that should be locked away for eternity.

"I was just about to enjoy a glass of sherry." She removed the stopper of a crystal decanter. "Do join me."

"Sherry would be lovely, thank you."

Helen smirked. "There's no need to be formal, Kennan. And do have a seat, you're making my neck sore."

He obliged. "You've never been one to stand on ceremony."

After she poured, she handed him a dainty glass. "If I were, I never would have left England."

"Cheers."

"Hmm." The widow watched him over the top of her glass while she sipped. "Msizi tells me you have a cabin boy tagging along with you."

Kennan cringed. "Brought him along for errands." What else had the butler said? But that's not why he was there. And who gave a rat's arse if Helen knew Divana wasn't really Davy?

"So, tell me. Why are you here…with your cabin boy?" Helen licked her lips and arched her brows. "Not for a rendezvous I'll venture."

He set his glass on the table beside him. "I'm looking for Jackson Vane."

"The bane of the high seas, that man." Her eyes grew distant as she sipped again. At one time she'd been on friendlier terms with Vane. Until the pirate betrayed her—joined together with Anne Bonny and had stolen an entire cargo of silk and tea from one of the lady's merchant ships. The theft had nearly ruined Helen. Nearly. But the widow sitting before him was as shrewd as they came. "Jackson Vane would murder his own mother and hang her naked body from the old fort if it led to treasure."

"I reckon you're not wrong there." Kennan eyed her, not wanting to reveal any more of his hand than necessary. "I've a bone to pick with him as well."

She gasped, her face genuinely shocked—though Kennan had seen her in action before. "Do not tell me Vane got his hands on your silver."

Shite—she knew—she'd most likely heard about the *Highland Reel* as well. "The bastard stole from me, and I'll not sit idle whilst he gloats."

"I see. So that's why you're here with your *cabin boy*, sipping my sherry."

"I'll nay deny it." He picked up his glass and drank the rest of the sweet wine. "Now tell me, where is Vane hiding these days?"

The woman harrumphed. "It is not likely any of the miscreants about town would divulge such a thing to me."

"You have your sources. Do not deny it."

"But it would be so much more fun if we slipped up the rear steps and started where we left off."

"Your offer is tempting, madam, but I aim to set sail as soon as my purser has acquired supplies." Hat in hand, he scooted to the edge of his chair. "Please, Helen. If you harbor any fondness for me at all."

"Oh, very well, but I cannot guarantee the accuracy of my information. 'Tis months old."

"Go on."

"Word is he and his band of pirates have found an oasis somewhere south of here."

"How far south?"

"No one knows." She stood and moved to the globe sitting on a table in front of a lace-clad window. Turning it, she pointed. "Here's Nassau, and if you trace a line south, you run into Cuba, and then Jamaica."

Kennan studied the line she'd drawn. The area had little in the way of islands—nothing but the larger ones. And he'd spent enough time sailing through the Antilles isles to know there were literally hundreds, many of them away from the trade routes. He tapped the empty sea to the southeast. "What about the cays?"

Something in her eyes flashed, but then she turned and leaned against the table. "Your guess is as good as mine."

"But you have a fleet of merchant ships sailing these waters. What have your captains reported?"

"I've told you what I know. He's south of Nassau, and I thank God he hasn't plundered one of my ships of late."

Kennan bowed. "I thank you, madam. You have been of great service."

"At one time that meant so much more." She held out her hand and let him kiss it. "Next time, do not bring the boy."

* * *

Divana spotted a Bible on a table across from the settee, wandered over to it, and smoothed her hand over the soft leather. She opened the cover and turned the pages until she found one with three large words. "The Old... Te-st-a-me-nt," she sounded out the letters as Kennan had taught her.

"The Old Testament," said a man with an unusual accent.

Divana instantly dropped her hands to her sides and skittered away from the table. "I-I was just having a wee peek."

"Ah, *ma chérie*, There's nothing wrong with reading the word of God."

"Are ye a holy man?"

"I cannot say that I am." He was heavyset and sweat beaded along his thinning hairline, but he had a friendly smile, though he was missing a tooth right smack in the front. "What is it that brings you to Nassau?"

"I-I'm a cabin boy and my ship arrived this morn."

"Is that so?"

"Aye."

"And if I were to venture to guess, you hail from Scotland, do you not?"

"I do. The Highlands." She pressed her fingers to her lips. Surely it wasn't wrong to admit she was Scottish.

"Only two ships dropped anchor today. You must have been aboard the *Lady Heather*."

Divana didn't respond.

"You've a Scottish captain, no?"

How could she phrase it without reciting Kennan's name and everything she knew about the *Lady Heather*, including the fact that the ship was purchased from the Baronet of Sleat? "What with a Scottish cabin boy and a ship named *Heather*, I reckon that might be a good guess."

"What business have you in Nassau?"

"I'm attending the captain."

"I see. He has dealings with Mistress Evans?"

Divana glanced away.

The Frenchman closed the Bible and tapped it. "I can only imagine."

Needing him to stop asking questions, Divana's mind raced. "Ah...the captain never tells me anything about his affairs. I just take orders and do his bidding."

"*Oui.* I'm sure you do."

Perhaps she ought to turn the tables and ask the questions. "Where do ye hail from, sir?"

"Have you never heard a French accent?"

"I haven't heard many accents aside from English— and not all that often." No, no, no, she wasn't about to carry on about Sergeant Corbyn and how he'd rescued them from Hyskeir, only to lock them in the room at the mill, after which he badgered Kennan until he shot him and ended up court-martialed at Fort William.

The man bowed, then set his tricorne on his head. "Well, young sir, it has been a pleasure."

Blast it all, Divana almost curtsied before she managed a clumsy bow. "Good day, sir."

It wasn't but a blink of an eye after the man slipped out the door before Kennan came into the entry. "Who was that?"

"He didn't say his name—just asked what ship I was with."

"Did you tell him?"

"There was no need. He guessed as soon as I opened me mouth."

"Bloody meddler."

"He spoke with a funny accent, said he hailed from France."

"What?" With the speed of a cat, Kennan drew his dirk and barreled out the door. Dust kicked up around his ankles as he skidded to a halt in the middle of the street. Holding his knife aloft, he turned full circle. "Where the hell did he go?"

Divana joined him. "Is something amiss?"

"I bloody hope it isn't." He grabbed her by the wrist and tugged. "I do not trust the French, is all."

She hastened her step to keep pace with Kennan's long stride. Good gracious, the Frenchman seemed friendly enough. Must the captain distrust everyone?

"Where are we off to now?" she asked.

"The regisrar's offices. 'Tis where they keep a list of ships that have come into port. And if the clerk has done his job, we'll aslo learn who the masters of those vessels are as well as the contents of their cargo."

Chapter Twenty-Two

*K*ennan turned the lock on his cabin door while Divana plopped onto the trunk and removed the square-toed shoes he'd purchased for her after they left the useless registrar's offices. The merchant who'd peddled the brogues claimed they'd hardly been worn. Though there hadn't been time to order a new pair from a cobbler, if Divana had to guess, these shoes had been worn once if ever. The leather was as stiff as oak bark and had already caused blisters on her heels.

She rubbed her foot. "I do not see why sailors have to wear shoes."

As Kennan faced her, his eyes shone in the lamplight. "Only heathens go barefoot."

"I'm no heathen."

He strolled past her, capturing her hand and tugging her along toward his velvet-padded chair. "I do not ken about that. I rather like you with a wee bit of heathen coursing through your blood."

Divana put up a wee struggle when he sat and pulled her onto his lap—but not too much of a struggle. On the inside she bubbled with anticipation. "How can ye say such a thing?"

He tugged the woolen Highlander's bonnet from her head and dropped it to the floorboards. "No proper lady can set my blood to boiling like you do."

"Not even Mistress Evans?" Divana shouldn't have asked, but she'd been rankled ever since visiting the woman's home. Good heavens, Kennan had entertained relations with the lady, who clearly was wealthy in her own right. Imagine being a widow and owning a stately home with servants and all.

He grasped her chin, his expression growing dark and serious. "Especially not that woman."

As she settled more comfortably on his lap, warmth swirled through her insides. Divana had tried to ignore her jealousy when they went to see the woman, but knowing he'd been friendly with anyone had made her inexplicably irritable. "N-n-nay?" she asked. "Can ye tell me why?"

"Let's just say she enjoys being a widow."

"How so?"

"Must I spell it out?"

"Please."

"She has a reputation for setting her sights on younger men…especially younger captains who might be in a position to help her further her operations."

Divana blinked, the realization of the extent of Mistress Evans's scandalous nature sinking in. "Ye mean she beds them and uses them for her own devices?"

"Smart lass."

When a knock came at the door, Divana flew off Kennan's lap, clutching her fists beneath her chin.

"I've your supper, Captain," announced the disembodied voice.

"Davy, attend the bloody door," he growled like a grumpy curmudgeon.

She shook away her alarm and started off. The idea of playing a cabin boy was beginning to wear thin. But at least she was where and with whom she wanted to be. "Straightaway, sir."

She opened the door wide for the sailor to come in with an enormous tray of cooked pork medallions and gravy, freshly baked bread, and an assortment of interesting fruits. Perhaps playing the role of a lad was a small price to pay for happiness.

Though after Kennan dismissed the sailor and they started in on the delicious meal, a flurry of questions swarmed around Divana's mind. Kennan had told her about Vane's attack in the Irish Sea, but he hadn't said much about what had happened before the attack. And why had he run out of Mistress Evans's house as if he were about to challenge a hideous scoundrel to a duel?

He pushed a plate of some hard-looking chunks of white toward her. "Remember the coconuts we saw in the market?"

"Aye."

"This is the fruit. Try some, 'tis delicious."

She picked up a piece and nibbled. "Och, ye're right." Immediately, her mouth watered and she ate the entire slice. "I...um...was wondering...," she said, wiping the moisture from her lips.

"Yes?"

"Why do ye not like the French?"

He broke the bread and slathered butter over a

portion. "'Tisn't the French as much as one particular Frenchman."

"Hmm." She stopped chewing and looked to the windows. "After today I've ended up having more questions, as if there are enormous gaps between the things I ken about ye."

"For instance?"

"Well, how did ye come to befriend Mistress Evans, and how did ye come to be enemies with some man from France, and why the devil was Jackson Vane after ye in the first place?"

Kennan pushed back his chair and strode to the windows. "I reckon it all started with the Duke of Kingston-upon-Hull and his aversion to paying taxes whilst he encouraged the vote in the House of Lords to impose crippling duties on the Scots—duties so high, we had no chance of selling anything to England."

"That hardly seems fair."

"Believe me it isn't. 'Tis why so many Highlanders have banded together for the Jacobite cause."

"To put Prince James on the throne?"

"Exactly. He's the heir, and as far as we're concerned, he's first in line. At least he would be if he weren't a Catholic."

"Why does it matter?"

"Because Queen Anne is terrified of popery and has enacted legislation to prevent Catholics from sitting on the throne."

"That makes no sense at all." Divana took another piece of coconut. "So, how did ye end up at odds with the Duke of Kingston-upon-Hull?"

"It wasn't at odds exactly. Word arrived that the duke had captured a Dutch ship that was carrying stolen

Spanish gold. The Jacobite loyalists came together and agreed that James—"

"Who is exiled in France, aye?"

Kennan nodded. "That James needed the gold more to support his cause than Hull. So, to make a long story short, my men and I spirited aboard Hull's ship and took it."

"An act of piracy?"

"I prefer to say privateering for the prince. Besides, the gold had already been stolen twice over." Kennan turned away from the window. "Remember the Frenchman I despise?"

"Aye."

"He had letters which he claimed to be from James— very convincing forgeries, mind you—which claimed he was an emissary from the prince. To avoid suspicion, those loyal to *the cause* decided to entrust the gold to him—Claude Dubois is his name, and I should have killed him when I had the chance."

"What happened? Did it have anything to do with your being wrongly accused in Dundee?"

"Dundee was part of it, aye. I think I mentioned the queen's man was padding his pockets and trying to force me to pay twice the normal duties, for a shipment of tobacco from the Continent. I was arguing my case when one of the soldiers on the pier fired a shot, and a riot broke out. And it so happened on that very pier the Earl of Mar and his wife were searching for me—as well as the gold."

"Is that how ye came to befriend the earl?"

"Let's say what happened afterward bonded our friendship."

"Saint Columba, I wouldn't have dreamed all this up if I were telling a tall tale."

"I suppose it seems like quite a jumble now." Kennan opened the journal on his desk and flipped through the pages. "Anyway, we found Dubois and the gold at Versailles, took the coin to James, where it should have gone in the first place, and he rewarded us each with a portion."

"Of gold? But I thought Vane stole your silver."

Kennan closed his journal and poured a tot of rum. "He did."

"Och nay, ye cannot stop now. I need to ken the rest. What happened to your gold and why did Vane seek ye out?"

"Most of the gold is in a strongbox at Achnacarry—Lochiel is the only man a party to its whereabouts. I took enough to buy silk, coffee, and rum—from Mistress Evans, mind you. But beforehand, we came across a Spanish vessel that had run aground on a reef. When we set foot on her decks, the officers were ready to go down with the ship—but she had silver aboard. After a wee battle, we sent the officers ashore in a skiff and helped ourselves to the silver."

"You stole it?"

"Let us say salvaged. Besides, no lives were lost."

"But what about those poor Spaniards?"

"I reckon they've found another ship and are somewhere sailing the high seas." Kennan took a healthy swig. "But when Vane attacked, he knew I had silver aboard my ship."

"Mistress Evans told him?"

"I never suspected her. She hates Jackson Vane almost as much as I do. But remember I said I never should have left Claude Dubois alive?"

"Aye."

"He was aboard Vane's ship when they attacked. Don't

ask me how, but I ken to my very soul someone told Dubois about our plunder and then he found a ruthless pirate to steal it."

"And so many men lost," Divana whispered.

Kennan slid into a chair and cradled his head in his hands. "Fifteen good men gone—all because of that bastard."

Divana moved behind him and kneaded his shoulders. "Their deaths were nay your fault."

"It was all my fault. I shouldn't have plundered the silver. Or I should have sailed a more circuitous route home. I should have been more vigilant as we entered the North Channel."

Divana hated how he tormented himself, thinking of all the things he ought to have done to prevent the attack. But even if he'd stayed on deck throughout the night or sailed a different route, there was every chance the *Highland Reel* still would have been plundered. "Did ye tell Mistress Evans about the silver?"

"She was the only one. But I gave my men shore leave in Nassau, and somehow the news made its way back to Dubois and Jackson Vane."

* * *

Kennan closed his eyes, reliving the torture of the battle. As clear as if it had happened yesterday, the gruesome aftermath shredded his gut. He'd never forget the bloody corpses strewn across the deck of his beloved *Highland Reel*. During the past month he'd tried to block the rage and guilt from his mind and focus on his duty, but retelling the past tore open those wounds and hit him with the force of a mallet.

"Relax," Divana whispered in his ear as her magical fingers plied his muscles. God, he adored the lass.

A voice at the back of his mind told him he didn't deserve her—told him to storm out of the cabin and sleep on the planks of mid-deck. But how would that look to his men? Och, the captain of the ship brooding and thrust from his own cabin?

"Ye'll soon find Vane and when ye do, I ken ye'll make him pay for the friends ye've lost."

Kennan balled his fists. "Bloody oath I will."

She kissed his neck, her fingers sliding down his chest. "How can I make ye feel better?"

The lass had done so much for him—always giving, always helping. "It is I who should be tending you."

"But I am nothing but a lowly lass."

"Do you truly think so? How many times have you helped me?"

"Och, but I did no more than me duty."

"I beg your pardon, but you are gravely mistaken. You gave me shelter after I'd been forced overboard and mauled by sharks. You went without sleep and tended my sickbed after I was shot."

"Aye, and then I spirited aboard this ship against your wishes."

"True." He released his belt. "But I reckon everyone's entitled to a misstep now and again."

She slipped her shirt over her head while Kennan unfastened her falls and shoved her breeches to the floor. "Do ye ken what I like most about you being dressed as a lad?"

A coy twinkle sparked in her eye. "Me shapely arse?"

He chuckled. Oh, how she distracted him. "Of course, your shapely arse drives me mad. But the thing I like most is it only takes a few flicks of my fingers to strip you bare."

Completely naked, she unfastened his plaid and drew his shirt over his head, exposing him where he sat. "Do ye ken what I like most about stripping ye bare?"

"I've no clue."

She took his member between her fingers. "Every time I reveal your manhood, ye are hard as iron."

He caressed her cheek. "I like how you've taken to the sport of the bedchamber."

She licked him. "So, Captain. What will ye teach me this night, or have we tried every position there is to master?"

An eager moan rumbled from his throat. "I reckon there's a few yet to go—and even more yet to invent."

"Oooh, I like your sense of adventure."

She slid to her knees and took him fully into her mouth. The warmth set his blood on fire, making him powerless to object. Even if he wanted to object. But presently there was no conceivable reason to utter anything but a satisfied growl. He rocked with the rhythm of her mouth milking him while her fingers slid down and swirled around his balls.

He'd never met a bed partner so eager to please. Growling with lust, Kennan untied the thong clubbing her hair back and then raked his fingers through her silken mane. He wanted to be inside her any way she wanted.

As her wicked tongue teased him, a bit of seed leaked from the tip of his cock. Much more of that, and their lovemaking would be over before it began. He tugged her up. "What is your desire, Divana?"

She blushed while she chewed the corner of her mouth. If a woman could seduce a man with the shift of her eyes, she'd mastered such a trick. "Ye said we haven't tried everything yet. That makes me curious. Tell me more."

"There's..." He stopped himself.

A lovely pink tongue slipped across her bottom lip. "What?"

"Nay. 'Tis crude."

"Nothing between us is crude, nay if it pleases ye." She twirled a lock of his hair around her finger. "Tell me."

Why not say it? Then Divana could make up her own mind. "What if you were to bend over a chair and I made love to you from behind?"

"We can do that?"

"In this cabin we can do anything if it pleases you."

Grinning like a hellcat, she strode toward the bed, red hair sweeping her shoulders while the shapeliest buttocks he'd ever seen swayed with her gait.

She peered over her shoulder and took ahold of the bedpost. "What about here? 'Tis sturdier than a chair." Good Lord, this woman was a natural-born temptress.

Kennan's cock grew so hard, it tapped his stomach. "You mean you would be willing?"

"Aye, why should I not?" she whispered. "I trust ye."

In two strides, he crossed the floor and grasped her creamy hips, burying his face into her neck. "I've died and gone to heaven."

"Ye like it backward?"

"I like it any way it pleases you, *mo leannan*."

Slowly, she bent at the waist, presenting a temptation no man could resist.

As he entered her, he slipped his hand around her front and ever so gently tantalized the tiny slick button.

"Oh, oh, oh my," she sighed, swirling her hips along with his languid thrusts.

"You like this, aye, *mo leannan*?"

"Faster."

On the edge of losing control, Kennan was only too happy to oblige, watching his cock disappear inside her. His balls clenched as tight as his fist as he ground his teeth and forced himself to wait for her release.

She arched her lovely spine, a cry catching in her throat, the tiny noise all Kennan needed to send him over the edge. Bending his knees, he pumped into her like never before. Higher and higher, passion drove him.

God damn, he wanted to explode inside her. She was wild and brazen and touched him deeper than any woman had ever done.

Fighting with his demons and bellowing at the peak of his release, he forced himself to withdraw and spill onto the floor. Bending forward, he wrapped his arms around her and held on for dear life. "Dear God, woman, you have beguiled me body and soul."

Chapter Twenty-Three

*K*ennan tilted his chair back while Divana served, pouring three drams of whisky. "Thank you, Davy. You may leave us."

MacNeil reached for his drink while Lachie Mor rested his elbows on the table and watched her go, shutting the door behind her. "Och, why do ye continue with the ruse whilst we're in your cabin?"

Kennan squared his seat and leaned forward. "I reckon we ought to stay in character at all times."

Wiping his mouth on his sleeve, Mr. MacNeil snorted. "You cannot tell me you're pretending she's a lad once you're locked away for the night."

"That's none of your concern."

"Mayhap ye think not, but the men are talking." Lachie Mor swirled his whisky.

MacNeil gave a nod. "Aye, they are."

"Bloody hell, this is a ship." Kennan threw back his tot

and slammed the cup on the table. "When aren't the men talking? They're like a gaggle of hens."

Lachie's shoulder ticked up. "Suppose it matters not."

"Nay. It does not." Kennan poured another. He figured sooner or later someone would start rumors. "What are they saying?"

A bit of color shot up the old quartermaster's face. "Ye do not want to hear it."

"For the love of God, why did you bring it up if it's too trivial to mention?"

"'Cause the men are wondering if ye have...ah... changed your preferences." Lachie Mor spread his arms, shooting a pleading glace at the boatswain across the table.

Not one to mince words, MacNeil looked Kennan in the eye, the scar down his face menacing. "They're saying ye prefer arse to quim."

Kennan's jaw dropped while he considered whom he should throttle first.

"Ah...er...um," Lachie stammered. "Ye must admit Davy is quite bonny for a lad."

MacNeil had the audacity to laugh. "Hell, she...er... he's quite bonny for a lass."

"Remove your minds from the stinking bilges, ye pair of flea-bitten maggots." Kennan shoved the flagon away. "And mind you, I'm responsible for her—him."

His companions threw their heads back with hearty belly laughs.

Kennan scowled. "The pox on you both. Now, tell me, what did you learn in town today?"

Lachie Mor took a bannock from the plate in the center of the table, crumbs peppering his beard as he bit into it. "A wee lassie at the brothel told me Vane found a treasure—and 'tweren't plundered."

"Randy bastard," said MacNeil. "Ye told me ye were off to the tavern."

Lachie Mor's eyes grew as round as those of a puppy caught in the meat larder. "Aye, but I ended up sidetracked along the way."

"How did the wench ken?" Kennan asked.

"Said she heard it from one of Blackbeard's own."

Kennan blinked. Edward Teach and Jackson Vane were sworn enemies. "Blackbeard?"

"Said Vane and his pirates put a score of villages in Trinidad to fire and sword—robbed the Spaniards of everything—jewelry, coin, weapons. They even killed the livestock, murdering anyone who stood in their way."

"I can attest to that." All eyes shifted to MacNeil. "I took a stroll to the old fort as we agreed—some of Vane's outcasts are holding court there of late. And they told me he's claimed his own bloody island—calls it Jackson's Hell—said he acquires his supplies in Port Royal just like the lassie told Lachie."

Thrusting himself to his feet, Kennan ground his knuckles into the walnut table. "God's blood, man, why did you not tell me this as soon as you stepped into my cabin?"

MacNeil sat back and crossed his arms. "Weeeell, Miss Divana was serving us whisky—and then we were led off on a diversion."

Lachie helped himself to the flagon and poured for the boatswain. "Och, Captain, I reckon we'll be setting a course for Port Royal come the morrow."

"Aye, we shall. We'll sail after the stores are loaded—and I'll tolerate no dawdling, ye ken?" With luck they'd be weighing anchor by midday.

* * *

"Arf!"

Divana's ears pricked as she hastened up the forecastle deck steps, mop in hand. At the top, she was met by a pair of paws slamming into her chest, followed by a wet tongue slurping across her mouth. "Och, ye wee beastie," she laughed, catching ahold of the rail before she toppled backward.

Runner gave the dog's collar a tug. "Hop down, Bannock."

The dog dashed around in a circle, then rubbed against Divana's legs. "Ye are a friendly sort, are ye not?" She glanced to the lad. "Where'd he come from?"

"I was sitting on the beach, having my nooning with the others, and the laddie filched a bannock straight out of my fingertips."

Divana dropped to one knee and gave the enormous dog a scratch. He had quite an interesting coat of fur, not long but not short, either. And he stood about as tall as a deerhound with one black eye and one blue. When he closed his mouth, one of the canines on the bottom stuck out. "So ye brought the poor rascal back here to do penance?"

"Nay, he wouldn't leave me be after he ate—followed me through the market with his nose in my hand."

Smoothing her fingers over the dog's thick coat, she felt ribs. "He's too thin."

"Mayhap that's why he stole me bannock."

"And hence his name?"

"Aye." Runner tugged the dog's rope leash. "I thought it suited him."

"Well, I like it."

"Ye do?"

She leaned on her mop and stood straight. "It makes him sound important."

The lad puffed out his chest. "He's a sea dog now."

Divana filled a pail of seawater from the cask strapped and bolted to the bulkhead. "What does the captain say about having the wee beastie aboard?"

The lad threw his arms around Bannock's neck. "He's mine. I gave him a bath and everything. And I'll clean up after him, I swear I will."

Divana dipped her mop. "Mayhap I should have a word with Sir Kennan—let him know what a nice—nice...what breed do you reckon he is?"

"No clue, but he's a Highlander, if ye ask me."

The dog sauntered up and licked her hand. "Well, then, the captain will fall in love with him just like we did."

"Thank ye." Runner motioned for the dog to hop up into one of the skiffs. "Stay, Bannock. We're swabbing the deck."

The dog wagged his tail and watched while they worked.

"The fellow obeys ye already."

"He's savvy, I'll say."

It was still morn, yet the sun already made Divana perspire. She stopped and wiped the sweat from her brow. "Does it nay seem a bit much to swab all the decks every day?"

Runner sloshed his mop around the skiff. "Working salt water into the wood helps preserve it."

"Truly? Who would have kent such a thing?"

Ethan stepped onto the deck, carrying a pail of something stinking to high heaven.

Burying his nose in the crux of his arm, Runner coughed. "Why the devil did ye bring that up here?"

The blackguard just looked at Divana and smirked. "Och, the golden *laddie* here needs to ken what real shite smells like."

As Ethan tossed the piss and excrement at her feet, Divana hoisted herself up on the rigging to the tune of Bannock's barks. "Saint Columba, ye are the vilest brigand on the seas!"

Ethan tipped his hat and grinned like a scoundrel, tobacco stains yellowing his teeth. "I dare ye to complain to the captain."

"Bugger off!" Runner shouted as he threw a bucket of seawater over the stench, flushing it out through a scupper hole. Bannock whined, scratching the side of the skiff. "Stay. If ye hop out of there now, ye'll need another bath for certain."

Divana jumped to the timbers, fetched another pail, filled it from the barrel of seawater, and joined in. "That man's a menace."

"Lachie Mor never should have brought him on."

"Why did he?" she asked.

"Ye want to ask him?" Runner picked up his mop and started swabbing all over again. "Besides, I reckon Ethan kens how to talk his way onto a crew. And I've been at sea long enough to ken there's always a rotten apple or two on a voyage."

Divana glanced over her shoulder. Curse the varlet, Ethan shook his finger at her right before he headed down to the lower decks. For the love of Moses, she'd already promised to give him her share of the prize. Why didn't he leave her be?

"Hey, look there," said Runner, moving to the rail.

"That schooner's figurehead is sparkling in the sun-light."

Bannock finally couldn't stay put and hopped down, moving in beside Divana, rubbing against her. She scratched him behind the ears before she looked at the ship, its sails flapping as they unfurled. "Och, she's beautiful."

"'Tis a mermaid."

Holding her hand up to shade her eyes, she squinted, trying to read the words on the bow of the ship. "Aha. She's called the *Sil-ver Mer-maid*. Such a beautiful name is suited to the likes of a graceful schooner."

Runner dropped his mop. "Ye can read?"

"I'm learning."

He seemed a bit cranky as he snatched the wooden handle from the deck. "It seems there are many advantages to being under the captain's protection."

Her cheeks burned. Thank heavens the lad didn't know the extent of the advantages. But the dog distracted her. He leaned against her as if he craved a woman's gentle hand. And he happily yowled as she petted his back.

"He likes ye."

Divana looked into the dog's eyes and couldn't help but grin. What was it about this wee beastie that made her want to hug him? He was scraggly and droll yet entirely lovable. "Mayhap he kens I've been abandoned, too." She swirled her fingers behind his floppy ears. "We're kindred spirits, Bannock and I."

But the dog's wily nature made her think. Where had he come from? What hardships had he experienced? Divana had faced a great many herself. And though she was determined to win Kennan's love, she was a survivor. No matter what may come, she would survive.

She could serve in a fine house. She was learning her way around the decks of a ship. And now Kennan had started teaching her to read. What an adventure life had become since the sea captain had washed onto the shores of her wee isle.

Chapter Twenty-Four

*W*hy does that mangy mongrel have to be in my cabin of all places?"

Divana glanced up from writing her letters as Kennan strode inside, looking as fierce as some of the wily pirates they'd passed in Nassau. But she'd seen him cross before, and she wasn't about to be bothered. Instead, she bent down and scratched Bannock behind the ears. "'Tis only whilst Runner finishes his watch."

The fiery captain untied his neckcloth. "The lad should have asked before he brought a stray aboard."

"Oh? And why not leave him be? The dog's very bright. He already obeys Baltazar." She dipped her quill in the ink pot. "And he's been lying by my feet since I brought him in here and told him to stay."

"Next thing he'll be wanting to sleep atop the four-poster bed."

"Och, do not utter those words too loudly, else I reckon he'll take ye up on your offer."

"It wasn't an offer."

Divana chuckled to herself and wrote a capital *M*, which was so large, it drained the ink from her pen, making her dip it again. She chewed the corner of her mouth as she used smaller strokes for the *e-r-m-a-i-d*.

Kennan leaned over the back of her chair. "What are you writing?"

"I saw a schooner setting sail this afternoon. She had a beautiful mermaid with a silver tail at her figurehead."

"Was her name the *Silver Mermaid*?"

"Aye."

He rubbed her shoulder as he pressed his lips to her temple. "Your letters have improved markedly."

Sighing, Divana set her quill in the holder and held up the parchment. "If only I were better at reading."

"What say you? I've been quite impressed with your progress."

She tsked her tongue. "I cannot read half as well as ye."

"Wheesht. I've been reading since I was a wee lad, and you've only been at it a month."

Sitting back, she regarded her work with a critical eye. "I suppose."

"Would you have kent the name of the ship if you hadn't been learning your letters?"

"I might have guessed, given the figurehead and the silver paint."

"But you wouldn't have known for certain."

"Nay."

"And you wouldn't have been able to sit down and write it."

"Not unless I was copying what I saw."

"Well, you've made good headway. Do not discredit yourself."

"Thank ye." She gathered up the writing materials and returned them to Kennan's writing table. A great deal had happened this day, but the thing that stuck in her craw was Ethan and his boorishness. What kind of brute would throw excrement over the deck? He was lucky the officers were meeting in the captain's cabin, else he would have been lashed for certain. "Are ye aware some of the men on the ship are expecting to earn a finder's share of any treasure ye find on this voyage?"

"Aye, 'tis the way of things, and it gives the men something to look forward to during the long stints at sea." Kennan removed his sword from its sheath and turned it over in his hands. "What have you heard?"

She pretended to examine her work, trying to appear unworried. "I've overheard some of the Glasgow sailors talk. They're hungry for riches."

"I suppose I would be if I were in their shoes."

"But ye nay sail the high seas bent on piracy?"

"I'd say I'm a king's privateer—I do his bidding, and if it entails securing riches in the name of James, then I will carry out my duty—just as is expected of all sea captains."

"James? King?"

"I misspoke." Kennan set the oil and a whetstone atop a cloth. "Prince James. Remember? He's the rightful heir."

"But does the queen nay see Jacobites as traitors?"

He spilled a few drops of oil on the sword, then methodically swirled the edge on the stone. "Anne has been misled on a great many matters, the exile of her brother being the most egregious of her errors."

"Good heavens, why is it people see fit to turn their

backs on their own blood relatives? I cannot imagine being so cruel as to exile me own kin."

"Nor can I, and those of us who are loyal to her brother consider ourselves true royalists. Our goal is to preserve the succession, not to invoke legislation to prevent it."

"I did not realize the gravity of the situation."

Kennan used the pad of his thumb to test the blade for sharpness. "I wouldn't expect you to, especially after being stranded on Hyskeir for two miserable years."

Bannock moved to her side and rubbed along her thigh. "Ye'll let him stay, will ye not?" she asked, giving the dog an extra-long scratch.

"You oughtn't touch him. He'll give ye fleas."

"But Baltazar has already bathed him." She parted the dog's hair in several places, searching for vermin. "Please, Kennan. I like him."

He resheathed his sword and set it aside. "Well then. If you like him I suppose he can stay, but do not tell a soul you were the one who convinced me, else they'll all think you have me wrapped around your little finger."

She twirled across the floor. "They already think that."

He caught her by the elbow and tugged her into his arms. "Do they now?"

Divana's breath caught as those green eyes stared into hers with a hunger she, too, felt deep and low in her body.

He kissed her while the flames of passion surged, coiling tightly in her loins. Only moments ago she'd been worried about Bannock and ensuring the dog would continue to live in comfort aboard ship. Now she swooned, kissing Kennan as if nothing else in the world mattered. Would it always be like this when in his arms?

What might happen after they found Jackson Vane

and returned to Scotland? She clutched him tighter and deepened the kiss, rubbing her mons across his hardness, her heartbeat racing with his guttural moan. By the saints, she would do everything in her power to make him fall in love with her. And by the end of this voyage, Divana prayed he would.

* * *

The sun shone low in the eastern sky when Claude Dubois took a skiff from the *Silver Mermaid*, which was moored at the tip of the harbor, where she'd be able to make a hasty escape if need be. He disembarked on the beach at Port Royal. Heading into town, he took a parcel of almonds from a merchant and tossed the man a coin, then found Jackson Vane at the rear of a brothel, sound asleep with a buxom woman in his arms.

"Cannot stay away from the ladies, *oui*, Captain?"

Within the blink of an eye, Vane had a dagger at Claude's throat while the woman on the bed yelped, pulling the linens up to her chin. "You know better than to wake me."

"Perhaps." Claude chewed the almonds in his mouth, albeit gingerly. "But before you kill me, I thought you'd be interested in who's paid a visit to Nassau and Mistress Evans."

Vane lowered his knife and dismissed the wench with a flick of his hand. "Who?"

"The Highlander—Cameron." Dubois grinned and pointed to the gap in his front teeth. "The same bastard responsible for this."

"Let him search all he wants, he'll never find Jackson's Hell."

"He won't need to if you continue dallying here."

"What say you?" Distrust filled the pirate's slitted eyes. "Tell me you didn't rush aboard the *Silver Mermaid* and lead him here?"

Claude popped a few almonds into his mouth and chewed nervously. Though Vane had been eager to learn about the treasure aboard the *Highland Reel*, their relations had always been tenuous at best. The sooner they dispatched Kennan Cameron, the sooner Claude would take his share of the spoils and return to France.

"The only Scot I spoke to was the woman dressed in the disguise of a cabin boy—and she is as ignorant as a sea urchin." Thanks to Msizi for pointing her out. Claude swallowed, the almonds sticking in his throat. "He never saw me. Nor does he know you have any ties with the *Silver Mermaid*."

"And I intend to keep it that way." Vane shrugged into his black leather vest. "So, you think you're smarter than me, aye?"

Claude smirked. "I knew where to find you, didn't I?"

"Please, Dubois. You found me because you are one of the few I've allowed into my confidence—and you'd best not forget it." Vane polished his signet ring on his waistcoat. "What about Mistress Evans? What have you said to her?"

"She knows nothing."

Vane brandished his blade in front of Claude's throat. "And she had best not. That woman has forever been a thorn in my side."

Claude glanced at the blade, sweat stinging his skin. No matter. He'd be rid of this madman soon. "How long are you in Port Royal?"

"I came up for supplies—there's a lumber shipment

here from the Americas. Why? Do you believe Cameron will pay a visit?" He aimed his blade at Claude's eye. "Have you lied to me?"

"Bless it, man, sheathe your weapon! You have the Highlander's ship. What must I do to prove myself?" Claude wiped the sweat from his face. "When I set sail, he and his men were asking questions."

"I should have killed the bastard when I had him in my grasp."

"And I was hoping you would have."

Vane finally sheathed his damned dagger. "I wouldn't worry about him. He's the heir to a Scottish lairdship— well-born men set to inherit aren't suited for a seafaring life."

"As I recall, you said the same after he leaped over the rail of the *Highland Reel*. I caution you not to underestimate Cameron, *mon ami*. He's a viper, that one."

"Well, then, if he shows his face in these parts, we'll have to lure him into a trap he'll never escape."

Dubois grinned, rubbing his hands. "And I think I know exactly how to ensure that Highlander will not interfere with us again."

Chapter Twenty-Five

*K*ennan took his time sailing around the isle of Jamaica before he gave the command to drop anchor in Kingston Harbour. This caution took an extra day. Port Royal had become a lawless haven for pirates since an earthquake had swallowed most of the town over twenty years past. Kennan ducked into his cabin and found Divana clomping across the floor with a limp.

He stopped midstride. "What have you done?"

She thrust her finger downward. "These miserable square-toes wore a blister on my heel and it hasn't yet healed."

He kneeled to examine the shoe, cursing that there hadn't been time in Nassau to engage a cobbler to make a pair to fit the lass. "Rise onto your toes."

She grunted as she complied, her heel slipping out. He untied her garter and rolled down her sock, finding a red-raw, popped blister.

"Och, the heels are not tight enough. I'll fetch a salve."

He stood and headed for his medicine chest. "Fold up two slips of parchment to use at the back of each. That and my ointment ought to set you to rights at least for today."

"I didn't have blisters when I was barefoot."

"Would you prefer to stay aboard ship?" he asked, removing a pot of salve from his cupboard. He knew she'd put up an argument, so he added, "It might be best."

"I beg your pardon?" She took a bit of parchment from her growing stack of writing papers and used a pair of shears to cut two strips. "I thought ye said no one can best me with a slingshot. Who else will watch your back?"

"Lachie Mor with his matched pair of flintlocks, to begin with." Kennan gestured to a chair. "Perhaps you might be a tad overconfident with that strip of leather."

"Och, ye already said I could go and I'm going." As Divana sat, she tugged the ends of her weapon—it had made a fine belt thus far, and knowing she was wearing it gave him some peace of mind. "I ken, I'm no match for a swordsman or a musket, but me slingshot kept me fed for two years, mind ye. I'm more comfortable with this bit o' leather than a slew of daggers up me sleeves and in me hose."

Kennan rubbed in the salve, then resituated her hose and tied her garter. "Let me worry about carrying the blades. And do not stray from my side—Port Royal is far worse than Nassau."

"Aye, aye, Captain," she said with a bit of sauce, slipping the paper into her heels.

After Kennan hid a pair of *sgian dubhs* in the flashes holding up his hose, Lachie Mor met them at the winch. "I already sent some of the men ahead in one of the skiffs."

Kennan checked his pocket watch. They'd only been at anchor a half hour. "Couldn't they wait?"

"I didn't reckon it mattered overmuch."

Sighing, he looked to the shore. He supposed it didn't as long as everyone knew they had to be back on deck by dusk.

"Where's Runner?" asked Divana.

Lachie Mor thrust a thumb over his shoulder. "He went on ahead—took the mutt with him."

Kennan held the gamming chair for the lass, forcing himself not to take her hand and help her aboard. "Why?"

"Said Bannock needed a good run."

Kennan eyed his man. "You never should have let him bring the dog aboard in the first place."

"Me?" asked Lachie Mor as if he'd known nothing about it.

"Och, let the lad have the wee mongrel. He's no troub..." Divana's voice was carried away by the wind and surf while the winch lowered her to the skiff.

The quartermaster snorted. "I reckon Davy's a great deal more trouble than Bannock."

Kennan fingered the hilt of his dirk and arched an eyebrow. Why Lachie Mor always chanced to make an offhanded remark about Divana, he had no idea. Once the lass had recovered from her fear of heights, she'd proved a valuable member of the crew. Never in his life would he be able to imagine his sister, Janet, keeping watch in the crow's nest or swabbing the decks for that matter. Such menial labor just wasn't done by gentlewomen.

Too right. Before Janet married Robert Grant, Kennan had carried his sister across the muddy street at Inverlochy so her riding habit and boots wouldn't be soiled. Bless her, Divana would have marched across barefoot and thought nothing of it.

The idea of the redheaded spitfire traipsing through the Highlands with naked toes had him grinning all the way to the shore. Until Divana climbed over the edge of the boat, shoes and stockings in hand, only to have Bannock charge through the water and nearly knock her arse-first into the surf.

Lachie Mor scowled. "Keep your footing and be firm with the dog, lad."

Kennan climbed out of the boat and steadied Divana by the collar—to help her more than anything, and to keep up appearances. Of course, the daft dog didn't help matters by running in circles around them, kicking up water. "Runner, put a lead on your bloody stray."

"Come behind, Bannock," the boy called, beckoning from the shore.

When finally on dry land, Kennan brushed himself off, somewhat surprised that the dog had obeyed without being told twice.

"You should have left him aboard," said Mr. MacNeil.

"Enough. He's here now." Kennan looked between his two officers. "One in every four buildings in this crumbling town is a tavern or a brothel—too many for us to visit all. I want you to find a chair and mind your own affairs whilst you nurse an ale and listen to the talk."

"Aye, just like afore," said Lachie Mor.

"Except..." Kennan gave the quartermaster's shoulder a shove. "I do not want to hear about being waylaid at a brothel."

The man's face fell.

"I mean what I say." When Runner sniggered, Kennan tweaked his ear. "And you pair will come with me."

"Me and Bannock?" asked the lad.

"Bloody hell, I don't give a rat's arse about the

dog—you and Davy. And there'll be no dawdling in the market."

"Aye, sir." Tugging Bannock beside him, Runner rolled his eyes at Divana. "He thinks me irresponsible."

"Nay, he's just irritated that Mistress Evans didn't ken more about the whereabouts of Captain—"

"Enough." Kennan sliced his palm through the air. "When that name is uttered, I'll do the uttering."

"Very well, but where are we off to? Another fine house owned by a wealthy widow?"

"I don't reckon you'll find any fine houses here."

Nassau was a kindly place compared to Port Royal, with fewer merchants and more scoundrels. But the town still lay in the midst of the trade routes, and thus goods were loaded, unloaded, and bartered here. Kennan stopped outside a shop bearing a shingle that read "Jack's Mercantile."

Divana peered into the window "A haberdashery?"

Kennan glanced over his shoulder to ensure no one was close enough to eavesdrop. "Word is Vane comes to the port for his supplies. That implies two things."

"What would those be?" asked Runner.

A bell rang as Kennan opened the door. "I'll tell you later."

A shopkeeper stood behind the counter, his beard long and unkempt. He regarded them with steely, untrusting eyes veiled beneath a jungle of eyebrows.

A true mercantile, the place was lined to the rafters with everything from thimbles and cloth to hammers, and pots for cooking. The only patrons were a pair of ladies carrying parcels, who sidled past them and out the door.

"Saint Columba," Divana whispered under her breath as she stared up at a cerulean-blue gown.

When the man said nothing, Kennan moved nearer. "Are you Jack?"

"Jack's dead." The man's black eyes shifted between Runner and Divana. "What are ye lookin' for?"

"Perhaps a wee bit of information."

"You're on the wrong island."

"I think not." Kennan placed his palms atop the counter. "And I'll reckon you can help."

"Not likely."

"I'm looking for a man."

"Everybody is lookin' for someone. If ye're not here to spend your coin, ye know where to find the door. And your two sidekicks can wait outside with their dog. I don't allow no sticky fingers in my shop."

Kennan motioned to Divana and Runner. "Wait for me outside the door. I won't be long." He returned his attention to the shopkeeper. "How much for the blue gown?"

"Fifty pieces of eight."

"Fifty?" Kennan guffawed. "That's thievery."

"'Tis the price of conducting business in the islands. Ye want it or nay?"

There were a hundred items or more that would cost a penny or less, including a basket full of shiny stones right beside his hand. But Divana wouldn't be wearing breeches for the rest of her days. When the time came to reveal her true identity, it would be delightful to see her in such a gown—red hair, eyes made bluer by the color of the fabric. "Aye, wrap it up," he said, tossing a handful of coins on the board.

The money immediately disappeared somewhere below the counter. Kennan watched as the man retrieved the dress from the nail on the wall. "What can you tell me about Jackson Vane?"

"He's a cutthroat pirate."

"He is. And I have word he purchases his supplies right here in this very shop."

"Ye're mistaken."

"Och aye? He comes to Port Royal for his supplies—thinks he won't be caught now most of the blackguards have moved on. Now tell me, when was he last here?"

"Why should I tell ye?" asked the man, heading back to the counter.

"Because I aim to see him to his grave."

"Ye sound awfully confident—especially for a man I've never seen nor heard tell of afore."

"Do you want to keep your fifty pieces of eight or nay?"

The man folded the dress and set it in the middle of a square of parchment. "Sometimes Vane sends his men for supplies."

"Are any of his men here now?"

"I can't say."

"Cannot say or will not?"

Pulling out a length of twine from a spool, the shopkeeper said nothing and set to tying the parcel.

Kennan took one of the shiny stones and rubbed it between his fingers. "What happened to Jack?"

"Succumbed to the bloody flux."

That wasn't the response Kennan was hoping for, but he wasn't finished yet. "You have a nice shop here. It would be a shame if you were robbed of everything you held dear—just as I was."

"I have protection."

"From whom? Pirates like Vane? At what cost?"

"Well, sir, I reckon ye just touched on why my prices are so high. And ye'll find the same from every merchant in Port Royal. Aye, Vane visits from time to time as ye are aware, but I cannot tell ye the last time I saw the man. And if it is Vane ye want, I wager ye'll have a long holiday in hell, 'cause that's where ye're headed."

Kennan picked up the parcel and looked the man in the eye. "I think not. After all, I'm nay the bastard who's sold his soul for a morsel of false protection."

* * *

Divana gaped at Kennan as he came out of the shop. "Ye've a parcel?"

Kennan scowled. "What of it?"

When Runner shot her a vexed expression, she couldn't help but snigger. Aye, the captain forbade them from shopping, while he had quite a sizable bundle under his arm. "Was the shopkeeper of any help?" she asked.

"Nay. Though he did confirm Vane and his men do come here for supplies." Kennan led them away. "Runner, how many ships were at anchor in the harbor?"

"Four, sir. A frigate, a cutter, a schooner, and a galleon looking as if she was full of rot."

"And not a one of them belonging to Jackson Vane?"

"At least none that attacked the *Reel*, sir."

"Och, we're so close I can feel it in my bones." He gestured with an upturned palm. "Lad, take your dog down to the wharf and see what you can learn about the ships in port."

"Straightaway, sir."

Divana gave Bannock a pat before the boy led him away. "Where are we off to, Captain?"

"Perhaps we ought to pay the market a visit."

She straightened, trying not to grin. "More shopping?"

"Not today. Mayhap we'll happen upon someone Vane doesn't own in this pirate cove."

She didn't let her excitement show, but for the first time in her life Divana had a few coins to spend. If only she weren't impersonating a lad, she'd buy something feminine—ribbons or a necklace, or a bit of lace to make her look bonny for Kennan.

For a small town, plenty of people mulled about— far more men than women. And everyone looked as if they'd been in the midst of the wars. Children dressed in little more than rags darted between the tents and stalls, chasing each other and laughing.

Divana closely followed Kennan while he browsed and she stole peeks at the myriad of colorful items. Merchants shouted and dazzled them with beautiful cloth, figurines carved from dark wood in human shapes—but unlike anything she'd ever seen, depicting long faces and noses, enormous eyes, and gargantuan earlobes. Gold jewelry adorned with shiny rocks sparkled in the sun. And the rich aroma of food sizzling on open grills made her mouth water.

Kennan purchased two helpings of meat on a stick and gave one to Divana. "Are you hungry?"

She nodded, taking a bite. "Mm, 'tis spicy and sweet at the same time."

He pulled the entire portion off with his teeth and chewed. "Do you like it?"

"Aye."

A bit further on, he stopped to talk to a merchant about glass floats and the various vessels that came into the harbor to buy them. Beside his stall, a boy sat with a basket full of beautiful shells twice the size of a man's fist.

Divana reached for one. "I've never seen colors so bright."

"If ye clean dem wit' salt water, da color don't fade. But freshwater ruins dem."

"Truly? Is that the same with all shells?"

The boy shrugged. "It works with conchs."

She took another and held it up to the sunlight and studied it, vaguely aware that Kennan was no longer right beside her. "Is this one your finest?"

As she spoke, a hand slid over her mouth—

No!

Ice shot through every muscle in her body. It wasn't Kennan's hand but one smelling of dirt, the fingers coarse. Divana's heart hammered as she shrieked into the palm, frantically thrashing, shifting her gaze from side to side.

"Shut it," growled a man with a menacing voice as he yanked her away through the shroud of tent linens.

Struggling against his iron grip, she bit the filthy palm, flailing her fists and jabbing backward with her elbows.

A brutal hand smacked the side of her head. "Bitch!"

"Good work, Petey. Bind her wrists and gag her," said an oily, burlap-faced scoundrel. "Quickly now. The captain's waiting."

Chapter Twenty-Six

*F*rustrated as all hell, Kennan glared at the merchant standing across from him. "Why does no one ken a bloody thing about Vane's whereabouts when he so clearly has every last one of you in his talons?"

The man squinted. "British patrols come through here oft enough. Ye sound as if you're one of them, as well."

"I'm not with the Royal Navy," Kennan snapped, turning away before he did something he might regret. "Davy! Let's head back to the skiffs. Everyone in this town is yellow."

He looked left and right, then turned full circle. "Davy?"

His breath caught in his chest. "Divana!" he shouted.

The hair on the back of his neck stood on end while the air suddenly became too heavy to breathe. Where was she? Running, he retraced his steps. She'd been right behind him the whole time. Hadn't she?

As he moved, he quickly scanned every stall, every tent, every table.

When did I last see her?

The blue glass of a float caught his eye. Yes. She'd been right there. He'd heard her talking.

"Where is s—he?" Kennan demanded from the merchant who'd sworn he'd never seen a cutter, let alone Vane's ship.

"Beg your pardon?"

"You bloody well ken what I'm asking. The cabin boy who was with me. What happened to him?"

As his mind raced, a trigger flickered in his head. Something was different about the stall. Something was missing. He squinted when he spotted the empty space. "Where's the boy with the basket of shells?"

The man shrugged, feigning complete ignorance. "There are no shells here."

"Aye." Kennan pointed to the empty spot, clearly recalling Divana in conversation with the young man who'd filled the small space between the vendors' tents. "But there was a lad right there. His basket was full of conch shells."

"Mayhap there was, mayhap there wasn't. I cannot pay a mind to every vagrant who happens past." The man rolled up a net with floats woven throughout. "If I were a lively boy ashore in Port Royal for the first time, I'd be peeking in the windows of the brothel or hunting for coins on the floor of a tavern—go have a look for your young whelp there."

Kennan grabbed the varlet by the collar. "Where's the goddamned lad with the shells, and don't tell me you do not ken!"

All around him, at least a dozen swords hissed through their scabbards.

"Release him, ye bloody Highlander," a man with

a cutlass growled as he pushed the tip of the blade into Kennan's neck. "Take your crew and sail back to Scotland. Your kind aren't welcome here."

For a fleeting moment, Kennan considered fighting. If he pulled the merchant over the table and used him as a shield, he'd be able to fend off a half dozen of the men for certain. But ending up bloodied in an all-out brawl wouldn't help find Divana any faster.

He pushed the varlet back as he released his fingers and held up his hands. "I'm not looking for trouble."

"Is that so?" asked the bully with the cutlass. "Could have fooled the likes of me."

Slowly Kennan turned and panned his gaze across the circle of miscreants scowling, their weapons at the ready. "I challenge each one of you to tell Jackson Vane I'll find him. And when I do, I'll show no mercy."

At the name of the hellion pirate, all eyes shifted. No one wanted to confront Vane. Kennan lowered his hands, affecting a scowl every bit as menacing as that of the man they feared. His fingers twitched over the hilt of his sword while he strode straight ahead, pushing his way out of the circle. The slight breeze rushed in his ears as he listened for movement—listened for one of them to act the hero. When an attack didn't come, he'd almost wished it had. Dear God, how he wanted to throttle the lot of them.

Once out of danger, Kennan hastened back to Jack's Mercantile. Of course, the shopkeeper hadn't seen Divana, either. A hollow cavern stretched in his chest as time marched on.

How in God's name did she disappear? She was never out of my sight. At least not more than a minute or two.

Kennan ran to the shore, where he found Mr. MacNeil standing over Runner on the beach. Sitting in the sand, the lad had tears streaming down his face. "We were walking side by side when all of a sudden he took off. I chased him. I called him over and over, but he was too fast for me—"

"The dog?" Kennan asked, but didn't wait for a response. "We've far worse problems than that. Davy's been kidnapped."

"God, no," said MacNeil.

"Right under my nose. I reckon everyone in this town is Vane's man, 'cause no one kent what happened in broad daylight, mind you."

"No one here kens anything." MacNeil kicked the sand. "They're all scared, if you ask me. Moreover, they certainly aren't living in luxury."

Runner wiped his eyes. "Mayhap Bannock is with Divana."

Did she see the dog and run after him? If only it were so—but Kennan hadn't spotted Bannock anywhere near the market. Stroking his chin, he looked to the horizon. "'Tis nearly dusk."

"We have to find her...er...him," said MacNeil. "If they find out that he's really a—"

"There's no need to say it," Kennan growled.

Lachie Mor came tottering up the beach with a band of sailors in his wake.

MacNeil beckoned them. "So much for nursing an ale."

Kennan shook his head and scoffed. What a ragged lot he'd pulled together. "You all had best be sober."

"What news?" Lachie asked, his expression growing wary.

Kennan quickly explained about Divana's disappearance. "He can't have gone far. I want men armed to the nines, watching the harbor, searching every skiff that leaves this beach."

"Search? By whose authority?" asked a sailor.

"On order of Queen Anne of Great Britain." Tossing out the queen's name might hold water long enough for someone to make a quick inspection of a wee boat.

"And keep an eye out for Bannock," added Runner. "He's gone missing as well."

Standing wide, Kennan thrust his fists into his hips. "We'll fan out—north, south, and central. Check every room in every tavern and brothel. Mr. MacNeil, post the remainder of the crew on the gun deck and keep lights burning in the portals whilst they're manning the cannons. If they want a bloody war, I'll be happy to oblige."

"Aye, aye, sir."

"Ask no questions. Besides, you cannot expect a straight answer from these worthless asps. If anyone sees him, send a runner—"

"I beg your pardon," said a child holding out a missive. "Would ye be Captain Cameron?"

"I am."

Without another word, Kennan swiped the letter from the lad's fingertips and hastened to open it.

What he read made the fires of hell swell throughout his chest. *I have your woman. And I will continue to take everything you hold dear as long as you pursue me. —Vane.*

Dear God, the bastard already knew Divana was a lass.

* * *

The enormous scoundrel pulled Divana down from the donkey and threw her to the sand. She thrust out her bound hands to break her fall, her gaze homing onto two pairs of square-toed shoes with silver buckles. As she scrambled away, her gaze trailed from the shoes all the way up to the faces of the men who wore them, and she immediately recognized the Frenchman from Mistress Evans's house. He was podgy and vile—how could she have thought him anything but despicable?

Shifting her gaze, all horrid thoughts of Claude Dubois escalated into a new form of dread. The brigand beside the Frenchman posed the most fearsome picture—a man whose face struck terror in her heart. Cloaked in black, he wore a tricorne low over his brow. Thick, black whiskers hid his expression—but she knew it was menacing. The whites of his eyes glared, piercing through the shadowy light.

Divana's mouth grew dry as she realized she was staring into the eyes of Vane himself.

The big guard stopped her retreat with a boot to the middle of her spine. "That's far enough."

Dubois lunged in, reached around her head, and untied the leather thong from her club. Scowling, he yanked it away, making her hair fall about her shoulders in waves. "See? I knew she was Cameron's woman as soon as I saw her in Nassau."

She eyed him. "Ye sailed here on the *Silver Mermaid*?"

"Shut your mouth," said the lout from behind.

Flinching, she dodged his vicious boot.

A low, wicked laugh pealed from the depths of Vane's throat. "Mayhap you're smarter than your lover." Oddly, the rogue spoke with a highborn English accent.

Her face burned as she clutched her hands to her stomach. "Why are ye doing this?"

"I own these waters. If anyone is foolish enough to threaten me, he will pay dearly with his life and the lives of all for whom he cares."

Divana clutched the slingshot wrapped around her waist. They'd captured her to provoke Kennan? She mustn't let them think her disappearance would hurt him. "But Captain Cameron doesn't give a fig about me."

"Liar!" Dubois slapped her across the face. "My informant confirmed it. She's Cameron's woman."

Vane smirked. "No longer."

As Divana drew a hand over her burning cheek, her mind raced. An informant? Who?

Ethan.

The Frenchman bent downward, thrusting his face an inch from hers. "Your beau stole something from me I intend to reclaim in blood."

Divana met his gaze, dropping her hand and squaring her shoulders. "But ye already stole it back when ye and Vane plundered the *Highland Reel.*"

"Not by half."

"Ye ken he will not come for me."

Again Vane laughed. "She does have a backbone, does she not?"

Dubois snorted, cutting her a menacing glare. "Even if she speaks true, she'll fetch a high price."

The blood drained from her face. "Price?"

"Shut it," the big man growled, with another shove of his boot.

"Yes, you see, Jamaica is quite a large island. There are literally hundreds of places to hide—and by the time Cameron realizes you're gone forever, you'll be out of my hair and sold to Joshua Finnes. Perhaps you've heard tell of my comrade. He's the shrewdest slaver on the high seas." Vane circled his hand over his head. "Prepare to shove off as soon as the skiffs return from supplying the *Mermaid*." He started away, then looked over his shoulder. "Petey—guard the prisoner. If anyone comes near, gut them."

Divana put her back against a boulder to prevent Petey's boot from kicking her again. He'd brought her to the southern tip of the shore and, though she heard the roar of the surf, she couldn't see the water. An enormous fortress of rocks surrounded them, keeping her hidden from view. And the sun had just disappeared in the western sky, the light growing dimmer with her every breath.

"We're setting sail on the *Silver Mermaid*?" she asked.

The pirate gave her a scowl.

But when they'd checked the registrar's records in Nassau, none of the vessels belonged to Jackson Vane.

"Who owns her?" Divana asked, steeling herself for a strike this time.

But Petey just smirked. "That's the amusing part. She's captained by the illustrious Mr. Dawson."

Though the air was as warm the heat from the hearth in Cook's kitchen at Achnacarry, a shiver coursed down her spine while the wind whipped her hair into her face. "W-where might one find Mr. Dawson?"

"Hmm." The man scratched his thatch of a beard. "I reckon he's in the belly of one of them giant sharks about now—or playin' whist with the ghost of Jonah, where you'll be if ye don't shut your gob."

Divana shifted her gaze to the sand and the thong Dubois had viciously ripped from her club. Was Kennan searching for her now? Where were Vane and his pirates taking her? Where would this auction be held? When?

"Hey, Petey," said a lanky brigand, his tongue slavering around his lips. "She's a damned mite prettier with her hair down. What say ye? Let's 'ave a bit o' fun afore we sail."

The two men ducked behind the rocks—out of sight. "The captain says 'e's saving her."

"For 'imself?"

"Most likely. But if anyone touches the wench it'll be me..."

While the men talked, Divana pulled the slips of parchment from her heel. Perhaps she could find some way to leave a note. She unfolded the first slip, but it had too much writing on it already from all her practice copying out Kennan's logbooks. And on the second...she was surprised and delighted to see that it was the one where she'd written *Silver Mermaid*. She could scarcely believe her luck! Now all she needed was a hiding place. Perhaps if she untied her slingshot and placed it and the note with the leather strap sticking out, Kennan or his men might find it.

From her right came a whine. Then a lick to her wrist.

"Bannock?" she whispered.

The dog slurped her face.

Leaning forward, she searched the sand for the thong and quickly reeled it in with her fingers. "Take this," she whispered in his ear. Her fingers trembled while she quickly used the thong to secure the message around the dog's rope collar. "Find Runner. Haste ye."

"Avast!" hollered Petey, throwing a rock at Bannock. "Be off, ye mongrel stray."

Divana bit her lip and cast her gaze downward. *Run, Bannock. Please do not fail me.*

As the pirate moved, she ducked and covered her head. Had he seen her?

Another brigand stepped into the fortress and beckoned with a wave of his hand. "Petey, bring the wench. We sail."

Chapter Twenty-Seven

*B*altazar paced in front of the skiffs with a musket slung over his shoulder. He hated being the one left behind to guard the boats. When it came to real fighting, the captain always assigned him to something to ensure he kept out of danger. Bloody hell, he was almost seventeen years of age and taller than most of the men on the crew.

All the rest of them were in the town muscling their way around the taverns and brothels. He ought to be out there looking for Divana, too, not marching around a pair of empty skiffs. He hated tending the stupid boats. Blast it, he could hear the laughter and music above the sound of the surf. Who knew what those heathens were doing with Divana? Surely he'd be able to find her afore anyone else, save the captain, of course.

"Arf!"

Baltazar stopped dead in his tracks and peered in the direction of the bark. Through the shadows, an enormous dog raced along the shore.

"Bannock!" Runner fell to his knees and beckoned the dog into his open arms. He'd only found the big fella two days past, but he clung to him as if he were already kin. A big, wet tongue licked his face. "Where the blazes were ye?"

Bannock rubbed his neck against Baltazar's chest, turned in a circle, then yowled while he rubbed his neck again, faster this time.

"Och, I missed ye, too." He took the dog's face between his hands. "Why did ye run away like that?"

He threw an arm around Bannock's back, but the dog whimpered and squirmed away.

"What the—" Runner carefully rubbed his hands over the dog's coat. "Are ye hurt?"

But Bannock yipped and persisted to rub his neck on Baltazar's chest. Then the collar scratched his palms until the coarse rope gave way to something soft.

Runner tugged the dog closer and examined the rope. "What's this?"

Bannock excitedly pawed the sand with his front feet while Runner removed a thong and a bit of parchment. He held it up to the moonlight, and though he was unable to read, he thought he recognized the name of the mermaid ship they'd seen in Nassau—the same one that had set sail just after dusk.

"Holy Mother Mary!" Runner gripped the paper in his fist and scanned the darkened buildings. Where the blazes was the captain?

Making a quick decision, he tugged on the dog's collar. "Ye found me, now let's make haste to find Captain Cameron!"

* * *

"Be gone with ye and never darken these doors again!" shouted the haggard madam while Kennan and Lachie Mor backed out of the last brothel in Port Royal, pistols in hand.

"I reckon this is the most unfriendly town I've ever had the displeasure of searching," growled the quartermaster. "Och, they're even more cantankerous than Campbells."

Kennan honed his gaze on the closed door, ready to fire if anyone dared come after them. They stood silent for a moment, the only footsteps coming from the beach, approaching at a sprint.

Both Kennan and Lachie Mor shifted their aim toward the sound.

"Captain!" yelled Runner, his youthful voice pegging him.

"Why isn't he with the skiffs?" grumbled Lachie under his breath. "I'll not tolerate a wee mutineer."

"Wheesht, perhaps he's bearing news." Kennan lowered his flintlock and hastened toward the lad . . . and that miserable hound. "What is it?"

"Bannock had this tied around his collar," he said, waving a slip of parchment.

Taking it, Kennan arched his brow at the dog before he inclined the paper toward the moonlight. "God blind me, she's aboard the *Silver Mermaid*."

Lachie Mor snatched the parchment and shook it. "But that's not Vane's ship."

"Ye reckon? Who in this town has told us the truth?" Kennan started back toward the shore at a run. "Find MacNeil. Tell him all hands onboard at once. Lachie Mor—I want you on the first skiff. We sail within the hour."

"What can I do to help?" asked Runner, taking the lead.

"What was the *Silver Mermaid*'s heading?" Kennan asked as they arrived at the beach, the sand slowing their progress.

"She headed due north, then tacked northeast once she cleared the rocks."

The sound of the boatswain's whistle pierced through the night air. Dear God, they couldn't cast off fast enough.

* * *

Locked in a small chamber below the gun deck of the *Silver Mermaid*, Divana sat on the plank floor in darkness. Inside, there was nary a stalk of straw let alone a chair or anything to provide a modicum of comfort. The seas were rough, making the ship rock, her timbers creaking and groaning with her sway. The wind rushed beyond the single porthole, from which a blue ray of moonlight shone onto the floor in front of her feet. The pall of salt pork and pickling wafted from below, as did gruff voices and hideous laughter.

Though the air was heavy and hot, she clutched her fists beneath her chin to calm the chill thrumming through her blood. She was to be sold? To a slaver—the vilest criminals in all of Christendom. No! This couldn't be happening.

This was far worse than being stranded on Hyskeir with nothing but her wits and her slingshot. And the measly slip of leather would be of no use at all—not when there wasn't a stone to be found anywhere in the middle of the ocean.

"Oy, Ricky, bring me one of them ales," bellowed Petey just beyond the door.

Licking her parched lips, Divana nearly hollered for Ricky to bring her a pint as well. How long had it been since she last ate or drank? This morning when she'd broken her fast? Would they feed her on this journey, or would she die of thirst locked in this miserable chamber?

"Ye're a good hand," said Petey. "Ah, 'tis nectar of the gods for a parched throat."

"Just as long as ye'll do the same for me when my turn comes round."

"Ye know I will."

The man who must be Ricky snorted. "I'll remember ye offered."

"Do ye reckon the captain will give us our share of the plunder once we arrive in Jackson's Hell?" asked the guard.

Divana turned her ear to the conversation. Is that where they were taking her? Jackson's Hell? *Vane's hidden island.*

"If he doesn't, 'e'll have a mutiny on his 'ands."

"I reckon ye're not wrong." Petey's sinister chuckle rumbled through the timbers. "What do ye aim to do with your share?"

"Find me a woman—one with a big, round backside."

The guard belched. "Too right, and udders large enough to bury my face in."

"What about the bit o' muslin right 'ere?" asked Ricky. "She mightn't be as buxom as I like, but a fellow could lose 'imself in all that red hair. Why not let me slip inside for a poke?"

"Not unless ye want to face Vane's cutlass. 'E said the wench was 'is, the bastard."

Hissing through clenched teeth, Divana pushed her back flush against the wall. She swore on the graves of her parents that if any vile brigand touched her, she'd bite a chunk of flesh out of his face. But no matter how much she vowed to fight, the hollowness stretching in her chest refused to stop. She rocked in place, trying not to cry.

"Do ye reckon Cameron will come after 'er?" asked Ricky.

"'E's set to inherit, is 'e not?"

"That's what Dubois said—but that French bastard speaks out of both sides of his mouth."

"Then what would Cameron want with a lass who dresses like a cabin boy and talks like she comes from the gutter?"

"Dunno, mayhap she's a tigress between the linens."

"Mayhap she's the daughter of a duke. Why else would she be dressed like a lad?"

"Do ye reckon she's feignin' an accent?"

Divana bit her lip to keep herself from shouting the truth. What if they thought she was highborn? Would she still be sold? Aye, most likely. They surely wouldn't return her to the *Lady Heather* and apologize.

"One thing's for certain," said Petey. "Cameron will chase after the wench if she is 'ighborn."

"I'll wager Vane is bankin' on it. Then we'll flank him and blast his brig out of the sea when he crosses through the narrows."

No!

Divana pushed to her feet and paced. Saint Columba, Kennan mustn't come for her now. He'd be sailing straight into a trap. Destroyed by Jackson Vane once again. The entire crew would be lost—Kennan, Runner, Lachie Mor…Bending forward, she nearly heaved.

No, no, no! They'll all be killed if they try to come after me.

Besides, those brigands were closer to the truth than they realized. Her affair with Kennan was fleeting at best. No matter how much she wanted to believe he loved her, his heart was duty-bound. When they returned to Scotland, he'd have no choice but to find a highborn lass to wed, and push Divana away while he and the future "Her Ladyship" raised bairns in the castle.

She hid her face in her palms while she tried to will away her tears. This was no time to turn into a simpering maid. She was alone again, and only her wits would see her through this nightmare.

The lock screeched, making her jolt.

"Come, wench," barked the guard. "Vane is asking for ye."

Throwing her shoulders back, Divana clenched her fists at her sides. "Whyever would he be keen to see the likes of me?"

A wicked grin spread across the brigand's whiskered face. "He's a man, is he not?"

She gulped.

The wretched guard stepped into the tiny chamber. "Will ye come on your own two feet or must I toss ye over me shoulder?"

Somehow, Divana managed to sweep past him. "Do not touch me."

"Oy, ye think ye're miss 'igh and mighty, do ye now?"

She said nothing and followed him through the middeck.

"Ye'd best face it, the life ye may 'ave 'ad afore is gone. If ye defy anything the captain wishes, 'e'll feed ye to the sharks. And there are monsters around these parts as big as the *Silver Mermaid* 'erself—swallow ye with one gulp, they will."

Divana wished Petey would stop talking as they climbed the steps aft. The wind blew a gale as they stepped onto the main deck, forcing her to cling to the rail before they proceeded in through the corridor leading to the officers' cabins.

Once she was announced, the guard unbound her wrists and pushed her inside, then slammed the door behind her. Again, Divana jolted with the noise. She tightly gripped her arms across her midriff as Vane looked up from his writing table, looking every bit as sinister as he had on the beach.

The ship pitched, making her lose her balance. After a stutter step, she bent her knees and surfed with the rocking. A storm was brewing for certain.

Vane's cabin was smaller than Kennan's with an enormous four-poster taking up half. Lanterns creaked, swinging from the rafters. Trunks with crosses and symbols carved into dark wood lined the walls. She craned her neck to peer inside an open one.

Undaunted by the shouts coming from the helm above, Vane poured a dram from a flagon into a stout pewter cup before he spoke. "A tot of rum?"

Divana rubbed her outer arms. "I've nay eaten since dawn. Rum would serve me no good at all at the moment."

He grabbed a bunch of grapes from a plate and tossed them at her. "Eat." He poured a second dram. "Then drink."

She plucked a grape and chewed, filling her mouth with tart sweetness. Unable to help herself, she plucked an entire handful and shoved it into her mouth, then wiped the juice from her chin with the back of her hand.

"Good?" he asked.

She swallowed, unwilling to admit they were delicious. "Where are you taking me?"

"We call it Jackson's Hell—"

"Your den of thieves."

"Not exactly." His black eyes watched her as he swigged his rum, while the ship continued to sway to and fro, the howl of the wind growing. "When we arrive I expect to meet Captain Finnes. He sailed under my command until he grew wealthy enough to purchase his own ship."

Divana feigned a spit. "A slaver—a man with no soul."

Vane pushed his chair back and strolled up to her— too close. She stepped away, but he caught her by the hair. "Easy, wench. I'm not planning to hurt you." He pulled her tresses to his nose and inhaled. "Sweet nectar of womanhood. Finnes will pay thrice for an untouched redheaded woman."

"Then you'll be sorely disappointed." She tugged away, but he held fast, making her roots sear. She clapped her fingers to her scalp. "Release me."

"Has Cameron bedded you?"

How dare he! "You're a vile pig!"

Snorting, he pulled harder while he slid a hand over her breast and cupped it, his eyes filled with malice. "Haste not, sweeting."

She thrust her shoulder forward, knocking his arm away. "Keep your filthy fingers to yourself."

He chuckled. "I think I have my answer."

She pursed her lips tightly together as she skirted his writing table. "Sir Cameron will not come for me."

"Hmm. You are unconvincing." Vane sauntered forward. "Why were you dressed as a lad?"

"I stowed away. Sir Kennan thought the disguise necessary to keep me safe."

"From the men or from him?"

Casting her gaze downward, Divana covered her cheeks with her palms, praying her face would not betray the love she harbored for Kennan.

"Honestly I care not whether he follows us, but I reckon he will."

He cannot! "Why?"

"You tell me." He drummed his fingers atop some sort of ledger. "Why would Cameron protect a stowaway? Aye, you are a pretty girl, aside from the faint scarring on your cheek."

Divana covered the marks as she stared at the document beneath his fingertips. At the top, it read *The Silver Mermaid — Contents of the Hull*. "I-I do not ken what ye mean."

"Or have you become his dalliance?"

A lead ball dropped to the pit of her stomach. Did the pirate suspect the worst? "I wanted an adventure is all."

Vane rapped his knuckles on the document, then planted his large palm over the writing. "A woman? Wishing to sail the high seas and risk life and limb, let alone courting scurvy? Was your family unkind?"

Still staring, she read the list above his fingers— *2000 silver pieces of eight, 1 chest of gold, 50 barrels of rum, bolts of silk, tapestries* ... It had to be a complete manifest.

"I believe I asked you a question," Vane demanded, his palm covering the rest.

"Ah…my family is dead. All died of smallpox, save me."

The black-bearded brigand shrank as he moved away from the table. "Recently?"

She read another entry—*sixty barrels of tobacco*. "Would my scars be so faint if I still had the sickness?"

"I reckon not." Vane's stance relaxed while he snatched the parchment from his table and rolled it up. "When we reach Jackson's Hell, you need to look like a woman."

He marched over to one of his trunks and pulled out a burgundy gown and tossed it at her. "Put this on."

"Here?"

"Aye here, and if you continue to ask questions, I'll rip your shirt and breeches off your scrawny body myself."

She clutched the dress to her chest. "Then turn your back."

"I think not. I need to know exactly what I'm selling."

"You will not..." She cast her gaze to the bed, making her tense all the more. Dear Lord, what if he tried to force her?

"Only if you defy me." He rubbed a hand across his loins, one corner of his mouth twisting upward. "If you were truly a lad, preserving your virtue might be another matter."

He liked to violate lads? Such a thought did nothing to calm her. Divana quickly removed her shirt, but as she pulled the dress over her head, he grasped the damask and tugged it from her grip. "Remove the bounds from your breasts."

Divana crossed her arms over her chest. "But I have no stays."

"Fie," he cursed, marching back to the trunk and rummaging through it. He held up a set of stays. "These ought to suffice, though the woman I stole them from was a bit larger."

"You stole a woman's stays?"

He shrugged, seeming oblivious when the ship pitched so far to port, Divana was thrown against the wall. "She no longer had need of them—met her end in a watery grave."

Laughing, he shoved the garment into her hands. With a rustle of fabric, she turned her back, trying to keep her balance. "Then what they say is true. You care not if you murder women and children."

"Only those who defy me." He approached so near, his acrid breath felt like steam against her nape. "Let that be a warning to you. Never defy me, or you will meet your end—I give you my solemn oath."

He rocked with the ship's sway as if he'd been bolted to the floorboards, breathing like a dragon while she unwound the length of linen from her breasts. As soon as the cloth fell to the deck, he grabbed her shoulder and whipped her around, forcing her wrists apart. "Imagine that, love. There's more there than I would have thought."

She wrenched away and crossed her arms over her chest. "Leave me be!"

"Ha! A modest tart, have we?" He sniggered with a sneer. "Carry on, then."

Trembling, she again faced the wall, teetering with the lurch of the ship while she pulled on the petticoats, then began lacing the stays in the front.

"Shift the laces to the back. I'll tie them," he barked. "And hold on to the bedpost for God's sake."

Divana gripped the dark wooden upright, swearing she'd gouge his eyes out with her thumbs if he tried to push her to the mattress. "You'll cinch the breath out of me."

"Remember what I said about defiance?" he said, his voice menacing and surly. "Turn the bloody stays around now, wench."

Gulping, Divana glanced at the man over her shoulder. If he stifled her air, she'd die quickly, and that would be far better than being sold into slavery. But instead, he made quick work of tying the laces—just loose enough to allow her to breathe. "You've done this before."

He scowled. "Sisters."

"You have a family?"

He snorted. "Believe it or not, even men like me were born of mothers—though mine was a whore in baroness's clothing."

So, he was highborn—or illegitimate. "Why did ye have this gown?"

"Never mind the reason. I'm just glad to be rid of it."

By the time he finished with his ministrations, he'd raked a comb through her hair and tied it up with a red ribbon. And when she regarded her reflection in his mirror, the balcony of the brothel in Nassau came to mind. The dress stank of camphor and age, and the bodice clung so tightly to her bosom, it made her breasts swell above the scalloped neckline, adorned with garish yellow lace. Divana was no expert in fashion, but there was no way around it—the gown was cheap, old, and most likely a castoff from a lady of easy virtue.

The ship pitched to starboard so far this time, they both were hurled against the wall.

"Captain!" someone bellowed, banging on the door. "We'll not last much longer!"

Divana looked toward the windows. The night was black as coal, and rain pelted the glass with a deafening torrent.

Vane thrust a finger beneath her nose. "If you value your life, you will stay inside this cabin. 'Tis the safest place on the *Mermaid.*"

As the ship listed, she latched her elbow around the bedpost and held fast while Jackson Vane headed for the storm.

Will I survive this night? God be with Kennan and the Lady Heather!

The half barrel containing the manifest Vane had rolled up toppled. Holding on with one hand, she stretched as far as possible, her fingers grazing the edge of the parchment.

Just a wee bit farther.

Chapter Twenty-Eight

*H*eave to!" Kennan shouted as he cranked the ship's wheel with all his strength. The *Lady Heather* fought him, her timbers groaning as waves crashed over the brig's topsides.

"Are you mad?" bellowed Mr. MacNeil.

Gnashing his teeth, Kennan clutched the wheel, his arms shaking with the force of the resistance. "Sound the order, I say! Else we'll capsize for certain."

A bolt of lightning flashed overhead, immediately followed by a thunderous boom so loud, the sound reverberated in his bones. Kennan blinked to clear the driving rain from his eyes as the boatswain's whistle screeched above the roar of the tempest, giving the order to shift the booms and head directly into the wind.

Damn, damn, damn! Changing course now and heading west would put them off Vane's trail, but it was the only way to save the ship and the lives of his crew.

Once the storm passed, he vowed to navigate every inch of these waters until he found the varlet's hideaway and rescued Divana.

I swear I'll not fail you, lass.

All hands scrambled to shift the booms and change the heading. Groaning like a dragon awakened from a thousand years of slumber, the *Lady Heather* began her turn, the wind and waves pushing her leeward. The ship rolled and listed. Foaming seawater crashed over the starboard side.

A sailor lost his footing and slid across the deck, barely catching himself on the tie-down of one of the skiffs. Kennan's muscles burned as he held fast to the wheel, watching and willing the man to stay put. If any of his crew went overboard in this torrent, he'd be lost forever.

Below, Lachie Mor gripped the rail and pulled himself up to the quarterdeck. "Runner must come down from the crow's nest."

As the ship began to climb a thirty-foot wave, Kennan brought the wheel back to center, casting his gaze upward. But there was no sign of the lad. "God's blood, where is he? Why didn't you order him down when the storm hit?"

"It came on too fast."

The enormous wave crashed over the bow as if the ship were but a twig floating in the rapids of a raging river. If the lad stayed up there, he'd be thrown for certain. "Call him down and send him below decks!"

Lachie cupped his hands to his mouth. "Runner!"

But there was still no sign of the boy.

Mr. MacNeil blew his whistle in a cadence demanding attention.

"Runner!" Kennan bellowed.

The lad finally peered over the edge of the barrel. And Lachie beckoned him down just as a bolt of lightning streaked above the center mast.

"He'll be struck for certain!" bellowed MacNeil.

"Haste ye!" Kennan shouted.

Nodding his understanding, Runner slipped one of his legs over the edge as the ship jolted, heaving portside. With an adolescent cry, the lad lost his grip and plunged to the deck. Jolting to a sudden stop, the boy dangled, caught by the rope around his waist. Runner scrambled for the rigging, but the erratic movement of the ship's mast whipped him from side to side, slamming his body against the wooden barrel of the nest.

Lachie faltered, catching a grab rail before he fell. "He's trapped."

As another rogue wave approached, Kennan turned the wheel right. "Take the helm."

"Och, you're not going up there, are you, Captain?"

"I'll not have anyone else risk their lives." He relinquished the helm to the quartermaster. "Head into the storm—we'll fare better once we've sailed out the other side."

As he headed down the steps, he tore off his soaked doublet and cast it away. A swell of water rushed over his feet as Kennan reached the mainmast. He latched onto the rigging and hoisted himself upward.

The wind's force was enough to carry him to his death if his grip faltered. And it only grew worse as he ascended. Higher, the ship's listing felt ten times more powerful than on deck.

"Hold fast, lad!" He bellowed, peering through the stinging rain.

Hand over hand, Kennan dragged himself upward, fighting with every bit of strength he could muster.

As Runner swung past, the lad stretched out his fingers. "Captain!"

Thank God he was still alive.

Kennan wrapped his elbow and one foot around the rigging and caught the lad's wrist. "I have you."

"I-I'm sorry, Captain. I n-never fall."

"Wheesht, wrap your arms around the ropes. I'll try to untie you."

Moving upward, Kennan clawed at the knot tied at Runner's waist. His wet fingers fumbled. The coarse rope had cinched too tight. "I need to cut it."

The lad's teeth chattered as rain made his face gleam with a sheen of water. "Careful with your blade, sir."

"There's nay other option." Kennan drew his dirk, but rather than wield the knife near the lad, he launched himself into the crow's nest where it would be safer to saw through the hemp. "As soon as you're free, skitter down to the deck! Ye ken?"

"Straightaway, sir."

Wrapping an arm around the mast, Kennan held tight. He sawed his blade back and forth for what seemed like an eternity. Slice after painstaking slice, the rope began to unravel but refused to give way. Just when he thought it would never cut through, all at once it snapped. The lad's body plunged downward with a bloodcurdling scream. But years of climbing the rigging had made Runner strong. He caught himself on the lattice rigging, looking up with a grin that expressed both fear and youthful confidence.

"Go on now!" Kennan bellowed while thunder shook the mast. He, too, needed to descend, but first he took a moment to scan the horizon. Black clouds surrounded them to the east, but to the west, a bit of moonlight lit the gray. As the ship crested a wave, he caught sight of a dark shadow on the water.

A ship? Here?

He swiped the rain from his eyes, but his view was blocked by waves and pelting rain. How far off course had they sailed? They shouldn't come across another ship for leagues unless the vessel had been thrown outside the trade routes. Nonetheless, the churning in Kennan's gut was not to be ignored.

* * *

Divana turned her head away from the bright sunlight as Petey led her onto the main deck. The blackguard had bound her wrists again, leading her with a rope as if she were a goat.

All hands must have come up top, because the sultry air stank with sour male sweat. The sea of pirates looked on with their mouths agape as if they'd never seen a woman in a garish dress before.

Claude Dubois stood beside the captain with an ugly smirk. If only the Frenchman knew how much Vane detested him. Divana had seen the entry in the ship's journal—the captain considered Dubois to be a gluttonous thorn. Aye, he'd been useful in leading Vane to Cameron's treasure, but since, he'd become "expendable." So, Dubois wanted to commandeer a slaver ship? In payment for his informant services, Vane had just the vessel for the snake—one with plenty of rot.

Perhaps 'tis the only decent idea the pirate has ever conceived.

Jackson Vane glared down on them from the raised dais of the helm. "It appears Captain Finnes has been deterred by the storm. Lock her in the pen," he boomed, shifting his gaze across the deck. "Guard the wench around the clock. If any man dares touch her, he'll be shot."

Divana didn't know what revolted her more—being accosted by one of these rank brutes or watching Vane shoot one in cold blood.

"Hasten your step," growled Petey. "I have a thirst."

By all the ale the man had consumed over the past few days, Divana couldn't see why he'd be thirsty. More likely, he just wanted his guard duty to be over with.

The seas had calmed to a gentle roll. The only sign of the ravages from the storm were the piles of seaweed and debris lining the beach. Gulls squawked overhead as they dove and scavenged for food among the rubbish.

Once seated in the skiff, Divana craned her neck, straining around the oarsmen to see the shore. Beyond the turquoise bay and the white sand, small timber and reed dwellings peppered the landscape, each separated by green brush. The isle appeared to be narrow, cutting through the middle of the sea in a wide arc. It wouldn't be easy to spot from a distance because it was flat like a skerry with nary a hill of substance in sight.

A group of women flanked by a few musket-bearing men hastened from the settlement, cheering and waving their arms and weapons, not as if a vile pirate ship had anchored offshore, but...

Divana squeezed her hands, making the bindings bite into her flesh. Of course they were excited. She'd read the manifest. The people on the shore were part of Jacksons's Hell and, from what she'd discovered, every last one of them expected riches. Vane had plenty. He'd left her in his cabin for hours before he returned and sent her back to her prison cell. But she'd not only read the manifest of the *Silver Mermaid*, she'd memorized all the places where Vane kept his plunder and more. As she'd searched the trunks in his cabin, she happened upon a false bottom, finding the map of Jackson's Hell and the tiny string of isles curving northeast, each marked with the location of ships and treasure. She'd taken a slip of parchment and copied it, though in the storm, her writing was blotchy at best.

Divana had folded her parchment and hidden it in her bodice—right before Jackson Vane pushed through the door and ordered the guard to take her away.

After they disembarked and waded through the surf to the beach, Petey dragged her to the rear of the village and locked her in a latticework pen covered by a roof of reeds. She grabbed the rungs and shook the rusty cage. "What's the point of keeping me behind bars when there's no place to run?"

The lout jangled a ring of skeleton keys with a hateful grin. "The captain's nay worried about ye escapin'. 'Tis others sneakin' in 'e doesn't want."

Bearing down with all her might, she shook the cage again. Drat it, the rusty heap was sound enough. Groaning, Divana paced—all of three steps. Her prison was even smaller than the bothy on Hyskeir, with a dirt floor and not a thing to sit upon.

Why hadn't she just told Kennan to leave her on Hyskeir? No, it hadn't been a happy life, but at least she'd been free.

Sliding downward, she sat on the ground, crossing her legs and burying her face in her hands. She silently cried and rocked herself, unwilling to give Petey the satisfaction of knowing the despair clawing at her heart.

And when her tears subsided and her vision cleared, she stared down at a stone—a weighty one nearly as large as her fist.

Chapter Twenty-Nine

*W*e're following that bloody carrack because you have a feeling?" asked Lachie Mor, his voice shooting up.

After the *Lady Heather* came through the storm, Kennan had spotted the ship on the western horizon—and it appeared to have sailed off course by leagues. But there was something about it he couldn't put his finger on—a feeling he'd never be able to explain to either one of his officers.

"Aye, and if we hadn't trusted my gut when we were sailing off Hispaniola, we wouldn't have plundered the silver."

The quartermaster gave the wheel a slight turn. "Oh, to have our reward end up in Vane's sticky web."

Kennan peered through his spyglass. The ship was not only sitting low in the water, she flew no colors. "She's tacking north."

"That would be right. Heading north to marry up with the trade route to the Americas, I'd reckon."

"Mayhap you're right." Kennan's gut clenched. He'd swear on his life that ship was up to no good. And if his intuition was worth a farthing, that vessel wasn't lost. The heavy-built carrack waited out the storm, and once it passed, she unfurled her sails as if she knew exactly where she was heading, and it wasn't in the direction of the trade routes. "Follow her northward until I give the signal to turn east. I don't want them thinking we're on their tail."

"The signal? From where?" asked Lachie Mor.

Kennan pointed up to the crow's nest. "Your belly-aching has given me enough cause to go up for a better view."

"Runner can tell you what he sees. He has the youngest eyes, after all."

"Perhaps." Kennan tucked his spyglass into his belt. "But my eyes have the better experience. Not to mention I'm nay about to lose another ship and crew."

Lachie Mor knew the perils as well as Kennan. They were sailing uncharted waters—seas infested by priva-teers and pirates. Aye, he'd sailed under the same guise as well, but he'd never ventured outside the shipping lanes this far north of Hispaniola.

The crew on deck heckled him with a few choice phrases.

"Don't slip, Captain!"

"Tell us how the weather is up there."

Kennan replied with a vulgar flick of his fingers, bring-ing on a round of raucous laughter. Though he didn't manage to crack a smile. He'd never smile again until he found Divana. All the gold in the world didn't amount to half her worth.

It was his fault she'd been taken. Disguising her as a cabin boy had done nothing to keep her from the vultures.

And it is all my bloody fault.

Reaching over the crow's nest barrel, Runner offered his hand. "What are ye doing up here, Captain?"

"Thought I'd get a better look at that carrack before we tack east."

"We're tacking east?"

He gave the lad a wink. "I wouldn't want her to think we're following, now would I?"

Kennan opened his spyglass and trained it on the ship. "Have ye been able to make out her name?"

"Nay, we haven't been close enough."

"Ye may have eagle's eyes, lad, but it would be a mite more convenient if you had eagle's wings as well."

"Aye, sir." Runner chuckled. "I'll be sure to request a pair of wings in my prayers this eve."

Kennan panned the spyglass west and east of the vessel. "I'd be careful with that—God might mistake your request for angel's wings."

The boy chuckled. "May I ask a question, sir?"

"You may."

"Will we find her?"

A lead weight sank to the pit of his gut while Kennan turned the barrel to improve the focus. If only there were a stack of Bibles handy, he'd give his solemn oath right here and now. "You'd best believe it. If it takes the next decade, I'll not lose her to those bastards."

"Well, I reckon I'll stay with ye."

Kennan thought better than to ask the lad if he had feelings for Divana. Who wouldn't? She was selfless and funny and bonny. When she smiled, not only did the room fill with sunshine, everyone's hearts overflowed with happiness as well.

He blinked, refocusing the spyglass yet again. "She's heading to that speck of land yonder."

Runner leaned out over the barrel. "Land, sir?"

"Dead ahead." He squinted, straining for a better look. "Two specks."

"Side by side?"

"Aye, and a good place for an ambush."

Runner shaded his eyes. "I can't see a bloody thing."

"You'll see it before Lachie Mor turns the ship." Kennan held out the spyglass, looking the lad in the eye. "This was a gift from my da, and if it should break, it will be sorely missed."

"Holy bloody Mary." Runner turned the telescope over in his hands. "'Tis a fine piece, sir."

"Keep your eye on that ship—and the land yonder. I'll man the helm and sail as close as possible without alarming the carrack. After we've given the appearance of sailing past, I want a full report of everything you've seen."

* * *

It took less than a day to circumnavigate the islands. Once they had sailed north, Runner reported two ships in addition to the carrack moored in the natural harbor between the two isles.

And Kennan knew in his bones this den of thieves was inhabited by Jackson Vane. It took every ounce of control he possessed not to sail straight through the narrows with cannons blazing. The only thing that kept him away was knowing the snake expected him to do so. Vane hadn't stayed alive all this time not to post big guns at opposing sides of the inlet that were powerful enough to sink intruders. And shallows on the north side prevented any ship from mounting a northerly attack. Aye, the blackguard had found himself a sea fortress, and the only possible way for Kennan to save Divana was to hold on to his wits and outsmart the devil.

He tried not to dwell on what the bastard might be doing with the bonny lass. But every time he closed his eyes, he saw her face. Why had they taken her and not him? The lass had never done anything to hurt a soul, yet most of her life had been fraught with misery. She'd been raised so poor, her family couldn't afford shoes. When she fell ill and needed mercy, her clan had sent her to Hyskeir to die. But no one could bring Divana Campbell to her end. She was a fighter from the top of her luxurious red locks to those tough feet that hated shoes. She deserved to be put on a pedestal and worshipped. She deserved to be queen of the high seas and have all those bloodthirsty bastards kiss her bare toes.

God, he missed those toes. Her smile, her teasing, her presence in his chamber. Kennan hadn't allowed himself to consider what life might be like without her. However, now the thought terrified him to his core. She'd become a part of him—a far better part. He loved her more than the sea, his ship, and his every worldly possession. Bugger clan alliances and Lochiel's expectations. If he must search the rest of his life, he would find Divana and make her his wife and then face his father's ire.

God save him, Divana meant more to Kennan than the very clan he was born and bred to lead.

Before he climbed down the *Lady Heather*'s portside rigging to the waiting skiffs, he grasped Lachie Mor's shoulder. "MacNeil and his crew ought to be moving into place on the western isle." They'd seen no sign of habitation on the smaller side, so Kennan had sent a party of men to take the cannons there. "I'm allowing myself three hours to reach the cannons on the eastern side. Once I give the signal, sail through. If you're fired upon, fire back, but I'm guessing the battle will be ashore—that's where I expect our gunners to set their sites."

The quartermaster gave a wink. "We'll blast them off the island."

"I need your sword as much as your cannons. When you do fire, make sure it is not aimed at any of my crew, including Divana Campbell."

"Aye, aye, sir. I'll do my best to shoot only pirates."

"Good man."

Though the sea was calm and the skiff's crossing smooth, Kennan still clamped his jaw so tightly, his teeth ached by the time they stood on the shore. Sixteen men faced him. "We're heading around the southern tip single file. Affix bayonets and have your muskets charged. If you fire your weapon, everyone on the island will ken we're here. This is the battle of your lives, men. Aye, 'tis said Vane's treasure is vaster than the queen's coffers. Remain vigilant and you will survive to enjoy the spoils!"

Kennan led the way, passing a wherry tucked behind the rocks. "It looks as if there might be someone about. Step lightly."

The scrub grew thicker as they traveled inland. Each man in the queue had his assigned checkpoint—Kennan took the nose, sweeping his musket from side to side. At his right flank, the man guarded the right quadrant and the next in line took the left and so on down the line, with the rear man sweeping the scene behind.

A flicker of movement ahead made him stop. Pressing his hand downward, Kennan signaled for everyone to drop. Grunting came from beyond. The brush in front of him rustled.

His heart hammering in his ears, Kennan set his musket aside, rose to his knee, and drew his dirk. If he had to kill a man, he damned well would do it without waking the dead.

Footsteps grew louder, snapping twigs.

Kennan tightened his grip on his hilt, readying himself to spring with deadly force. With a booming snort, a wild pig barreled straight into his path, followed by a mob of sows and piglets. But once the boar spotted him, the swine stopped and squealed, stamping its front feet.

"Off with you," Kennan growled, baring his teeth.

The boar shook his head and backed off, then led his mob on a different trail.

"Holy hellfire," said Cuthbert from behind him. "I nearly shite meself."

Kennan smirked over his shoulder, imagining their entire mission being foiled by a passel of hogs. He wiped a hand across his mouth and collected his musket as he stood.

It took about an hour to reach the base of a small crag, right behind the narrows. Kennan took three of his best fighting men and ascended the rocks. Taking cover behind an enormous boulder, he peered out over the promontory. Just as he suspected, five enormous blackened iron cannons stood pointed at the inlet. And two of Vane's guards sat atop one of the barrels.

"'Tis a boon Captain Finnes sailed in today," said a pirate. "I can smell the pork roasting from 'ere."

"I can smell the women."

Dirk in his fist, Kennan motioned for Cuthbert to follow. Silently, they crept behind the cannon.

One of the guards emitted an ugly laugh. "Nothing better—rum, a good meal, and a saucy wench moaning beneath me."

With a burst of speed, Kennan reached over the cannon's barrel and slit the throat of one pirate while Cuthbert did the same.

Kennan stood and wiped his blade on his victim's shirt, the bile churning in his gut over what he'd heard. "Finnes is a notorious slaver. Word is he used to sail under Vane until he bought his way out. No wonder he's here."

The sailor sheathed his weapon. "Do you think Vane's planning to sell Davy?"

Kennan cringed. He hadn't told the crew about Divana's disguise. "The lad's a lass. I had her dress as a cabin boy for her protection."

"Och, we all kent that, sir. We just reckoned ye didn't want us to know ye'd fallen in love with her."

"I beg your pardon?"

"Are ye planning to marry Miss Divana?"

Good Lord, how long had they known? The only person he'd been fooling was himself. "Hold your tongue. We've only managed step one of the plan. We mightn't make it through till dark and you're yammering about bloody weddings?"

"Sorry, sir."

Kennan pulled out his spyglass and spotted MacNeil and the team across the way. The boatswain used his hands to signal that they were off to cross the sandbank to the north as planned. Panning the glass out to sea, Kennan spotted the *Lady Heather* making her turn. He used the sun to make a flash that would be seen by Lachie Mor and Runner in the crow's nest. She'd be crossing through the straits within the hour.

And when she did, Kennan and his band of men would be ready to pounce.

Chapter Thirty

*D*ivana stood against the rear wall of her prison and stared at Dubois, Vane, and the master of the slave ship, Captain Finnes, an older, portly man. The buttons on his waistcoat strained over his rounded belly. Atop his head he wore a tricorne with gold cording. Muttonchop whiskers sprouted on the sides of his face, and his jowls flapped when he talked.

And at the moment, Finnes eyed her from head to toe with a hardened glare. "She's untouched, you say?"

"I am convinced of it." Vane leaned his shoulder against the cage. "Besides, who gives a damn? She looks pure, and that's what will matter when she's standing on the auction block."

"The bidding will turn rabid," said Dubois, rubbing his pudgy hands. Of course he'd say anything if it meant he'd have a chance to ruin Kennan.

Finnes beckoned with his fingers. "Move closer, girl. I want to see what I'm purchasing."

Divana gripped her arms across her midriff and shook her head. "I'll never yield to the likes of ye."

Vane drew his musket and aimed it at her heart. "Move your feet, wench, else I'll put a ball of lead in your belly," he said, his face bearing the grin of the devil. "'Tis a slow death, being shot in the gut. Painful as well."

Clenching her arms tighter, she inched forward to the sound of Claude Dubois's snigger. She leered at the Frenchman. "How's the gap in the front of your smile feeling? I never kent Sir Kennan was so efficient with a pair of tongs."

"Tais-toi!" Dubois swung a slap through the bars, but she was faster, ducking away from his reach. "Your arrogant beau is not long for this world. And I'll have the last laugh whilst I watch his woman being sold to a malicious master."

Divana opened her mouth to issue a retort, but Finnes reached in with the speed of an asp and gripped her chin. Hard. He forced her head from side to side. "She's marked. They won't pay a premium for that."

Vane tugged the bow from her hair, making it fall about her shoulders. "They will when they see her red tresses. How often do you find hair as lustrous as burnished copper. Just look at how it glistens in the sun."

"Hmm." Finnes released his grip. "The hair will help, but 'tis too short. I'll give you sixty pounds."

"Sixty?" Vane asked incredulously. "She's worth twice that."

"On the block, mayhap, but what about my profits? And I'm the one who has to feed the wench."

Divana skittered against the wall, jamming her fists into her hips. "Stop talking as if I'm nay here."

"Your life isn't yours," growled Dubois. "And 'twill never again be."

Vane smirked and shoved Captain Finnes in the arm. "Come, let us discuss the terms over a tankard of ale."

Shuddering, she watched them walk away. Dubois lasciviously flicked his tongue at her before he followed.

"It appears as if you'll be leaving this fine establishment soon," said Petey, laughing at himself. "At least ye'll be off my 'ands. I only regret I won't be there to watch when they sell ye into bondage. Ye won't be so 'igh and mighty then, will ye?"

Divana spat on the ground—wishing she was unmannerly enough to spit in his face. She absolutely could not leave Jackson's Hell with Captain Finnes. If she smacked Petey with a rock, she might escape her cage, but then where would she go?

"When is your next adventure?" she asked, trying to sound civil. The more she knew about Vane's plans, the better.

"Why would ye care?"

"Why did ye become a pirate?" she countered.

"Ye ask too many questions."

"Och, Vane and his pirates have stolen a king's ransom. Why continue to plunder?"

Petey rubbed his loins. "Coin is made round to go around. The merchants earn it, we take it—spend it on women, gambling, and drink. Once it's gone, 'tis time to find another victim."

Ye wretched, lawless scoundrel.

"Is that what happened with the plunder from Captain Cameron's ship?" she asked.

The blackguard smacked the cage door, making it rattle. He drew a dagger and clanged it between the bars. "Shut your bloody gob, or I'll cut out your flappin' tongue."

Divana turned her back, the walls closing in around her. This was the end. If she didn't do something, she'd never see Kennan again. Such a notion was unthinkable. Captain Finnes would be sailing on the morrow or the day after. She had no more time. Making her decision, she tapped the rock with her toe. Come dark, she'd make her escape—and then she'd improvise. Now all she must do was bide her time.

But when the blast of cannons shook the ground, she gripped the bars and looked toward the sound. Her pulse raced. Her breath swelled in her chest as one thought consumed her mind. *Kennan!*

"What the—" said Petey. He hopped to his feet and gaped in the direction of the blast.

Moving like a cat, Divana tugged the slingshot from beneath her skirts and scooped up the rock. It took one forward lunge to slip her arm out the latticework and hurl the stone straight at the base of Petey's skull. The brigand dropped to his knees and froze for a moment, near enough for Divana to reach the keys on his hip—right before he fell on his face.

Muskets cracked above the shouts of men while the cannons continued to boom. Whoever had come to do battle was an enemy of Jackson Vane and thus a friend of hers.

* * *

A fly landed on Kennan's nose while he hid in the brush, waiting for his chance to attack. Blowing upward, he didn't dare swat the annoying insect away. The mosquitoes and midges were sucking his blood like vampires as well, yet one errant twitch might draw the attention of the black-guards only paces away. Gulls screeched overhead while the hammer from a smithy shop clanged.

Laughter came from the center of the village, if a man could denote such a civilized name to this mishmash of run-down huts. Though he'd oft been called a pirate, Kennan had never considered himself low enough to be one. Not like these disgusting louts. They were lazy, rank barbarians without a scruple among them.

Kennan's sweaty fingers slipped on the oiled steel of his musket. He scanned the positions of his men. All were ready. Even MacNeil's party had moved into place, each one of them dying to scratch the welts forming on any exposed skin.

Where the hell are you, Lachie Mor?

The thought had barely skimmed through his mind when the blessed sound of cannon fire reverberated across the isle.

Pushing to his feet, Kennan raised his musket to his shoulder and took aim. "Fire!"

Crack, crack, crack! The battle began. Stunned pirates darted about the hellhole, grappling for their weapons. Kennan ran forward with his bayonet, taking out a brig-and wielding a pair of flintlocks.

"Reload," he shouted while the *Lady Heather* contin-ued to pummel the shore with cannon fire.

Attacked from the flank, Kennan spun, crashing the butt of the musket into the forehead of his assailant. Drawing his sword, he swung the blade in a figure eight, his gaze darting through the mayhem. *Where is Divana?*

Pulling his dirk, he surged forward, taking on pirate after rotten pirate.

Brigands materialized from nowhere as he battled onward, thrusting with his dirk, defending with his sword. Three men ambushed him head-on, making him blindly step backward. God only knew what was coming from behind.

"I'll send ye to Hades now, Cameron," growled a deep voice. By the hairs prickling on Kennan's nape, he had a fraction of a second to turn. He sliced his sword, driving two away and cutting down a third.

As he spun, he aimed an upward strike to the body of the blackguard behind. Out of the corner of his eye came the glimmer of shiny steel. Time slowed as he bobbed, yet he knew with his next blink he'd feel the cold blade of a pirate sword slice through his flesh. Gnashing his teeth, he fought on, thrusting his dirk into the belly of a murdering fiend. When he sidestepped to take on another, the killing strike didn't come. His foe dropped to the dirt, bleeding from his head.

"Och, I thought ye'd never come!"

The voice at his side was soft and gentle, like none he'd ever heard in battle. And he knew exactly who had saved him.

"Thanks for having my back, lass," he shouted, protecting her from attack, sending another brigand to hell. As the fighting ebbed, Kennan managed to give Divana a wink. "You haven't exactly been easy to find."

She swung her slingshot over her head and released a stone. "Thank heavens for Bannock."

"Miserable dog."

When there was no one left wielding a weapon, Kennan pulled Divana into his arms and kissed her. "Are you all right, lass? Did they harm you?"

"Only me pride."

She was warm and wonderful, and though she'd been through a terrible ordeal, sunshine radiated around her. "Thank God." If only he could hold her like this for the rest of his days. "I'm going to take you back to Scotland and—"

"Haste!" She thrust her finger toward the shore. "Look at the skiff! Dubois is spiriting away with Captain Finnes—the slaver who paid a measly sixty pounds to auction me to the highest bidder."

Kennan grasped her shoulders and held her firm. "Can you keep out of danger?"

"Och nay! I just found ye." She took a cutlass from the ground. "I'm not leaving your side for a single moment."

She grabbed his arm and tugged. Bloody hell, if he left her alone, she'd most likely end up at the wrong end of a pirate's dagger.

"Come, men," Kennan shouted, taking Divana's hand, running for the shore. "Charge your muskets!"

The lass pointed her sword. "They're heading for the carrack."

A handful of his men barreled ahead, muskets in hand.

As they neared, Kennan pulled Divana behind him to keep her from being hurt. "Shoot to kill, men!"

The first man to reach the shore kneeled and took aim. *Crack!*

Claude Dubois clutched his heart and crashed into the water.

The oarsmen quickened their rowing as two more men took aim.

"I call quarter!" bellowed Captain Finnes, throwing up his hands.

Kennan pointed to the skiff. "Bind and gag them all." He turned full circle. "Where is Vane?"

Runner came out of a hut, leading a woman at knife-point. Bless the dog, Bannock was growling at her heels. "He's gone, sir. This woman said he ran off with two of his men."

"Yellow blackguards, the lot of 'em," cackled the wench. "Cap'n always makes everyone do the work whilst he sits back and enjoys the spoils."

The Cameron men led Finnes and his crew onto the beach.

"Hold them here." Kennan took Divana to the skiff. Damn it all, now that he'd found her, he wasn't about to let her out of his sight for a second. "'Tis time to board that carrack and unload her cargo. Mr. MacNeil, come with us."

By the time they boarded the slaver, Lachie Mor had already moved the *Lady Heather* alongside her and had what was left of her crew under arrest. No surprises, they were a downtrodden lot, most likely men who'd come from the jails and had accepted a pittance for pay.

"Are ye aiming to hang Cap'n Finnes?" asked one.

Kennan ignored him. He headed straight for the hold and threw back the hatches.

"Beg your pardon, sir," said one of the crew. "The 'old's empty."

Thank heavens for small mercies. Though he would have freed any captives, it was a blessing to have none aboard.

Still, he eyed the man. "Then why is she sitting so low in the water?"

The man didn't answer.

There was treasure hidden below decks for certain. "Mr. MacNeil, select your crew and sail this heap of worthless timber to Scotland."

"Me, sir?"

"Aye, you. If you're willing."

"Absolutely, sir. Straightaway."

After the plans for MacNeil's voyage were settled, and they were alone on the deck, Divana took Kennan's hand. "We mustn't tarry. I ken where the *Highland Reel* is, and if my guess is right, Jackson Vane is heading there now."

Her words were like heavenly music. He drew the lassie's fingers to his lips, closed his eyes, and kissed her knuckles. "You found my ship, *mo leannan*?"

"I did."

"I've always thought you were astounding, but now there is no doubt. You are the most incredible woman I've ever met."

"Truly?"

"Aye, you amaze me at every turn. You're smart and saucy, and you make me feel as if the sun is always shining in my heart. I love you, Divana. I've been in love with you from the moment I saw you digging for clams on the shores of Hyskeir."

With a catch in her breath, her eyes twinkled. "Ye love me?"

"More than anything."

She grinned, making his heart swell. "I love ye as well, Kennan. More than ye ken."

He kissed her, savoring the moment, running his fingers along silky fabric.

Silky?

"What the blazes is this?" he asked, pinching her sleeve.

She scowled. "Vane's attempt at preparing me for the auction block."

Kennan's gut clenched. He wanted to wrap his fingers

around that varlet's neck so badly, bile burned his throat. "I must go after him. He cannot demean my woman and slip away like a snake."

"Are ye certain about that?" A bit of mischief sparkled in her eyes. "I reckon ye may change your mind."

"Oh?"

She stepped very near and raised her lips to his ear. "When he told me to don this dress, he left me in the captain's cabin. 'Tis a good thing ye taught me to read some, 'cause I pored over his charts. Not only is there a fortune on the *Silver Mermaid*, Vane has treasures hidden up the 'strand of pearls' that make up this chain of isles."

Kennan threw back his head and laughed from his belly. "God, woman, I love you!"

Chapter Thirty-One

*I*n Vane's cabin on the *Silver Mermaid*, Divana spread the charts across the writing table. "This is the map of Jackson's Hell and the Strand of Pearls. See?" She pointed. "He named the two isles at the bottom Hell and Pur-ga-tor-y."

"Have a look at that." Kennan leaned over her, the comfort of his body soothing against her back. "I cannot believe how well you've taken to your lessons." He caressed her neck with a feathery kiss, then gaped at the chart. "Good heavens, the others are named Hades, Satan, Lucifer, and Beelzebub. The varlet must have a preoccupation with the devil."

"He is a devil." Sighing, she leaned against him and unrolled the next chart. "This is the one with the treasure." They'd already found the barrels of tobacco and rum in the hold of the *Silver Mermaid*, but Divana had kept mum about the rest until she and Kennan were behind closed doors.

"He's been hoarding his riches. He gives his men and those who support him in Jackson's Hell only enough to keep them happy—but never enough to make them rich. And he has jewels and coin hidden all along the Strand of Pearls."

More of Kennan's kisses caressed her neck. "And I'll reckon you can tell us where to find it."

She beamed, pulling a slip of parchment from beneath her bodice. "I copied his chart, but now we're aboard Vane's ship, I don't reckon we need me scratchings." She moved to the chest filled with treasure. "And have a wee peek in here."

"My God, gold ingots, doubloons, reales." Kennan scooped a handful of plunder. "There's enough here for him to start his own country."

Divana took a coin and let it drop, clinking atop the others. "If he hadn't made enemies of all the nations in Christendom."

"This is stupendous. Every single man in the crew will be wealthy beyond their wildest imaginings."

Divana's shoulders tensed. She'd been captured and nearly sold into slavery...and before that she'd suffered on Hyskeir. Bless it, 'twas time to stand up for herself. Besides, everyone knew her secret now. Moreover, Ethan had been assigned to the *Silver Mermaid*, and if that man caught wind of the size of Vane's plunder, he might attempt mutiny and keep it all for himself.

"There's something of grave import I must tell ye straightaway." She twirled out from Kennan's embrace and faced him. "One of the men threatened me when we were sailing from Scotland."

"One of *my* men?"

"Aye, hired by Lachie Mor in Glasgow."

Kennan's jaw took on a hard line. "Which one?"

"Ethan. He said he kent me secret and he'd tell all the crew if I did not give him me share of the plunder."

Rage flashed through the braw Highlander's eyes. "He threatened this and yet you said nothing to me?"

"If I had, he would have told everyone I was really a lass—a-and when I asked him what he'd do if there was no prize, he said he'd incite a mutiny."

"The bloody scoundrel. And I discovered everyone kent your true identity all along. The only person we fooled was me." Kennan adjusted his sword belt and headed for the door. "I'll rearrange his priorities."

"Wait!" Divana dashed ahead and blocked his path. "Ethan said he has allies who support him—what if they band together? Are ye certain ye want to face him this night?"

Kennan groaned, scratching the stubble on his chin. "Mayhap it would be best to wait until we drop anchor off Hades. I can think of no better place for the swindler to spend a year or two pondering his lot."

Her hips swayed as she stepped into him and cupped his face in the palm of her hand. "Ye are a wise man, Sir Kennan."

"All wise men are inspired by wiser women," he whispered as he moved his lips closer to her ear.

Divana closed her eyes, releasing an enormous sigh as he slid his fingers around her waist. "Och, I feared I'd never see ye again."

His arms felt like heaven, even if they were sailing through the isles of Hell. "If I had to spend the rest of my life searching, I wouldn't have given up. God, you are my world."

Her heart swelled so much it nearly burst. "I ken ye

cannot marry me, but I love ye with my heart and soul. It drives me to the brink of madness to think that one day ye'll belong to another."

"No." He grasped her shoulders firmly and focused his gaze on her eyes. "I will marry you this night. The Highland way, if you'll have me."

"But what about your da—your clan and kin?"

"If they do not love you as I do, then they can all join Vane in hell." He dropped to his knee and took her hand gently between his large palms. "Divana Campbell, I ken in my heart there will never be another woman as caring, smart, brave, or as bonny as you. I beg you as a man to accept me with all my imperfections. Please, please, please, will you be my wife?"

Good glory, perhaps this was all a dream. Perhaps she'd died and gone to heaven. She might believe it if his hands weren't quite so warm. A tear spilled from her eye. "Ye—ye want to marry me?" she whispered. "Are ye certain? But what about your da?"

"I've never been surer about anything in all my days, and no one's opinion matters except yours." He squeezed her hand. "Say yes. I'll give you my solemn oath as our forefathers did, and once we reach Scotland, we'll have the grandest wedding you've ever dreamed of."

"Aye. I will marry ye, and none other—but I need no grand wedding, I only need your love."

"And you have it." In one powerful motion, Kennan rose and swept Divana in his arms. "This day when we join as one, I will be claiming you as my wife in the eyes of God."

"And ye will be mine for all of eternity?" she asked, her head swimming as he rested her on the bed.

She lay very still and watched her brawny Highlander

remove his belt, shoes, stockings, and shirt, and at long last, away fell his kilt. Never in her life would she grow tired of gazing upon his naked form. He was hard and sleek and desirable beyond anything she'd ever imagined.

Nestling into the crisp linen pillows on the pirate bed, Divana raised her arms to him. It didn't matter where they were, only that they were together, pledging their love for the rest of their days. "This time I want your seed to spill inside me."

As he kneeled over her, a low chuckle rumbled from his throat. "'Tis the only way to seal the bond." He urged her to roll to her side. "But first we need to rid you of this hideous gown."

"'Tis nicer than the rags I wore on Hyskeir."

Unraveling the laces, he nibbled her neck, making gooseflesh rise across her skin. "I'll buy you gowns of silk in every color you desire."

He pulled the bodice away and tsked his tongue. "Stays as well?" he asked, sounding disappointed.

"What did ye expect? Aren't all lassies supposed to wear stays? That's what Mistress Barton says."

"Does she now?" Deftly, he unlaced and cast them to the floor. "Not to worry, *mo leannan*. Taking a wife should never be done in haste."

By the time he'd finished removing every last stitch of clothing, pausing between each garment to kiss and caress the multitude of sensitive places on Divana's body, her flesh was steaming and tingling with want. Eager to have him beside her, she patted the mattress. "Are ye certain ye do not want to be just a wee bit hasty?"

Kennan joined her and smoothed his fingertips around her nipple. "Och aye, I want you to soar among the stars." He slid the pad of his thumb down the center of her body, stopping when he reached the patch of red curls. "Shall I go further?"

Her tongue tapped her top lip as Divana nodded. "Ye ken I want ye to."

His eyes grew dark as his finger skimmed the sensitive button and swirled into her moisture. It took but a few strokes to make her breathing ragged. Down and up, down and up, he teased with each stroke of his finger.

"Open," he growled, encircling the tiny nub that always drove her mad.

She thrust her body toward him, her need already ravenous. "But—"

He pushed inside her, making slow, leisurely, torturous circles. "Wheesht."

Needing more, Divana moved in tandem with his devilish strokes. "I need ye now."

"Soon."

His thumb brushed her while his finger continued to work inside, each swirl making the pleasure coil inside her, tighter and tighter. Her heart raced as her desire ratcheted higher.

Grasping his muscular shoulders, she bore down and tugged him over her. "Och, I said now, Kennan!"

"Now?" he asked, laughter shining in his eyes.

"Aye. If ye want to be me husband, ye'll take me now, ye brawny fiend!"

A low growl rumbled through his throat as he licked her breast. "Fiend?"

"Ye ken what I mean, ye're torturing me."

He rose slightly and slid his member along her channel. "Is this what you've been asking for?"

With a saucy grin of her own, she reached between them and grasped him, guiding his hard shaft to her entrance. "The question is, are ye ready for me? 'Cause I'm feeling like a wildcat."

"I like that—you wild island sprite." He kissed her lips, her jaw, her neck. "Have I wooed you enough, *mo leannan*? Have I proved my worth?"

She writhed beneath him. "Any more wooing and I'll go mad."

Kennan's entire body shuddered as he slipped inside, his eyes growing glassy. "Dear God," he gasped. "There is no closer place to heaven than when I'm inside you."

Divana sank her fingers into his bum and tugged until he was buried to the hilt. "Lord have mercy, it feels like home."

He grinned, moving slowly, just as his finger had done. "Aye." His voice strained. "Wherever we may be in this world, we're always home in each other's arms."

She drew in a stuttered breath, tears stinging the back of her eyes. No more words came between them while Divana stared into the gaze of the only man she had ever loved—the man who had enchanted her from the day he came ashore and burst into her wee bothy. He was braw and rugged, and he was hers for the rest of their days.

And as they focused upon each other, the mounting pleasure he'd begun with his fingers inched higher with her every breath. Squeezing him tightly, she dictated the tempo, her breath coming in short gasps. "Faster," she whispered.

Kennan bared his teeth as he growled, his eyes growing more intense. "Be my bride! Say it."

The power of their love surged between them, forming a bond that would bind them for eternity. "I will be your wife forever and ever."

He dropped forward onto his elbows, thrusting into

her deeper and faster than ever before. "Then I am your husband. We are man and wife, and no one but God can separate us."

With his words, his seed pulsed into her, the intensity of his love taking her over the edge of oblivion. Thrusting her head from side to side, Divana soared to new heights far above the crow's nest on the *Lady Heather*. She shattered, sailing through puffy white clouds, clinging to her man.

After their breathing ebbed, Kennan cupped her face, his eyes glistening with happiness. "I love you more than anything in this world."

She slid her fingers up his back, the ridges of his scars reminding her of how much they had endured to make their fairy tale come true. "And I love ye—but then ye ken how much I do."

"But I'll never tire of hearing it, m'lady."

"Lady?" A tear of joy slipped from the corner of her eye. "I like the sound of that."

Chapter Thirty-Two

*C*aptain!" shouted Runner as he pounded on the timbers. "I've spotted the *Highland Reel*."

"I'll meet you on deck, forthwith," Kennan replied before he kissed his wife. "We've arrived sooner than I thought."

Stretching, Divana beamed at him, looking more radiant than sunshine. "Must ye go?"

He retrieved his shirt from the floor and pulled it over his head. "I'd prefer to stay."

"I ken it is an important day—not only because we are wed..." The bedclothes dropped as she slid up against the headboard. "But ye must reclaim your ship."

"Our ship."

"I love the way 'our' rolls off your tongue."

Kennan kissed her again. "I'd prefer it if you stayed abed. There could be fighting."

"And miss all the excitement?"

"If you join me at the helm, I need your word you'll duck inside at the first sign of danger."

She twirled a lock of hair around her finger. "If that is what ye wish."

After he'd dressed, Kennan found Cuthbert at the helm, manning the wheel. "You've come along well these past years. I must commend your courage in capturing Jackson's Hell. I was proud to have you fighting beside me."

"Thank ye, sir."

Runner joined them. "I hope ye don't mind, but I signaled the *Lady Heather* to flank her on portside whilst we take the starboard."

Kennan patted the boy's shoulder. "Good man." Then he returned his attention to Cuthbert. "How would you like to take command of the *Silver Mermaid* on the journey home?"

The young seaman beamed. "'Twould be a dream come true, sir."

"May I act as quartermaster?" asked Runner.

"I can think of no one better, but first we need to take back my ship." Kennan drew his spyglass from his belt. "Hold your course, men."

"Aye, aye, Captain," bellowed the sailors on deck. The air was charged with the excitement from not only the plunder in the hold, but the anticipation of riches yet to come.

Kennan swept his gaze across the faces of his crew. All but one was smiling. All but one man was giving his best. He should have pegged Ethan for a scoundrel sooner. The laggard had never pulled his own weight, and even Kennan had caught wind of an offhanded comment or two.

But he'd deal with the mutineer later. There were bigger fish to catch at the moment. He raised the spyglass to his eye, gazing upon the detail of his beloved ship for the first time since he leaped to the sea months ago.

Aft, he spotted Jackson Vane and two other men cranking the anchor's winch.

Only three?

Kennan made a complete sweep of the deck and saw not a single other man. An abandoned skiff bobbed in the water not far from the ship. He turned the barrel for a better look. Aye, 'twas the same wherry he'd seen when they landed on Jackson's Hell.

Damnation, if it is the last thing I do, I'll chart these isles and rename them.

Within the next half hour, both the *Lady Heather* and the *Silver Mermaid* had tied up either side of the *Highland Reel*.

Vane had moved to the quarterdeck with his men and wielded a pair of flintlocks. "Cast off now, else you'll be the first to die, Cameron."

Thank God that Kennan had convinced Divana to hide in the great cabin.

And because of his wife, he wasn't daft enough to run over and challenge the lout to a duel, no matter how much he wanted to be the one to put a musket ball between Jackson Vane's eyes. He stood proud on the main deck while his men held their posts on either side of the *Highland Reel*. "Throw down, ye bastard. I've a dozen muskets aimed at your heart."

One of the pirates lost his nerve, looking from side to side, the flintlock in his hand trembling. "They'll send us to Hades."

Kennan laughed aloud. "You're already there, ye flea-bitten swine."

The man took aim and fired, the bullet hitting the bulwark above Kennan's head.

With the blast, the men opened fire. Clutching his shoulder, Vane dove behind a barrel as the flash from the muzzle of each pistol ignited.

"Take back the *Reel*!" Kennan shouted, leading the charge across the wooden plank.

The Gaelic cry of the Camerons swelled through the air. "*Aonaibh Re Cheile!*" They shouted to unite, not to divide, not to conquer, but to defend their honor. Those three words meant more to Cameron men than any others.

Kennan raced up the stairs to the quarterdeck, where he'd spent many a day commanding the seas. The two pirates had met their end, but Vane crouched on his knees, clutching a bloody shoulder.

"Lock him in the jail."

"Kill me!" Vane shouted, while droplets of spittle dribbled on his black beard.

So now the tides had turned. Vane was alone, wild-eyed and feral. "Och," said Kennan. "Death would be too good for you."

The pirate captain turned toward the rail, only to be met with the point of Cuthbert's sword. "Then toss me over the side. I'll take my chances."

"Nay. I'm carting you home. If you survive the journey, you'll stand trial on British soil."

"No. Please," Vane begged. "I cannot go back to England."

"England?" Kennan chuckled. "I'll be dumping your bones at Fort William in my beloved Scotland. From there the colonel will most likely grant you a public hanging. You've a month or more to ponder how you'll shite yourself on the gallows whilst Her Majesty's dragoons heckle from the crowd."

When the men led Vane away, Divana approached them midship, a loaded slingshot swinging from her grip. She wore the skirt from the burgundy gown but not the garish bodice. Rather, she'd donned a linen shirt and a leather belt, the ensemble reminiscent of a pirate queen. The wind caught her red tresses and they whipped around her like fire, rendering her a fearsome woman to behold.

Kennan's jaw twitched. Would she cast her stone and end the pirate's life? He wouldn't blame her if she did, even though the man was already condemned.

As Vane passed with guards on either side, she raised her chin and slapped the rock in her palm. "Ye chose the wrong path and soon ye'll meet your end."

Filled with pride, Kennan joined her. "Unfortunate he's injured, else he might sell well on the auction block."

She flicked the slingshot around, catching it in her palm again. "I'd never sell any man into bondage, especially that one."

"Oh?"

"He's a liar, he's crafty and smart, and I've heard tell he'd kill his own mother if it would make him a farthing. Nay, the only place for Jackson Vane is Fort William's gallows—just as ye said."

* * *

Once Vane was in chains below, Kennan gathered his men. "I have an announcement to make." He grasped

Divana's hand and pulled her beside him. "I'd like you all to formally meet my wife, Lady Cameron."

There was an immediate uproar of gasps and laughter, and most every man on deck held forth, blurting out congratulations—except Ethan, of course. Interestingly, the man was standing off by himself. Perhaps the allies he'd claimed stood by him no longer.

Kennan returned his attention to the crowd and held up his hands for silence. "I've asked Cuthbert MacDonald to take command of the *Silver Mermaid* on the voyage home. Baltazar MacGee will act as his quartermaster, and I need at least ten volunteers to man the ship."

A few hands went up, and with a bit of coaxing, Kennan had nine willing seamen. "Come, lads, I need one more."

Of course, Ethan Crowder was the only tar who raised his hand. In fact, the lout appeared rather eager to join the crew of an untried captain. Kennan had planned to deal with the varlet next, but since he was so anxious to draw attention to himself, it was time to face him. "Sailor, I have a special position in mind for you."

The man stepped forward, thumping his chest. "Ye hear that, fellas? Ole Ethan's going to be promoted."

"I'd save your enthusiasm if I were you." Kennan said, beckoning Divana beside him, the act making Ethan's grin disappear.

Before he said another word, he gestured to two trusted Cameron sailors with whom he'd had a wee chat before he'd begun his address. They moved into position behind the scourge.

Kennan grasped Divana's hand. "Lady Divana, did not this man threaten you?"

"Lies!" Ethan shouted as the two men seized his arms.

"Her Ladyship never lies!" shouted Baltazar, bless him.

"Agreed," said Kennan. "Now, dear, as you were saying..."

Divana eyed her accuser. "Aye, Ethan threatened me and ye as well, Captain. Told me if I did not give him me share of the takings, he'd expose me secret."

"And what secret would that be?"

"That I'm a lass and not a lad." She batted her eyelashes and fanned her face. "Now me secret has been revealed, I would be remiss if I did not say this man also threatened to incite a mutiny against ye."

Ethan struggled against his captors. "More lies! The pox on ye, wench! How dare ye smear me good name."

Kennan shifted his fists to his hips. "How many aboard have not heard this man spew bile? I ken he's whispered in your ears about mutiny and he's cheated a few of you at dice as well."

"Aye," came the rumbles from the crowd.

"Ethan Crowder, I deem you guilty as charged. And no longer a member of this crew." Kennan turned to Divana. "Shall I put him in irons and let him keep company with Mr. Vane until the pair of them swing from the gallows?"

"Nay." She looked across to the isle. "Give him a barrel filled with stores and utensils, a few good blankets, and a shove. Then let him ponder his misdeeds in Hades for a time."

The man's eyes grew enormous with fear. "Ye cannot abandon me on a deserted isle. I'll starve!"

"Would you rather swing from Fort William's gallows?" asked Cuthbert.

"'Tisn't so bad especially if ye have a shovel to dig for clams." Divana brushed her fingers on the rail. "After all,

I survived on Hyskeir for two years, and there the winters are fierce and summer lasts but a sennight. Hades would be an improvement over that."

Kennan took her fingers and kissed them. "I reckon you're right, m'lady. Cuthbert, I'll leave it to you to sink the wherry—after all, we cannot make it easy for him to escape."

Would Ethan survive his punishment? Most likely. Eventually a ship would drop anchor off this isle, but whether they saw fit to take him aboard would depend on how well the scoundrel had learned his lesson.

Chapter Thirty-Three

*I*t took three weeks of days with excellent wind to sail back to Scotland. Three weeks of utter bliss. Kennan treated Divana like a queen throughout the entire journey, her every need catered to. She laughed as he balked when she set out to dust the cabin. God forbid she try to pick up a mop or set foot in the galley, lest the captain accuse her of anarchy. After all, she was a lady now—a member of the gentry.

Her trepidation grew after they disembarked at Loch Eil and worsened throughout the hour's ride to Achnacarry. It didn't help that Kennan had grown quiet as well.

"Are ye certain I look presentable?" Divana asked when they rode through the gateway into Achnacarry's courtyard. She smoothed her trembling hands over the skirts of the blue gown Kennan had purchased at the shop in Nassau.

He helped her down from her mount. "You're the bonniest woman within a hundred miles."

She tucked an errant lock of hair beneath her new bonnet and gave him a nervous smile. "Only a hundred?"

Tweaking her nose, he took her hand. "Bonniest in all my travels, I'll say."

Together they climbed the stairs toward the keep. "Let me speak to my father."

"I hope he doesn't cast me out."

"He won't. But if he tries, he'll be casting me out as well."

She gripped his hand as the butler opened the door. "But—"

"Kennan!" bellowed Lochiel, his arms stretched wide. "Och, son, I thought you'd be away for another year at least."

The captain squared his shoulders and faced his father. "We made good time of it for certain, sir."

"And what of Vane?"

"Handed him over to the queen's dragoons after we disembarked."

"Imagine that. My son captured the greatest scourge of the high seas."

"And claimed his fortune." Divana peeked around from behind her husband. "Grand enough to build an empire."

After they'd left Ethan on Hades, they found no fewer than fifteen chests filled with priceless jewels, gold, and silver. They'd given the men generous shares, but only Divana and Kennan knew the extent of the fortune they now possessed. Kennan said he wouldn't be surprised if they were the richest people in Scotland.

Lady Jean came below stairs carrying Adam, her wee son, on her hip. "Och, Divana, we thought you'd gone back to your kin. Cook will be ever so happy to see you. She said the kitchen had fallen into disorder after you left."

Biting her lip, she looked at Kennan. "Ye'd best tell them, else I'll be donning an apron."

"Forgive me." He grasped her hand and clutched it over his heart. "There's so much to say all at once. Most importantly, Divana is my wife."

Everyone in the hall gaped. "What—?" asked Lochiel.

"Before you go off asking questions, allow me to say that we married the Highland way. But for the family, we want a proper wedding just as soon—"

Lochiel raised his palm. "You mean to say you haven't been married in a church?"

"Nay," said Kennan.

"Then the marriage can easily be annulled."

Divana's breath froze in her chest. The backs of her eyes stung. Blast it all, she knew the laird wouldn't want her.

But Kennan gripped her hand tighter. "There will be no annulment. I've a fortune in my coffers, and I've chosen this bonny, smart, and fascinating woman to be my bride. And if you do not accept her, we'll be on our way forthwith."

Lochiel gripped the banister rail. "Just a moment, son. Let us retire to the library and discuss this man-to-man."

"I fail to see what there is to discuss."

"Humor me."

Lady Lochiel gestured to the drawing room. "Divana, perhaps we can chat over a cup of tea."

Rather than follow, she wanted to turn and run, but the determination in her husband's eyes made her stay. "Thank you, m'lady. Tea would be lovely."

Adam stretched out his chubby arms to Divana. "Hug!"

His adorable smile helped ease the tension in the hall, and suddenly the happy bundle was in her arms.

And the kiss Kennan applied to her cheek helped as well. "Go with my stepmother. I'll attend you anon."

Divana followed Her Ladyship and carried the bairn through to the drawing room.

"Please do have a seat."

"Thank you." Divana held the lad out to his mother, but he wrapped his arms around her neck. "Hug!"

"It seems you've won the heart of more than one of Lochiel's sons."

Taking a seat on the settee, Divana propped the lad on her lap. The fireplace where she'd once cleaned on hands and knees shoveling out the ash caught her eye. To be honest, it would be a great deal easier if she were shoveling ash or doing anything aside from worrying about what Kennan's father might be ranting about above stairs.

Mistress Barton brought in the tea service and set it on the low table. "Shall I pour, m'lady?"

"No, thank you. I'll do the honors."

"Very well." The housekeeper curtsied to Divana. "'Tis good to see you again, m'lady."

Adam clapped his hands. "M'lady, m'lady."

Mistress Barton had just acknowledged her title? Saint Columba. Divana hadn't expected a soul at Achnacarry to pay a mind to the fact that she was married to a knight. "Thank ye, mistress. 'Tis lovely to be here."

Lady Lochiel poured. "You must have been on a fantastic adventure. I am so utterly amazed. You simply must tell me everything. How on earth did you convince Kennan to allow you on his ship?"

Divana took the tea, but with Adam toying with the

ribbons on her bodice, she didn't dare drink. She set the cup on the table. "I stowed away."

"A stowaway?" Her Ladyship's expression went from utter shock to keen interest. "Mercy, the plot thickens. Go on, dear. I'm on the edge of my seat. Tell me all."

Starting with being discovered in the galley by Lachie Mor, she felt a great relief in reciting the details of their grand adventure. Though Adam didn't seem to think so. By the time she'd finished, the bairn was asleep in her arms and Her Ladyship had consumed the entire pot of tea.

Fiona came in and lit the lamps. "Good evening."

Divana looked at the lad. "Och, Fiona, if it weren't for the bairn in me arms, I'd embrace ye. Tell me, are ye wed?"

"Wed and expecting a bairn of my own come spring."

"I'm happy to hear it."

"And ye married Sir Kennan—I kent ye liked him, m'lady."

"Very much."

No sooner had Fiona excused herself than Kennan stepped into the drawing room.

Her Ladyship took the sleeping babe. "If you'll excuse me, I'll take this laddie up to the nursery." As she passed, she gave Divana's shoulder a pat. "I'll speak to Lochiel. He doesn't take to change easily, but I'm certain everything will be fine. Have nary a fear, all will be well."

Once they were alone, Divana braced herself on the back of the settee. "Your father hates me."

"He hardly knows you."

"But he sees me as a kitchen maid, nay your wife."

"He kens where I stand, and he has naught to accept it."

"Or what? He'll disown ye."

"Who cares if he does?" Kennan wrapped her in his arms. "You are my world now. Aye, I'm the heir, but there are three sons behind me. Besides, Da settled a wee bit after I told him of our fortune—told him to think on it as your dowry."

"Och, did ye now, ye crafty Highlander?"

"I did, and after, I sent a messenger to my sister, Janet. Told her I needed her help straightaway."

"But why?"

"'Cause if anyone can influence my father, 'tis her."

"So, will there be a sealing of the vows or nay?"

"Where Janet is involved, there won't just be a church wedding, there will be a celebration of all the clans in the Highlands."

Divana rested her head on Kennan's chest. "But we're already married in the eyes of God. I'm happy with that."

"I am as well, but we'll make it proper for clan and kin, and then no one in all the world will question our bond."

"Not even Lochiel?"

"Especially not him."

* * *

And Kennan was right. Janet Cameron arrived three days later with her husband, Laird Robert Grant. Kennan's beautiful sister was well-bred and proper, and Divana adored her after the first day. Janet knew the vicar and the dressmaker and ordered everyone about as if she'd been born the princess of Achnacarry, which she had been.

Her husband, Robert, was nearly as handsome as Kennan, and the two of them hunted and sparred while the women made arrangements. But the most special person of all was Emma Grant, Robert's sister. She had been afflicted with blindness since birth, but she didn't let her disadvantage hinder her in the least. She chatted endlessly about the most amusing things while her hands stayed busy with knitting. Every once in a while, Janet would inspect her work, but the lass rarely ever dropped a stitch.

Emma played the harp as well and serenaded the family after the evening meals, except Divana didn't attend. She had decided not to partake in family meals or anything that included her father-in-law until he accepted her as Kennan's wife. Sadly, when the day of their wedding arrived, the great laird of Clan Cameron was still keeping his distance.

Divana stood in front of the looking glass and pressed her fingers to her stomach. "He told Her Ladyship he wouldn't attend."

Janet stepped behind and placed her hands on Divana's shoulders. "If he doesn't, he's nothing but an old fool."

"But it would mean ever so much if he did."

"Do not let my stubborn father ruin your happiness. You are the woman with whom my brother has chosen to spend the rest of his days, and that is all that matters."

"Not to worry, m'lady," said Emma from the chair by the hearth. "If Lochiel becomes unbearable, you are more than welcome to visit us in Glenmoriston as long as you wish."

"Thank you. I truly hope it will not come to that."

"If it should, the pair of you are welcome always." Janet kissed her cheek. "But enough talk. You are radiant, my dear, and 'tis nearly time to walk down the aisle."

Emma set aside her knitting and moved toward the

mirror. "I want to see the gown." She held out her hands. "May I?"

Divana took her hands and placed them on her shoulders. "The bodice is the color of primroses, and the lace is like the foaming edges of the sea."

"I do love primroses—they have such a lovely fragrance." Emma skimmed her fingers along the lace at the neckline. "Goodness, your descriptions are so thorough, I can see everything in my mind's eye. Tell me, Janet, is she not the bonniest lass in the Highlands?"

"Today she definitely is. Our lady has hair the color of fire, and it is laced atop her head with a yellow ribbon. And remember the sea she mentioned?"

"Aye."

"Her eyes are blue like the shallows right before the water begins to foam."

"Och, all the lads will be jealous of Sir Kennan this day."

"I reckon they will." Janet turned to the mantel clock. "But now 'tis time to go."

"Already?" Divana's stomach fluttered. "I'm so nervous."

Janet took Emma's hand and started for the door. "But you're already married, sweeting. This is simply a formality."

"And the service will only last a wee hour," said Emma. "And then there will be dancing."

Divana didn't budge. "But there are so many people here."

"Aye." Janet beckoned. "Isn't it fun?"

* * *

At the front of the church, Kennan stood by Ciar Mac-Dougall, both clad in full Highland garb. The Chieftain of Dunollie, Ciar had been his closest ally since childhood and was the right choice to stand as his best man. The pipe organ in the kirk began to play, and he still hadn't seen his father—blast his bullheaded nature. Lady Lochiel had been good enough to attend, and she sat in the front pew, with baby Adam on her lap. Kennan's brothers, John and Alan, sat beside her. And he gave a nod as Janet and Emma slipped into the seat beside Grant.

Ciar leaned in. "'Tis good to see Miss Emma."

"Is it?" Kennan eyed his friend. "Have you a fondness for the lass?"

"She has been an acquaintance of mine for years, though with the current unrest in Scotland, I haven't had the opportunity to visit Glenmoriston as of late."

"Then you'd best make good use of your time here."

"Perhaps I will, my friend."

As the rear doors opened, had Ciar uttered something else, Kennan would have heard it if he weren't dumb-struck. He stood spellbound, gazing down the aisle at the most stunningly beautiful woman he'd ever seen. But what made the moment exquisitely special was that the man who offered his arm and walked the lass down the aisle was none other than the Great Lochiel himself.

As Kennan smiled, not only did a lump grow in his throat, but he found himself blinking away the moisture in his eyes. Of course a braw sea captain would never shed a tear when standing in front of two hundred guests, nor would he admit he'd had any difficulty keeping the tears at bay.

When Divana joined him, radiantly smiling like his queen of the high seas, Da took her hand and placed it in

Kennan's palm. "You have chosen the woman who will preside alongside you when you become clan chief. I'll admit I had my misgivings at first. But then I recalled a time when she tended you without sleep, fiercely protecting you from all ills, trusting no one else to mind your bedside. I do believe this lass would have gladly given her life for you. And her spirit embodies the essence of what it means to be a Cameron."

Da squeezed their joined hands tightly. "I approve of this union and welcome my new daughter into the clan."

Kennan blinked, forcing himself not to shed a tear, but his throat choked up on his next words. "Thank you, Father."

As the service proceeded, Kennan saw nothing but the kind, generous, and remarkable woman standing before him. She'd conquered the gravest of adversities and come out stronger and wiser than anyone he knew. And his father was right. Divana would be unmatchable as the next Lady Lochiel.

She smiled and whispered, "What are ye thinking?"

He inclined his lips to her ear. "I'm the luckiest man in the world."

Author's Note

Thank you for joining me for *The Highland Rogue*. I've been wanting to write Kennan's story for a long time, but because he's been such a bad boy in the past, I first had to redeem him and show the man coming into his own in *The Highland Earl*, where Kennan had a supporting role. In fact, he has had supporting roles in *The Highland Renegade* and *The Highland Chieftain* as well.

I fashioned Kennan after John MacEwen Cameron, Eighteenth of Lochiel and Chief of Clan Cameron. He was the son of Sir Ewen Cameron, the Great Lochiel (who lived to the ripe age of ninety), though in fact John married Isabel Campbell of Lochnell. On that note, I must say that Divana's character is completely fictional, however I did make mention of Isabel's father, Laird Alexander Campbell of Ardslignish, in this story.

John MacEwen Cameron succeeded to the title of clan chief after the death of his long-lived father in 1719. The record shows John had three sons, Donald (the nineteenth chief), Archibald, and John. I took literary license in developing Achnacarry Castle for this book, because the structure presently standing in its place was built in 1802.

Achnacarry is now considered the ancestral home of the chiefs of Clan Cameron, only five miles northwest of Fort William on the River Arkaig. My literary license was in describing the castle as having been built by generations of Cameron chiefs, when in fact the castle that would have existed at the time of this story was built around 1655 by Sir Ewen Cameron to take advantage of a strategic position between Loch Lochy and Loch Arkaig. Of note, Sir Ewen's bard referred to Achnacarry as a "generous house of feasting." The 1655 castle was destroyed by government troops after John (Kennan) fought with the Jacobites in the 1746 Battle of Culloden. The 1802 castle was built in the baronial style and can be seen today.

Another point of mention is Divana's abandonment by her clan. Though there is no record of persons being abandoned on the isle of Hyskeir, I have read accounts of victims of pandemics being deserted and left to their own resources on uninhabited Hebridean isles, and such accounts gave me the idea for Divana's circumstances.

Don't miss Amy Jarecki's next thrilling Scottish
adventure in

THE HIGHLAND LAIRD

Available in Fall 2020.

About the Author

Known for her action-packed, passionate historical romances, Amy Jarecki has received reader and critical praise throughout her writing career. She won the prestigious 2018 RT Reviewers' Choice Award for *The Highland Duke* and the 2016 RONE Award from InD'tale Magazine for Best Time Travel for her novel *Rise of a Legend*. In addition, she hit Amazon's Top 100 Bestseller List and earned designation as an Amazon All Star Author. Readers also chose her Scottish historical romance, *A Highland Knight's Desire*, as the winning title through Amazon's Kindle Scout Program. Amy holds an MBA from Heriot-Watt University in Edinburgh, Scotland, and now resides in Southwest Utah with her husband, where she writes immersive historical romances.

Looking for more historical romances?
Forever brings the heat with these sexy rogues!

FOREVER AND A DUKE
by Grace Burrowes

Eleanora Hatfield knows from experience that dealing with the peerage can only lead to problems. But she reluctantly agrees to help Wrexham, Duke of Elsmore, sort his finances. What starts out as an unwanted assignment soon leads to forbidden kisses and impossible longings. But with scandal haunting Ellie's past and looming in Rex's future, how can true love lead to anything but heartbreak? Includes a novella by Kelly Bowen!

Discover bonus content and more on read-forever.com.

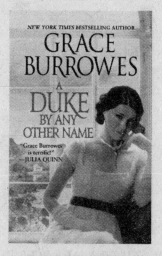

A DUKE BY ANY OTHER NAME
by Grace Burrowes

Lady Althea Wentworth has little patience for dukes, reclusive or otherwise, but she needs the Duke of Rothhaven's backing to gain entrance into Society. She's asked him nicely, she's called on him politely, all to no avail—until her prize hogs *just happen* to plunder his orchard. He longs for privacy. She's vowed to never endure another ball as a wallflower. Yet as the two grow closer, it soon becomes clear they might both be pretending to be something they're not.

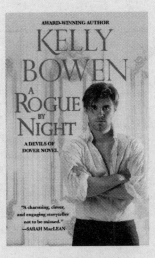

A ROGUE BY NIGHT
by Kelly Bowen

Baron. Physician. Smuggler. Harland Hayward is living a double life as an aristocrat by day and a criminal by night. As a doctor, Harland has the perfect cover to appear in odd places at all hours, a cover he uses to his advantage. He's chosen this life to save his family from financial ruin, but he draws the line at taking advantage of the honest and trustworthy Katherine Wright. But when Ketherine's own identity proves to be as secretive as his, will he be able to trust her with his life—and possibly his heart?

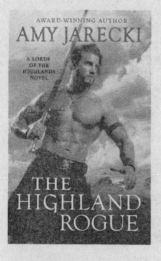

THE HIGHLAND ROGUE
by Amy Jarecki

Abandoned on a deserted Scottish island by her family, Divana Campbell is both terrified and relieved when Highlander Sir Kennan Cameron drags himself from the surf. Trusting Kennan is her only chance for survival—and by the time they arrive at his castle, she can barely imagine life without him. But as the heir to a powerful chieftain from a rival clan, Kennan could never marry the likes of her.

THE HIGHLAND EARL
by Amy Jarecki

Evelyn has no desire to wed John Erskine, the widowed Earl of Mar, but at least she'll be able to continue her work as a spy—as long as her husband never finds out. Yet the more time Evelyn spends with the rugged Scottish earl and his boys, the fonder she grows of their little family, and the last thing she wants to do is put them in danger. As alliances shift and enemies draw closer, soon everything they hold dear is at risk: their lands, their love, and their very lives.